our thing

our thing

NICCI HARRIS

also by nicci harris

The Kids of The District

Facing Us

Our Thing

Cosa Nostra

Her Way

His Pretty Little Burden

His Pretty Little Queen

Their Broken Legend

ISBN ebook: 978-1-922492-00-5

ISBN print: 978-1-922492-02-9

ISBN Hardback: 978-1-922492-11-1

Edited by Writing Evolution. @writingevolution. www.writingevolution.co.uk

Proofreading by Deborah Richmond (Kat's Literary Services)

Internal graphics by Nicci Harris

Cover design by Books & Moods

Nicci illustration holding kindle by @lamdin.designs

for the goodest boy

—that ever lived.
I lost you this year.
And I'll miss you forever.
Archie.

our thing

song list

Kids of the District

Our Thing

Book one & two

1. Dance of the Sugar Plum Fairy – Royal Philharmonic Orchestra
2. Riptide – Vance Joy
3. The Way You Look Tonight – Frank Sinatra
4. Rosaries – Nbhd Nick
5. Numb – Linkin Park
6. Nothing Else Matters – Metallica
7. Wild Horses – The Sundays
8. Somewhere Over The Rainbow – Leanne & Naara
9. Tears in Heaven – Eric Clapton
10. The Unforgiven – Metallica
11. M.I.A. – Avenged Sevenfold
12. Over The Rainbow – Judy Garland
13. The Bones – Maren Morris
14. Tangled Up In You – Staind

15. Nothing's Gonna Hurt You Baby – Cigarettes After Sex
16. Angel – Theory of a Deadman
17. All I Know So Far – P!nk
18. Remember Everything – Five Finger Death Punch

Go to Spotify to listen.

"i thought love

—would be warmth in my chest and heart, and peace and contentment in my soul. But it's not contentment. It's not peaceful. It's terrifying. It's so strong that I know it could undo me. It could unravel everything that I am, strip me back until I'm nothing but bare bones and a swollen heart."

CHAPTER ONE

SWEAT BEADS on my forehead as my ballet partner pulls me into our final sequence. The other performers are in a semi-circle formation around us. The music has peaked, and the audience is in a state of silenced awe.

I'm en pointe, floating across the stage in an ethereal motion, when the spotlight bounces around the audience. As it momentarily illuminates the faces of the people seated, I catch a glimpse of a boy I haven't seen in many years. So many, in fact, that I'm surprised I've recognised him at all. Joshua, I think his name is.

One summer on my front lawn, he and my brother started fighting. Fists and bats were swung. He nearly knocked my brother unconscious.

But that's not why I remember him.

Warmth spreads through me.

I remember him because that was the first time I saw the notorious bad boy of the District. Oh, he was only young then, so his reputation hadn't yet formed roots, but there was no mistaking his strength. His single mindedness.

Dominance. That boy with the grey eyes was a complete stranger to my brother and me and yet, he jumped into the rumble. After dragging Joshua away, he effortlessly laid him out across the grass. Then he wandered up the street as if nothing had even happened. Well, something had happened... He'd made an impression.

A lasting one!

My attention is drawn back to my dance partner as he pulls me into our closing position. We still, smiling and breathing heavily. The crowd stands and coos. As the curtains slowly draw shut to the sound of applause, his name lingers in my mind.

Max Butcher.

He is the boy I dream about at night. Until recently, I never saw much of him, but my sister Flick has started to date someone in his circle and now he's *everywhere.*

Much to my delight and discomfort.

Lost in thoughts, I'm taken off guard as my ballerina squad ambushes me in our private sanctuary behind the fabric that separates us from the audience. They jump and squeal with excitement, congratulating me on my successful final show as Nikiya. I hug a few girls, two or three. The exact number of embraces is unknown because I'm so drained from my performance.

I hope no one can notice.

Rushing down the hall toward my dressing room, I pass by dancers who are being embraced and gifted flowers under waves of excitement. It's not until I'm pushing the door open and the silence and stillness of my dressing room surround me, that I'm able to focus on myself. Not on Max Butcher or the day he'd rescued my brother from a bully.

No. Not on that!

Sitting down in front of the mirror, I stare at myself and sigh. "You're eighteen today."

Right now, Flick is probably blowing up balloons and ordering caterers around in preparation for my arrival.

Today was the final day of my tour as Nikiya, the main female role in *La Bayadere*. It was a beautiful production about how love conquers all despite the three big As—Angst, Action, and Anguish. And I showed the audience that emotion in motion. I expressed it through movement and lived with it in my body for the past six months while really absorbing her character, and yet I have *no* real-life experience with any of the *As*.

I am, for lack of a better phrase, A-*less*.

Leaning closer to my reflection, I focus on myself. "Why are you thinking about Max Butcher and Angst and Anguish and Action? Cassidy? Are you listening to me? He doesn't even know your name..."

A knock at the door snatches my attention. Clearing my throat, I swivel in my chair to face it. "Come in."

The sound of the girls celebrating another successful show suddenly radiates into the room. On a flood of energy and good vibes, my bestie enters, holding a bunch of white tulips. "Darlin', you were amazing!"

He struts over to me and places the bouquet on my dresser. "Oh, my." His mouth drops open as he cups his cheeks in mock horror. "Are you talking to yourself in the mirror again?"

The truth plays with my mouth. My lips twist into a grin. "It's a very one-sided conversation."

Despite his overly broad shoulders, and thick waistline, Toni is still one of the prettiest guys I know. He is half-Chinese, half-Italian, and rocks the best of both worlds, with his delicate features and long ink-black lashes under thick chocolate-brown hair. His skin is the perfect tone of caramel. He is pretty and butch—it's a beautiful combination.

Grabbing a stool from the corner of the room, he pulls it up beside me and makes himself comfortable. He faces the mirror, giving himself a once over before rubbing his jaw to check for stubble. "You were incredible out there, my queen."

"Thank you." I turn back to my reflection and now another name plays on my mind. A big sigh escapes me. "Konnor didn't come tonight. He's not coming at all."

Toni's over-the-top attitude softens. Despite his usual humour, he knows that when it comes to my brother, I don't appreciate jokes. Konnor is, without a doubt, my favourite person in the whole world, and he's been through so much. He's adopted, but I'd like to see anyone tell me he isn't my real brother. They'd soon be sporting a Cassidy-shaped fist in their abdomen.

Toni's smile is tight. "He lives on the other side of the state, aeons from the District. It's too far. He's got classes and rugby and heterosexual male stuff to do. Darlin', you'll have more fun without him tonight, don't worry. He's kinda a drag when it comes to you."

"Yeah, I know," I huff. "But I'd still like him here."

"I know you would. But you have *this* drag."

I grin at him and lift my feet onto his lap. He immediately gets to work, unwrapping the ribbon from my pointe shoes and peeling me out of my confinements.

"Oh my gawd, that feels so good." I wiggle my toes. "Flick says his punishment is 'Crazy Grandma Duty' next Christmas."

Toni's eyes crinkle as he laughs. "Does she still call him 'The Fake Grandson'?" Toni asks as he rubs my feet.

I try not to giggle because she's harmless, and Konnor knows it. "Yep, every time. But they both get drunk, argue, and then end up discussing the universe and religion and communism. It's like clockwork."

"Are they for or against communism?"

"Hard to say. I think they both agree on a kind of socialism?"

Toni laughs again. "Your brother is so intense."

"I know."

"So can you get your fanny up and get a move on!"

Nodding, I face myself in the mirror. "My birthday... Lots of people. Profiteroles, maybe. Cocktails, definitely. Speeches, I hope not! Presents... Maybe I'll get the Bert and Ernie leotard I've been asking for... Hey, have you ever noticed that Bert has a monobrow, while Ernie doesn't have any eyebrows at all?"

"No, I didn't. But I did notice they sleep in the same bed, so I blame *Sesame Street* for my homosexuality."

I pull my feet from his lap and twist to face the mirror. "You should write to thank them."

"I will. Now let's get that makeup off, because you kinda look like a baby prostitute."

"I think I'm the last person in our entire city you can call a prostitute," I point out as I begin to wipe the makeup off my eyes and cheeks.

"You have no one to blame for your abstinence but yourself. Guys wanna get up in there." He smirks and thrusts his hips suggestively. "You just won't let 'em."

I copy his thrusting and giggle. "I don't have time for guys to get up in here."

"Get a dick up ya already." He laughs loudly. "You're all wound tight! We're not living in a John Hughes movie; you're not gonna lose it to the boy you will marry and have annoying little brats with."

I scoff as I continue to remove my makeup. When

someone knocks at the door, I immediately sing out, "Come in," without thinking.

My casual attitude changes as soon as I see who strides in. Two middle-aged men in coats greet me—one with a wide smile and open arms. I don't need an introduction to know who he is. It's a formidable sight to see Jimmy Storm striding into my dressing room. I've never met him before.

Why would I?

But I've seen him on The District News enough to know that he's Barack Obama to some and Al Capone to others. I swallow, finding it hard not to notice that Toni's suddenly ashen beside me.

"*Cassidy*. What beauty. Thank you for that performance," he says, his accent so thick it's like he's only just left Sicily.

"Hi, Jim— I mean, Mr Storm."

"Jimmy, please." He extends both hands and sandwiches mine between them. He smells like smoke and bourbon and something else—something like... shoe polish?

I grin at him and feel my cheeks heat. "I'm glad you liked it."

"Liked it? *M'arricriài*!" He gestures theatrically. "You are a very talented young lady."

My eyes move to the man beside him, who is standing so staunchly I reckon a bullet wouldn't chip him. I wonder if he's intending to appear intimidating or if he's just antisocial. I glance back at Jimmy. "Thank you."

Jimmy releases my hands and croons, "I love the ballet. Did you know it originated in my country? Not France. It was Sicily. The romance. The passion. The drama. Ballet is my soul, Cassidy."

"Well..." I chuckle awkwardly, unsure of what to say to a stranger who talks with such sensibility. "Well, mine too."

He laughs loudly. "Yes. I could see that when you were on

stage. I had to come here and thank you." His eyes haven't left mine. "You need to dance at one of my events."

"Yeah, for sure," I find myself saying. Dancing in front of people comes as naturally to me as breathing, so why wouldn't I just say yes? And given he's incredibly famous and somewhat of a philanthropist, he's probably just referring to a charity event or a play he's sponsoring...

Well, that and he's Jimmy Storm, so it's not as if I even have a choice.

But maybe I do? Maybe I should have said, 'Maybe'?

Stop maybeing!

"For sure," he nods, repeating my words. "I will see you soon then, Cassidy Slater."

"Okay," I say with a half giggle that sounds nervous even though I'm not.

I'm not.

He turns and walks out, tailed by the other man. As soon as the door clicks shut, I swivel to face Toni. "What. The. Actual. Frick? Did that just happen?" I say, my mouth nearly as wide as Toni's eyes.

"Oh my, you're in trouble," he says, his lips now a mischievous curve.

"Who would have thought that Jimmy Storm likes ballet?" I rub my cheeks in disbelief. "Hey, why am I in trouble? Don't say that."

He looks at me, animated as usual. "A private viewing for Mr. Storm."

"Stop it. He never said he wanted a private viewing. Jebus, Toni!"

"*Jesus,* darlin'. It was subliminal."

"You're subliminal." I chuckle as I turn to the mirror to finish removing my makeup.

Toni sighs with disappointment. "I'd like to be subliminal in a sexy boy by now, but we're still here. Here, instead of being at your party."

I turn my nose up. "I don't get it."

He stares down at his phone, which is always pinging away with gossip. "That's because you are an asexual pigeon."

"I'm not an asexual pigeon," I sulk, giving my face a final wipe before dabbing moisturiser below my eyes.

"Yeah, you are." He lowers his phone, and I already know he's about to start a monologue. "You're scared and way too picky. You know, you could have anyone you want... Nearly anyone—not me. I mean, I'd give you a pity hump, but I'd be thinking about Mark Wahlberg. But no, you, my girl, have big girl-boners all the time, but you tuck them in your leotard and get back to acting like an asexual pigeon. You are too afraid that a slice of cock will derail your ambitions." Toni coos like a pigeon.

I scowl at him half-heartedly and feel the need to say something dirty. "Well, I think the guy I like has a whole cake, not a slice."

Toni cracks up laughing. "Look, let's go get feral, and I think you should just, like, purr all over someone's face tonight."

"I'm not going to lose my virginity on my eighteenth birthday. It's too cliché."

Looking straight at my reflection, dead serious, he raises a sharply tweezed eyebrow. "Look, darlin'. Firstly, purring on his face isn't going to take away your V-card. I know most guys are dickheads, but it doesn't work like that."

I giggle, pulling the bobby pins from my hair and letting it cascade over my shoulders.

"And secondly." He suddenly frowns at me. "Are you leaving your hair like that?"

"What's wrong with it?"

Toni looks exasperated. "You have incredible hair. Long. Strawberry-blonde. Wavy. Don't you want to wash it, so it isn't all sticky and stiff from that hair Viagra they spray on you?"

I laugh. Grabbing my leave-in hair conditioner from inside my cosmetic bag, I spray it all over my hair and rub it in. "Better? Why does it matter? Everyone knows I'm coming from a performance."

Toni smirks, a secret clearly lingering on his smug lips.

My eyes narrow. "What do you know?"

"I saw a tweet just before I got here," he says, still brandishing a big grin. "And, well, ya know, apparently, a certain Butcher boy might be coming to *your* party."

I clear my throat but wish that I didn't because Toni is now smirking like a fricking fox that's just caught a hen. "Okay," I say. "Look, I know I have this little crush and I said a few things, but it's not a big deal. *Please...* please, don't make it a big de—"

"Firstly, I'd call it an *infatuation*, not a crush. You're seconds away from drawing hearts with little Ms in them on your leotards," he objects. "And secondly, you have never crushed on anyone. Ever. Before. And then you happen to crush on the most notorious manwhore in the District? This. This is a sign. Prove you're not an asexual pigeon and take his enormous cake and eat it. Tonight!"

I stand and turn from him evasively before sliding my leotard down my shoulders and shimmying it past my legs. My heart begins to race. I shift from one foot to the other, trying to pull it off. "I doubt he even knows my name," I mumble.

"Maybe not. But he will after toniiiiight. Purr. On. His. Face."

My pulse thunders in my ears. Max Butcher is the last person on earth who would find me the least bit interesting. I have spent my whole life studying and dancing. I have no social skills. I'm awkward and weird and completely inappropriate and so very uncool, especially whenever I open my mouth around intimidating people—*like him.*

Finally managing to tug my stockings off, I chuck them towards my bag. "He's coming to hang out with Flick, you know that. It has nothing to do with me."

I don't want to keep talking because talking to Toni right now is just going to freak me out. But if I don't talk to him, then he'll know I'm freaked out. Which I'm not. Unless he talks to me.

Feeling my skin flush, I don't look at Toni, but I can sense his eyes on me. When I'm down to my underwear, I riffle through my bag to find clothes for tonight. Clothes that I know aren't in here because I didn't pack any 'Max Butcher' appropriate clothes because I didn't know I would be fricking needing them! After moving the same three pieces of clothing around again and again, I finally pull them out. Acting like that didn't just happen, I turn to face Toni with a feigned grin. "So red playsuit and cream ballet flats, it is."

CHAPTER TWO

IN EVERY DIRECTION there are strangers dressed to the nines, wishing me happy birthday and embracing me tightly. My party has become a major social event and has brought people from all over the District. From across the river. From important businesses. From important families.

My sister is a socialite. Popular. Beautiful. And she loves attention and crowds and noise. Being more of a homebody myself means I have a handful of real friends and the equivalent in acquaintances.

There are nearly fifty people here whose identities are a complete mystery to me. It's a beautiful party, but despite her best intentions and efforts, it just screams *Flick*. From the live DJ and neon-lit dance floor to the over-the-top polaroid booth, to the gift covered pool table, and finally to the pink and red balloon garlands that are, like, everywhere.

Although, I do like pink.

My mum is bouncing between the kitchen and the game room, topping up cocktail dispensers and repositioning food. My dad is setting up some kind of projector, and I know I'm going to need more than a few drinks for whatever he has planned.

Suddenly, through the laughter and drum-and-bass, I hear Flick's voice. "You like it? You love it, right?" She emerges from the crowd, her shapely body and long molten-red hair swaying.

"Wow. It's... *big*," I say. The grin on her face is hard to ignore. Infectious. It's enough to make me love this party as much as she clearly does. I nod. "I love it."

Appearing on the verge of happy tears, she says, "I know you don't usually go for the elaborate thing, but I wanted tonight to be epic. I know you're probably a bit embarrassed, but that's why I had to do it. To get you out of your comfort zone and get you drunk. Loosen you up." Her eyes gloss over. "Sorry, I just had two shots from Stacey's belly button. I'm feeling a bit emotional. She has a beautiful belly button." She laughs and wipes a single tear that dared to break free. "I just love you so much, little sister, and you're so beautiful and I'm so proud of your determination and how strong you are." She embraces me tightly.

The backs of my eyes begin to prickle. Must be something in the water—like alcohol. "I love you too!"

She begins to giggle. "And I wanted to milk the District of presents for you. And ya know, just because I tend to favour the fairer sex doesn't mean I haven't noticed the male hotties around here. Hey? Dillion? Cute. Athletic. *Riiiight*?"

"Flick, stop it," I say as I take a few steps toward the bar. My eyes bounce around the desserts, landing on a cupcake. Smiling, I grab the cupcake and take a bite. I talk to her around a mouthful of delicious chocolate. "He's not my type. We dance together. I don't want to date the male version of me. I want someone..." The word gets lost; the name, however, doesn't. *Max Butcher.* I swallow and take another bite. "I don't know. Different."

"You're so graceful on stage. What the hell happens when you step off?" She says, using her perfectly manicured finger to wipe icing from my top lip.

"I get hungry," I laugh.

Her smile widens, and I know it's because she's so happy and loves me so much. "You're eighteen. Come have a body shot!"

I wrinkle my nose. "Not off Stacey."

She giggles and grabs my hand, steering me through the crowd and out onto the alfresco where people are gathering in groups. It's nice outside tonight. Slightly cool. Perfectly still and cloudless.

"Get a shot for Cassidy!" Flick yells to the people at the bar cart. "But not a Slippery Nipple." She cracks herself up. "A tequila shot. Hell, make it a Flatliner!"

I jolt to a stop, my hand suddenly slipping from hers. My cheeks begin to smoulder.

Standing casually behind the outdoor bar table is Max Butcher and his gang. I will my feet to keep moving forward, but they don't. His level of hot is uncomfortable. That is the best way to describe him—hot to the point of physical discomfort. I study him quickly, and both love and hate the way his jeans are tight around his thick thighs and hips, the way the sleeves of his white V-neck shirt are bunched above his elbows 'cause, like, why have long sleeves if you're going to roll them up? Because the sleeves probably couldn't accommodate his thick, tattooed forearms, that's why. I don't really know why, of course, but—

"Cassidy?" Flick says.

I swallow hard as I look at her. "Sorry. I just remembered Toni." I do not sound convincing at all. "He needs a Flatline...

er or whatever it was called. He'd probably have a Slippery Nipple, actually, if that's a real shot. I don't know. I'm just rambling now. But I should go get him."

Her brows raise, a smirk now plastered across her cheeks. She sees straight through me as she points to a guy sitting down at a table a few metres from where Max is standing. It's Toni.

Frick.

"Oh, cool," I say breathily.

Double frick.

She grabs my hand again. "Come on."

I'm pulled over to the group by the bar cart, but plonk down just short of them, seeking refuge with Toni.

He eyes me and smacks his lips. "You look so awkward right now."

"Stop it. Don't say anything, Toni." I stare out over the grass that is darkened by the night sky. The moon's big tonight—lots of big things here tonight...

Shut up, Cassidy!

Toni wraps his arm around my shoulders and squeezes. "That boy is bad news. Bad. Bad. Sexy." He chuckles. "Sexy, bad news."

I think I like bad news.

He takes a sip of his cocktail and crosses his legs. "Personally, I'm more of a Xander Butcher fan myself. Oh my giddy aunt, he's just yummy. Classic boy next door look. Don't you think?" He nods his head and grins. "And, well, Max scares the shit out of me. His biceps are bigger than my hopes and dreams for the future... And Jamie just told me that he bit some guy's finger off and swallowed it. I mean, I still think you should purr on his face, but maybe with witnesses, ya know?"

I turn to face him. "Come on, that rumour doesn't even

sound real. No more real than"—I drop my voice—"The Clay Butcher one. You know where he rips a guy's head open with his bare hands? Or the one where Bronson Butcher gets into a bar fight and slices a guy's neck open with a glass. Or the Xander Butcher one where he killed that cop with a taser. They have to be lies."

He shrugs. "Either way. Sexy, bad news. The lot of them."

I pretend to massage my neck from side to side so I can peer over at Max. He's standing with Xander, Stacey, and a few nameless faces. Beautiful girls hover around them, but the Butcher gang is more focused on laughing amongst themselves than paying their spectators any real attention.

Max's eyes are near black from this distance, narrowed and deep, with so much intensity—almost weighed down. A pretty, golden-haired girl circles his bicep with her hand. He flicks her his attention, only to say something that has her grimace and storm off. Her reaction makes him laugh, menacing and gravelly and sexy as hell.

"Cassidy," Flick says, stepping in front of me and handing me two shot glasses with a lemon wedge balanced on top of each. "This is a Flatliner. It's basically just tequila and Cointreau and lime, but with tabasco. See, the tabasco makes a little line in the tequila."

I blink at her. "You want me to have both?"

She grins. "Yep. It's liquid confidence."

After a quick glance at Max and the biceps *I'd* love to wrap my hand around, I nod. "Let's do this." I tip the shot glass into my mouth. The refreshingly cold liquid gives me a false sense of security before the heat rips through my throat. Swallowing it, I quickly drain the other.

When the heat in my chest slowly dies, I turn to my sister. "Tell me about Stacey."

Tell me about Max.

Flick looks over her shoulder at Stacey and smiles. "She's beautiful, hey?"

"She is," I agree. "Beautiful skin. She reminds me of Natalie Portman. So are you two serious? I kinda thought she was straight."

"So did she," Flick states smugly.

Toni laughs. "Everyone is gay for the right person."

"Nah, I'm just kidding," Flick interjects. "Seriously though, Stacey doesn't like labels. She likes me. I happen to be a girl."

"Wasn't Stacey dating Xander?" Toni asks.

She scoffs. "Hell no. They're just besties. No sex as far as I'm aware."

Toni sips his cocktail and studies Flick. "Wouldn't you hate it if she had, though? 'Cause like, I'm not sure a girl could come back from that boy and what's snuggled up in his boxers."

Flick rolls her eyes. "I have ten dicks on my hands and an intimate knowledge of what's between a girl's legs. I think I'm fine."

Toni looks at me. "Maybe you can tell Cassidy what's between a girl's legs. She's an asexual pigeon."

I feign a chuckle and coo, and then steer straight away from that topic. "Are the rumours true? The ones about Max and Xander and their brothers?"

"I don't know. I doubt it. But we're new mates, Cassidy. We haven't traded diaries yet."

Toni pretends to read a diary. "Max's diary: Had sex. Had sex. Had sex. Played rugby. Bit a guy's thumb off. Had sex."

I giggle. "Flick's diary: Did hair. Did nails. Did Stacey—"

Flick interrupts, "Cassidy's diary: Danced. Danced. Danced. Ignored my obvious beauty and played the part of a hermit. Danced."

I scoff and stand to get another drink. "Cassidy's diary: Danced. Where are my tits? Help, I've been robbed. Danced."

"You do have tits!" Flick exclaims. "They're pretty perfect actually. You're only a little person."

"They're pretty frickin' small." I giggle, grabbing a glass of champagne from the cart and quickly moving back to my spot beside Toni.

Toni bounces and slaps his thighs. "Oh, do me next. Do me. Do me."

Flick obliges before I can. "Toni's diary: Entry 1,000,005: I love cock. I love myself. Good day, sir. I said good day!"

As laughter erupts from me, I grip my stomach. We all crack up.

Toni beams. "That sounds just like me!"

My face begins to tingle. "Come on, I need to dance before I get too tingly."

A lot of alcohol passes my lips over the next few hours and even more strangers wish me, 'Happy birthday.' I'm surprised at how smooth and velvety a Flatlin*er* becomes after a while.

My birthday party quickly becomes a mirage of smiling faces, cuddles, and alcoholic beverages. It's not until I stumble away to get a moment of quiet and my feet cross in an awkward manner, sending me to the ground, that I realise just how drunk I am. I pull myself up and brush my legs clean. I vaguely remember someone telling me I'm wasted... just a few minutes ago. I can't remember who.

Pressing my back against the outside wall of my house, I relax. This is the first moment of silence I've had since before my performance started this afternoon. Down the side of the house, in the direction I've just stumbled from, I can see the flicker of multicoloured lights. I can still hear the music, but it's more bass than drum from this distance. Several stragglers are sitting on the grass a little further from the building, but I'm all alone over here. The cool air surrounds me, making me shiver. I wrap my arms around my waist. It's nice to get a breather. Gather my thoughts...

I try to focus on objects ahead of me, but they're all circled in a ring of haze.

I'm squinting at what I'm pretty sure is a dog when an aggressive female voice draws my attention towards the front of my house. Curious, I navigate my way along the edge of the render in order to get a better position. I stop walking when I see a guy and a girl arguing near the turning circle. A red sports car idles nearby.

"Frick." I cover my mouth and press my back into the wall. Although a bush conceals me, I have to peer around it to see the commotion. I should just leave. But I hesitate when I hear her tone and I find myself leaning around the shrubbery to watch them. He has his back to me. She is seriously angry. Thrusting her hands around, she yells at him. Her face is tight and twisted in anger. Her lips are a red line of aggression that moves and snarls.

The guy is all cool and calm, and oh my God, I think that's Max. Leaning a little closer, my foot kicks a rock and it rolls out from behind the wall.

Oh, frick!

My breath gets lodged in my throat, and I straighten out of view. I breathe for a few minutes and then hear the red-lipped woman say something like, 'Look at me' or 'So you're not even going to look at me' or something like that. After a few seconds, I peer back around and watch as she pokes him in the chest.

Woah.

I should walk away. This is none of my business. I will my feet to move, but they don't, and when she slaps him, I cover my mouth to smother a gasp. She'd slapped him so hard, but his head barely moved. And now there is no way I can look anywhere but at them.

My head is swimming, and it's both a result of what I'm witnessing and the unmeasurable amount of Flatli*ners* I've ingested tonight. I feel my brows tighten with shock because this is embarrassingly the most scandalous situation I've ever been a part of—well, not really a part of, but have seen.

Max... It's hard to believe he'd just stand there and take it. It's also hard to believe that any girl would treat him like that... No, that's not true. I'm sure lots of girls hate him. Frick, I'd even like the opportunity to hate him for the same reason they do.

The royally peeved woman growls and then stumbles on her stiletto. Her ankle flops to the side momentarily. Max pulls something out of his back pocket and hands it to her. She slaps him again, but this time his head turns ever so slightly. He doesn't retaliate. He barely says a word. After putting the mystery item in her bag, she stumbles to the red car, gets in, and drives off. Max still hasn't moved.

He waits until her car disappears out of sight before shoving his hands into his pockets and turning around, walking... Straight. Toward. Me.

Frick.

I spin around and rush away, but to my absolute mortification, I trip and land on my knees, my palms slapping the pavers. Defeated, drunk, perhaps a little mentally slow, I roll onto my bum and lean against the outside render. I sigh and stare straight ahead as the sound of his feet gets closer to me and then stops. I'm now staring at the hem of jeans and dark shoes.

"You look a little out of place," I hear a deep voice say, and it's the first time Max Butcher has ever spoken to me. His voice is clear, confident, and articulate, yet with a gravelly aftershock that does things to my breathing.

I clear my throat. "It's funny."

"What's funny?"

"I was going to say, 'It's funny you say that because', but then couldn't be bothered finishing that sentence."

My head is heavy, but I manage to arch my neck and look up at him through my lashes. I sigh, my drunken vision distorting his face at this distance and creating a fuzzy fisheye around him. "Hi, Max."

"Do I know you?"

"You're so tall," I whine.

He's suddenly squatting next to me, a grin playing on his lips. "Better?"

Gazing into his eyes, I feel as though he's looking inside me. Through skin. Through muscle. Into *me*. He studies me unapologetically as if it's his right and my privilege. Everyone says that all The Butcher Boys have blue eyes, but his are so much more than just blue. They are a stormy ocean, hinting at the powerful chaos beneath their blue-grey depths.

Ugh... He's perfect.

He must be a witch. Or like, the male version... a warlock?

I smile and feel my eyelids get heavier. "Yeah. And no, I don't know you. I mean, you don't know me."

He's still grinning, his lips a provocative slash across his face. "Okay."

I look down at my legs stretched out in front of me and then at him. He's still there, nailing me with his stare. "Oh my gawd. You're too hot, Max. Seriously, just stop it."

I can't believe I've just said that.

His grin gets wider, becoming slightly crooked and naturally cocky in nature. He has a single dimple on his left cheek. Of course, he does. I want to poke it. I'm going to poke it.

Do not poke it!

His mouth moves and I'm fixated on that dimple. "I'll work on that for you," he says.

"Good." I nod. "Go get fat or something."

He chuckles a little and it's my new favourite sound. White teeth flash at me for a moment, and they're straight and perfect. My eyes go back to his dimple.

Do not poke it.

Swallowing down the knot in my throat, I say, "You're probably wondering why I'm on the ground, right?"

He studies me, eyes shifting around my face for a moment. I can feel them everywhere, their path from my eyes to my lips palpable, and I'm pretty sure I'm now panting.

"You fell," he says, amusement in his voice.

"Right." I giggle nervously. "So, you're not so much wondering as... Not wondering. Because you know."

Oh my gawd, Cassidy. Shut up.

I'm not sure what he thinks is so funny, but he's still grinning, his eyes fixed on me. Thick silence settles between us, charging everything within a kilometre radius. Maybe further. The moon looks extra bright. That might be because of us. Because of what I just witnessed and the fact that he knows that I witnessed it, and his proximity to me and his annoying level of perfection that isn't annoying at all, and of course, me—goofy me—on the ground, unable to stand without wobbling. That's a lot of charge.

He holds his hand out, and I just stare at it. "Need some help?"

I take a deep breath. Placing one hand in his big palm and the other against the ground, I push myself up as he helps stabilise me. When my legs attempt to take my weight and balance, I stumble. His hands catch my waist and, *frick,* I'm so aware of them on me right now. Warm. Strong. I look down at them, blinking in confusion as the two hands gripping my middle become four.

Standing up quickly was not a good idea. My legs are already giving out again, knees buckling, and it's not me that's wobbly but the room. I'm not in a room. The planet? Yep, the planet just tilted, and now my feet are no longer on the floor because Max has me cradled against his chest. Attempting to focus, I blink a few times, but my vision has disappeared. My head rolls onto his shoulder. And when I let my eyes close, they don't open again. A tide of darkness sweeps me out, taking me away from the conscious world.

I like it here.

CHAPTER THREE

drink me, alice

"TELL me again what happened last night," I plea, running the razor from my ankle to my knee. The faucet above me is on high, spitting hot water down onto my body. I can vaguely distinguish Toni's silhouette on the other side of the shower curtain.

His outline moves and the curtain is suddenly jerked open. "How many more times must I narrate this for you?"

Straightening, I frown at him. "Really, Toni?"

He points between my legs, looking disgusted. "Are you going to shave that?"

"It doesn't bite, Toni. And, no, I wax. It needs to get a little longer first. Go back and sit on the toilet and tell me again." He flicks his head as if he has hair to flick—he doesn't—and closes the curtain.

The dark shape of his body slumps down on the toilet lid. "Okay. *So,* I'm getting sweaty with a gorgeous hairless gentleman in your game room when I look up and see Max Butcher with a dead-to-the-world, stubble-between-her-legs Cassidy Slater in his arms. And he's carrying her up the staircase towards the bedrooms! He was up there with her for at least three minutes too."

I can't help but grin. When my eyes finally peeled open this morning, I found two Panadols and a glass of water on my bedside table along with a note that read,

'Drink me, Alice.'

"Were you even going to go check on her?" I tease. "She could have been in some kind of trouble."

"Oh, darlin', I was hoping she was, but no." He begins making pigeon noises.

"I have no memory of that! I barely remember talking to him," I admit as I begin to shave my other leg. "When did he leave? Did he leave with someone?"

"I don't know. I was 'subliminal' not long after that."

I laugh. "What's his name?"

"Braidy. He's a police officer, and he promised to arrest me the next time he sees me," he coos.

"He's a cop? How old is he?" I ask.

"I dunno," he says whimsically. "Twenty. Twenty-one. Twenty-two. Twenty-three."

I giggle. "So, you two *really* got to know each other then."

He chuckles. "I could map his mouth."

"That's a start, I suppose. But maybe next time, try pulling your tongue out and let him get to know you."

"Why would he want to get to know me?"

I hate it when he does this. Shaking my head, I scold him, "Toni, you're more than your body."

"*Well*, I suppose I could go out on a date with him if my queen accompanies me."

I reach for the curtain, tugging it open to glare at him. "No."

Sitting on the toilet and eyeing me with enthusiasm, he claps his hands together in a prayer-like position. "Please. You know I don't do dating well. They don't like me when they realise I only have a one-track mind."

I lift a blonde brow at him, my expression dubious. "They do like you. You have issues with liking yourself."

He scrunches up his face as if he's just eaten a lemon. "What cockamamie is this? I love myself. Haven't you read my diary?"

I close the curtain to finish shaving my legs. "You just wanted to say cockamamie."

"Never had an opening before. I just took it."

Sighing, I think about how very few people get to know Toni. Beneath the BS, innuendos, and mockery, there is a really considerate and loyal person. "You struggle to accept that you have more to offer than your hot bod—"

"*Eww*. No. Stop it," he mocks.

"You can do this on your own," I press, but I can feel my resolve slipping.

"*Please.*"

"I'd be a third wheel. It'd be *weird*."

"He has a hot friend named Luke," he says, hope lifting his voice a decimal.

I cringe and put the razor back on the ceramic shelf. "*Toni*. You know I hate it when you try to hook me up with people."

"It's not a hook up," he assures me. "Just people getting to know each other. Just like you said."

"*Oh my God*." I give my body a final rise off. "How did I get roped into this?"

"Ropes won't be involved." He laughs. "Luke's a cop as well. He'd probably use handcuffs."

I roll my eyes even though he can't see them. "Not helping, Toni."

"My, my. You get Max Butcher's attention once and you're a Mean Girl."

I don't know what to say to that.

He continues, "Come on, darlin'. You'll have fun. Meet new people. Maybe get your fanny wet?"

Feigning disgust, I wrinkle my nose. "Stop it. Or I definitely won't be going."

"So, you're saying yes then?"

I squeeze my eyes shut and sigh. "You're a suck hole."

"Yes, we have established that already."

Pulling the curtain all the way back this time to stare at him, I warn, "No pressure!"

"No pressure. Is that a yes?" He smiles, lips set in a wide and triumphant curve.

"Fine." I exhale in defeat and turn the water off. "But it's not a date!"

Water splashes into the tub and down the drain as I quickly ring out my hair. As soon as I step from the shower and look at Toni, he's grinning at me with wide hopeful eyes. I tilt my head at him and wrap myself in a towel before wandering into my room to get dressed. "I said fine. Now go home," I say as I riffle through my clothes. "I've got to meet Dillion in my studio."

Toni suddenly appears at my shoulder. "I know. That's why I'm still here. Can I watch? He's so yummy."

I moan. "No. Go home."

He glares at me. "You're a Mean Girl. You're a witch with a B."

"You need to get new material!" I yell out as he walks from the room.

"Your mum's chest hair!" Toni replies and then laughs.

God, I wish *Mean Girls* was never filmed because he finds a *Mean Girls* quip to nearly everything I say.

When I hear the front door shut, I decide it's an animal-print leotard kind of day. And even though I'm really hung-over, I'm dressed and out the door by eight fifty-five.

My studio is a hundred metres behind the main house with its own driveway and two parking spots. It looks just like another house on a rear block and has all the modern commodities to match. Bathroom. Kitchen. It has excellent acoustics and high ceilings completely covered in LEDs—the more lights the better. Mirrors line the inside walls, and the flooring is a kind of vinyl plank. Dad had the studio built specifically for Flick and me when we both needed a place to dance. But Flick gave up ages ago.

I, on the other hand, attend a professional academy five days a week, and my goal next year is to secure a higher-paid position as a ballerina. It may be a bit ambitious, but I'd love to join an international company; I don't want to be stuck in the District my whole life.

Rome maybe. Or Paris...

Bonjour, je m'appelle, Cassidy Slater.

Ciao...

On top of that, I teach two senior dance classes on Monday evenings. My students pretend not to fondle each other while they waltz and I pretend not to notice. I also offer personal classes and have a few advanced students that I coach on Sunday mornings.

Dillion is one of them.

None of this pays much. It works out to be just enough to cover the electricity, WI-FI, costumes, props, alterations to the studio, and maintenance, while leaving about $50 a week left over for personal stuff. But it's not about the money. Dad just really wants me to contribute to the costs associated with my business even though my parents are pretty rich.

I think they're rich...

We don't discuss money in my household.

Dillion arrives not long after I switch the lights on and start to warm up. After an hour of practising lifts, he places me on the ground with a sigh. "You're so easy to lift."

"Oh, stop it." I shake my head. "I was able to balance very easily. That was a great lift."

He scoffs. "That's because you're amazing! Not because I'm any good. When I'm holding you, you're like an extension of me. You're so light and easy to manoeuvre. The girls at my studio are just not as good as you."

I make my way over to the foam mats. Sitting down, I begin to stretch out my hamstrings. "Well then, you'll need to get better to accommodate them."

Dillion meanders over and sits beside me on the mats, pressing his chest to his thighs. "You're incredible at what you do, Cassidy. You're good even after a night on the piss. Your movements look so natural. You don't even look hung-over this morning."

I sit up and cross my legs. "Well, they only look natural because I spend like fifty hours a week practising, but trust me, I'm hung-over today. I'm faking a lot of it." I giggle and try to be reassuring. "Listen, you're a good dancer, Dillion. That one-handed presage lift you just did was really strong, but you need to get out of your own head."

"I know," he moans. "I just can't think straight today."

"I can tell. Your mind should only be on me." I study him as he stretches. "Your mind should be on my body and yours."

"It is," he mutters.

"Well, good."

A deep mechanical growling sound from outside grabs my attention, and I frown at Dillion. "Is that a motorbike?" I jump up and rush towards the porch. The noise is rhythmic and intense as I open the door and step outside onto the deck. Leaning around the side of the studio, I watch a red bike and a big, black four-wheel-drive park up on the grass beside our pool. Flick and Stacey bounce from the back seat of the four-wheel drive as Xander and Max jump out of the front.

Oh my gawd.

And I'm back inside as fast as I can, closing the door behind me. "Frick."

Dillion is standing at the entry. "Who is it?"

I try not to smile because I'm painfully obvious. "Um, some of Flick's friends, I think."

He narrows his eyes at me, dubious. "Why are you hiding all of a sudden?" He scrutinises my face. "It's Max, isn't it?"

My mouth drops open. "Oh my God, does the whole District know I have a crush on him?"

"Yes." He grimaces. "Because he carried you up to your room last night, Cassidy."

I look at him wide-eyed. "Were you there?"

He scoffs and shakes his head in utter disbelief. "At your birthday? Yes. And we danced. But, even if I wasn't, there's a picture of you in his arms circulating socials."

I hate the internet.

Slapping myself on the forehead, I exclaim, "Yes, of course! I remember seeing you at the beginning. I'm so sorry, Dillion!" I reach out for him, but he takes a defensive step back. His emotional response completely throws me because we are not even good friends.

His brows draw tightly together. "We danced for like an

hour and you were kinda... flirty. I dunno... you were sorta... sexy."

As I stare apologetically at him, my cheeks burn. "I'm so sorry. That's so unprofessional. I swear, it'll never happen again."

He glances at the ground and frowns, before turning to collect his things from the bench. "Okay."

"Dillion?"

"You have your head in the sand, Cassidy. Max and his brothers are trouble."

"You need to stop listening to rumours."

"Go onto Google. Check out some articles. Literally, I'm not kidding. Just google Butcher and you'll see."

"I'm not interested in what The District News has to say about them." That seems to annoy him even more, but before I can press him for an explanation, my studio door swings open and Flick struts in.

"Hey, my little love, how are you feeling?" She glances at Dillion. "Dillion, looking toned in those tights. Hot."

He continues to grab his things and then walks towards the door. I think he is probably feeling patronised, but I'm sure she'd only meant what she'd said as a compliment. Flick is so confident, she's often oblivious to how she can make people feel uncomfortable.

"Yeah, do they make them for men?" I hear a voice say from outside the door.

Well, that definitely wasn't a compliment.

Annoyed by the comment and how comfortable everyone is invading my studio space, I walk out onto the patio. Xander is chuckling to himself, and Max is standing staunchly behind him. I freeze.

My eyes meet Max's momentarily, and I'm again consumed by insecurities. *Frick.* I'm only wearing a skin-tight leotard and stockings. Nothing is left to the imagination. That might be the intent in ballet—visible and obvious lines—but in the real world, I might as well be wearing lingerie.

And I have no tits.

So now he knows I have no tits.

Flick stops Dillion in the doorway. "Come for a swim with us? Cassidy, you coming?"

Dillion halts and then turns to me. Enveloping my shoulders with his arms, he whispers in my ear. "We okay?"

I squeeze his waist. I'm not happy, but I still feel a sense of relief. "Of course. We'll talk soon."

His breath hits my ear as he says, "Don't go there, Cassidy." He grips me tighter. "He'll destroy you."

The relief is replaced by discomfort.

My arms flop to the side and Dillion leaves, walking past the boys and straight to his car. I glare at the brick wall for a moment, confusion and irritation both wrestling for first place in my mind.

He'll destroy me? Like destroy my reputation or does he mean emotionally?

It's almost unfair. Last night was the first time that I allowed myself to make a few bad decisions. I'm not going to be destroyed by anyone. I'm not a delicate little flower. I'm a frickin' ballerina—I'm always working on swollen toes, bruised knees, and cramping muscles. I'm a machine. I'm a model of self-control.

I grin at Flick and nod adamantly. "Yep. I'll come for a swim." I massage my quadriceps. "It'll be good for my muscles. I'm just gonna run to the house and grab my bathers."

I dart across the patio, taking very little notice of Max on my way. Well, except for a few minor details, like he's wearing a casual white tee-shirt with short sleeves and navy boardshorts that display every wave of muscle on his arms and legs. The definition of some of those bad boys can only be achieved by a rugby player or someone who does CrossFit every day. His biceps and forearms even seem to have somehow grown since last night too... Or maybe they just appear that way because they're now folded across his chest. But his eyes are definitely bluer in the daylight.

He turns his head slightly as I rush past and I inhale deeply, fighting the blush threatening to creep up my cheeks.

By the time I stroll back to the pool in my pink one-piece bathing suit, my nerves are replaced by annoyance.

Five-minutes-ago-Cassidy has some explaining to do.

What was she thinking, choosing the suit that sits high on my hips, riding up each bum cheek? She's a little tart.

But thankfully, as I unlatch the pool gate and walk in, my emotions once again shift. I'm just in time to see Max remove his shirt by pulling the back of his collar up and over his head with one arm.

Oh my gawd.

I glance away and take a big breath, wishing that I wasn't so into him. That it wasn't so obvious. That I wasn't an asexual pigeon. Kicking my flip-flops off, I drop my towel on the chair. He's diving into the pool and it's then that I notice the other brother. I've never seen him before, but I know that he's Max's brother because they look so alike. It's hard to tell with them both submerged, but I think he's taller, maybe less built.

"Who is this then?" The other brother smiles at me as he swims a little closer. "I don’t think we have met."

Flick throws a pool noodle at Stacey, who catches it, straddles it, and jumps into the water. "That's my sister, Cassidy," Flick says.

He lifts himself out of the pool just enough to offer me his hand. "Nice to meet you, sister Cassidy. I'm Bronson." *And* he's as annoyingly gorgeous as his brother, with clear, opal-blue eyes and a soft, infectious grin. He even has that signature Butcher dimple on his left cheek. The only ugly thing about him—and I'm not even sure if it's ugly or just tacky—is a terrible chopper-style moustache. I hope he wears it ironically. I shake his hand and within a second, I'm pulled from the step and into the water. A yelp escapes me as I'm submerged. Within another second, I'm surfacing again.

My grin is huge as Bronson playfully pushes my wet strawberry-blonde hair away from my face. "You okay, sister Cassidy? Sorry, couldn't help myself."

"Bronson ya dickhead," Xander groans from across the pool. "You don't even know her."

"Bronson!" I hear Flick growl.

I cough a little and then laugh. "Yeah, I'm fine." I wade backwards, purposefully splashing him as I kick over to the corner. It's somewhat refreshing to not be coddled.

My hair is all over the place, so I dip my head back and smooth it down my crown. By the time I wipe water from my eyes, Xander is jumping into the pool, and Flick is splashing Stacey. Water goes everywhere as they chat and mock each other.

I stay in my own corner, a little overwhelmed by the three boys. I kick hard to stay afloat and watch everything unfold.

My gaze is suddenly snagged on blue-grey eyes just as they lock on me. And my chest is rising and falling faster to keep up with my quickening breaths. Max is swimming towards me now and I'm wading backwards, all the way backwards until I'm hitting the fibreglass boundary. *Frick.*

He grins. "Do I know you?"

I giggle nervously. "Funny." While I work to keep afloat, he stands with his shoulders above the surface. "Oh my God, how tall are you?" I almost moan.

"Six four." He studies my body as it moves underwater. "Want to wrap your legs around me, birthday girl?"

I burst out laughing and cup my face, nearly dunking myself in the process. "No."

"Come here." Chuckling, he reaches for me. He pulls my legs around his waist and my arms onto his shoulders, and although our torsos aren't touching as water flows between us, his face is only inches from mine. And instantly I'm not smiling anymore. I'm lost in the dark grey outline of his irises, and I'm sure he can identify the exact hue of every one of my freckles.

"Hands off my sister, Max!"

"Mind your own hands," he yells over to Flick, but doesn't turn his head. "Mine are wherever I want them to be."

Flick splashes us. "Just scream if you need me, Cassidy."

Electricity crackles between us. I'm not naive enough to say it's surreal or unexplainable; it's just sexual energy, I know that, but it's intense. His eyelashes have beads of water on them, and his hands are wrapped around my waist, and come to think of it, they are big. He has really big hands. My lips part and his eyes drop to watch me breathe. I want more than anything to just get it over with and press my mouth to his, exploring this feeling, but I don't think that's what girls do in a situation like this. I'm sure they seduce or act coy or say something clever like...

"You have big hands."

Oh my God, shut up.

He flexes his fingers around my waist. "What do you imagine they're good at?"

My cheeks burn. "Oh my *gawd*. Stop it."

He grins at me. "So why don't I see you around the District much?"

I try not to get sucked into the vortex of his eyes. "I'm busy."

"Busy doing what?"

"Dancing. That's kinda all I do."

"That's good. Did you take the Panadol?" His voice is even and authoritarian.

I blink at him as we float together. "Um, yes, thanks, and sorry about the whole passing out thing."

"That made my night."

My cheeks feel a pinch as I fight back a giggle. "Care to fill me in on before that?

He leans in a little closer. "Which part?"

"Um, the part where... Well, any part that involved you and me? I don't remember talking to you much."

"You told me to stop being so hot." His lips part and his white teeth show. "It's the cutest thing I've ever heard."

"Ah..." I stammer. "Your level of, like, self-love, is like, so over-the-top."

"Like, is it?"

"Yes." I nod and lose the fight with my mouth and just let a goofy grin show. "I would have never said that... *to your face*."

He grins, his lips set in an amused and mischievous curve. "Really?"

"Yes, really."

The corner of his mouth draws out further until his dimple is on display. "So, you don't think I'm, 'Oh my gawd you're too hot, just stop it' kind of hot?"

Frick.

I pull my arms from his shoulders and shield my face. "Oh no, Max. Go away. I did say that, didn't I?"

"Like I said." His hands move from my waist down to cup my backside and he pulls me into him. My chest touches his, my nipples growing so hard they hurt. "Just helping you stay afloat, Little One," he claims with a smirk.

I drape my arms over his shoulders again even though my heart is racing and my breathing becomes something I have to concentrate on. His eyes move around my face and down my neck as his fingers draw little circles on each of my cheeks. I suppress a moan, and he grins even further when my eyes slowly start to close.

I'm not a fricking asexual pigeon...

"You have a serious girl boner for me, hey?" Max laughs.

My eyes fly open and I glare at him. "Oh, stop it, Max. You're being a jerk."

"I *am* a jerk," he declares, his tone brazenly unapologetic.

"No, you're not. A jerk doesn't put Panadol out for a girl. A jerk doesn't carry a girl to her room and not even try to sleep with her."

His eyebrows are level and he fixes me with a stare. "You were unconscious. That's not a jerk; that's a rapist. You keep saying shit like that and it's gonna worry me."

I glance away. "I know. I didn't mean..." There is this silence between us now and it's so palpable that I can't breathe. "So what if I do have a girl boner for you? It's just primal."

He moves his hands back to either side of my waist and I sink down a little. "It's a bad idea."

My forehead tightens. "What is?"

"You and me."

"Why?"

"Because you're clearly a girlfriend girl, and I can't think of anything I'd like less."

"That's a heavy statement. What about polio? Bet you'd like that less."

"Nah." He curls his lips and shakes his head. "I think I'll take the polio."

"You don't even know me. Maybe I'm only interested in one thing from you, Max Butcher."

"Is that so?"

My eyes are suddenly drawn to Bronson, who is climbing out of the pool butt naked, and I can't believe I didn't even notice that he's been naked this whole time. He casually struts over to collect his towel. His thick, powerful thighs are wrapped in beautiful vibrant tattoos. An intricate family tree design runs from the base of his spine to his neck. I struggle to look away when he turns around and begins to pat himself dry. He starts at his lean muscular abdomen and works his way down each leg. His penis hangs thick and long between his thighs. There are colourful tattoos on nearly every inch of his body. It's intense and sexy and awkward, and I really need to look away now. I glance back at Max.

He's eyeballing me. "You checking out my brother, Little One?"

My cheeks catch fire; I know I'm blushing off the charts. "Oh my God, he's completely naked, Max."

"Yeah. He does that. I really wish he wouldn’t."

Bronson calls over to Max. "Time to hit the road, Maxi-pad. Boss called!"

Max lets go of me and swims towards Bronson. He lifts himself out of the water and I push back to the pool edge, where I watch the hottest man on earth stride away from me. Max has mostly black ink on his arms and chest and the exact same family tree tattoo, but the rest of his skin is smooth, bare, and bronzed.

I stare at them as they converse. He dries himself off quickly and pulls his shirt on. He's definitely built bigger than Bronson, with large defined muscles that create visible curves beneath his shirt.

His jaw is tight as he talks to his brother, but then softens when he looks over at me. "Until next time, Little One."

I sigh, knowing that he was right—I'd want more than just one thing from him.

I'd want everything.

CHAPTER FOUR

i'll fuck you on this slide

"I LOVE THIS SONG," I announce. "Turn it up, pretty please."

Using the button on his steering wheel, Braidy turns the volume up as he glances at me in the rear-view mirror.

Luke listens intently from the seat beside mine. "What's the song?"

“"*Riptide*.” It's my jam." I bop my head and begin to sing, peering out the window as we roll down Old Coast Road towards the marina.

Toni sings over the top of the music. He twists to grin at me from the front seat while making a jerking-off motion with his hand. *"Your left-hand, man."*

I just laugh and continue to sing, lost in my own world of Vance Joy and ocean views.

When we get to the marina, we wander the docks for a while, pointing out the boats we like and enjoying the final rays of the sun.

"Where is our boat today, Toni?" I ask, smiling widely.

He chuckles. "Fucking Manu," he says, and we hip and shoulder each other lightly.

An amused look passes between Luke and Braidy.

"Who is Manu?" Braidy asks.

"When Toni and I were younger, we used to pretend that our boat was being cleaned by our boat chauffer, Manu. I don't even know if there is such a thing as a boat chauffeur, but that was our lie for why we didn't have a boat docked here."

"You guys have known each other for a while then?" Luke asks.

Toni laughs. "She's like an addiction."

As we pass by the bar, Gypsy's, Toni persuades us to go inside. It can be pretty rough in here at times, but then again, we are with two of the District's finest. And the food is always good, huge selection too.

When our meals arrive, Luke stares at my plate. "Wow, I've never seen a girl order that much food."

Toni tsks. "My friend, you never mention what a girl orders. How many dates have you been on?"

My eyes narrow at Toni and they inaudibly scream, 'This is not a date!'

Grinning at Luke, I give him my attention. "Eating is like my third favourite pastime." I pause, thinking on it. "Fourth favourite. Dancing. Fireworks. Arcade games. Eating."

"Do you want to hear mine?" Luke asks, focusing his attention on me as Braidy whispers something in Toni's ear and they both chuckle. We twist even further to face each other. Our knees touch, but I don't mind.

I take a sip of red wine and focus on Luke's crooked canine. "Yeah. Shoot."

"Movies, cricket, playing guitar, and sleeping. Although, I'd say sleeping can creep its way up to number one under certain circumstances." Luke grins at me. "And I think it's great you eat. I love food."

Using my fork to point at his plate, I ask, "Then why did you order a tuna salad?"

He glances at Braidy and then back at me, searching for words. "Trying to be healthy?"

"You don't sound sure." I giggle.

Toni plays footsies with me under the table. "You don't make friends with healthy."

I laugh and dunk my potato in sour cream. "Toni's allergic to healthy."

"Isn't it, you don't make friends with salad?" Luke points out.

"Is it?" Toni curls his lips in contemplation. "All these years. *Hmm*."

I begin to really enjoy the wine and find myself signalling the waitress for another... And another. Luke's crooked canine gets cuter and cuter with every sip. He pushes his blond hair back from his face and finishes his fifth pint before asking for the check.

He goes to pay, but I object. "No. I can pay for myself."

There is this grin playing on his lips now. "Seriously, Cassidy. Let me pay for you."

When he says my name, I think of Max, just for a second. Because Max never says my name. He calls me 'Little One'. And I'm still not sure if that's a term of endearment or if he's being patronising, but I like it anyway.

I shake my head. "No. I don't feel comfortable with that."

His eyes search my face, measuring me up. Perhaps wondering if I'm being serious or testing him, which is so not in my nature to do. "I'm serious," I press. "I work really hard and have my own money."

"Hmm." He nods in agreement. "How about we rock

paper scissors for it? I win, I pay. You win, you can pay for yourself."

I smile. "I love that idea."

We both put our fists in and count, "One. Two. Three!"

My fist flattens into paper, and he throws two fingers out, making scissors.

We are both smiling at each other now. He's nice.

"Okay. You win," I say.

We walk hand-in-hand towards the carnival rides, but it's very G-rated between us—coy and flirty, but suitable for all ages. Toni and Braidy disappear into the crowd, leaving Luke and me to continue the night on our own.

He seems to enjoy my silly side and even joins in. We sit on the teapots and spin, shoot ducks and miss, throw coins and sink them, and now I'm genuinely having a really great time.

We leave the rides and games and head up the hill, where we plonk ourselves down on the grass steps that overlook the water. Conversation with Luke has become completely natural.

"So, you're a ballerina." He tugs on his earlobe and cocks his head. "I've never been to see the ballet before."

I cross my ankles in front of me. "You should."

He sighs. "I'm not sure I'm cultured enough."

"What?" I say, genuinely surprised. "You don't have to be cultured to watch ballet."

"Okay. Show me something? Let's see if I like it."

I giggle nervously. "What?"

"Yeah. Seriously. Show me a move or whatever."

"Like, now?" I look around the hill. It's pretty dark, but people are scattered around us for fifty metres or so. I'm not hesitant to dance in public, but in order to do so, I'm going to need to adjust my skirt... "Here?"

"Why not?"

"*Okay*." I kick my heels off and stand on the grass in front of him. I hike my denim skirt up until it's around my waist, putting my white knickers on show for far too many people. And what the hell am I doing, flashing half of the marina? It doesn't matter, I decide. It's dark. Tilting my chin up, I raise my arms, forming a loose circle above my head. I relax my neck and smile at him. A little heat hits my cheeks when I see his eyes are trained on me. Slowly, I lift my working leg up, toes pointed, until my calf is beside my face, my legs forming a perfect line. I hold the développé position with ease and glance back at Luke, who is now squirming in place. I lower my leg until my toes meet my knee. Then I kick with that leg. Whipping around, I hold my head stationary and complete three fouettés—which after a bottle of wine is impressive—before finishing gracefully in first position.

"Are you cultured enough to watch that for a few hours?" I grin at him.

There's heat behind his eyes now that has my stomach flipping. Or maybe that's the wine? He stands, takes my hand in his, and pulls me towards the old waterpark.

We duck under a fence and walk through the ruins of the park. Stopping suddenly, he lifts me onto the lip of an abandoned slide. The cold plastic on my thighs sends a shiver down my spine. He stands in front of me and as he presses his mouth to mine, he moves his hips between my knees. I close my eyes and welcome him, feeling a fuzzy sensation rush through me and a complete lack of concern because Luke is a cop. This feels nice too. Luke feels safe. His hands caress from my knees to the plump parts of my thighs. There he grips me, tilting me up and wrapping my legs around him. I hum and his tongue finds mine. His jeans rub against my knickers, and a moan escapes me with every movement.

And it's inadvertent and unwelcome, but now I'm thinking about Max.

I close my eyes and imagine for a second that Max is the one touching me. Guilt makes me squirm and I force my eyes open, trying to acknowledge Luke. For Luke. His kiss is chaste. I get the feeling Max's kisses wouldn't be. I imagine they'd consume me.

Stop thinking about Max!

Forcing Luke to the front and centre of my mind, I lift my hands up and feed my fingers through his thick, blond hair. He touches me with intimacy and longing, making this all feel okay. I'm sure he won't take things too far. But then his hands start pawing at my thighs and his breathing becomes laboured and mixed with groans.

His hands are up my skirt now, skating around the seam of my knickers. "Cassidy, you're so hot here."

Out of nowhere, Luke is pulled back from me, leaving me open-mouthed and flushed. Luke growls, "What the fuck?" just as Max swings his fist into Luke's jaw.

Max?

What. The. Frick.

I wince when blood sprays from Luke's face. He doubles over, cupping his chin and groaning gutturally. It looks like he's about to fight back, but there is no opportunity for him to retaliate; Max is already dragging him towards the fence line. His superior height and build make Luke look like a petulant child in trouble with daddy.

"Oh my God! Stop it!" I yell out.

Max throws him through the gap before turning to glare at me. I'm speechless.

Luke attempts to come back but stops when Max stares him down. "If you climb back through that fence, your knees won't work for a month." Luke looks at me, and Max takes a step towards him. "A year," he warns.

I nod at Luke, but it seems unnecessary because he's already decided he's not going to take Max on tonight. Turning, he disappears into the dark.

"What the hell, Max?" I crane my neck to glare at him as he dissects every inch of me. His jaw clenches as his eyes scroll down my body, skirt around my waist, and linger at my spread thighs. I slam my knees together, wipe my mouth, and pull my clothes straight.

Max nails me to the spot with his glare. "I just overheard the strangest thing. Apparently, Cassidy Slater is finally putting out tonight."

I cringe at his words. "Max, what have you done?"

A vein in his neck bulges. "I just saved him a lot of pain, Little One. If his hands had gotten any farther, I would have had to break them."

"Who the hell do you think you are?" I shuffle on the slide and try to squeeze past him, but it's an attempt to no avail. "Get out of my way, Max."

He stands staunchly. "I saw your peep show, Little One. You were seconds away from crawling onto his lap. No wonder he took you back here."

My breathing becomes shallow. "You were watching me?"

"Half the fucking District was watching you spread your legs for him."

"I was dancing. Not spreading my legs for him! Why are you so mad at me?"

He glares down at me over a tight jaw. "Do you know how easy it would have been for him to rape you back here?"

"He wasn't going to do anything to me, Max. He's a cop."

"Then tell me this" – he leans towards me – "if he wasn't

going to do anything, why did he take you back here? Why didn't he just kiss you on the hill?"

Swallowing hard, I reach for an answer to that question, but come back empty. "I'm safe," I whisper. "I'm here with Toni."

"Yeah?" He looks around the dark, derelict water slides. "Where. *The fuck.* Is Toni?"

I glance at the ground between his feet. "I don't know."

"Are you fucking stupid?" he scolds. "Are you in heat or something?"

I feel both the sting of his words and my welling tears. As he glares down at me as if I'm some naive idiot, too many feelings swarm around inside me—most of them completely contradictory. There is this skip in my heart that inadvertently relishes his attention, concern, and what looks and sounds a lot like protectiveness. But the weight in my belly churns because I was alone in the dark with a stranger. That's true. I still don't believe Luke would have done anything, but I don't know for sure, do I?

"You're being a jerk again," I say.

He shakes his head. "I don't like it."

"I was just kissing him."

His body makes a shadow over mine. "I. Don't. Like it," he states, and I flinch even though his words were spoken softly. "Does Flick know her little sister strips off for guys and disappears into dark corners with them?"

I stare up at him. "Flick would encourage me to express myself. I don't do it enough."

"Express yourself?" He near snaps the words. "Express yourself all over his fingers."

"*Max*. Stop it."

"Is this what you want? To give up your virginity to a stranger outside a waterpark?"

My eyes widen. "How did you know I was a—"

"It hurts." The words come out through a growl. "The first time can hurt. It isn't meant to be done like thi—"

Anger bites at the heels of humiliation. "Excuse me! I don't want to discuss my virginity with you, *Max Butcher*. It's none of your business. And as if you care about my virginity. As if you care about any girl's virginity. It's not a prize, right?"

He fixes his eyes shut, making no noise or movement for a few seconds. His eyes open and find mine again. "Who said it wasn't a prize?"

"I don't know. Everyone in my life? It's the norm. Toni. My brother, who's had more girls than I can count. Flick. Guys like you who treat sex like it's as casual as eating breakfast. Guys who think having a girlfriend is the worst thing in life. Worse than polio!"

"That's what this is about? You're that desperate to get fucked? Fine! Get in my car right now. I'll fuck you." His tone is harsh and authoritarian, making me recoil. Heat prickles the backs of my eyes. He growls when I don't instantly move. "Okay then!" He unzips his jeans, pins my legs apart, and grasps my upper arms, handling me roughly as he forces me to stare at him. "Want me to fuck you right here on this slide?"

I tug my arm from him and cover my face with it, trying desperately to smother the sobs building in my throat. I've lost my fight against him. Lost my resolve. "Shut up!" In an instant, the tears start to flow, and I hold myself tight.

Through my pooling eyes, I see something like regret flash across his face, but it's gone so quickly I could have imagined it. He fastens his jeans, pulls me up by the elbow and drags me over to his car.

His black four-wheel-drive is parked not far from the

grass hill Luke and I were sitting on less than half an hour ago. He lifts me into the passenger seat and leans across me to buckle my belt, a semblance of urgency to his movements. I'm rendered speechless, wanting to scold him, reason with him, and ask him to forgive me, all at the same time.

What?

Forgive me for what? Kissing a boy? Getting myself into a position in which he felt I needed rescuing? The door slams shut. I stare at my bare feet as he climbs in behind the wheel and sets off down the road at an aggressive pace. A heavy bass vibrates under me.

Frick, my heels.

"My heels," I mutter.

He points to the backseat, and I twist to see my black Steve Madden stilettos lying there. I blink and turn back to watch the dark road as it rushes under us. From the corner of my eye, I can see Max scowling straight ahead. He thinks I'm some kind of naive idiot. It was nice to feel wanted. Sexy. That's all. And this all started because of him, because of my attraction to him. Next time I have a crush on a boy, I should just tape my mouth and vagina shut. Call it a day.

"He's a cop, Max," I say. He doesn't respond, just stares unwaveringly at the road. "He wouldn’t have hurt me." His hands tighten around the steering wheel. "You could get into heaps of trouble for hitting a cop." He presses the volume button and turns the beat up until it drowns out my voice.

Giving up, my eyes move to the little tree hanging in the centre of the windscreen. The plastic packaging hangs half off, preserving the scent inside. His car feels new. Leather seats. Digital display. It smells new.

I'm in Max's car.

Is he taking me to his house? I swallow hard at the thought of him pulling me into his room and teaching me a lesson about men. I squeeze my thighs together. As much as I want Max, I don't want him in this headspace. He's... intimidating.

"I don't want to do anything," I whisper, but he can't hear me over the music. "I don't want to do anything!" I yell. Max's hand is on the volume button in seconds, lowering the beat until I can hear my own breaths of courage.

"Say that again," he says, his voice salacious as if he's trying to get me to understand something.

I swallow past the tone and how it makes me feel. "I don't want to do anything. I didn't want to do anything with Luke either. Things just got out of control."

The tension in his face softens. "We're not going to, Little One. We're just going to sleep."

This time when he says 'Little One', my heart races and an uncomfortable level of arousal spikes inside me.

I move my knee to the side and stare at his profile. His mouth is in a tight line. He grips the wheel firmly and his biceps bulge, stretching the sleeves of his shirt. He's too hot. He should come with a warning label. "Are you taking me home?"

He offers me a quick glance. "I won't be able to sleep tonight unless I know you're next to me." Every part of my body feels those words, including parts I didn't know could respond to words alone. My heart is beating so fast it threatens to jump right out of my chest. That's the single, most intimate thing any guy has ever said to me. And if it wasn't obvious before, it is now. I'm brandishing that goofy grin because Max Butcher cares about me—even if only a little.

I should still be angry with him.

But I'm not.

I'm becoming one of those girls I have always pitied.

When he pulls onto my street and turns down my driveway, I feel disappointment curdle in my belly. Why are we at my house? Does this mean he doesn't want to sleep next to me tonight? Was that just a fleeting moment of something growing between us? Now over? *God*, he's giving me whiplash.

Without a word, he switches the headlights off as we approach the front porch, perhaps trying not to wake my family. He drives the car out the back and up onto the grass beside my studio.

My brows pinch tightly together. "I don't understand."

He switches the ignition off and looks at me sternly. "Go upstairs."

"But I thought—"

"Go upstairs," he orders. "Do you want me to meet you up there?"

My breath lodges in my throat, but I manage to whisper, "Yes."

"I need to hear you say it." He stares down at me, locking his eyes on my mouth. "Say, Max, I want you to sleep next to me tonight."

"Max, I want you to sleep next to me tonight." The words are uttered softly, because I'm completely breathless. His eyes are still focused on my lips, making my pulse drum in my skull.

"Good." He nods towards the house. "Go upstairs. I'll meet you up there."

I climb out of the car and race towards the house. I can feel his eyes on me. Once I'm inside, I sneak up the stairs and into my room. Shutting my door softly behind me, I press my back to it and stand like a statue for a few moments, trying to catch my breath.

Max Butcher is going to sleep in my room tonight.

Oh my God!

Rushing into the ensuite, I quickly throw water on my face and brush my teeth like a machine. I run around my room, grabbing clothes, and then change into my pyjama shorts and tank top. My reflection catches my eye and I stare at myself. My cheeks are flushed and my hair is messy around my shoulders.

A sudden knock at my window draws my attention, and oh my God, Max is at the window. He must have climbed up the lattice.

I stare at him for a moment, the magnitude of this moment settling inside me. First, I kiss Luke. Max acts like a damn caveman, and now he's here. Should I be nervous? Not excited-nervous, but fearful nervous?

He frowns at me through the glass. "Open up."

Walking over to the window, I slide it open. As he pushes the screen in and climbs through with little exertion, I step back.

And now he's standing in front of me, in my room and intimidating as hell. I crane my neck to watch him take in my most personal space. He looks out of place amongst the white furniture and overly feminine décor. This feels strangely intimate. I think he almost grins.

He peers down at me and lifts a hand to my face, brushing one of my blonde waves over my shoulder. My eyelids grow heavy as his warm knuckles stroke my cheek.

"Go to sleep," he states, but it isn't a suggestion.

I crawl into bed as he kicks off his shoes. Under the false sense of safety the sheets give me, I watch him pull his shirt off and unbutton his jeans before sliding them down his legs. I gasp. He is so fricking beautiful.

He leaves his clothes sprawled out across the carpet, and they improve the space—a lot. I like them there.

He walks towards me in white boxer shorts that leave very little to the imagination; the form of his penis beneath them is a large bulge that moves under its own weight. Muscles cut up his physique, creating definition on every inch of skin. The sight of him is uncomfortable. It's hot tingles. An uneven heart rate. It's breathlessness. I scoot over and he slides in beside me. As he lies on his back, frowning at the ceiling, I stare at his profile.

"I thought you were going to take me to your house," I admit, resting my face on my hands and trying to pretend I'm unaffected by his presence.

You're failing, Cassidy.

"So did I." He pauses for a moment with his thoughts. "It's not a good idea."

"I seem to hear that a lot from you."

"That's because when it comes to you, it's true."

"I don't get it. You seem to like me." I search his face for emotion and feel a spike of panic when he doesn't respond. The silence between us is crushing me. "Well, at least I think you do." He clenches his jaw. "What are you thinking about, Max?" I press.

He exhales. "I'm thinking about that fucking sound." He looks at me and his eyes thin. "The one you made when he had his cock pressed between your thighs. And I'm thinking about how he's probably thinking about it too while he rubs one out."

I breathe out fast. "*Max.*"

"Should've broken his hands."

CHAPTER FIVE

be mindful of the company you keep

I WAKE to the sound of Toni barging into my room. "Eeee, I need to check my panties!"

As he charges into the bathroom, I slowly sit up and rub my groggy eyes, my dry mouth, my tight forehead. I listen to the water running from the faucet and try to discern what he's doing, but it's way too early in the morning to think.

"False alarm!" When he reappears, his smile is incorrigible. "I just got schooled by Max Butcher. He gave me a semi. I also thought maybe I'd crapped my panties. He makes angry look like you'd risk your life to be manhandled by him. I couldn't understand a word his luscious mouth was saying with all my brain blood in my cock. What's going on?"

I squint at him. "Huh? Max yelled at you?"

Gripping his waist, he leans on one hip. "It was more of a deep, threatening tone than a yell. But I'm in trouble, that's for sure. I've been a naughty boy and he needs to spank me. At least... that's what I heard."

"Wait." I shake my head. "What time is it? Where did you even see him?"

"At the gym, darlin'. I'm there at five most mornings. This body doesn't come without maintenance."

"Was he okay? Like, was he acting normal?"

"He was boxing with his dad; they do that a lot." He wiggles his eyebrows. "I like to watch."

An image of Max boxing out his frustration from last night invades my mind, warming my skin. I struggle to swallow. "He's ah—"I clear my throat. "He's probably mad at you for leaving me."

"Uh, exqueeze me? We left each other. Mutually."

"Yes, I know that, Toni," I say as my eyes land on a glass of water and a note:

'We gotta stop meeting like this, Alice.'

My heart flutters at the words.

Max slept next to me last night.

I stare at the spot where he'd dropped his clothes and get that uncomfortable feeling again.

"What is that?" Toni lunges toward me and snatches the note from my tabletop. He reads it, eyes sparkling. I can't help but smile at my best friend's enthusiasm.

"Oh. My. Giddy aunt! Is this from Max? You hooked up with him? He stayed the night? What did you do? How big was it?"

I roll my eyes. "Technically, I hooked up with Luke."

His jaw gapes. "You hooked up with them both?"

"No, it wasn't li—"

He reaches for me and caresses my cheek, his eyes feigning earnestness as he begins to serenade me. He sings "Wind Beneath My Wings" by Bette Milder. I throw my head back and break into laughter before joining in the song. "You're everything I would like to be."

We have a good giggle together. Before I roll out of bed and get ready for ballet school, I fill Toni in on last night—the whole eventful lot.

His shoulders sag. "I'm so disappointed. So, he never touched you? Not even a little finger action? That is so... un-Max Butcher. You really are an asexual pigeon."

I make pigeon noises as I pull on my sneakers. "I fell asleep. I can't believe I just fell asleep." I run my fingers up through my hair and pull it into a high ballet bun.

I'm completely packed and ready to go when I glance out the window and see a police car roll onto my driveway. Braidy and Luke step out, both dressed in uniform.

"Oh, crap." I wince.

Toni gasps. "Did you just swear, Cassidy Slater?" He rushes over to the window and his eyebrows shoot up. "Oh crap."

"I swear my life is too eventful now," I moan, grabbing my bag and rushing down the stairs to answer the door before they can ring the bell. As I swing the door open, I feign surprise. "Oh. Hey?"

Braidy is standing with his finger in the air, having been about ready to press the button. When I appear in the door jamb, he takes a polite step backwards. He's very formal. "Cassidy, I'm glad you're still home... Is he here?"

I nearly cough. "Who? Max?" I bounce my eyes between Luke and Braidy. Oh my God, I'm in some kind of trouble. I stare at Luke's face; the lower part is bruised—red and purple and swollen. "Oh, Luke. I'm so sorry. Are you okay?" As a shadow hovers over me, he glances past my shoulder, swallows hard, and takes a step back. When it's just Toni who appears at my side, Luke relaxes instantly.

Toni peruses their police uniforms. "What's with the formalities? Am I in trouble? Please tell me I'm in trouble!"

Braidy takes a deep breath. "I didn't realise you'd be here."

"You should always assume I'll be here," Toni says with an edge to his voice.

Braidy's eyes crinkle as he forces a smile. Then he looks back at me and says, "We were just on patrol in your neighbourhood and thought we'd make a quick house call to see if you're alright after last night."

"Um." I falter and glance quickly at Luke. "Okay. Yeah, I'm fine. But I'm not the one who got hit in the face."

Luke clasps his hands in front of him. "I'm fine, Cassidy. We just wanted to make sure *you* were."

"Well, thanks. I am."

Luke's face is tight and his eyes are evasive. "Good to hear."

I brush a non-existent strand of hair off my face and give a small shrug. "*Kewl.*"

Toni presses his shoulder to mine. "Awkies."

"So," Luke pauses with his own thoughts. "Just be mindful of the company you keep." He nods once and walks back to his car. Opening up the passenger side, he puts one foot in and stops. "That's all," he says, looking at his partner.

Braidy's eyebrows lift and he gives his thighs a single tap. "Alright then. I'll call you, Toni."

"Arrest me," Toni purrs.

Braidy chuckles, but it doesn't reach his eyes. "Maybe next time."

We watch them drive from the house and out onto the main road before finally relaxing enough to look at each other. "What was that all about?" I ask, wide-eyed.

Toni grabs my bag and slings it over my shoulder. "Max Butcher."

"Yeah, but it just doesn't make sense. I can't... I don't even know what to say." Shaking my head, I stand on my tippy toes and kiss Toni on the cheek. I've probably missed warm-up already. "I don't have time. I've got to go."

I run to the garage as Toni shouts, "Good luck!"

"What?" I stop and face him.

"With Sugar Plum." He gives me two animated thumbs up. "You'll get it."

I exhale loudly. "Thanks, Toni. You really do listen to me when I talk, hey?"

"I judge you too" – he shrugs – "if that makes it less creepy."

"Naw, and I appreciate that." I jump into my car, turn the ignition on, and scroll through my song library until I find Tchaikovsky. My mind races with thoughts of Max and Luke. A strange flutter fills the pit of my belly. I rub my cheeks and will myself to focus on the music to drown out all other distractions until after five p.m.

When I finally run into the hall, I stare straight at my locker, ignoring the girls already halfway through a sequence at the barre. I've completely missed our morning Pilates session. As Kelly offers advice, her voice breaks through the loud music playing. "Loose arms, Kate."

Sitting down on the floor, I pull my pointe shoes out and quickly pull them on.

"Relax your shoulders, Lucy," Kelly calls out, walking around the room.

I take a deep breath, stand, and join in the sequence. My arms arch backwards before sweeping forward and moving into position as though I have been here the whole time. We concentrate on our upper body, moving through five shaped positions, focusing on our lines and the elongation of our necks and décolletage. It quickly becomes me. I love the way the music and my movements seem to be one entity. It's hard to think about anything other than my body.

After several more sequences and four more hours, we retire to our small group training sessions.

"Cassidy." Kelly rushes over to me as I drink water from my bottle. I prepare myself for a tongue lashing, but she just says, "I hope you're going to audition for the role of Sugar Plum. I know you're usually Clara, but the ballet mistress and I both think you're ready for some diversity."

I breathe out fast. "Oh, yeah. I will be."

"Good." She nods and tilts her head. Her neck is long and elegant; it's as if she'd been engineered to be a ballerina. "You know the choreography inside and out. You've been distracted this last week with other things, but I know you and nothing has come between you and ballet before. Just let me know if it's something you need help with, okay?"

I force a smile. I'm finding this attitude towards my recent social activities tiresome. They are underestimating me; I can be both a girl interested in a boy and an athlete moving ahead in her field. In fact, I find it a little bit sexist that everyone thinks I'm going to suddenly lose my identity just because I've found another facet of myself. "I'm fine but thank you."

Several girls are standing behind Kelly, eyeing me every so often. Their giggling and chatting can only mean one thing, they are eager to discuss more about the image of Max and me from my birthday. I tell them the truth—just like I've been doing every day since it was posted.

Nothing happened.

I'm not sure why they don't believe me. Maybe it's got something to do with the big frickin' goofy grin that stretches my cheeks whenever I hear his name.

I drive home and it's only when I pull into my garage that I check my phone. I lean back in my seat and watch the roller door hit the pavers. I could just fall asleep right here. I have a voicemail from a private number and a message from Toni, but my eyes get heavy as I stare at the screen. I bat my eyelids and then close them completely. I wiggle my toes, getting comfortable. My breathing deepens. Suddenly my phone vibrates and I jerk upright. Fumbling to pull it to my ear, my eyes open at half-mast. "Hello?"

"Is this Cassidy Slater?" a strong, sturdy voice asks.

I sit up and rub my eyes to life. "Yes."

"My name is Michael. I'm an associate of Mr. Storm's. He has a proposition for you. When can you meet him?

Frick.

"Um." I rub an increasingly moist palm down my thigh.

"Will tomorrow at twelve p.m. suffice?"

"No." I clear my throat and try to keep my voice steady. "Um, I have rehearsals."

"After five then?"

"Ah..." I squint at nothing in particular and strain to find a reasonable excuse to object, but I come up short. "Yes. Yes, I can do that. Where will I be meeting him?"

"I will send a car to collect you tomorrow. What time suits you?"

"A car. Fancy."

"Not really. It's just general procedure, Ms. Slater."

"Um, no, I didn't mean, like, *fancy*." I chuckle nervously. "Not like I was being treated or ya know, fancy, like, la di da..." I slap my forehead. "I'll be home by five-thirty."

His voice is mirthless. "We will collect you at six then."

"Do you know what this is about?"

"No."

I take a quick, uneasy breath. "Ah. Okay."

"See you tomorrow."

"Okay."

CHAPTER SIX

the godfather

IT'S A BLACK STATESMAN, I think. I've told my dad who I'm going to see, as well my mum and Toni. I've written a big note on the fridge just in case I end up in a trunk.

That's a joke.

Sort of.

My dad believes Jimmy to be very refined and generous, but without a doubt, also a man you do not want to cross. I'm not even sure how to cross a man like Jimmy Storm, but I sure as hell don't plan on doing it. I clutch my bag and thank the man holding the passenger door open. As I step inside the car, I begin to fidget.

The windows are pitch-black on the outside, but easily seen through on the inside, which I didn't think was legal. But then, he is Jimmy Storm.

The car begins to move, and I riffle around in my bag for a while even though I'm not searching for anything. It's an awkward journey. The man in the front seat peers at me every so often, so I keep my head low and pretend I'm preoccupied with my misplaced belonging.

It's a half-hour drive from my town to Connolly. Knowing I can't riffle around for that long, I pull out my phone, open my kindle reader, and continue *Ugly Love* by Colleen Hoover.

I've just gotten to a juicy bit when a picture message from Toni drops down from the settings bar. I click on the notification and a picture of Max pops up. He looks pissed off with the person snapping it; there is no wondering why. He's bent over a redhead. Her thighs are spread, dress pulled down below her bra and bunched up above her underwear. She looks flushed and excited to have him over her.

I would be too.

He's probably moments away from ripping her black, lacy underwear off her annoyingly perfect body. His tattoo-covered back is bare, but I can see a peek of denim at his hips though, so he's not completely naked. He's glowering at the camera, his eyes slits of stormy grey.

Ugh.

God, he's gorgeous.

There is a little monster in my belly, sitting high and alert. So, while I was dancing myself into a near coma and then falling asleep alone in bed, he was at a party, humping a gorgeous redhead with perfectly voluptuous breasts. The little monster pinches the walls of my belly. It's green-eyed, lonely, and needy.

The caption reads, 'Redhead caught red-handed between a couch and a hard place. Does Max even know this one's name?'

All of a sudden, anger wrestles jealousy to the ground and stomps on it. So, I'm not allowed to kiss a boy, but he can have long legs wrapped around his body any time he likes? I swipe the picture away, although I'm sure it won't be the last time I look at it.

Study it.

We finally roll onto a driveway and I press my cheek to the window. The front yard is a large concrete jungle with huge potted plants and very little grass or natural vegetation other than ten-foot-high hedges separating its various sections. There are security cameras everywhere. We pull into the turning circle and stop alongside a central water feature. The three-story house is raised and the front door is accessible by several steps. It has columns and archways, and it's grand and beautiful. I don't see a garage, though, nor any designated parking bays on this side of the property. Presuming this entry is specifically for guests being dropped off, I wonder what the main entry must look like. Does it have gold crusted pillars and a fountain of youth?

My legs are already shaking with fatigue from rehearsals today, and as I take the steps up towards the double doors, they start to feel infinitely weaker. I stop to smooth my dress down my body and adjust a strap on my wrap-around heels. When I peer back up from my shoes, Jimmy is smiling at me from the doorway.

He claps his hands together. "*M'a scusari.* Cassidy, I feel I must apologise."

I sweep my hair to the side. "For what?"

"Your father contacted me while you were on your way here. He was a bit unsure of why I might want to speak with you. It's occurred to me that my inviting you here without asking him first was poor manners. *Se?* You're a young girl and that may have been..." He motions with his hands as he appears to search for the word. "Perceived as inappropriate."

"Oh, that's okay," I assure him, feeling slightly more at ease now. Although, not nearly as at ease as I'll be once I know what this is all about. Why he hasn't just come out and told me, I don't understand. Supposedly, it's not polite to talk business over the phone or maybe his phones are tapped and we're planning on going to the mattresses... I'm not entirely sure what that even means, but I heard it on *The Godfather* once.

"Well. That's very kind. Please come inside. My daughter is waiting to meet you in the living room." He moves backwards and I walk past him. "To the right." Stepping inside, my heels clip-clop on the marble flooring. The circular foyer leads off in many directions and I'm unsure about which one to take. Up the stairs? Through the door beside it? Or into one of the many others on the right?

Coming up behind me, Jimmy says, "I'm afraid I have some business to attend to, Cassidy. I'm terribly sorry. Aurora will take good care of you."

I watch him as he strides away. "Oh, okay. Um, thanks."

"Cassidy?" someone calls.

My heels start clip-clopping again as I walk left into a lounge-type area. "Hi."

"Oh, thank goodness. I'm so stressed." A leggy brunette paces around charts on easels and two people sitting with clipboards, looking rattled. "There is so much to do. I've still got seating plans to finalise and the table settings to fix and you to organise."

My brows shoot into my hairline. "Me?"

"Yes." She stops rushing around to scrutinise me. "My dancer."

I tilt my head and contemplate feigning understanding. "Ah... "

Her dark eyes grow wide. "No one told you."

"Not in so many words."

"In any words?"

I wince. "Not so much."

She throws her hands around. "Madonna mia!" The two holding clipboards flinch and I try not to laugh. "You'd think he could handle something this simple. I mean, the man runs half the District, but his daughter's wedding? No. Forget about it. That's just too hard."

"I'm sorry."

"No, don't be. This is just classic." She points to the couch. "Please sit."

Nervously, I sit opposite the terrified two. She grins and scoots in next to me.

"Sicilian weddings are big, Cassidy. Mine is a four-day event. I need performers and entertainment and activities. I have this amazing orchestra flying over from Sydney and I really want you to dance."

"Oh." I swivel around to face her.

"I've seen you on YouTube." She smiles at me. "You're beautiful. The ballet is so romantic. Please. I've budgeted $1500 for your pocket, plus accommodation and food."

"Wow." My voice squeaks slightly because a stranger who resembles some kind of a stunning Italian manga character has called me beautiful. And because $1500 will cover my studio's utility bills for six months.

Plus...

"Accommodation?" *Food!*

"Yes. It's a destination wedding." She interlocks her long, elegant fingers, the rock on her forefinger nearly blinding me. "Clay and I want to get married in Bali. I know it's been done, but we fell in love hiking in Ubud."

I nod and smile sweetly, trying to appear professional when what I really want to do is jump up and down and squeal with excitement. "When is it?"

"Two weeks from Saturday."

"*Oh my God*, that's soon."

"Yes. You're the last act I need to finalise. A last-minute act, but my favourite." She stares at me with big brown doe eyes. "Please. My father thinks you're wonderful and that man is not easy to please. I'd know. He really wants this. So do I. What do you think?"

My cheeks feel warm. "Sure. I'd love to."

"Yes!" She claps her hands. "I'm so excited."

Her glee is infectious, so I can't help but giggle. "What choreography would you like?"

"I'm happy for you to create your own. Romantic. Intense. Meaningful. My father loves to see fouettés. The *Black Swan* is his favourite." I'm in no way surprised to hear that Jimmy Storm's favourite choreography is one of Odile's. It is dark. Intense. Sensual. Odile is the epitome of a sexy female antagonist.

"Okay." I bite my bottom lip, not wanting to argue with her. Aurora seems to get what she wants. Still..."Odile is a bit dark for a wedding."

"Well, you'll be on the night before the wedding, during the final dinner before I leave Clay and go to my villa with the girls."

"She's probably still a little dark even for a pre-wedding dinner. I'll incorporate some fouettés, though, for sure."

A phone buzzes on the table in front of us, but Aurora completely ignores it. Staring at me, she asks, "Can you do twenty-five in a row?" She smiles without blinking. "I'd love to see that."

"That's a very specific number." I chuckle uneasily. Fouettés are challenging, especially twenty-five in a row. Talk about a head spin. Ballerinas have vomited after completing less than that.

"It's my lucky number," she presses.

"Okay." I nod once. "I'll try."

She turns to look at a piece of paper on the coffee table and scowls. "Honestly, look at this. Such incompetents."

I swallow hard and stare at the table. "What am I looking at?"

"The seating chart should say, Clay Butcher and Aurora Butcher! Not Aurora Storm. I mean, it's not that hard."

When I hear the name Butcher, I fumble for words. I take a big breath in and cross one thigh over the other, biding myself time. I want to ask if that means all The Butcher Boys will be at the wedding?

In frickin' Bali?

"Yeah," I manage to get out. "That's a big mix up."

"Yeah, it's a *big* mix up." Her phone begins to buzz again and this time she grabs it, her long manicured nails curling around the display. "I have to take this. I'll email you the details and also check in with your sister. She's Max's plus one. You'll be staying in the same villa as her, so you won't be alone."

Oh, my gawd.

I cover my mouth with my hand to hide my inexplicable smile. She's up and pacing again with the phone clutched to her ear. I lower my hand and glance at the terrified two, who haven't moved since I walked in. I want to, like, cuddle them or something.

Feeling a little dazed and in need of a Toni and Cassidy conversation dissection, I walk towards the door. As I glance behind me to wave at her, I slam into something hard. Two hands grip my shoulders and centre me. Startled, I look up and find myself staring at a scowling Max. My mouth drops open when I see he's in a black suit with a black tie pulled loosely around his neck. His white shirt is unbuttoned slightly, showing the licks of a tattoo on his neck.

There is no way I'd guess this guy was only twenty-four. He has the appearance and presence tonight of someone in his thirties. He looks pissed off, as if I have no right to be here. As if he didn't punch my date in the face. As if I'm an annoying little sister.

"The fuck are you doing here?"

My heart races. "Wow, it's nice to see you too."

Xander appears by his side. "Cassidy, I should have known it was you. Only you could make my brother forfeit his hand because he'd heard your voice."

Max throws Xander daggers before aiming them back at me. "Why are you here?"

As I arch my neck to see him properly, I try to ignore the harshness in his eyes. "You know, my mum has always said that if the wind changes, your face could be stuck like that."

He lets go of my shoulders and folds his thick arms across his chest. "When it comes to you, this is my default expression."

"I seem to have quite the effect on you then," I say smugly. And I'm so impressed with the wit I'm pulling out in the face of Max Butcher's intimidation that I grin.

"When did you become such a smart arse?"

I swallow hard. "I'm not sure."

He glances around and then back at me, the dark look in his eyes stealing my breath. "You shouldn't be here."

My chest tightens when I realise we are not just playfully sparring with words. He actually doesn't want me here. Scoffing softly at his attitude towards me, I say, "You're giving me whiplash, Max. What's your problem?"

He snorts. "Every time I see you, you're asking for trouble."

I glance at Xander and feel my cheeks glowing with

embarrassment. He smiles tightly, eyes pitying and apologetic. I hate that look.

Stacey pokes her head out from an adjoining room and her brows draw together when she sees me. "Max, I've dealt you a hand. You coming back in here?"

Well, she clearly isn't a Cassidy Slater fan. Apparently, neither is Max today. The image of him bent over that redhead suddenly jumps into my mind, igniting me with annoyance.

Butthead!

"I'm leaving anyway," I say as I rush past him, down the steps and towards the statesman.

Xander jogs after me and holds his hand up to the driver. "Just give us a minute." He studies my face for a moment. "Hey, don't worry about Max. If it's any consolation, he doesn't want me here either."

"He's such a jerk sometimes." I stand next to the car, shuffling in place, desperate to get away from Max before he sees the effect he has on me. As if he doesn't already know.

"Yeah. He can be." Xander grips my shoulder with one hand and rocks me slightly. "But he's also the best person I know."

The statesman idles beside us.

I scoff and stare up at Max as he watches us from atop the steps. "Then you need to get out more."

"When you've had the kind of upbringing we've had, the qualities you admire are different."

I frown at him. "I don't understand."

He just smiles at me and opens the passenger door, waving me in. "I know you don't. That's why he likes you so much."

"He doesn't like me that much. I irritate him."

Xander chuckles and shakes his head as I step inside the

car. He closes the door and taps the roof. As the car pulls away, I twist in my seat, watching Max get smaller and smaller until he's out of sight.

I slump back in my seat and try to process everything. He's so hot and cold with me. Touching me in the pool. Teasing me. His attention is intoxicating, and I'd do just about anything for those moments when I have it. Like, I'd do anything for that chuckle. For the small touches. For the moments he seems almost... protective of me.

But his personality flips from flirt to butthead in seconds and I never know which Max Butcher I'm going to get. My mere presence this evening seemed to infuriate him, so he humiliated me in front of Xander. And if Stacey also heard the way he spoke to me, then her too.

And why? He could have just ignored me. Not forfeited his hand to give me a hard time about being in his superior presence...

And what were the chances that he'd be at Jimmy's at the same time as I was? Is he friends with Aurora? I suppose they are family now.

So Max and his brothers are associated with Jimmy Storm. My eyes shift to the rearview mirror and I catch the driver's eyes just before he glances back at the road. I shuffle in my seat and take a big breath in, trying not to overthink this situation, but it's hard to ignore so many red flags.

Be mindful of the company you keep.

Max is trouble. That's for sure. What I'm struggling with now is how little I seem to care.

CHAPTER SEVEN

you're a jerk

I'M WRITING notes for Aurora's wedding when I hear a soft tapping at my window. My eyes dart to the clock. It's nearly midnight. I slide off the mattress, walk around the bed, and sweep my curtains aside. Max stares at me from the other side of the glass. I frown at him.

I mouth, "You're a jerk."

He scowls at me and mouths, "Open the window."

I sit on the ledge and brush my hair over one shoulder, feeling strangely empowered. "What do you want?"

His eyes turn into slits. Big biceps flex as his grip tightens on the lattice he's perched on. "Open the fucking window."

I slide the window open and step back. He pushes the screen in and jumps over the sill, his presence filling the room. He isn't wearing a suit anymore; he's looking casual—his age—in faded jeans and a black V-neck tee-shirt.

He peers around as if he's looking for something or someone and then fixes his eyes on me. I take another step back when he tries to close the gap between us. He halts when he notices my trepidation.

His brows tighten. "I was a dick to you, and I don't like the way it's making me feel. I'm sorry."

My fingers find the hem of my pyjama shorts, fiddling with them. "You embarrassed me."

"I know."

Unable to think with him so close, I step back, but he steps towards me again. "Stop it." I hug myself because I'm not wearing a bra; I'm half-naked and he's fully dressed. My hands fumble around my body, adjusting my singlet and shorts before covering my exposed midriff.

"*Cassidy*." The word purrs from his lips and it's the first time I've heard him say my actual name. "Little One, I was a dick. I overreacted. I'm sorry."

I continue to hug my waist, unable to make eye contact with him. I'm no longer feeling in control. He moves until there isn't any space between us, and I breathe out in a rush at the heat of his body. I stare straight ahead at the black shirt that covers his chest.

Big, warm palms enclose the crook of my neck and his thumbs caress my jawline. I gasp and close my eyes, drawing in big breaths. Time lapses.

With his thumb to my chin, he tilts my head. "Open your eyes, Little One."

I open my eyes and peer nervously up at him.

Oh my God.

His eyes narrow as he studies my expression. I glance down and try to collect myself for just a moment, but when his thumb moves to my mouth, I can't help but look back up. He traces the swell of my lower lip, folding it down to expose the pinkness inside. My heart begins to thunder against my ribcage. Yearning and fear both heat my skin. He tastes so good, like salt and man and him. Sliding my tongue out, I lick the tip of his thumb. He clenches his jaw, so I wrap my mouth around his thick pad and suck on it. A quiet groan escapes him, and he pushes his thumb between my teeth and into the hot depth of my mouth, moving it possessively inside me.

"Fuck," he says through clenched teeth.

All I can manage to say with his finger in my mouth is his name. "*Max*."

His thumb pops out and he cups my cheeks with both hands. "What do you want?"

My cheeks heat beneath his palms. "You know what I want."

"I'm not monogamous. You know that, right?"

I swallow past the flashing image of Max and the pretty redhead, and I disregard the monster inside me that screams my true discomfort. "*Yes*."

"I need to hear you say it." His thumb strokes my cheek. "Say, I understand this is just sex."

"I understand this is just sex."

"You can't expect anything more from me. I won't be giving it to you."

"I know," I whisper.

When his hands start moving around my neck, my head rolls and my breathing speeds up. I close my eyes and moan a little, the sensation both relaxing and arousing.

"What have you done with other guys?"

My eyes open, but I don't look at him. "Nothing."

"Nothing?"

I look up. His eyes are smouldering. "Max, nothing. I've done nothing. I've made out with boys, that's all."

A slow grin spreads across his lips. "What do you do to yourself?"

I cover my face with my palms. The silence between us thickens like glue, pulling us together.

"Answer the question," he orders, pulling my hands down and putting them on his hard chest.

My fingers flex over the fabric of his shirt, which does little to soften the feel of his muscles beneath. "I um," I stammer. "I touch myself, a little."

"Do you put your fingers inside your pussy?"

I laugh nervously. "Oh my God, you really do need a warning label."

"Do you?" he repeats.

"No," I say breathily. "I just... play with my clit a little."

He grabs the collar of his shirt and pulls it over his head before pressing my palms back to his chest. Naked. Warm. "Can you make yourself come?"

"Yes." I drag my fingertips down the ridges of his abdomen. "Sometimes."

He walks me backwards and lifts me onto my chest of drawers. "Do you think about me while you touch yourself?"

We are eye to eye now. His lips are so close to mine, I can feel the heat from his breath. "Yes."

"What do you imagine me doing?"

My hands tremble against his perfect abdominals. "You're inside me."

He leans in. Lips meet my ear. "Which part of me?"

My head dips back slightly as I moan. "Your tongue."

He breathes out fast and presses his forehead to mine. "Do you want me to fuck you with my tongue, Little One?"

Oh God. That is such a great question.

My jaw quivers as I nod. And I'm so tightly wound, I may explode.

When his nose touches mine, my eyes close. His mouth wraps around my top lip and I'm humming as he tugs on it. And then he kisses me deeply, our hot, needy breaths mingling. He feeds a hand through my hair and another around my waist, pressing my body against his. My knees part to welcome his breadth.

I'm kissing Max Butcher!

I try to stay out of my head, but I'm so conscious of the kiss, wanting it to be good for him, wanting my lips to be soft and skilled like his are. I caress my fingers up his back, making his muscles contract. His tongue caresses mine, and our lips massage and pet each other. It's completely beautiful. He smells like man and whiskey and a scent that is all his own. The small hairs on his cheeks and chin brush against my face. As his lips move down to my chin, my neck, and back up again, they paint a hot trail of friction.

His lips never leave mine as he lifts me up and walks me over to the bed. He crawls on with me wrapped around his torso. He leans on one elbow, putting only a tiny part of his weight on me, but it's the part between his legs, the part that is hard as a rock and pressed into my thigh. His fingers glide up my belly and under my singlet. My stomach trembles.

He breaks our kiss. "What's this?" He tickles my upper abdomen, making me giggle.

Cool air rushes between us when he leans to the side and lifts my singlet off over my head. As he stares down at my stomach, I cover my face again, grinning into my palms.

"Is this a little four-pack I see here?" he says. "Little One, you're toned."

"I'm a ballerina," I mumble into my hands.

He pulls my hands from my face again. "Don't hide from me."

I stare straight into his blue-grey eyes and swallow uneasily. "But I have no tits."

His brows draw together and he cups my breast, his fingers teasing my nipple. I bite my bottom lip to stifle a moan, my nipples becoming painfully hard. He buries his head between my breasts and begins to lick and suck and squeeze. The skin on my chest muffles his groan as he rubs his erection into my thigh.

He sits up abruptly. "I've got to get these off." He unbuttons his jeans and kicks them onto the floor before moving straight back to my nipple. This time I can feel the whole tense ridge of his penis rubbing against me through his boxers. I breathe in and out fast. *Suck, suck, blow.*

My nipple pops from his mouth and he leans up to watch my expression. His hand slides down my trembling belly, into my shorts, and between my legs. I'm relieved I waxed yesterday. He watches as my eyes close. His fingers stroke the valley between my lips. I'm wet. I'm really wet. His fingers slide around and when he parts me, my mouth opens. *Suck suck blow.* He presses down on my clit, causing me to whimper.

He inches a finger inside me and then stops. "Fuck." His voice is deep. "You're so tight. I think my cock should have the honour of stretching you open."

My eyes widen when I feel the bed dip. As he crawls down my body, I tremble from each kiss he leaves in his wake. By the time he's pulling my shorts off and pushing my knees up, I'm already on the edge. He nestles his shoulders between my legs.

The back of my head hits the pillow as he kisses from my knee to the inner flesh of my quivering thigh.

"You've got fucking amazing legs."

I feel the cool air and my cheeks instantly flush, knowing he's looking at me—open to him. Then his thumb begins to stroke me worshipfully, exploring my lips and clit. I let out a slow, longing moan. And as I do, his tongue dips and that beautiful friction from his cheeks and chin rub on the most sensitive parts of me. I dig my fingers into the pillow on either side of my head. A soft whimper leaves my mouth. God, he knows what he's doing.

He hums when my hips thrust up on their own accord. I can't stop them. As his tongue starts to lap with more purpose, his lips devouring me, I become completely undone. Unravelled. His hand slides under my backside and when his fingers skate around my bum hole, I let them. Like them, even. Nothing is off-limits to Max Butcher.

My belly button and toes tingle.

My knees and thighs quiver.

He takes his time with me, but when the tide of my orgasm rushes up my legs, my clit buzzing against his tongue, he abruptly stops and blows on my skin.

"*Max*," I plead.

"Ask me to make you come." There's amusement in his voice.

I groan. "Make me come, Max."

He chuckles. "Say please, Little One."

"Please make me come, Max."

He rubs the rough of his chin between my lips, creating an intense feeling I don't want to stop. And then his mouth is on my clit. His fingers are pushing back the hood and it's too overwhelming. Consuming.

I whimper. "*Max*."

I feed my hands through his hair, rubbing myself along his face. His skilled mouth inches the tide back up. And then away. And then up some more. My knees try to close around his head, but he doesn't stop the repetitive stimulation. My clit begins to throb with sensitivity.

I cry out. Ripping the pillow out from under me, I shove it over my face to mute the sound of my orgasm. My cries only intensify as he licks me through my climax, wringing it out of me with every lap of his tongue.

After several seconds, the mattress moves again. When I finally pull the pillow away, it's to see Max staring at me.

"You okay?"

I want to cover my face, but I don't. "Yep." My giggle makes him smile, and it reaches every part of his face, drawing me to that darn dimple of his. I really like him like this—playful and relaxed. We share a sweet, contented moment.

"Did I... " I roll my eyes. "Did I taste okay?"

"You taste fucking *amazing*."

My skin is still humming when I hear a knock at the door. Max jumps up and pulls his jeans on, while I fumble around, searching for my pyjamas.

"Cassidy, you okay, baby?"

Mum.

We freeze. I almost answer her, but Max holds his hand up to silence me.

I stare at him, wide-eyed, and tilt my head.

"Cassidy?"

He grabs his clothes and swings out of the window, climbing down the lattice.

The door slowly opens. My mum creeps cautiously in, relaxing when she sees me up and awake. "Are you okay, my love? I heard you cry out. I thought maybe you had a bad dream."

CHAPTER EIGHT

sugar plum fairy

I STAND with my left leg extended, my hand gently touching the barre. The District News team snaps several photos of me. My smile is genuine and a little silly. It's awkward posing for strangers.

"That was perfect, Cassidy," Lilly says as she leans over to view the camera. She nods at her photographer. "That one, definitely."

I pull my legwarmers up and walk over to her. "Did you get everything you need?"

She smiles at me. "Just a few more questions. *The Nutcracker* is a constant every year at Christmas and has become a District tradition. We have seen you play Clara every year since you were fourteen. We love you as Clara. So, will you miss her?"

Still reeling from the news of my new role as the Sugar Plum Fairy, I answer with excitement. "I won't miss being on pointe the whole time." I laugh. "But yes, I think I will. It's Clara's journey, ultimately. That role is a huge responsibility. I won't have as much stage time this year, but being the

Sugar Plum Fairy means I'll get to do some iconic choreography—including a pique ménage sequence I'm still trying to wrap my head around."

Lilly nods. "Ah, yes. Can you explain this sequence to us?"

"Well, a pique is one move. But to do the pique ménage, like the one the Sugar Plum Fairy does, I'll need to push off my left leg on pointe and turn and repeat this over and over. It sends me in wide sweeping circles around the stage. It's not just about technique, but stamina and keeping my head level or I'll fall over. It's dizzying. Not only that, but I often can't feel my left ankle the next day."

Lilly smiles at me. "That sounds like a lot of work."

"It is. But I love it."

"How do you feel about your headline: 'Golden Girl Cassidy Slater Our Sugar Plum Fairy'?"

Oh, my gawd.

I blush. "Honestly? Flattered. Awkward." I giggle and Lilly's smile widens.

I didn't realise I was the 'Golden Girl' of the District. I wonder if I'd still be their Golden Girl if they knew what I let Max Butcher do to me last night...

The entire time they're packing up, I can't wipe the beam off my face. I wave goodbye to Lilly and the crew before going back inside my studio to call Toni. I put him on speaker phone. Laying the device on the floor beside me, I begin my stretches.

Toni's voice sings through the phone as soon as he picks up. "Did they make you wear something God awful?"

"No." I move into the thread the needle position, twisting my hips so my shoulder touches the floor. "I'm just in a leotard and legwarmers."

"I can't talk to you anymore. You're just too fabulous for me these days."

"I'm a Golden Girl." I laugh.

"Oh, my giddy aunt, is that what they're calling you?"

"Yep."

"I'm mortified and jealous. I'm jortified."

I giggle. "Tell me what's the next move I make... with Max."

"You don't make a move, Golden Girl. He will."

"Um." I swap arms and press my shoulder into the mat. "We kinda parted in an awkward way. I want to like apologise or something."

He tsks at me. "Apologise for the blue balls you gave him? Yes, they hurt, Cassidy. You hurt Max. I hope you're happy."

"You're not helping."

He chuckles. "Then we are right on track."

"I want to make it up to him."

"Good! Suck his dick."

"*Toni.*" I sit up and stare at the phone. "I have no idea how to do that. And it's Max Butcher. He's probably had more blow jobs than hot meals."

"He'll appreciate the effort. Trust me."

I move into the downward dog position, walking on the spot and stretching my calves. "Fine, how do I do it?"

"I'm so thrilled we're having this conversation! This is where I shine. So first, forget the term blow job. You don't blow on it. Well, *you* don't blow on it. I might."

"Gross, Toni."

"Alright, so you suck him slowly. Leisurely. Keep the foreskin up... if he has foreskin. I imagine he would because they're all Catholics."

"Max is Catholic?" My mind drifts to his mouth between my legs. "He must go to confession *a lot.*"

"Well, his dad is part Sicilian and they are very Catholic, so I presume so."

"How do you know all this?"

"Twitter."

"*Riiight.* You know that if YouTube, Twitter, and Facebook all became one platform, it could be called You-Twit-Face." Which about sums up my feelings towards those social media platforms.

He laughs. "I'm stealing that one."

"Go for it."

"So," he continues, "make sure your mouth is really wet. You want to fold your lips over your teeth so there is pressure, but no grating. Don't grate his cock, Cassidy. Suck him in long strokes and use your tongue on the underside where the skin meets..." He makes a squirming sound. "I'm getting a semi having this conversation."

I roll my eyes. "Toni."

"Okay. Keep his foreskin up while you do this, but if it slides down by itself, lick the tip, but be gentle. Don't overstimulate. I repeat, do not overstimulate. You will struggle to make him come if you go hard and fast. A guy like Max Butcher won't be easy to make come. Tease him. Change up the movements and then when you think he's ready, you pump him like you're milking a cow."

I scrunch up my face. "I'm grossed out by that analogy."

"I'm grossed out by your fanny."

"Toni, for your information, my vagina happens to be beautiful and smooth and very satisfied right now."

My studio door swings open and Flick rushes in, squealing, "This is so great!"

"I gotta go," I say to Toni and hang up the phone.

My sister's red hair sways around her shoulders as she

bounds toward me. Falling on top of me, she envelops me with her long arms.

"Oh my God, you're not my type," I laugh, rolling around on the floor with her.

We flop side-by-side with our legs folded over each other and sigh.

Her grin is infectious. "I'm so excited."

I twist my head to stare at her. "Why are you so excited?"

"Um, duh, you're coming with me to Bali!"

"Oh yeah." I stare up at the downlights in the ceiling. "I actually forgot all about that with everything going on."

"Oh, well, don't! Aurora is expecting *the* Cassidy Slater to entertain everyone. I set it up so Stacey and I are in a room together. You have your own."

"Oh." I frown at her. "I thought I was sharing a room with you?"

"I thought I wasn't your type."

"Hahaha," I snicker.

"Don't worry, we're in the same villa. I'll be right next to you." Her eyes sparkle as she describes our accommodation. "It has a private pool and outdoor kitchen and like a common area. It's just stunning. The boys let us choose from a few close to the reception."

"Oh." I curl my lips together to keep a smile at bay. "So we're in the same villa as the boys." My chest feels tight. I couldn't be more excited to spend a holiday with Max, but I'm not sure he'll share my enthusiasm. We aren't friends. We aren't anything according to him.

She nods. "Yeah."

"Why are you Max's plus one?"

"Well, because Xander can pretty much get whatever he wants from his big brothers, and Stacey can get whatever she wants from Xander. She wants me there, so that's that. Plus, I think Max likes the idea of having a girl on his arm who won't cramp his sexual prowess, know what I mean? He's a complete manwhore, but he has very little respect or time for women. That doesn't stop them though. It's strange because the other boys aren't like that at all. Xander is very considerate and open, and Bronson has been in love with the same girl since he was thirteen."

Discomfort knots my belly. "Sounds like you've finally traded diaries." I picture Max's smile last night after he'd made me come. A smile that lacked his usual arrogant demeanour, instead seeming raw and revealing. I think about the night we slept beside each other without touching. He respects me.

"Stacey knows the boys really well and she seems to worry about them a lot."

"So what's the deal with Stacey and The Butcher Boys?"

"They don't have a sister, but if they did, it'd be Stacey." She twists to face me. "You don't mind that I said yes to going with Max, do you?"

I feign indifference. "What? Why would I mind?" She lifts a beautiful auburn brow at me and says nothing. "What? I don't care." Her eyes stay glued on mine and amusement tugs at her lips. "I don't mind. Why would I mind?" I cover my face and grin into my palms, my cheeks flushing. "Okay. Yes. I have a crush on him. But I know the score. It's fine. I'm fine with it." She's analysing me dubiously and her lack of verbal communication is getting under my skin. "Flick, don't just stare at me!"

"I'm just reading you like a book, my little love."

"Well, that's good," I stammer. "It's been a while since you, like... read."

She grins at me. "Is that the best comeback you have?"

"Yes." I smile back, knowing I've lost this round with my

sister. "Your grin is so annoying right now; I want one of those pies to squish into your face."

She rolls over onto her knees and stands up. "I'm really glad you're coming, my little love. I'm going to stay in Connolly with Stacey for the weekend. Tell Dad, okay?" She dances along the mats towards the door and then swivels to wink at me.

CHAPTER NINE

action

ALONE IN MY STUDIO, I turn the music up. I turn it up loud. The bass vibrates through the speakers. The music moves into me. My programmed body sways to its rhythm. I bourrée, fouetté, jeté, and pique around the studio, mixing routines and having fun. It becomes a free, wild workout of my body and ballet skills, and I have "*Riptide*" to thank for it.

Love this song.

The studio door swings open, and I catch a glimpse of someone in the mirror. I pivot to a halt, halfway through a fouetté, to see my favourite person standing with his hands stuffed in his pockets, a wide grin on his lips.

"*Konnor*!" I yell out and rush towards him.

He steps backwards when our bodies collide, but then his arms go around me and lift me up as I kick with excitement. He's here. He's here, and he's okay. The last time I saw him, he was a drunken, grieving mess with intense girl troubles like I had never seen before.

He lowers me onto the mats and turns to the pretty

blonde girl blushing by his side. He steers me with his arm towards her and introduces her. "This is Blesk."

Blesk fidgets with her ponytail and glances at the floor and then nervously at Konnor. She's stunning and my brother is gazing at her with infatuation. This must be *the* girl. He's a bit tightly strung as if her unease has become his.

"Hi, welcome to the Thunder Dome," I say, breaking the awkward moment.

Her face relaxes and then Konnor relaxes, and it's like a magnetic effect. I stare at my brother and take him all in. Even though he's freshly shaven and still so beautiful, his eyes look tired.

I shake my shoulders and stretch my hands out for him to take. "Come dance with your sister."

He digs his heels in. “Pipsqueak, no.”

I do a silly dance. "Come on, come on."

Konnor groans at Blesk. “See what I have to deal with.”

“Come on, you’re a beautiful dancer."

He shakes his head adamantly. “No, Cass.”

“You owe me for missing my birthday!”

Konnor sighs, tilting his head back in defeat and rolling his eyes. “Thank God, Jax isn’t here.” Jax is one of Konnor's best friends and they play rugby together. They are all manly and butch about it too. But Jax is fun, and I have no doubt he'd dance with me if he were here right now.

Konnor joins me in the centre of the studio, and we formalise our stance. I kick his foot into position. Sticking our noses in the air, we giggle. My feet take the first step, but I pretend to let him lead.

We waltz together just like we used to do when we were children. I stare up at my big brother and he grins down at me. I love it when he's home.

It's a special occasion when he bothers to make the long

drive from his campus accommodation to stay with us. And even more so because he has brought his best friend Jax and Blesk's friend Elise—who is so my spirit animal, it's not even funny.

Later that evening, as we all sit around the dinner table, laughter fills our home. Elise is just as weird as me. Blesk is sweet. She's a little shy, but clearly adores my brother.

After dinner, Blesk places a box full of cupcakes on the table. My face lights up. But everyone else is too full. Well, except Jaxon. I mock-frown at him over the chocolate fondant.

We share, like, twenty cupcakes in a cupcake battle that ends with me puking in my bathroom. All the while, Blesk and Konnor drink a little too much. The night quickly becomes eventful when Konnor and my friend, Faith, get into an argument. I end up having to kick her out. Konnor often gets into arguments with people...

At least I won the eat-off.

Good times.

THE FOLLOWING MORNING, I'm setting the timer, which is strapped to my bicep, all ready for a morning run, when I see Konnor, Blesk, and my dad sitting on the patio. As I approach, I hear Blesk ask, "How did you make the tap water green?"

A chuckle vibrates in my chest because the time Blesk is obviously asking about is the day my brother decided to dye everything green.

He often 'acted out,' a polite way to describe his past behaviour. My brother's story is long and full of trauma. He was kidnapped when he was four years old. And if that wasn't bad enough, when the police found him years later, his mother had already passed away and his father hadn't wanted him back. We have no idea why. It sickens me to think about a father not wanting his son. We don't talk about this though. It's been swept under the rug.

But his broken little soul couldn't be healed by hiding the injustice. So he'd misbehaved. He'd drank too much... *drinks* too much.

Sometimes I wonder if he had tried to push us away as a test of our commitment. Would we still love him after it all? We did. We do. We won't abandon him like his father did.

"Well, Duchess," Konnor begins, making me smile. I've come to learn that that's his pet name for Blesk—too cute.

"I'm so glad you asked," he says. "I put green jelly crystals in the faucet under the washer."

Bouncing over to them, I plonk down on my dad's lap and kiss him on the cheek. "I remember that!" Dad's hazel eyes brighten as he gives me a bear hug. "What's up, Daddy-o?"

Konnor leans over and lightly pinches my stomach. "You're too old to sit on Dad's lap, Cassidy."

"*Daaaaad*, Konnor's hitting me."

Dad squeezes me tighter. "Now now, Konnor, let me keep my little girl for a while longer. God knows I lost Flicker as soon as she came out of the womb." My dad doesn't have any favourite children, but the two of us have a special bond. We spent a lot of time together because I was more of a homebody than either of my siblings. We liked watching quiz shows and playing board games together while Konnor and Flick preferred to socialise with their friends.

Konnor lets out a big sigh and smirks at me. "Such a bloody princess." He leans back and looks at Dad. "Where is Flick? Cassidy just said she was away for the weekend."

Dad peers up at me. "Isn't she with her new lady love?"

I stare down at the spread on the patio table, grinning at the sight of Konnor's signature waffles. He cooked Blesk breakfast. He must be pulling out all the moves for this girl.

I pick up the fork and shovel a piece of waffle into my mouth, chewing and answering at the same time. "Yeah, but I don't know where. Probably in Connolly somewhere."

Konnor's brows furrow. "Who? Why Connolly? Who's she seeing?"

My big brother has always had an apprehension toward The Butcher Boys. They have a bad reputation. I take another piece of waffle so I don't have to elaborate. "You don't wanna know."

Konnor glares at me and it's a hostile look I very rarely see directed at me. "Who, Cassidy?"

Salty waffle chunks muffle my words. "Stacey Grange."

"I know Stacey." Blesk smiles sweetly at Konnor. "She was friends with Erik for a while. She went to Connolly High." I don't know who Erik is, but that doesn't seem to impress Konnor at all.

He stiffens. "Great. So she's been hanging out with that crowd."

Dad feigns laughter and I know he's trying to lighten the mood. Konnor is overprotective and often irrational. It's all to do with the way he handles conflict. He struggles sometimes to channel his emotions.

"Don't worry, Konnor," Dad says. "The boys know to behave here. They've grown up a lot since you left to study."

Blesk glances between us as she fidgets with her clothes. "Are you talking about The Butcher Boys?"

I tilt my head at Blesk. "You know them?"

Blesk and Konnor share a significant look before she says,

"Not really. But doesn’t everyone in the District know of The Butcher Boys?"

They sure do.

Konnor grumbles. "Yeah, alright. I’ll have a chat with Flick when I see her next, but you stay clear of them. Please, Cassidy. They are just bad news."

I glance up at the sky and then back at Konnor, internally shaking the negativity from this conversation out of my mind. "Yes, big brother."

They continue to talk as I wander off. Jogging out the front door, I head towards the track that circles our property. Flick doesn't understand the exercise thing. Konnor and I have been running since we were children, and when I don't run in the mornings, I dance or do Pilates. Exercise has always been a part of my morning ritual.

After a light run, I take a shower in the studio and get ready to practise Sugar Plum's choreography. To really get in the mood, I put on some music by Tchaikovsky. I pull on my favourite white leotard and my pink knee-high legwarmers.

It's a warm day, but I always wear legwarmers. They're essential for minimising the chance of future injuries. My torn ligament last year reminded me of that and I've never forgotten them since.

Barefoot, I go to warm up at the barre. My eyes are focused on my form in the mirror when the door to my studio swings open to the stopper. Max's tall, broad form appears as a reflection. He has something in his fist, but he's staring at me in the mirror, his eyes caressing every inch of my exposed body. My lips part to allow for bigger breaths. The door bounces off the stopper and swings shut, leaving me alone and secluded with his piercing gaze. As I turn to acknowledge him, he turns from my reflection to meet my eyes.

"What's this?" He raises the newspaper rolled up in his grip.

"You tell me," I say with a nervous chuckle, but he just stares at me. "Okay... I got a very special role and they printed an article about me." My heart skips in time with each of his steps toward me. I lower my leg from the barre and pivot towards him just as he stops an arm's length away.

He smirks. "Golden Girl?"

The corners of my cheeks pinch as I try not to smile. "Apparently."

"Congratulations."

"Thank you." The word comes out breathlessly as his consuming stare wraps me up in warmth and tingles. I swallow and look towards the unlocked studio door. "You can't be here at the moment, Max. My brother is home for the weekend and you're not his favourite person." Max's narrow grey eyes start to strip me of sanity. He drops the paper before closing the space between us. Stepping backwards, the barre presses against my lower back and I gasp. "You should probably go."

His fingertips meet my hand before brushing up the full length of my arm and enveloping the arch of my neck. "I should probably go... say hi."

"You're a menace," I whisper as he tilts my chin up with his thumb.

His face is suddenly filled with amusement. "A menace?"

I giggle shakily. "Yeah."

He suddenly lifts me onto the barre and wraps my legs around his waist. Feeding his hand through my hair, he kisses me passionately. He presses his pelvis between my thighs and rubs against the thin fabric of my leotard. I moan and tighten my legs around him. His tongue enters my mouth. His hands begin to move around my body, stroking me with a tender, yet demanding level of pressure. I slide my fingers under his shirt, break our kiss to help him tug it over his head, and then desperately find his lips again. His cheeks have that perfect level of roughness. His mouth and tongue are all over my chin. My neck. My ear. The warmth of his heavy breathing caresses my skin.

Wrapping his fingers around the straps of my leotard, he begins to peel it down my body. My breasts bounce free, squishing against his toned abdomen.

"*Max*," I beg as his lips leave mine and circle my chin and neck again. "Max, we can't. The door."

He groans. Pushing himself away from me, he walks over to the door and locks it tight. I glance at myself in the mirror. I'm sitting on the barre, shoulders rising and falling with each big breath. My leotard is bunched below my navel. My nipples are pointed, and I actually look as sexy as Max is making me feel.

My eyes dart back to him. He's stalking toward me, his torso wrapped in taut, flexing muscles. The inked design under his skin ripples as he moves. His face is completely emotionless.

He pulls a foil packet from his back pocket. Stopping inches in front of me, he unbuttons his jeans, slowly pulls them off, and stands with his thick, toned thighs between my knees. I grip the barre until my knuckles feel tingly. He reaches into his boxers and pulls his erection out, fisting the root and giving himself long, slow strokes to the tip and back. Precum forms as a glistening bead on its head.

Peeling my fingers off the barre, he moulds my hand around his penis. It's so thick, my fingers are unable to circle it fully. While he holds my gaze, he begins to show me how to stroke him.

I peer down at his long, heavy penis, which looks even

bigger in my tiny hand. I'm overawed by how rock-hard his erection is, how I can squeeze him with all my strength and yet, that doesn't stop him from throbbing against me.

As Max pants beside my forehead, his lips brush against me, breath fanning my arousal. He squeezes the barre on either side of my thighs; the dramatic music of Tchaikovsky flowing through the speakers intensifies the moment.

Taking him in both hands, I lick my lips, wondering what he tastes like. As I massage his penis up and down, his hands move between my legs. He circles the buttons at the crotch of my leotard with his fingers for a while, slowly, as if he's unsure about what he's touching. But then it clicks and he's snapping them open in quick succession. And he's pulling it off, leaving me with only my pink legwarmers on.

A soft kiss meets my earlobe. Another graces my jawline. His lips take mine again when he grabs my hands and pulls them off his erection.

I hear the foil from the condom wrapper crinkling, and then he's positioning me on top of his erection. Using the tip of his penis, he stimulates my clit. Arching on a spasm, my legs tighten around his waist. My arms begin to tremble around his neck. Our kisses now mingle with whimpers and deep, longing groans.

"Don't worry, Little One. I'll try to go slow."

A tear escapes my eye, but I'm not sad. "Please, Max."

"Tell me you want this." He's almost growling. "I need to hear you say it."

"I want this."

With one hand cupping my bum, he lifts me slightly. His fingers are between my cheeks, pressing on the hole between them. The other hand grasps his cock and feeds his erection into me. Slowly. Inch by inch until he stops on a groan. His shoulders are taut from his restraint. The pace is perfect for me, but I imagine he wants to thrust. But he isn't.

I'm feeling a lot of tightness, a lot of stretching. And I'm so full. So utterly taken.

"Fuck." I barely hear the word, but I feel it against my lips. "Relax, Cassidy."

He uses his hand to push his erection further in, but he's not fitting—it hurts. I begin to wriggle my hips and mewl. He curses again and thrusts harder. And then I feel a sting like an elastic band being flicked inside me. And now he's sliding in deep and I'm crying out in pain and pleasure.

"*Relax*," he groans as he kisses my face, his penis pumping inside me.

Heat from his skin radiates against mine. There's an intense, mind-blowing sensation when his whole erection stretches me open. Our breathing becomes laboured. Our lips are everywhere.

As he begins to speed up, I hug his neck and look over his shoulder at his reflection. I watch as his muscular, tattooed back tightens and his perfect backside thrusts into me, clenching and releasing with each buck of his hips. My legs and body shake from the force of him. It's voyeuristic. Erotic. My ears start to burn. The muscles inside me, circling his penis, begin to squeeze together and pulse. And it seems to affect Max because he's groaning louder beside my ear.

He lifts me to straddle his waist, supporting my weight with ease and bounces me on top of him.

He's not slow anymore.

But he's not rough.

My stomach tenses up. My toes curl. And Max is so fricking strong. He moulds my body wherever he wants it and even though I want to crawl away, the sensation coming on too fast, too intense, he's taking me, handling me.

My legs begin to shake as heat shoots up my thighs and down my abdomen, crashing together in a powerful orgasm. I cry out, but Max swallows my sounds.

My body feels weak, muscles fatigued and trembling. He continues to bounce me on top of him until I feel him grow even bigger inside me. He's growling next to my ear now and thrusting up once more. Holding me close, he pulsates on a wave of pleasure. His groan is deep and sexy—my new favourite sound.

He buries his head in the arch of my neck, exhausted. As he nuzzles me, I brush my fingers through his thick, dark-brown hair. The sweetness of this moment makes my heart skip.

When he finally lowers me down, his penis slips from inside me, wet and amazingly beautiful. But at the sight of the blood on the condom, my chest tightens. Glancing between my legs, I spot my blood-mixed arousal sliding down my thighs like a pink snake.

Max grabs my chin and lifts my wide eyes to meet his soft, supportive ones. "It's normal. I'm a big guy."

I breathe out fast and with urgency, not even realising I was holding my breath. He pulls the condom off and ties the end before walking over to the waste bin and disposing of it.

I detail his body from a distance. At the sight of the smug grin plastered all across his face, my cheeks flush. "Stop it, Max."

Staring at me in the mirror, he tucks his penis into his boxers. "I was watching your sexy little arse bounce on my cock in the mirror."

I cover my face, which is ridiculous because I'm naked from the knee up. "Oh my gawd."

"Big tick for the choice of venue." He laughs and I look up

from my hands to see that relaxed smile again. Max appears lighter for a moment.

He moves towards me and scoops me into his arms, cradling me as he walks into the bathroom. We smile at each other. He places me on top of the vanity and helps me clean myself up. I'm not at all uncomfortable—he's incredibly attentive.

I throw on a yellow tee-shirt and a pair of denim short shorts.

When I'm completely dressed, he says, "I gotta go, Little One."

My heart sinks.

My mouth gapes as I watch him pull his jeans and shirt on. He can't seriously be leaving. Not straight after that. Not straight after taking my virginity.

He turns to leave, so I rush after him and grab his wrist. "Don't go."

He stops. When he faces my direction again, I take a step back. A long sigh escapes him as he studies me with a tight expression—seeing every desperate and pathetic inch of me.

"I got shit to do," he says as his finger strokes down the shaft of my nose before tapping the tip playfully. "I'll see ya soon."

"One hour. Hang out with me for an hour?"

Oh my God. Stop it, Cassidy!

"This is just this. Sex. I fucking told you that."

His words cut into me, but they bring anger rather than pain. "What? So we can't be friends?"

After a quick glance at the door, his head dips back in defeat. "Fine."

His fingers feed through mine and he pulls me outside onto the porch in a form of defiance, knowing full well that Konnor is around somewhere. He releases my hand and when I try to protest, he slumps down onto the daybed and positions himself against the backboard. He smirks at me while patting the cushion between his outstretched legs. "Sit."

I scowl at him. "You're a menace."

"So I've heard."

I falter and gaze across the property, my eyes landing on a red motorcycle. "You rode Bronson's bike?"

Max watches me hesitate and clenches his jaw. "Yeah. Look, stop searching around for daddy. I saw Konnor when I pulled up. He was getting blind drunk out front. Don't worry."

My breathing stammers. "Is he okay?"

He shakes his head and smirks. "I don't really care. Your brother is too much drama."

"You actually are a jerk," I bite out.

"Another thing I've heard."

My cheeks are still warm and tingly. I run my hands down them as I contemplate. Narrowing my eyes at Max, I stroll over to him because there is literally nowhere else I'd rather be. It's frustrating as hell.

As I crawl onto the daybed, I settle between his thighs, my back and head pressed against his chest.

Moments pass and we breathe together in comfortable, pleasurable silence. I hate that my irritation towards him is dwindling.

The last minutes of the day are displayed in an orange and pink glow above the rooftops. I can smell Max all around me. I can feel his deep breaths behind my spine. I find his tattooed forearm draped across the armrest and drag my nails softly through its soft hair. As his skin prickles, he twists his wrist to encourage me to keep stroking him.

“Tell me about this role,” he says, kissing my temple.

His interest in my life makes me smile. I'm glad he can't see it. "What do you want to know?"

"Anything you want to tell."

"Well, the Sugar Plum Fairy is the guide for the Land of Candy, which sounds weirder than it is. The whole story follows Clara on this adventure. It's kinda Alice in Wonderland-esque, but instead of the Mad Hatter, you have the Sugar Plum Fairy. She's sweet and spice and everything nice. She's sort of like a conductor. Her choreography is playful and even a little flirty."

I think he chuckles, but it's barely audible. "Is it the main role?"

"She's one of the main roles." I roll my head across his chest and wonder if he's making conversation for the sake of it or if he's genuinely interested. Max doesn't usually banter. He doesn't sugar-coat. His words are like knives that stab straight to the point. "She has some very complex sequences."

"Have I said congratulations?"

I bite back another smile. "Yes."

A few moments pass. Before I was content in our silence, but my comfort is weighed down by my insecurities. "Max?"

"Yeah?" he asks, his tone wary with suspicion.

"I'm going to the wedding. Did you know that?"

"Yes," he states, the word curt.

"Do you... *mind*?"

I imagine him frowning. "Why would I mind?"

"I don't know." Because I'll cramp your sexual prowess? I wish I could see his face. His body is tense behind mine and his breaths have become more exaggerated. "You were so angry when you saw me with Aurora," I press.

"I was. I am. It has nothing to do with you."

"Well, it seems to have had *everything* to do with me... Are you fighting with your brothers or something?”

"No, Little One."

I drag my fingernails up the curve of his bicep, making him twitch. "Wanna talk about why you're mad?"

"Nope."

I huff. "Why not?"

"Don’t be pushy or I’ll bend you over this couch."

I press my knees together and try not to wince.

Max must have sensed my discomfort, though, because he caresses my outer thigh and then cups a hand between them. "Are you in pain?"

I'm familiar with muscular tearing—fatigue or throbbing of overworked muscles, and this feeling is no different. "I'm fine... *Max?*"

As he gently strokes between my legs, he says, "Yes?"

I draw in a breath for courage. "Why can’t we–"

"So, how’s your dickhead mate, Toni?"

I can't help but laugh. "Ladies and gentlemen, I introduce the Master of the Subtle Transition."

He slides his hand inside my shorts and continues to tenderly caress the swollen valley between my lips. "I like the master part."

I try to ignore his touch, but it's soothing and sensual and I don’t want him to stop. "He isn’t a dickhead. He's my best friend."

"Great friend."

"What makes you say that?"

He pulls his hand away. "He left you in heat while some dickhead was trying to get inside you."

I twist on the daybed to glower at him. "Firstly... not in heat. Secondly, he isn’t my keeper."

His face tightens. "Right."

"I'm a big girl." I turn a little farther toward him. "I can look after myself."

"Not from where I'm sitting."

"Well, sit somewhere else then!" The air around us thickens. His teeth grind. For a second he looks like he wants to punch a wall.

But then he slumps down and grins. "Nah."

I twist back around towards the main house. "You aren't so good at this 'getting to know you' stuff, are you?"

"Nope."

"Master of the Single Word Responses."

He laughs loudly and presses his lips to my ear before pushing his hand down my shorts again, stroking me softly. "I'm the master of a lot of things today."

I swallow and drop my head to his chest. "I'm sore."

"Get inside." His tone is salacious. "I'll lick you all better."

"I thought you had things to do?"

"I prioritise."

A distanced yell makes me jump. It's coming from the house and is soon punctuated by loud slamming. My feet are on the ground and running across the grass before I even register the motion. In the next step, I slam into Max, who has outpaced me and is now holding me back.

"Get out of my way!" I yell at him.

"I'll go." He throws me over his shoulder and tries to walk me back inside the studio.

"I swear to God, Max Butcher, if you don't put me down!"

"Shut up!"

"Max!" My voice breaks.

He freezes. With a curse, he places me back onto the grass and grabs the nape of my neck hard, manhandling me to focus on him. "Go up there, but I'll be listening. If things get out of control, I'm coming up."

CHAPTER TEN

dustin nerrock

RUSHING INTO THE HOUSE, I follow the voices until they become clearer. As I steady my pace, I listen to my dad and Konnor arguing. Their words are like an auditory panic attack to my senses. Hate and distrust are being thrown around, threatening to unravel the family unit we have worked so hard to knot up tight.

As I approach my father's office, the snarling gets louder. I hear my dad's pleading voice ask, "Konnor, what do you remember about why Dustin Nerrock gave you up for adoption?"

His tone makes my lips tremble and my eyes well up. I peek inside to see Konnor standing stiffly over my father, who is seated at his redwood desk. Blesk is sitting on Jaxon's lap, watching them intently.

Konnor growls and thrusts his hands around. "I have a better idea. Why don't you just talk? Tell me what I know or what I don't!"

I swing the door open and they both stare at me wide-eyed. "What's going on? Why are you yelling at each other?"

Konnor is in front of me in seconds. I've never seen him look so unlike my brother. So angry. So filled with suspicion. "You should leave, Cass."

I frown up at him and hold my own. I'm not letting him push me away or test my loyalty today. Dad is suddenly beside us, trying to control the situation, but it's seemingly uncontrollable. "Cassidy, sweetheart, this is Konnor's business. It isn't something you need to be involved in."

I glare at my dad because I want him to know he can't just dismiss me. I'm a part of this family. I was there when Konnor ran away. I was there when he punched holes in every door in the house. I was there, and it's not fair to treat me like I don't have a place in this conversation. "If it's his business, then it's mine."

"Sweetheart, it's—"

"No. I'm not leaving until I know why my two favourite people are yelling at each other." My dad nods. Walking back to his chair, he falls into it. The defeated look on his face makes me want to cuddle him, but I don't know whose side I'm on yet.

Konnor stares at me and I cross my arms.

He almost smiles. "Fine, Cassidy."

I wait for Konnor to say something like, 'Bloody princess,' but he doesn't, and when Dad talks, we all start to listen. "So, you don't want me to ask questions, Konnor. That's fine. But then I can't distinguish what information you have, and so I'm going to just lay it all on the table and between the two of us, we can sift through the pieces and hopefully come out with a puzzle that looks like a picture." He takes a big breath in. "I went to school with your mother, Madeline. I'm yet to meet a woman who could summon the kind of infatuation that woman could. She was wild and intriguing and sharp as a razor with the biggest green eyes and a strange mind. But she was also very insecure and often troubled. She thought too much, and that always led her to the horizon, looking for something more."

My heart contorts. I want to scold my dad and find my mum to cuddle her tightly because he's clearly in love with Konnor's biological mother.

Dad's lips slump. "She married Nerrock not long after high school. They had a son. They looked beautiful together and their son was picture perfect. It wasn't until later that these rumours started to circulate. You all know what the District is like with gossip. Well, the rumour was that Deakon Nerrock..." My father's voice falters. "That *you* weren't Dustin's son.

"Now Dustin's family has a lot of money. They are one of the founders of the District and are deeply rooted in Catholicism. Adultery was completely reprehensible. People loved the rumour. I mean, Dustin and Madeline were political celebrities and the envy of everyone. Their love, life, and every moment were caught on camera and plastered all over the District which made what happened even more impressive because, Christ, the whole world had been watching them. And yet this happened right under everyone's noses. You were taken. Missing."

I stare at my kind-hearted, gentle dad, who is now tightly wound with nerves. He doesn't notice me; his eyes are lost in the whirlwind of his son's emotions. Konnor has his head pressed against the wall. A whimper and a groan vibrates through him, but he's not alone because Blesk is there comforting him. I wonder how much she knows. How is this girl such a comfort to him? How has she become his rock so quickly when we have fought tooth and nail to gain his trust for over a decade?

Who is this girl?

Dad clears his throat. "I'd be lying if I said I liked Dustin, but I never thought he'd go so far as to have a child kidnapped. I thought he might, well... I worried about your mother's safety, but not yours. You were just a child. Who would hurt a child? Especially not you, the golden child of the District. I didn't realise how far he'd gone until now. I don't know for sure, Konnor. I have no proof. But if this statement is true, then someone paid that man to take you."

Covering my lips, I gasp and stare at my dad from above my hand.

"And I know in my heart that it wasn't Madeline, so that leaves... Well, it's Dustin and Madeline's account."

I look at the papers my dad is shuffling around on his desk. A statement of some kind. Is he saying that money came out of Konnor's biological parents' account to pay for the kidnapping? That's sick.

"That's bullshit, such bullshit," Konnor yells. "Money came from that fucking account for my tuition! How's that possible? Answer that question! I saw it, Ben." He cuts us both up when he refers to our dad by his Christian name. I wait with bated breath. "The invoice was clearly made out to the university for my tuition."

Wait? What?

My parents pay for his tuition. Don't they? So, that can't be true. That would mean *my* parents paid for him to be kidnapped. Is that what Konnor is accusing him of? Is that why he's yelling at my dad and calling him by his Christian name?

Shaking my head, unable to believe any of this, unable to rationalise this information, I listen to Dad talk.

Dad stiffens. "Konnor, your mother handed the rights to that account over to me a few weeks before she died. She said it was for you and you alone if you were ever found or ever returned. That money would have gone to Dustin's other children, his future children, and she knew she didn't have much time left. So, I have been using the funds for your tuition and for anything else I see fit. We didn't need the money, of course, but it was important to Madeline that it went to you."

A bit of relief fills me. It wasn't my parents' account that the money had come from. Dad now has the rights to that account, though, because Madeline wanted to make sure Konnor would get his inheritance. It's confusing as hell.

Konnor blinks at him. "You loved her."

As I watch my dad fall apart from all these secrets, I don't know what to do. I can't even imagine what my brother is going through right now. Blesk leans into him and whispers in his ear. I glance at the window behind Dad's desk. It's open all the way. Max is probably below that window, listening...

With a sudden thought occurring, I look directly at my dad, wondering if we're all sharing an infidelity that my mum knows nothing about.

"I love your mum, Cassidy." My dad's voice is soft and pained as he reads the accusation in my eyes. "But, yes, Konnor, Madeline was my first love."

Konnor looks desperately at our dad. "Okay, so are you my dad? I mean, are you my biological dad?"

My dad—our dad—shakes his head. "No, Konnor. I wish I was." We all sink together. "You're my son, but you're not my blood. I'm sorry. I don't know who is. She never told me."

Konnor's face contorts. "So you two planned my adoption? Before they even found me? That's such crap."

I shake my head, clearing my throat, "That makes zero sense. This sounds like fricking BS, Dad. When kids go missing and they aren't found for four fricking years, don't people just, kind of—" I hesitate. "Assume they're dead?"

Dad's response is sad, but also almost... robotic. "Madeline never gave up hope, not for a second. I don't know if she suspected foul play because she never told me. We very rarely spoke, Konnor. We'd never discussed the adoption. I received a letter in the mail one day, and it just said that I was entrusted to make sure you'd receive the money if you were found or that it went to her charity if you weren't. It was from a lawyer. She didn't even send it herself."

He stares directly at Konnor. "I'm not sure if you have heard about this, but Madeline started a charity for you. Nerrock Missing and Beyond. It's for lost children and their families. This is your legacy, Konnor. If you were never found. If you were just... gone. All the money would have been donated in your name. That was Madeline's wish. Well, that was what the letter said."

Konnor grimaces. "You never tried to talk to her? Face to face?"

"Of course I did. I was completely disconnected from her. No one would let me speak to her."

"Did she know? Did she know Dustin had something to do with my disappearance?"

Dad rises from his chair and holds up shaky hands. "Slow down. Firstly, we don't know he did for sure. We are just speculating here and only because you came in here, guns blazing. But since we are, I can admit it crossed my mind. It was very peculiar that months after the rumours of your legitimacy as a Nerrock began, you went missing."

Konnor's whole face tightens. He glances at Jax, perhaps seeking comfort in his friend. "She stayed with him anyway?"

"Even if she did suspect him, you don't divorce people like Dustin Nerrock. It's too... dangerous."

"I don't understand," Konnor mutters.

Dad smiles tightly and shifts his weight in the chair. "I know you don't. Because I have worked very hard to keep you kids out of that world." I hold my breath as he continues. "The District's streets are run by The Families. The whole structure is corrupt. They are just dangerous company to keep and even more so to marry into."

Dangerous company to keep...

Jax's eyes widen. "So, what, like the mob?"

My eyes shoot across to Dad as he answers, "Something like that."

I try to control my breathing, having known the truth this whole time. The District is run by the mob. It's a collective secret that no one agreed to keep, but everyone strictly adheres to. *Everyone* knows that Jimmy is at the head of the table, but most people in the District respect him. Fear him too.

"And Nerrock is involved?" Blesk presses. Her interest stretches outside of the realm of a concerned girlfriend and into something else—something I don't understand.

"Well, he would deny it. They're just businessmen, Blesk."

Konnor's jaw clenches as he steps toward our dad. "Are you involved with them?"

Dad coughs. "God, no!"

Blesk speaks delicately and apprehensively. "Is my... I mean, the man who took Konnor, was he involved?"

"I don't know, Blesk."

Jaxon shuffles in place and even though I really like him, I wish he wasn't here to witness such a private conversation. "Whoa, this is a bit intense. Konnor, you're a mafia kid."

Konnor tightens. "No, I'm not. I'm a Slater." He claims our name above all else and that makes me yearn to hold him close. He is a Slater and no new information will ever change that.

But right now I need to know for my own aching self, inside and out. "Is Butcher one of them?"

As I imagine Max's eyes turning into slits at the question, my pulse begins to shudder in my throat. I think I want him to know... that I know he's been brought up in this world—as have I, in many ways, with Konnor as my brother.

Konnor glares at me. "Cassidy, why? Why would it matter?"

Evading his eyes, I stare straight ahead at my dad. "Just wondering. Flick hangs out with them a lot now."

Konnor steps in front of me and I crane my neck to look up at him. "You're lying," he states. "Why do you care about The Butcher Boys? Why is that name even coming up?"

I feign indifference. "They're our friends, Konnor. That's all."

"Oh, so now they're *our* friends? Not just Flick's friends anymore?"

Blesk touches his arm and pleads, "Konnor."

"Son, what is your qualm with them?" Dad asks. "Do you know something I don't?"

Konnor eyeballs me before glancing across to Dad. "Don't like them, that's all. I don't want Cassidy hanging out with them."

I snort. He's not even here most of the time and he's barking orders at me? "Well, I guess it's a good thing I'm not five anymore and can do what I fricking like."

"Cassidy, calm down." Dad tries to settle me with his gentle tone. "Your brother just worries."

My brows weave. “Great, now I have a restriction on friends."

I don't know why I'm getting so worked up by this. I guess I'm just sick of being treated like a child. By Konnor. By Max.

“You’re acting like a brat, Cassidy," Konnor spits out.

"I’m acting like an eighteen-year-old girl who is being interrogated by her brother because she has ‘boys’ who are friends. Can you be more of a cliché? I bet you wish I was gay like Flick."

"Not boys, Cassidy," he says. "Butcher boys."

My dad intervenes. "We are digressing. These aren’t conversations we should be having. Nor are they necessary. Luca Butcher’s sons are not the issue here and you’re not in any kind of danger. This should go without saying, but this is Konnor’s business. None of this can leave this room. Konnor, if you want to make arrangements to discuss this further with other parties, then you can, but it should be discussed here, with me, first. I can’t stress this enough. Everything I’ve done, all the truths I’ve withheld, have been for you. Promise me you won’t go ruffling feathers. Okay?”

Konnor slowly nods. "Does Nerrock know? Does he know where I am?"

“Yes, of course,” Dad says. “He knows who you are, Konnor, and where you are. But you’re not in any danger. It’s over. You’re mine. Trust me.”

Uncertainty flickers in Blesk's eyes. “How can you be so sure?”

“Trust me." Dad approaches Konnor. "Do you? Do you trust me?”

Konnor's shoulders fall slack. “I trust you, Dad.”

Leaning into him, Blesk comforts my brother in a way I cannot. Despite loving Konnor more than anything in the world, I've never really been able to breach his walls. He's always kept me at a distance. But with Blesk... with Blesk he finds comfort. It's like she is physically taking away his pain.

Touching his forehead to hers, Konnor sighs, proof that a bit of tension is already fading. As I watch Blesk comfort him with a mere squeeze of his bicep, my heart aches for that kind of love.

"We're going to go rest," Blesk says as she leads Konnor out of the room.

Strolling over to his desk once again, Dad falls into his chair. "Cassidy, baby, can you get your old man a drink?"

My eyes begin to sting. "Okay."

I pour him a drink from the bottle of whiskey on his cabinet and place the tumbler down on a coaster in front of him. As he takes a mouthful, I watch silently with furrowed brows. When he finishes the glass, I pour him another. "Is that all true, Dad?"

I study him, not convinced he's told us the whole truth. He looks too exhausted to have gotten everything off his chest. The truth is supposed to unburden you, not cripple you under even more weight.

Shaking my head, I say, "His own dad paid to have him kidnapped?"

When he finally looks up at me with sunken eyes, his gaze darts over my shoulder and his face pales. His eyes widen for just a split second. My heart pummels inside my ribcage and I spin to see Max filling the doorway.

"Max," my dad says with a closed smile. The room suddenly has no air.

Max is blank. His stare doesn't waver from my dad. "Ben, sorry to interrupt. I just wanted to say goodnight to Cassidy."

My mouth falls open as I observe the soulless interaction. A knot rolls up my throat. My dad's hands tremble as he folds them in his lap. He smiles. This time it meets his eyes, but I can tell his teeth are clenched by the way his jaw moves.

"Of course." Dad's voice is strained. "Don't keep her up too late. She has ballet school tomorrow."

"I wouldn't dare."

CHAPTER ELEVEN

I FOLLOW Max as he steps outside into the cool night air. The weather is something I usually love about Western Australia. It's cool in the evening and warm during the day, but tonight the chill has ominous company. I haven't spoken because the words are caged in my throat, unable to leave.

Max stares deadpan into the darkness. A long moment passes, twisting the knot in my stomach before he turns towards me. I think of our day together. Of our intimacy. Of his light smile. I think of them because I barely recognise this man in front of me.

"You need to be very careful with the names you throw around. Don't talk about people you think you know. You know nothing. You're a silly little girl. Stop asking questions you'll never get the answers to. Focus on being a ballerina."

My pulse leaps as his detached eyes crush any hope I've ever had for us. "But... Konnor's part of—"

"This conversation is over."

I cuddle myself tightly, holding all the pieces of myself together in case I fall apart. Without another word, Max walks away, vanishing into the void between my house and studio. Silence lingers and then the lights of Bronson's bike flick on and stun my senses. The engine growls to a start and he disappears, neither speeding nor meandering; he just casually rides away from me.

CHAPTER TWELVE

TONI IS SITTING CROSSED-LEGGED on my bed beside my half-packed suitcase. "Are you sure you still want to go to Bali?"

I fold another pair of shorts. "Yes. I'll be fine. I'm focused." I motion with my hand, cutting the air in front of my eyes. "I'm focused."

He pulls out a lacy pair of knickers and wrinkles his nose. "I really don't think you should be going."

"It's business." I shake my head and glance everywhere except directly at Toni. Chuckling nervously, I add, "It's a lot of money. Plus, Jimmy is sponsoring me now. He's paying my way through Europe; he's gotten me offers from companies in Italy. I'm not going to mess this up. I will keep my distance. I have the power to ignore... I'm an excellent ignorer."

"Yes, I think every guy from high school will agree that you are an excellent ignorer. But we aren't talking about them. We are talking about—"

"Max Butcher. See." I shrug and smile with gullible

enlightenment. "I can say his name again. It's fine. Toni, I know what I have to do. I'll keep it professional. I'll go for bike rides during the day. I'll visit villages, temples, and fricking volcanoes, and I'll be fine."

He pointedly lifts up my new toffee bathing suit. Between its spaghetti straps and thin crisscrossing wrap-around midriff, the suit resembles a few pieces of string rather than bathers.

"It covers everything," I state adamantly.

His eyes widen. "I don't think you should be going."

Snatching the one-piece from him, I force a grin. "You underestimate me, my friend."

"No, Golden Girl, I don't. I estimate you. I estimate you right at the point of blinding, young, irrational obsession. That's my estimate."

"Well, um," I stammer. "Get a different ruler."

"Your comebacks are sad. I can't believe we're friends sometimes. Listen, you haven't heard from him in nearly two weeks. And the last time you saw him, he crushed you, calling you a silly little girl. Just leave it, darlin'."

I begin to pace around the room, riffling through cupboards and drawers that I know have nothing in them I need or want. "I was a silly little girl," I whisper into the closet.

Toni sighs. "Cassidy."

"I was." Stiffening, I turn to face him. The back of my eyes heat and my lower lip threatens to tremble. "I thought I could relate to his world. I thought that being Konnor's sister meant that we weren't so different because I'd known hardship too. I'd thought that meant he could let me in, but I was wrong. I know nothing about pain. I know nothing about responsibility. I know nothing about violence or torment. I know nothing about anything, just like he'd said."

"*Cassidy.*"

"No. I'm no longer an asexual pigeon, Toni." My voice cracks. "I've become very aware of my body and my sexuality since being with Max. I'm confident enough to wear something like that now," I say, pointing at the swimsuit. "It has nothing to do with him being there."

He stares at me with furrowed brows. "I don't think you should be going." Sighing, he adds, "But in the end, this is your life. If you want to be a glutton for the punishment that is Max Butcher, then fine. Flaunt your fanny around Bali, but what kind of friend would I be if I didn't warn you against it." He pauses. "No, seriously, what kind of friend would I be? Because I'm one more Max Butcher altercation away from locking you in a tower and guarding you with a dragon."

Laughing a little, I shake my head and finish packing. With a few more sarcastic comments, Toni drives me to the airport and waves me off at the gate.

Being only five foot three and petite comes in handy when flying on a small jet. Curling my knees up until they're touching the cold metal curve of the plane, I peer out the window as the urban patchwork of the District is replaced by the flat red dirt of the Australian outback. The plane will head north across the Kimberley and Indian Ocean before setting down in Bali in several hours. Flick, Stacey, and the others are all on Jimmy Storm's private jet, which is scheduled to land a few hours after mine.

As the Kimberley pans beneath me, I open the Indonesian language book I'd purchased in year twelve and practise simple terms of conversation. By the time we touch down at Denpasar Airport, I've learned the Bali words for 'thank you' and 'please,' as well as the numbers one through ten and numerous greetings.

Selamat pagi.

Terima kasih.

After grabbing my luggage, I step out of the airport and the humidity cloaks me like a blanket I can't kick off. My brow immediately moistens. The thick air smells of tea leaves and rotting fruit and spices. It's exotic, nice, and gross all at once. Bali is somehow both bright and hazy. The heat brings a kind of lethargy with it. Of laziness. Of leisure. Of romance. It's moist and hot. I want to strip off and swim naked in a pool.

A nice man named Atu picks me up and drives me two hours north to Ubud. As he navigates through the chaotic sea of motorbikes and scooters, I watch the rice fields and dense, lush greenery of this tropical island stream past the window.

"*Terima kasih,*" I say, thanking Atu when we reach our destination. After waving goodbye, I wheel my suitcase towards a lovely Balinese lady, who is wrapped in the most beautiful purple dress.

She shows me to the villa, which is carved into the side of a mountain and situated along the outskirts of a luxury resort boasting two pools with swim-up bars and two restaurants. The villa itself has its own access point with a private pool and outdoor kitchen.

The fridge calls my name, so I pull out a Bintang beer, pop the cap, and have a few mouthfuls. I stand still for a moment in the empty villa before taking another sip. Then I wander around the rooms, reading the names on the doors: Flick and Stacey, Bronson, Max, Cassidy, Xander, and Clay.

Walking into my room, I stare at the double bed, beautiful wooden furniture, and hand-carved ornaments. I take another sip and smile. I should jump on Max's bed and scruff up the blankets a bit. I don't, but the thought makes me happy. My room has a private ensuite with walls, but no roof. It's decorated with grey tiles, a single bamboo chair, and enough foliage to make it feel as if I'll be showering outside despite being completely private.

I place my beer on the bedside table before grabbing my luggage and tossing it onto the bed. Riffling through the clothes, I pull out my new toffee bathing suit. I strip off and squeeze into it. It's one-piece; the bottom connects to the top by thin bands. The seam of the panties cuts high, displaying the swell of my hips. The bands wrap three times around my belly and ribs. The top is a halter neck with a plunging neckline. It's pretty.

Toni was wrong, I tell myself as I slide my toes into my flip-flops. I'm not wearing these bathers for Max. I'm wearing these bathers because I like the way they make me feel and I don't care what that means. I grab my towel bag and bronze-tinted aviators and meander towards the main resort pool.

Kicking my flip-flops off, I lie on a sunbed by the pool and stare through my sunglasses at the brochures I picked up at reception. The sun and humid air caress nearly every inch of my body, creating beads of moisture on my skin. Strangers splash around me, laughing. Beautiful girls lie baking in the sun. Lovely Balinese people shuffle around, delivering cocktails and food, as well as offering towels and other comfort items. I focus on my book.

"Cassidy!" I hear my sister's voice screech a second before I'm in her arms. "You'll never believe what just happened."

I return her embrace, dropping my book. "Yay! We're in Bali."

"So?" she pants. "We jumped out of a fucking plane!"

I sit up and she slides onto the side of the sunbed. "You what?" I gasp.

"Yep. They didn't even tell us. They just strapped on

parachutes, connected us to them with harnesses, and jumped. Out. Of. The. Fucking. Airplane. I'm not even kidding you!"

I feel terrible all of a sudden. My stomach threatens to create knots because, for the first time since all of this Butcher boy stuff started, I'm concerned about Flick and whether she knows the depth of their secrets. I wonder if she'd care.

"Wow." She's clearly high on adrenaline, wired and smiling from ear to ear. "You're obviously all okay, though?" I ask.

"Yeah. They apparently do this kind of thing all the time."

Of course they do.

"That sounds amazing." As I slide back down onto my sunbed, wriggling a little to get comfortable, Flick moves to the bed beside mine.

She pauses, ogling me. "Cassidy Slater, those bathers are gorgeous."

I squeeze my lips to hide my smile. "Thank you."

She shuffles slightly to get a better view and observes every inch of me. "They are evil! I love them."

"They aren't evil... The red ones were evil."

"Um, I've never seen you wear anything like this before. Sexy as fuck, sister."

I laugh and glance over my sunglasses. "You're not my type."

Stacey joins Flick soon after we have caught up on all things light-hearted and have settled down to drink some cocktails. The sun's thick presence massages warmth into my muscles, and I bat my eyes closed as Stacey and Flick natter beside me. I drift into a fuzzy, warm world of muted, splashy giggles. Several long seconds pass before the sound of a playful scream causes my eyes to flicker back open.

I watch as a group of excited girls run down the steps. They're screaming and laughing, but all my attention is on Max. He and his brothers, one of which I don't know, are caught in the midst of the girls' chaos for only a moment. And then they're free and every inch of Max's beautiful form is bared to me. I stare directly at him, but he doesn't notice me.

Until he does.

Flipping over onto my belly, I rest my head on my forearm. I'm feigning confidence right now as my heart vibrates against the plastic cushions of the sunbed. Taking a big breath, I try to ignore the commotion and will myself to stay in my own lethargic, lazy, romantic Bali.

"Cassidy," Flick whispers. "Max is fucking you with his eyes right now."

I bite my lips to stifle the silly little girl smile—isn't that what it is? A silly little girl smile. "I'm sure he's not."

My skin is humming from just having heard her say those words though. I'm aching everywhere for his lips. And that is precisely why I'm trying to mentally escape right now. If I look up and see his eyes mentally stripping me, I'll turn into a smouldering puddle of need.

"Felicity, don't," I hear Stacey say, and I twist my head to face them.

Flick rolls her eyes. "Don't what? It's not subtle. He hasn't taken his eyes off her arse since he got here."

"Please," Stacey mutters. "Leave it. It's not a good idea."

It's not a good idea?

Stacey really is a Butcher; she even talks like one.

"What does that mean?" Flick asks. "Why isn't it a good idea—"

Stacey smiles tightly. "Look, this holiday is about the boys. You two need to behave or you won't get an invite next time. I've seen these situations go wrong because girls get on their nerves. Especially Clay and Max, okay? Just be good."

My loud sigh is inadvertent. Sitting up, I grab my purse and walk towards the bar.

I'm used to eyes on me, but today I can feel them caressing me, following each lift of my legs, each sway of my hips. It's as though Max's eyes have the power to physically touch me, though, so now I'm struggling to stay relaxed. My stomach flips around with nerves. It takes all my strength to not glance over at him.

Once I'm finally at the bar, I lean against it. It provides a semblance of protection from the eyes that were following me so intimately only moments before.

I smile at the beautiful white toothy grin of the Balinese man polishing glasses.

"Can I please get a mimosa... Sorry... *Jus jeruk and sampagne. Terima kasih.*"

His whole face brightens. "Yes, *wanita cantik.*"

I'm not sure what that means, but he begins to pour me a drink.

A stranger on the bar stool beside me presses his shoulder to mine for a split second. "He said, beautiful lady."

"Oh." I smile at the stranger, whose accent is clearly Australian. "That's nice of him."

His grin slants. "Nah, he's just being honest."

I try to ignore the fact that this man is quite attractive, but my blush gives it away. Laughing awkwardly, I say, "*Terima kasih.*"

He cracks up. "You're fucking adorable. Can I buy you a drink?"

"No," I state respectfully. "I can buy my own. Thank you, though."

"Come on, I've got a mining wage burning a hole in my

pocket and no one to share it with. It's like 0.20c. Let me buy you a drink."

I roll my eyes. "Okay, sure."

"Sweet. I'll pay for her drink and any others she orders." He swivels to face me. "Where you from?"

The bartender places a mimosa in front of me.

"The District."

He nods, one of his eyebrows raised. "Yeah, in WA?"

I grab the glass and take a sip. It's considerably stronger than what we'd get back home. "Yeah." Standing on my tippy toes, I slide up onto a stool and cross my legs. A bead of sweat drips down my hairline as I study his tanned, rugged face. He's as flushed and as sweaty as I am.

"I went there once," he says. "Some bloody good restaurants in that area."

My chair swivels slightly as I relax into the conversation. "There are. And museums and theatres. We're... *arty*." I giggle nervously; he seems to like it because his grin gets wider. "I mean, we're *cultured*. I'm an idiot. Sometimes I say silly things."

Stranger chuckles. "I haven't heard you say anything silly."

"Give her time," I hear Max say, his big form appearing in my peripheral vision.

My head turns towards him like a magnetic attraction and I stare at his naked, tattooed torso. His muscles shift hypnotically as he moves, and—oh frick—he's so close now I can see the beads of sweat on his chest.

I swallow hard. "Yes, Max?"

He stops right in front of me, unapologetically raking my body. "Tell me, Little One, did they run out of fabric while making those bathers?"

Stranger leans on the bar. "Hey, man, don't ruin it for the rest of us."

Max's biceps twitch.

I try to remain calm. "Just ignore me if you don't like my bathers."

His eyes are fixed on mine. "I didn't say I didn't like them." He signals the bartender. "A mimosa and a Jameson neat."

I glance at Stranger as he says, "Hey, man, I've already bought her a drink."

Max completely ignores him. Gripping the bar between us, his other hand reaches for my current mimosa. His eyes are firm and brazen as he drains the glass.

Stranger stands up abruptly. "Are you fucking serious?"

My pulse quickens when Max slowly turns to acknowledge him—all six foot four inches of scowling Max Butcher. He makes Stranger look like a little boy. He should probably have to declare his body as a weapon like people who do karate have to do... Or something.

"This is ridiculous!" I stumble to my feet. So he doesn't want me. But he also doesn't want anyone else to have me. Fricking caveman! "I'm going for a walk."

"Put something else on," Max growls.

"Of course, I was going to." I glare at him. Never breaking his gaze, I slowly slide on my flip-flops. His eyes narrow further as I walk out onto the footpath and wander down the cobblestone street.

I half expect him to chase after me. Throw me into a stall. Force me to cover up my body. I wish the thought didn't excite me so much. Literally, as soon as I'm far enough away from the resort, I duck into a little street market and search for 'something else to put on.' But there was no way in hell I was going to let Max Butcher dictate my attire. Especially since I haven't heard from him in two fricking weeks.

Browsing the dresses, I take my time. I find a few I like, and the woman is all smiles as I practise my Indonesian in an attempt at bartering. Of course, I pay the original asking price anyway. Each dress only costs me five Australian dollars. The white summer dress that cuts directly across at the knee is perfect for today, so I pull it over my bathers before heading out again to explore a few spots around Ubud.

CHAPTER THIRTEEN

silly little girl

BACK AT THE VILLA, I find Flick, Stacey, and the boys lounging on the wicker sofas in the private alfresco. The night is balmy. I've sweated the alcohol from my system, so I feel a little more content now. Eager to meet the groom and thank him for the opportunity he's given me by letting me be a part of his wedding, I meander over to them.

I suddenly freeze when I catch sight of two beautiful girls dressed scantily. They shuffle around, clearing empty beer bottles from the tables and making eyes at the ridiculously attractive gang of Butcher boys.

Great...

Bronson twists around and winks at me. "Hey, sister Cassidy. Lovely dress. See, Maxipad, she could just about join a convent."

Max appears unfazed by the comment and my presence in general, which is fine by me because I don't want to talk to him anyway. I sit down beside Bronson. He's so welcoming and charismatic that I instantly feel accepted beside him.

"Wanna drink?" Stacey asks me, bouncing to her feet and walking over to the fridge.

"Sit down, Stacey," Xander orders. "We have serving bitches to do that."

Bronson gasps in mock horror. "Xander! Serving *goddesses*. Seriously, who taught you manners?"

They all laugh and say, "Max."

"I don't mind, Xan," Stacey insists.

"Sit down. Relax," Xander says.

Shuffling to the edge of the sofa, I lean across to Clay. "Hi. I'm Cassidy. I'm-

"Our ballerina." He nods. He looks a little like Max, but with sharper features and salt and pepper hair in his beard. "I know. Aurora hasn't shut up about you."

"Try sticking your dick in her mouth. That usually works," Xander says.

Max laughs. "That's what your boyfriend told me he does with you, Xander."

I've entered boy land.

One of the serving girls passes me a beer. "*Terima kasih*," I say with a tight smile, trying not to scowl at her beautiful breasts, suddenly conscious of my own small ones.

"I apologise for my brothers, Cassidy." Clay smiles and leans further into his chair. He has a powerful presence. The way my throat tightens warns me to be cautious around him. "We're not heathens. They're just not always around such beautiful girls."

"Now I know that's not true," I say, crossing my legs.

Max stares at Stacey. "On the subject of beautiful girls, where are you three fucking off to on Thursday?"

"Eloquent as always, Max." Bronson leans closer to me and mutters, "Buck's party."

My stomach rolls with unease. Toni's voice sounds in my mind. *You shouldn't be going.*

Stacey pats Flick's thigh. "We're all staying somewhere else."

"Yeah, you are," Max states, his gaze shifting to me for a brief moment.

Bronson grins at me a moment before I'm in his arms and being bombed into the pool. The water hits us. My dress floats up and when I surface again, all I can hear is laughter. "Oh my gawd! Bronson."

"You love it," he says, splashing me.

I crack up laughing, my hair dripping down my face. The feelings I'd felt when I'd heard about the buck's party have mellowed, replaced by his contagious playfulness. "You and me and pools are a no-no."

He shrugs. "It's our bit."

I beam at him. "Who decided this?"

"Ah, you did that day you were the last in the pool."

The next few hours are buzzing with laughter and playful insults, but at ten p.m. I decide to retire to my room. Stripping out of my damp dress, I step into the garden-style shower and spin the faucet to cold. But even cold water in this sticky humidity is perfectly warm. After washing the chlorine from my hair, I press my hands to the tiles, dip my head under the refreshing water, and think about Max.

He'd completely ignored me tonight. Of course, the exceptions being his many passive-aggressive comments.

Finished in the shower, I step out and let the thick warm air lick me dry. When I crawl into bed and lie down, I remember how Max and I share a wall—the wall behind my head.

As the soft white sheets bunch around my naked body, I grab a pillow and stuff it between my legs. My eyes close as I mount it. Rubbing into it, I imagine Max's lips on my clit, his erection pulsing inside me as he comes. His taut muscles. His hot breath.

Beginning to moan, I feel a tingle between my thighs. I fist the sheets and pull my body up, rubbing fast against the pillow.

But it's no use. I'm not getting there.

Frustrated, I give up and rearrange the pillow and sheets. At the sudden sound of the doorknob twisting, I sit up, my cheeks smouldering.

Max walks in and tilts his head. "You're a naughty little girl."

I frown at him. "I'm a silly little girl, remember?"

He grins and that darn dimple mocks me. "*Cassidy*."

"No!" I pull the sheets up. "Get out. You've been nothing but a jerk to me."

He closes the door behind him and presses his back to it. "I thought you knew I was a jerk?"

"I'm not playing this game anymore," I say, my voice shaking.

"Little One, you just put on a little auditory show for me."

"No." I bunch the sheets around me. "You can't do this to me. You humiliate me every time I see you." I did just put on a show for him and now I'm angry with him *and* myself.

He frowns and takes one step forward. "How could I humiliate you? No one knows about us."

"Bronson does." I watch him intently.

He pauses. "Yeah."

"It's pretty obvious he's, like, damage control for you."

"Like, is he?"

I tighten my arms around myself and scoot backwards

until I hit the headboard. "Yes. Why is he so nice to me when you're such a jerk?"

"He likes you. And that's all him."

"And you don't, and that's why you're a butthead."

He chuckles and I hate that I love that sound. "A butthead?" he says.

"Does he know everything about us?"

His gaze bounces around for a moment. "Yes."

I breathe out in a rush. "What does he think?"

"He thinks I'm an idiot," he says with a shrug.

"You are!"

He rolls his head in frustration. "Yeah, and he also doesn't think... about you. Goddamn it... protecting *you*. Like I do."

I frown tightly. "You've upset me, Max. Leaving like that. Talking to me like that."

"I know." He nods, his gaze lacking its usual arrogance.

"And you think I'm a silly little girl?"

"Yes." He walks until he's sitting on the end of my bed. "Sometimes you are."

"Okay—"

"But... " He starts to speak and then changes his mind. "Sometimes I *like* it."

"You like silly now?" I say with mock amusement.

"No..." He exhales loudly and frowns at me contemplatively. "I like how you... *soften*... my life."

I take a big breath in and out. "I do?"

"Yeah."

I sigh, wanting to crawl towards him and hold him close, but I don't. "Is this still just sex?"

"Yes."

I laugh once in disbelief. "What!?"

"And..." He reaches for the word. "*Friendship*."

"Okay?" I'm not sure what I expected him to say, but I wasn't prepared for that blatant answer. I compromise... again, and a stone adds to the collection in my belly weighing me down these days. "But are you gonna disappear again?"

"Are you gonna stick your nose into places that might get it broken?"

"No," I say, and I really mean it. "Are you gonna—"

Before I can finish my sentence, he's pulling me to him. His lips are on mine, and he's crawling with me until we are lying on the mattress. His hands are everywhere, exploring. I moan, letting my body become mouldable as he nips and licks and gets carried away with my naked figure beneath his fingers.

"Fuck, Cassidy."

His clothes come off in a rush. Pressing his hot, heavy, naked body to mine, he rubs up against me, his lips unable to break away from mine.

"Just be a good girl from now on," he groans into my mouth. He's impatient as he lifts my legs over his shoulders and thrusts into me, pulsing with sharp pumps that send us both over the edge. We struggle for breath between kissing and moaning. It's not sensual like last time. It's needy. It's fast. It's desperate. He's pinning me to the mattress, thrusting harder and harder.

He groans again, "Fuck, Cassidy."

His thick erection sinks deeper inside me. All the way to the end before sliding back out again. And then in. As he grips the headboard with white knuckles, I wriggle in an attempt to adjust to his girth. "You're fucking beautiful." Those words make my body soften and relax around his. I slide my hand down his muscular back and onto the cheeks of his perfect flexing arse. I'm hot everywhere. He drops one of my legs as he slides down to lick the tight bud of my nipple. My other leg is still weightless over his shoulder. He growls, "Take me."

The muscles inside me hold his penis like a vice, squeezing with every inward thrust and outward draw. He strokes his hand between my legs, kneading my clit as his stormy grey eyes stare into mine. "Come, Cassidy. I need you to."

I wriggle around and then, out of nowhere, he flips me onto my belly. Lifting my backside, he spreads my thighs and enters me again in sharp, quick pulses.

"*Fuck*," he growls, "those bathers." I fist the sheets as he lifts me by the hips. Hard pumps. So deep.

"You're so wet, Little One. Such a tight fit but so wet." While he moves in and out of me, his fingers collect the slickness of my arousal and paints it across my bumhole. "I know what you want." Slowly, his thumb inches inside and I bite the pillow. Moaning into the soft fabric, I'm overwhelmed by being so completely taken by him. He's inside me—everywhere. A tickle twists at my clit, making me cry out. And a force rushes down to where he opens me wide. And I come hard around his precise thrusts, squeezing his penis and tightening around his thumb.

"Good girl," he says, pulling his thumb out and tilting my body up until my back meets his chest. His tongue is on my neck. His hands move around to my breasts.

He pumps his hips up into me until he starts to tremble. Groaning, his hips thrust with each grunt of his orgasm. "*Fuck*."

Breathing hard, we collapse onto the bed. He pulls me into his big arms, wrapping them around me as he buries his head into my hair. We stay like this for several minutes, breathing deeply together.

Tears begin to burn the backs of my eyes because I'm feeling so much right now—too much. It's uncomfortable. The way I want him. The way his presence makes my insides flip around. The way I give myself to him. I begin to shake.

I didn't seek out these feelings for him. I fell into them.

I'm still falling—hard.

I'm in trouble.

Max brushes the hair from my cheeks and shuffles to study my face. "You're crying."

I shake my head, eyes squeezed shut. "No."

"Yes, you are. Did I hurt you?"

"No, Max." I open my eyes and stare through wet lashes. "Not yet."

His brows tighten and he looks sad for a moment. "Don't say that."

I sniffle. "I'm sorry. I am a silly little girl."

His jaw clenches just briefly. "I'm gonna take care of things, okay?"

"Things?"

He pulls me down beside him and we share a pillow, facing each other. "You. I'm gonna take care with you. I'm not gonna hurt you."

"You might not mean to."

"Try not to expect anything and you'll be fine."

My eyes drop as I remember the image of him with the red-headed girl. He doesn't owe me anything. I know this. He couldn't have been clearer that day in the pool. Monogamy is worse than polio... Despite this, I'm feeling things. Excitement, yes. But also fear. An emptiness in my belly. A kind of tightening in my throat. "Easier said than done."

He brushes his fingers through my hair. "You're gonna be fine."

"What do you feel?" I whisper. "Like right now?"

A lazy grin spreads across his cheeks. "Which part of me?"

"I mean inside." I roll my eyes." After you have sex with me, do you feel anything?"

He keeps playing with my hair, his face relaxed. "I feel tired."

"Max." I blink at him. "Because I feel kinda emotional."

He wipes at a tear beading on my cheek. "I can see that."

"Do you feel emotional?"

"I wouldn't use the word emotional."

"Use another word then?"

He laughs once. "Well, I'm becoming *irritated*."

I can't help but smile. "A different word."

"*Agitated.*"

"*Max.*"

"Happy, Little One." He kisses the tip of my nose. "I'm happy."

CHAPTER FOURTEEN

the legend, luca "the butcher" butcher

"YOU'RE WHAT?" Toni's voice sounds through the speaker as I riffle through my suitcase to find a pair of strappy sandals and my favourite playsuit, the one with the zipper at the front.

"I'm going to watch a boxing match. It's a thing, apparently. They're into boxing. I wasn't going to hang out with them during the day. I mean, it's kinda a buck's week, but Max actually wants me there. He invited me."

"Oh, I'm so jealous. I love watching two men sharing blows... obviously."

"Your innuendos have no bounds." I get dressed and lean over to wrap the spaghetti straps of my sandals around my ankles. "Toni?" I pause for a moment, staring at myself in the mirror. Blushing cheeks, moist skin, and wild natural waves cascading down my shoulders... "We were careless last night."

"Don't tell me."

"I mean... He didn't wear a condom."

"So now you have officially had sex with everyone he has." He makes a sound of disgust. "That's a lot of fanny."

I stare at my reflection, my brows drawn together in contemplation. "Can I get the morning after pill here in Bali? Aren't they super religious?"

"I don't know, darlin'. You can always take it when you get home."

"No, I googled it. It has to be taken within seventy-two hours or the chance of it working can drop to below fifty percent."

"I'm so glad I don't have to worry about that side of things."

"Toni..." I shake my head slowly and smile at myself in the mirror, thinking about Max and me last night. The way his whole face was soft with affection when he'd said he was *happy.* That he *felt* happy. "You were right. I'm *so* obsessed with him. I want to be around him and smell him and hear his jerky comments all day. I'm in serious trouble."

My body feels different. Before Max, I couldn't care less about intimate affection. It was never really something I'd craved. But I'm an addict now. I crave Max. His approval. His mere attention. His rough, manly hands on my soft skin and that deep, manly scent. That fricking smile... I sigh just thinking about that smile. That sweet crooked smile that tells me he's just a boy, a boy who is enjoying a girl.

"Tell me about the sex?" Toni presses.

"No..." I stiffen as if he can see me. "It's private."

"Nothing is private between me and you."

"No. I don't want to."

"*Please.* I've waited so long to talk about sex stuff with you because of the whole asexual pigeon thing, and now you won't cough up the goods? It's not fair."

"Fine." I cover my face when my cheeks start to tingle. "So, apparently, I like... Oh God, I can't even say it."

He claps and squeals. "*Ooooh*. Like what? Like what?"

I scrunch up my face, cringing. "My... *bum* being played with."

Loud laughter creates crackling feedback in the speaker. "Me too!"

"Oh my gawd, stop it. I can't talk about this anymore. My cheeks are on fire with embarrassment."

"No, that's the chlamydia he's given you."

"That's not funny," I mutter.

He laughs again. "I got a kick out of it."

I WALK TOWARD THE ARENA, gripping the straps of my backpack as motorbikes and scooters scatter around me in a chaotic formation. People shuffle about. Beautiful Balinese girls strut towards the entrance in high heels, balancing perfectly on the cobblestone streets. Overwhelmed by the crowd and nervous about seeing Max, still unsure about which version of his personality I'll be graced with today, I search around for him, or Flick, or anyone.

A black motorbike pulls up alongside me. "Get on."

My smile meets my eyes when I see Max gripping the handlebars. No helmet. No jacket. Just a tee-shirt, shorts, aviators, and flip-flops.

It's Bali.

Grabbing his shoulders, I swing my leg over the bike and cuddle his waist, resting my cheek on his warm back. My arms tighten as the bike takes off.

This is a good start. Apparently, I get nice Max today.

When we pull up around the back of the arena, I slide off

and he kicks the stand down. He leans the heavy bike to the side before swinging his leg over.

He stills in front of me. "You prepared for this madness?"

"I'm a ballerina. There's nothing I'll see in there that can compare to what I've put my body through."

He laughs but has no rebuttal. "Good." His eyes drop to the zipper running down between my breasts. "I like this."

I swallow. "Good."

When I'm around Max, it feels like I've got a million things to say, but they all end up trapped in my throat.

His fingers entwine with mine and we walk into the arena. It's so hot with all the bodies in here that most of the men are shirtless. Max strides down the passage towards the ring, pulling me along behind him. People yell or motion to communicate over the racket. When they see Max, they tend to duck out of his way, so even though the arena is hectic to all of my senses, the crowd parts for us and we move around seamlessly.

He stops at the front row and motions for me to sit alongside Stacey. Then he sits down beside me. I peer down the line of seats, past Xander, Clay, and Flick, to wave at Bronson, who makes a funny face at me. He's such a child; I love it.

The final chair in the row is on the other side of Max. A middle-aged man sits down on it, his eyes trained on the ring. Max slides his hand down between my thighs, but doesn't break eye contact from the commotion of people now ducking between the ropes.

A bell rings. I cross my thighs over each other, snuggling Max's hand between them. The boxers are clearly identified by their gloves, waxed up faces, and the way they gnaw with anticipation on their mouth guards. They're both Caucasians.

I lean towards Max. "Where are the Balinese competitors?"

"This is heavyweight, Little One."

The speaker whines as it's switched on. "Ladies and gentlemen, welcome to the BBA championship round in Ubud, Indonesia. This event is brought to you by Storm Industries. This battle is sanctioned by the World Boxing Association and the Athletic Association Indonesia. Introducing our three judges: Mike Harley, Wayan Lempard, and all the way from the District, Australia, we have The Legend, Luca "The Butcher" Butcher!"

My eyes widen and I turn to see the man on Max's right raise his fist. The crowd goes mental—his name is chanted in adoration. So that's Max's dad... He would have been quite something when he was younger. Although he is still handsome, his nose has obviously taken more than a few hits and there is a scar under his left eye. It's clear just by looking at him that he has lived a fierce existence.

"The referee, the man in charge, is Tiuk Leyir. And now the moment we have all been waiting for—it's go time! On the left, we have the challenger from Melbourne, Australia—Steven Garrad, weighing in at 96kg! And on the right, from the District, Australia, weighing in at 101kg, is the defending BBA Heavy Weight Champion, Drazic *Marino*!"

I wish I had earplugs as the cheering blisters my ears.

The bell rings again. The crowd falls deadly silent until the first step is taken by Garrad. Then the room fills as shouts, fierce orders, and cries of disappointment bounce off the walls. Max, Bronson, and Xander are on their feet, punching the air and yelling out to Drazic, "Set the pace! Arms up! Get up! Hold him!"

I watch in awe as the fighters throw their big bodies around in sharp, jerking motions. Their power comes from the surprise and weight behind them. It's the opposite of everything I do as a ballerina.

My heart is racing with excitement. I'm suddenly caught up in the drama and the waves of emotions exploding from the crowd, the boys, and my own body. It's a blood bath. I cover my eyes, but peek through my fingers because the intensity between Drazic and Steven is completely captivating. I don't want to miss a second.

After several rounds full of splattering blood and heavy blows, Drazic is the last man standing. Facing the crowd, blood gushing from his split brow and fresh sweat pouring down his chest like rain, he chomps on his guard and raises his fist.

The audience detonates.

Max and the boys knock fists, Xander yelps with excitement and everyone starts to holler Drazic's name.

"*Drazic! Drazic!*"

As the fighters finally clear the stage, I'm still left staring at the ring. "Wow."

Max studies my face, sliding his hand back down between my thighs. "You liked that?"

"I feel bad saying I liked it." My cheeks pinch when I try to keep a straight face. "But yeah. I liked it. It was incredible watching their strength and resilience. And somehow, they're still agile. And quick... despite all that bulk... It was really exciting."

"I didn't expect you to say that."

My smile is coy. "Why?"

"Just thought you'd find it too violent."

"It was. I'd hate to see that outside of a controlled environment. I don't like violence. But they're both athletes, both up there willingly. So they know what they're getting into."

A satisfied grin stretches across his cheeks. "Very true."

"Why are you smiling at me like that?"

"Dunno..." His eyes roll around my face, amusement dancing in them. "Very few people surprise me. You, on the other hand, do it constantly."

"If you thought I'd find it too violent, why did you ask me to come with you?"

He considers my question for a moment. "Maybe I wanted to keep an eye on you."

I smirk and lean towards him, using his own words. "Which part of me?"

He moistens his lips. "All your parts."

"Let's go spend some money!" Xander yells across to us.

A vein in Max's neck bulges and he shoots a sideways glance at his little brother.

I peer down the line at Xander. "Why?"

Jumping to his feet, he rubs his palms together. "Because we just made a shitload!"

Luca pats his thighs once and slowly stands. "I'll see you all at the restaurant. We'll be having dinner together tonight, including you." He gestures to me and grins. I feel Max's hand twitch between my crossed thighs. "I don't know you, but I want to." Luca smiles down the line at his sons, but it's thin and filled with mixed messages.

When he casually walks away, he has such a presence that people part ahead of him. He's a big man. As tall as Max and just as built, but more tight-lipped. Everything about him is tight.

Stacey squeezes my knee and whispers, "Drazic is one of Jimmy's boxers." She twists to eyeball Xander. "And Xander's had too much to drink."

CHAPTER FIFTEEN

victoria

I HOLD Max tightly around the waist, my cheek pressing against his shoulder blade as we ride around the congested, lawless streets. Clutching him tighter around his middle and inhaling him, I imagine we are in love and he's my person.

He pulls up alongside a luxury, Balinese-style restaurant alongside his brothers' motorbikes and Flick's and Stacey's scooters and turns off the ignition. I watch his hands squeeze the rubber around the handlebars, his body hot and tight. When I bounce off the bike, I swivel around to face him, but he's still staring deadpan at the gravel ahead of his tyre. Usually, I'd be inclined to ask what's wrong, but if I've learnt anything from Max Butcher over these past few weeks, it's that I shouldn't—at least not right now.

With a long, deep sigh, Max finally swings his leg over and we walk side by side into the restaurant. There are no walls, only piers. Everything in Bali merges the outside world with the inner. Candles flicker on tables. Everyone is reddened by the humidity. He stops at the cane bar and a lady hurries over to him, bowing her head slightly.

"Whiskey. Whatever. And—" He stares at me, his eyes blank.

I force a smile. "Um, a glass of champagne, *terima kasih*."

She places a whiskey in front of him and he throws it back. Dropping the glass on the counter, he raises his fingers to indicate he wants another. After she hands it over, I follow Max towards a private canopy across the lily pond, where I see Xander, Stacey, Flick, Bronson, Luca, and... a stunning blonde woman I recognise. I halt for a moment. It's the girl from my birthday. The one who was outside the front of my house. The one who had slapped Max so hard across the face.

Flick taps the seat beside her and Max positions himself opposite me. His eyes look bored, but his jaw tics like crazy. Five pairs of eyes stare at me, making my breaths whirl around in my chest.

Flick wraps an arm around my shoulders while she grins at Luca. "This is my sister, Cassidy."

"Cassidy. My sons are so rude for not introducing you before," Luca says with a smile. "Thank you for joining us. Clay has told me you'll be dancing on Friday?" He has a subtle accent – Italian, I presume.

I nod and speak quietly. "Yes."

"Jimmy speaks very highly of you," Luca says, his opal-blue eyes an intense beauty set into a hard, worn face.

"He's been very generous," I say, shuffling in my seat.

The blonde woman smiles wryly. "Is that all you're doing?"

I cough on my champagne. "I'm sorry, what?" My mouth drops open and I stare directly across at Max, who is seething.

"Dancing? Is that all you're doing?" She raises a pencil-drawn blonde brow at me. Her elbow is on the table as she nurses her white wine glass. Long, red fingernails wrap around the stem. I wrinkle my nose as I smell her abundantly applied perfume.

"Ya know what? I hate poker," Bronson states loudly, causing everyone to turn and look at him. "If you count cards, you're a cheat, but if you don't, you're literally guessing. What's the point? There's no skill in it. I don't care what people say. It's just fuckin' luck."

The blonde leans back in her seat. "It's a game of intimidation, Bronson."

He's animated when he says, "Ya know what... I don't like blackjack either."

She curls her lips up in disgust. "What's gotten into you?"

He leans across the table to me and whispers, "Give me another game?"

I brush my fingers through my hair. "Roulette?"

"Or roulette!"

"Alright, Bronson." Luca lifts his hand. "Thank you for that... Well, it's lovely to meet you, Cassidy." He smiles. "I'm proud my boys keep such beautiful company."

The blonde sneers and I narrow my eyes at her, a million words knocking at my tongue.

Stacey stands up abruptly. Collecting her clutch from under her seat, she looks at me kindly. "I've just remembered I owe you a shot. I never had one with you on your birthday."

I blink up at her and then across to a wide-eyed Flick. "Okay."

She holds a hand out to me. "Come on. Excuse us."

As we walk away, she squeezes my hand. "She hates me too."

"Who?" I say, my breathing still laboured. "Who is she?"

When we stop at the bar, Stacey tilts her head at me and says, "She's their mum."

"What?" I wince, hurting for Max and his brothers. I've never wanted to hit a person. Not once in my whole life, and she slapped her own son so hard. My forehead feels hot. I glare over Stacey's shoulder at Max's mum, who is scowling at her own boys. "She's so young."

Signalling the bartender, Stacey orders two of something —I don't know what. "No, she's not that young; she's in her forties. She's just got a good plastic surgeon."

I observe her from a distance. "Is she always like that?"

"Vile?" Stacey asks without looking at her. "Yes."

I squeeze my eyes shut. "She's so... *cold*."

"She's always been like that."

"What about when they were babies?" I imagine a baby Max all alone in a house full of toxic masculinity and Chanel Number Five.

"They were raised by the nanny." Stacey touches my arm and I open my eyes again. "When the nanny wasn't busy screwing around with Butch... everyone calls Luca, *Butch*."

My eyes sting. "Who did they have to love them?"

"Each other..." She takes a shot. "And me. And Butch loves them as best as he knows how. He's always offered them friendship and protection and so much praise it would have been intoxicating. He's proud of his boys. She's just a shitty person."

"I can't sit with her."

"You have no choice now," she says.

Scrunching my nose up in disgust, I toss the liquor back. "She slapped Max across the face at my birthday party."

Stacey squints at me. "When was she at your birthday?"

"She came to the house to get something from him, I think, and then she slapped him. Twice."

Stacey stares at the ground for a moment before sighing through her own words. "She hits him all the time, Cassidy.

Butch had to travel a lot for Jimmy. He'd sleep around. She'd get drunk and then take it out on the boys. Max and Bronson got the worst of it. A slap is nothing."

My eyes pool. "Why do they put up with it?"

"What do you want them to do about it? Hit her back?"

"No," I mutter as one hopeless tear streams from the corner of my eye. "I can't handle that. I can't be polite to that woman."

"Stop being naive. Not everyone had the perfect upbringing you and Flick have had. When you're around us, you need to think before you open your fucking mouth."

"Woah. Don't be a jerk. You sound like Max."

She exhales through her nose. "That's because you're so clueless. You say the wrong thing in front of the wrong person... You just don't understand what these people are capable of."

I still. "What people?"

She stares straight-faced at me. "All of them, Cassidy."

I swallow down a lump. "Including Max?"

"All. Of. Them. Cassidy."

"Then why are you still here?"

She lifts her chin and speaks quietly while avoiding eye contact. "You don't know what they've done for me."

I shake my head in disbelief. "Why are you telling me all of this now? I thought 'it wasn't a good idea'?"

"It's too late." She draws her brows together. "You're sitting at our table. Max had his hand on your leg at the match. That will have been noticed."

"By who? Why don't you want us together?"

"It's not that I don't want you together. It's just that—" She considers her words with care. "I'm trying to protect Max."

I laugh. "From me?"

"I can't talk about this anymore. I just wanted to stop you from saying whatever it was you were about to say to Victoria."

I tail Stacey back to the table. At the sight of Max's empty chair, though, I make a quick detour to start looking for him.

My mind is swimming with images of his childhood. Of his mother's neglect and abuse. Of his father's stance on being a man. It makes me feel weak with sadness. I need to find him, to tell him... I don't know what because what I want to tell him, I know he's not ready to hear. And I'm not ready to say. Even if he wants to be alone, he shouldn't be. I want to show him comfort. I want to give him contentment, but he's nowhere to be seen.

With a heavy heart, I approach the bar. There is no way I'm going back to that table. I'm about to order a drink to calm my nerves when I spot the little Balinese lady from when we'd first entered the restaurant. She heads towards me, her steps deliberate as if she was looking for me.

"Come," she says.

Hoping she'd been sent by Max, I follow her out of the restaurant, past dogs and people sitting on the sidewalk, and into a little bar.

She points. "He's in there."

It's balmy and dark. My every step is taken with caution. I pull back the pendulous beads that separate the outside from the beating pulse of the club. Half-naked girls are sliding up and down poles. Men, blackened by shadows, turn to stare at me as I walk by their tables. The music is beautiful and enchanting and clearly Indonesian. I know I should leave. Perhaps I should even be mad at Max for being here, but I'm not.

I search the room, each table, every private booth. My smile is uncontrollable when I see Max sitting in a private canopy, tight faced, gaze lowered as he stares at his whiskey. He's contemplative—and alone.

I watch from a distance as beautiful, near-naked girls approach him, coy and flirtatious. But his expression never wavers from one of boredom and inconvenience. With a sad smile, I walk in his direction.

His eyes shift from his whiskey. He stares at me through lowered lashes, the whites of his eyes barely visible. "Come sit with me, Little One."

I take a step closer to him. "I don't like this place."

"Is that right?"

"Yes." I take another step. "Why did you bring me here?"

"I didn't. I just wanted to be here. I also needed you to not be there."

My brows dip as I think about his mother. "*Max*."

His fist hits the table. "Don't you fucking dare!" I flinch and cover my mouth to stop from talking. He's drunk. He's tense. Max relaxes his hand and leans back into his seat, lifting his gaze. He licks his lips while caressing my body with long strokes of his eyes.

My feet find their way to him and I swing a leg over his lap, straddling him. His eyes squeeze shut as he presses his forehead against my shoulder.

"I'm sorry," he mutters. "I should never yell at you."

A shiver rushes down his body as I stroke my fingernails up from the nape of his neck and into his hair. He rolls his head against me. His breathing is deep and long. His arms go around me, clutching at me as if he's afraid to let me go. My heart wants to jump right from my chest and into his. I find his ear and kiss it chastely, slowly. I'm not sure how much time passes by while I hold him. Several minutes. More maybe.

I hear the clipping of heels and then a salacious voice. "Do you want a dance, Max?"

"Are you serious?" he hisses, making me flinch. Sliding me gently off his lap, he glares at the woman. "You fucking blind?"

My breath catches.

The pretty brunette swallows. Her eyes drop to her feet. "I'm sorry."

"No." He shakes his head slowly. "I don't want a fucking dance. Not from you." He gazes at me under heavy eyelids. "Will you dance for me, Little One?"

I stand as she leaves, my legs shaking a little with the weight of his request. The music is hypnotising and laps through me in soulful waves. My eyes are trained on Max; the intensity between us makes his narrow. My breathing becomes shallow and fast as I search his expression. I want more than anything to show him how I feel, knowing I'm not ready to say it aloud. There is this need in his eyes, and I'd do just about anything to give him what they are silently asking for. Something intimate. Something more than just sex. His eyes leave mine to stab holes into the men behind me. I turn to draw the curtains.

After I pull the sheath closed, I freeze at the feeling of his eyes on me. My hands tremble as I unzip the front of my playsuit. The suit drops to the floor, leaving me standing in just lacy white underwear.

"Take it all off," he says, his voice huskier than normal.

My pulse vibrates through my whole body, making me quiver as I stare at the worn, faded fabric. I slowly unclip my bra, letting it drop to the floor.

Shaky hands find the hem of my knickers, and I shimmy them down over my knees before bending to my ankles to unhook them from my feet. Max groans at the sight of me bent and bare. My legs are like jelly.

I straighten. It takes a few breaths of encouragement for me to start swaying my naked body from side to side. My arms stretch up and I curve my neck, staring at the light flickering through the curtains. I can't see him, but I sure as hell can feel him—everywhere. It's a sensual beat I dance to—slow and rhythmic with a bass that beats in time with my heart. In this moment, I remember the feel of his eyes on me by the poolside as he'd watched me, each sway of my breasts and movement of my backside. This time, I welcome the feeling of his gaze.

As the song ends, I turn around, my stomach fluttering at the sight of his clenched jaw and smouldering eyes. Eyes that have the power to physically penetrate a girl. My pulse is in a frenzy now. Unable to hold his gaze and maintain my composure, I bat my eyes close and rub the beads of sweat on my skin, coating myself. My hands find my nipples. My quivering abdomen. My needy clit.

"Don't stop." I hear a loud exhale and when I open my eyes, he's gripping his erection. His bicep bulges as he draws his hand up and down. "Keep going."

His breathing becomes jagged. I'm more turned on than I've ever been, watching him seated in the shadows and stroking his magnificent penis while he studies me as I tremble and tease my clit. I moan. He bites back a violent grunt.

"Come here!" he growls. I hurry to close the gap between us, and he takes a fistful of my hair. Forcing me onto my knees, he shoves his erection into my mouth. He shoots hot cum into the back of my throat. His pumping motion is such a turn on, and I fumble to find my clit again, press down on it and come wildly with him.

CHAPTER SIXTEEN

WHEN WE GET BACK to the villa, everyone has already turned in for the night, so we make love in his bed. He might not call it making love, but I do. There is no other definition that suits our speed, tenderness, and level of intimacy. He falls asleep on his side with one arm slung over my waist and his head between my breasts. I watch him sleep, his breathing even and smooth in his slumber.

When I wake up in the morning, Max is gone. He's left a note on his bedside table, which reads,

> *'I fucked up the other night. I didn't wrap up. We can't do that. If you're not on the pill, take these. M.'*

Beside it, there is a small blue box with two pills inside it.

Looking at them, I feel a small knot start to grow in my stomach. Even though him taking care of a mistake we both willingly participated in is sweet and responsible, I'd have liked him to have given the pills to me in person.

Because this way makes me feel a little empty inside.

I'll be fine.

Rolling around in his soft sheets, I tangle myself up, stroking the slight divot his body has left in the mattress. It's Clay's buck's party today, which means I need to pack an overnight bag and move into the other villa, so they have privacy for whatever shenanigans they have organised. Unease slithers into me; I hate that it does.

I take the first pill. The other is to be taken in twelve hours, so I set an alarm on my phone.

I spend the day alone by the main pool, drinking cocktails and reading all about the origin of the Sugar Plum Fairy.

Swim. Eat. Sunbathe. For an hour, I practise my choreography for tomorrow night under the cabana. It doesn't bother me that people are watching. It's no different from doing yoga or tai chi in the park on a Sunday or working out at the gym.

When it gets dark, the staff begin lighting citronella lanterns. The thick, hot atmosphere relaxes my muscles and I roll onto my belly, nestling into the cushions.

Slowly, I fall asleep and dream of Max touching me. His hands against my skin. His fingers between my legs. His tongue on my nipple. I can almost feel him, becoming so needy and wet that I wake up. When I open my eyes, it's completely dark and I'm panting.

I stare down at my phone, lying on the sunbed beside me, flashing with a message.

I read a text from a mystery number and frown at the screen.

Unknown Number: You're a beautiful dancer.

Sitting straight up, I scan the area for Max or anyone whose eyes might be on me. I shift in the bed and feel a sudden urge to find the villa. I text back, hoping that it's Max. Hoping that he'd stopped by for a while to watch me dance by the poolside. Hoping that there is nothing sinister about this message.

Cassidy: Who is this?

Collecting my things, I ask a lovely Balinese lady to show me where we are staying tonight. As she leads me down the steps, I peer across the valley that drops between the two mountains. Tropical trees seem to disappear down into the dark and then reappear on the other side, climbing back up in a similar formation. When I stumble on a step, I decide to focus back on the path.

A rock rolls behind me. My neck prickles and a tingling sensation moves through me. I spin, squinting up the steps and to the side and through the trees—nothing.

You're being paranoid.

I follow quietly behind the lady to the new villa, my pulse a little faster than normal. Once inside, I push the latch across, locking the door. "Flick?" I look around the villa. It's much smaller than the other one. "Stacey?"

Flick bounces out from around the corner. "Hello, my little love."

"Frick." I exhale. "Make a noise. Don't just jump out at a girl."

"Huh?" She tilts her head at me. "You on edge, little sister?"

"No. I'm fine. Where's Stacey?" My voice gets louder as I wander away from her. Heading into the Balinese-style outdoor kitchen, I slump down into a wicker chair.

"She's out and about," she says, following me. "Anyway, I was hoping you and I could have a little chat."

My shoulders sag. "Oh no. Let's not do this."

"About Max... and you."

"Oh my gawd."

I wish we were more like guys sometimes. She would offer me her fist. I'd bump it.

'Did you tap that, sis?'

'Oh, you know I did!'

"Can we just fist bump or something?" I plea.

"Would you like something to eat?" She grins at me. "I can't imagine you've slept much lately and probably need to keep your energy levels up."

I chuckle once. "Subtle."

"I'm sorry, Cassidy." Sliding into the seat opposite me, she leans back in her chair. "I'd love to just talk boys, but I'm nervous now that it's actually happening. I didn't think much of your crush before."

I blink at her. "My *crush*?"

"How long have you been fucking Max?"

"Jebus, please transition me slowly into the conversation."

"I don't think we need to fliff-flaff."

"I like a bit of fliff-flaffery."

"Cassidy. You were supposed to tell me about your first time. It's meant to be under the covers with the lights off and in a bed. It's meant to be slow and awkward, and we are meant to laugh about it after."

I bite my lip to stop the grin that's tugging at it. "Well, it definitely wasn't that."

"What was it like then?"

I beam for a split second. "Insanity."

"How long have you two been fucking?"

"Fine." I groan the word. "We had sex for the first time a few weeks ago."

"You still can't say the word 'fuck'? Cassidy. If you're doing it, then you should be able to say it."

"We don't. We have sex. And I don't want to say that word because it becomes too... relied upon. For everything. Pain. Pleasure. Excitement. Shock."

"Whatever. I don't know what to say. I can't believe you didn't tell me. We used to tell each other everything."

"I'm sorry, Flick." I smile tightly at her. "It's just this is our thing, mine and Max's."

"Oh my God. This is not a thing. This is just Max Butcher."

My brows pull together. "And that's why I didn't tell you—"

"Because I would tell you the truth."

"No. Because you're not always right. This is a *thing.* It might just be a kind of friendship, but it's definitely still a thing."

She shakes her head slowly. "Please tell me you aren't in love with him."

"Okay," I state. "I'm not in love with him."

"Don't lie to me. I know you are."

"You just told me to tell you I wasn't!"

"I can see it on your little blushing face. I just never thought—" She reaches for the words. "He would—"

"What?" My jaw tightens. "You didn't think he would want me?"

"God no! What? He's been fucking you with his eyes

since your party. I just thought he'd care enough not to fuck with your emotions."

"He isn't." I take a big breath. "He made it clear."

"He just isn't emotionally available, Cassidy. As much as you think he might be, he isn't."

"Thank you for the insight."

"Cassidy, you don't know Max like I do. You haven't seen the things I've seen. He has zero respect for the girls he fucks."

"You don't know anything about Max. Trust me when I say, you're the one who doesn't know him like *I* do."

"It sounds to me like you two are discussing Max's personal life. Is that right?" We turn to see Stacey standing staunchly in the hallway, both of her hands clutching plastic bags.

Flick glances sideways. "It's Cassidy's personal life as well."

"Leave it, Flick." Stacey walks slowly over to us and places the bags of groceries on the table. "If Max finds out you've been talking to Cassidy about him and their relationship, he won't be happy."

She folds her arms across her chest. "Well, I don't really care if he's not happy about it."

I murmur under my breath, "Please, continue talking as if I'm not here."

Stacey lowers her voice. "Felicity, be very careful. If Max wants Cassidy, then let him have her. Leave it alone. If you get involved in his personal business, you'll regret it."

"Cassidy is my business," Flick states.

Stacey rolls her eyes to the sky. "Not anymore, she's not. She's his. That's how it works in his world."

I jump up and my chair slides backwards. "You know

what, I have to get some sleep. I have a performance tomorrow. Have fun discussing my life."

"Cassidy, I just worry about you." Flick follows me down towards the bedrooms. "Max isn't right for you. Max isn't right for anyone."

"Oh my God," Stacey growls. "I'm leaving before I hear anymore." The door swings open and then shuts with a bang.

I swivel to face Flick. "You sound just like Konnor. Max isn't the person everyone thinks he is." I pause for a moment and we both collect our thoughts before I continue. "He's complex and unassumingly intelligent and funny and... He has these sporadic moments of being so tender and considerate."

She smiles. "You love him."

I swallow past a knot in my throat. "I don't know how I feel. Can we not label it?"

Flick nods. "Look, Max is loads of fun. I like him. You're just headed for better things... You throw yourself into everything you love. I just don't want you to throw yourself into him. You just don't understand. You're my hero! You wanted to be a ballerina and you made that happen. I just don't want you to lose yourself in Max Butcher. He has the kind of identity that people get swept up in, losing all sense of self. The girl who ends up with him will need to fit into his box. He won't change for her. You two are just not compatible. He will never deserve someone like you. You don't need a Max to be someone. You're someone on your own."

"I hear everything you're saying. I do. I appreciate the sentiment. But Stacey is right. Max is very guarded with his personal life. He's very protective of his privacy. I don't even feel comfortable talking about us. It's ours. He makes me feel like this thing is just ours. I like it that way. You should just—"

Her mouth opens. “Is that what this is about? Protection?”

I squint at her, finding her revelation expression annoying. "What?”

“This is about Konnor. You were so young and he was so broken. You two were inseparable. We always thought he was looking after you, but sometimes I felt like you were the one looking after him. After everything that happened to him at such a young age, it makes me think about how those things might have affected you. You want someone who can look after you. You like Max so much because you want someone who can protect you.”

I fumble around for words. “This is such a bizarre path you've taken! This has nothing to do with Konnor. I like Max because he's gorgeous and for all the other reasons I've already mentioned. This is about Max. Max and me. And it just doesn’t have anything to do with you or anyone else.”

My phone vibrates in my bag as the alarm goes off. Ignoring Flick's concerned face, I open the door to my room and shut it behind me.

My room for one night only.

I sit down on the edge of the mattress and pull out my phone. Blinking at the display, I read the notification: It's time for *Plan B*.

CHAPTER SEVENTEEN

muzzles and straitjackets

I LIKE to wake up before the sun. I like to start my day before everyone else. The atmosphere is thick and dark as I jog outside. Glancing at the daybed, I see a white sheet and pillow. It seems that either Flick or Stacey slept there. I hate that they are fighting. Shaking my head, I clear my mind and begin my morning run.

I jog. I shower. I pack my bag. Then I join Stacey and Flick in walking up the stone steps in silence. They have sad eyes and tight smiles as we reach the resort's breakfast buffet. We eat in near silence. It's torture. I stare at my sister wide-eyed before darting my gaze to Stacey. Flick shakes her head as she peers down at the omelette she's shuffling around her plate. After giving up on the pretence of eating, we head back to see the boys.

Despite the mood that has settled around us, I can't help but be excited about seeing Max. I picture his face, brooding and conflicted, as is his default expression.

As we push open the door to the villa, empty bottles roll across the tiles. I glance at the girls, who look as concerned as me. My stomach knots as we walk in without hearing a word. It's nine a.m., so the boys are probably still passed out in bed. The villa smells like smoke and sex and vomit. After stepping over the smashed glass, crumbled up packets of crisps, and condom wrappers without so much as a wrinkle of my nose, I finally cringe at the blood splatter!

Stacey grabs my arm. "We should come back later."

I yank my elbow from her. "No way."

"Cassidy." Flick touches my hip. "Let's go outside. Go for a swim and wait for them to wake up. We aren't cleaning up this mess."

I ignore her. I have no right to do what I want to do, but I do it anyway. Making my way to Max's door, I push it open a few inches and peer inside.

My heart doesn't sink.

It plummets.

Max isn't alone. He's flopped over the mattress with one arm draped across his forehead and his legs spread, still in his jeans. His inked chest rises and falls with each deep, sleepy, relaxed breath.

She, a Scarlett Johansson lookalike, has her naked, shapely body wrapped around his leg. Her full breasts press into his side. I hate her. I hate Scarlett Johansson by association. As I stare at them, I experience a sharp stab in my chest. I squeeze my eyes shut, hoping that this scene doesn't haunt the rest of our relationship... our *friendship*.

When I open my eyes again, it's to the same scene, but this time I'm locked on the open top button of his jeans. So that sweet, pleasured look on his face right now is because of her—for her. I'd thought it was all mine. It isn't. And it never was. Every girl who gives him pleasure is graced with this version of him. But they probably aren't dumb enough to believe they are special. That they share something special with him. *Our thing*. There is no *thing*. I was wrong.

I should have known. It's not like he didn't warn me enough. Shame feels a lot like hunger—it's twisting my insides, begging for the antidote, but unlike hunger, food can't cure this feeling. Forcing a whimper down, I softly close the door and walk outside into the forest.

There is a little bench towards the bottom of the valley. I can hear water trickling, but I can't see it. Tears rush from my eyes as I stare at my bronze sandals. They shuffle grey dirt around. I lick tears from my lips, consciously trying to channel nothingness.

"Cassidy?" I hear Flick's voice calling through the foliage.

I wipe my mouth with my wrist. "I'm over here."

Stopping in front of the pathetic display that is me, she sighs. "That was a dick move."

I shrug and hug my knees. "I don't want to be upset. So I won't be."

"Sometimes it's good to cry, to get it out of your system."

I laugh and tears fall into my mouth. "When have you ever cried?"

She sits down beside me. "I cry. Just... in my own company."

My eyes are trained straight ahead into the forest. "Nope. I'm not crying. I knew. I just didn't think I would have to see it. Now the girl has a face and the relaxed Max who was all mine, isn't mine anymore."

"Yeah, like I said, dick move."

"Maybe he was making a point." I swallow. "Maybe he did it on purpose."

She spins to face my profile. "I don't think so. He's a dick, but I don't think he'd hurt you on purpose."

I pick up a stone and throw it down the valley. It clicks for a while and then nothing. "Whatever."

"What do you want to do now? We could leave. Do you wanna go back to the District?"

"No. I have a job to do here. I made a commitment to Aurora. I just needed a reality check, that's all."

"Okay," she sighs. "If you say so."

"Do you think there is any chance, however small, that she passed out there without him knowing?" The question is as pathetic as I feel. It's desperate and raw and hopeful where there shouldn't be any hope, but I can't stop myself from reaching for it.

"No, Cassidy. He knew she was there."

"Yeah... yeah, of course, he did."

"So, are you going to keep your distance now? Or what is your plan? Are you going to continue sleeping with him?"

"I don't know. I kind of can't say no. I'm just so weak around him, Flick. I want to pretend I'm in control, but I'm not. He has the reins one hundred percent of the time and when we connect, I convince myself that he really does care. Likes me even."

She strokes my shoulder. "He likes you as much as he's capable of."

"I suppose you were right."

"I didn't want to be right."

I squeeze my knees tighter. "There's something about him, Flick."

"Yep. The boys are kinda addictive. But you need to take your heart off your sleeve and put it back in your chest where it's safe."

"Okay, Dr Phil." I finally turn my head to look at her. "You and Stacey are fighting?"

She stares at me, her lips thin. "Yeah. It started about you and then... Well, she has a lot of secrets. That's all. It's getting on my nerves a little."

I laugh once. "You're dating a Butcher boy."

"I guess so."

"And she won't share details with you?"

"She's really closed off. Short-tempered. But..." She smiles. "Fucking beautiful!"

"Ugh, you're dating female Max!"

We share a defeated, sad little chuckle. After a few minutes, we make our way back to the villa.

Despite the fact that I have zero right to be mad at him, I still am. Not more than a few nights ago at that dingy strip club, I'd given him something—something I'll never get back. It wasn't just sex. Not just physical. We'd shared a very real, raw encounter. He'd wanted me for more than just my body. He'd wanted me for comfort.

But I'm not going to offer him that gentleness anymore. He can have my body, but only because I want his. I'm not going to offer him my heart to help heal his ever again.

When we get back to the villa, I decide to channel my feelings into dance. I change into black short shorts and a crop top before walking outside. The air in Bali is in an eternal state of thickness. After laying my mat down on the grass by the poolside, I begin to stretch.

My chest tightens when the door slides open and the smell of cloves seeps toward me. A new smell.

"Hi," a soft voice I don't know says.

Pressing my chest to my thigh, I shift my eyes up to Scarlett Johansson.

"Hi," I say, biting down on my lower lip as I move my gaze back to the grass below me. That green-eyed monster in my belly digs its claws into me, but I force myself to ignore it. It's not Scarlett's fault that Max can't keep his dick in his pants. If I were her, I'd jump at the opportunity to touch him too. She doesn't owe me a thing. I refuse to be rude to her. I won't be that girl.

She's smoking a cigarette and it smells sweet. "I've lived here for four years and still can't get used to the heat," she mutters from behind me.

"I think I like it," I say, but maybe only because I want to like what she doesn't.

Good job at being mature, Cassidy.

"The fuck are you still doing here?"

My heart stutters at the sound of Max's growl. So this is how he wants it? Is it because he'd shown me a moment of vulnerability? He can't stand my presence again? I'd thought we were past his ever-fluctuating personality crisis. Apparently, I was wrong.

Hiding the bruising of my heart, I angrily stand to face him.

Only, he's not scowling at me. He's drilling holes through *Scarlett*. He looks rough—groggy, scruffy hair, bare chest, jeans hanging low around his hips, his eyes red and glazed. He's squinting at the natural, ambient world as if it's physically disorientating.

Scarlett blows out another clove-scented puff. "I was waiting for a lift. Heidi's still with Xander."

My belly churns. Desperate to hide the emotion on my face, I sit back down and continue to stretch.

"Wait out front for her!" Max snaps.

She scoffs. "Why are you talking to me like this?"

As a sick kind of curiosity invades my mind, I turn back to watch them.

"Because despite the look on my face, you're still fucking here," he growls, and it's the first time I've ever seen him use his hands to talk—like a real Sicilian.

Pathetic and wanting to be noticed, I say, "She can wait here with me. I don't mind."

"No, she fucking can't!"

Scarlett's voice falters. "Is... is it something I did—"

"I swear to God, if you say another fucking word, you'll regret it. Now wait. The fuck. Out front!"

When Scarlett disappears inside, I push off the ground with my hands and step to face him. "The way you just spoke to her *disgusts* me."

He lifts his chin and peers down at me through his lashes. "Don't do this." The words are laced with warning. As he takes a step towards me, he reaches for my hip, but I shuffle backwards in disbelief. He thinks he can still touch me? He feels he still has the right?

"Don't touch me, Max," I warn.

"I'm too fucking tired for this shit, Cassidy."

"I bet you're exhausted!"

His jaw tightens. "I asked her to leave. What more do you fucking want?"

I shake my head slowly and speak quietly. "I don't want *anything* from you. Ever. Again."

His nose flares as he exhales. He didn't seem to like hearing that. "I knew you wouldn't be able to handle this."

"I suppose you were right. The silly little girl can't handle it."

We're both silent, and for a split second, I see the pain on his face before he moves toward me again.

"I said don't touch me," I say, stepping back.

His jaw tics like crazy. "I don't like hearing that."

"Get used to it," I whisper.

He takes another step toward me. "I didn't fuck her."

Immediately, I hate hearing those words. I hate how

much I wanted to hear them. I hate how they chip at the wall I've just built between us.

Arching my neck to look up into his eyes, I feel every cell in my body suddenly compress beneath his stare. "You can do whatever you want, Max. It's none of my business."

"Fuck," he growls before storming away from me. I watch him leave, my heart chasing after him; luckily, my body and mind are in control right now. He suddenly stops at the sliding door, spinning quickly to face me. "I. Didn't. Fuck. Her!"

After a few swallows, I manage to say, "You expect me to believe that?"

"I don't expect anything!" He walks towards me so quickly I'm afraid he'll bowl me over, but he stops an arm's length away. "You're the one with all the fucking expectations."

I glance at the grass for refuge because, once again, he's too much for me. Too consuming. "I just want to be alone, *please."*

"Look at me."

My breath shakes. "I can't."

"I didn't fuck her." He reaches for my hip again and his fingers coax me slowly towards him. Sighing, I let them take me closer because I want to seek comfort in *him* now. Comfort from him—in him...

Ugh.

I let Max press my body against his. "She was naked in your bed. The same bed we shared the night before. Doesn't that mean anything to you?"

He rubs the length of my spine up to my neck. Gripping the back of it, he tilts my gaze to meet his. "That's why I didn't fuck her."

Shaking my head, I stare straight into his groggy eyes. "You're so full of shit."

His lips twitch with a grin. "Did you just swear, Little One?"

I mouth the word, "*Shit*."

He smiles for a split second. "What do you want from me? I want to hear you say it."

Breathing out loudly, all I can do is tell the truth. Even if I hate the truth. Even if it results in pain. "I want *all* of you or none of you."

He lifts me into his arms and wraps my legs around his waist. "Okay."

I push out from his chest and frown at him. "*Okay*?"

His shrug is all confidence. "I can be monogamous."

"You?" My cheeks twitch with a laugh and then it's gone. "You'd need a straitjacket and one of those muzzles greyhounds have to wear because they chase and eat little animals."

A sleepy grin stretches across his cheeks. He moves his hands from my thighs to cup my backside, and I can't help imagining where those hands were last night. Cupping big breasts. Teasing Scarlett's nipples. The images churn my stomach.

"I do like to chase and eat little animals," he says with a purr to his voice.

I drown out that tone and how it makes me feel. "So, if you didn't sleep with her, what did you do with her?"

"Nothing. She got naked. Girls do that."

I laugh with derision. "No, they don't."

"It was a bucks party! She wanted me to fuck her. I could have, Cassidy. I fucking didn't! Xander got his dick wet. Bronson got his dick wet. I. Did. Not."

"Did you touch her?"

"I'm sure at some point I did."

The ambiguity in his answer infuriates me. "Did you get anything else *wet*?"

His bloodshot eyes narrow on my face. "No. But if you keep talking dirty like that, I'm gonna shove my cock down your throat to silence you."

I consider pushing him away in a form of protest, but then I'm filled with fear he'll let me, so I don't. "How hung-over are you?"

"I'm not hung-over."

I scoff. "*Right.*"

He tries to bat his eyelids, but they seem nearly too heavy to lift. "I'm still pissed. And I'd like to see *you* in a muzzle. Straitjacket. Nothing else."

"*Max*. You can't just say these things." My eyes squeeze shut as I shake my head, just once. I shouldn't be listening to a single word that comes out of his gorgeous mouth. Not while he's intoxicated. I doubt he'll even remember this conversation. And if he does, well, I'm sure he'll regret saying he can be a one-girl guy.

"Okay, no straitjacket," he says.

I open my eyes to find him smirking at me. "*Max*. Do you know what you're saying to me? I mean... *monogamous*."

His brows draw together. "Never tell me not to touch you again. I fucking hated that."

"You can't just touch naked girls! You can't just sleep next to naked girls whenever you want."

He laughs a little. "Oh really? Fuck, forget about it then."

"*Max*," I breathe. "That's what this means."

His head dips back as he groans. "Listen. I'm not concerned. You want me to be monogamous. Then fine. I thought it would be hard. But last night I managed it." I attempt to interrupt, but he fists my hair, giving me a light tug in warning. "And I fucking swear to God, if you make me say I didn't fuck her one more time—"

"Do you know how it felt to see her in your arms?"

"It wasn't a big deal, Little One!"

"Imagine if you walked in and I was naked, and my body was pressed against another guy. Would that be a *big deal*?"

As his eyes dilate almost instantly, the fingers knotted in my hair tighten. He leans in until his lips touch my ear. "Cassidy... You do *not* want me imagining that."

The heat from his breath cascades down my throat like a warning. "I was kidding."

"Well, I'm not fucking kidding. Be very careful," he growls as he walks me into the villa. "We can talk about this shit later. You can write me a long fucking list of all the things I can't do. I just gotta lay down and I need you next to me."

CHAPTER EIGHTEEN

the performance

MY PHONE RINGS, vibrating against the bamboo side table. When I search for it, Max's resting face brushes my arm. His chin hair is rough against my skin. My fingers fumble to find the phone's lock button, so I can stop its obnoxious sound before it wakes him. We are above the covers. Max is still in his jeans, unbuttoned and showing tight abdominal muscles that point towards his favourite appendage. He clearly has no boxers on.

I wriggle around on the sheets and then press my palm to his chest. I kiss his cheek. I want to be happy, but there is too much fear weighing me down. Fear of losing him. Of lies. Of deceit. I don't know Max well enough to know whether I can believe him. That he didn't sleep with her.

My fingers skate over the rugged bumps of his stomach and circle the little trail of hair that leads beneath his jeans. He should smell like man and sweat, but instead his scent is arousing. Hot. Max.

So even if he did sleep with her, his beautiful body is now mine. All mine. Perhaps I can believe that. I push my hand down the neat path of hair and fondle his penis and then his balls. He groans as his hips move up into my touch.

"*Cassidy.*"

Perhaps, I'm now the only girl who gets to touch him like this. I stoke him in his slumber. He expands, thickening and hardening, in my hand. He cups the back of his head. Wide biceps relax beside his face.

"Take me out. I wanna feel your little tongue on my cock."

And I didn't think this through because I have no idea what to do now. I swallow hard. My body slides down the mattress before settling between his thighs. When I pull his long, thick erection out, it reaches up towards his navel and pulses with need.

I stroke him hard.

"*More,*" he growls as he grips the headboard, his huge arms tightening with restraint. My belly flips around because I don't know how to make him come with my hand —or mouth. I remember what Toni had said.

Drawing my fist up the full length of his shaft, I lick the underside of his penis. His hips move up into my hand and mouth. Wanting to please him, I slide my lips down as far as I can go, which isn't far at all. At halfway down his thick shaft, the muscles at the back of my throat contract around him, causing him to let out a deep, longing groan. He starts to thrust up, his penis nearly sliding all the way down my throat. I gag and those muscles contract again, but he seems to like it, just groaning louder.

My breaths come in and out fast through my nose as he pumps up into my mouth. I lean back when it gets too much and lick him again. He's just too big, but I love tasting him. Love how much he's groaning.

Several minutes pass by as he lets me explore and taste

him. He releases the headboard and wraps his hand around mine, squeezing his erection tighter and thrusting into our joined fists. His abdominal muscles tighten, his breathing grows jagged and then ropes of cum land over my fist and shoot across my face—it's the hottest thing I've ever seen. My tongue runs along my lips, tasting the saltiness of his cum. I think I like it.

After I clean us both up—there was a lot—Max slowly slips back into slumber with a beautiful smoothness to his forehead and cheeks. It looks a lot like contentment.

The second time my phone buzzes, I collect it and stroll into Max's shower. The screen flashes with 'Toni.' I turn the water on, but tilt the faucet away from me. Sliding down the wall until my bum hits the tiles, I hold the phone to my ear.

I wriggle my toes in the water and answer, "Yes, Toni?"

"I just wanted to wish—" he pauses. "Are you in the shower?"

"Yes." I kick my legs in the water pooling around my body. "I've got to get warm and clean for tonight."

He chuckles. "You'll never be clean again."

I grip the phone. "What?"

"I dunno. Just sounds like something I would say."

I relax. "Okay."

He smacks his lips and hums. "You're short... Why are you short?"

"I was born this way."

"Mentally challenged, not vertically challenged, darlin'. Why are you short?

"I'm fine." I lift my knees up and envelop my legs, resting a cheek on them. "I've got a big day."

"Yes. Aurora's pre-wedding dinner. The crowd will hush. The men will get boners. It's Cassidy Slater in a leotard, twirling her fanny around."

I scoff. "Do you have any respect for what I do?"

He pauses. "*Yes*. You're my queen. You know this... You *are* short. What's going on?"

I breathe in deeply and exhale even stronger. "Max has told me he can be monogamous... for *me*."

"So..." He hesitates. "Just. Believe. Him."

My jaw drops. "What? So *not* what I'd expected you to say."

"You wanna be with him, darl—"

"I mean, I used muzzles, straitjackets, and chastity belt analogies, but you just say"—I shrug, feigning his nonchalance—"believe him... Who are you?" For a moment, there is silence, and I shuffle my bum on the slippery tiles. "Toni?"

"Braidy has a past. He wasn't completely *out* until me. That's a big thing. Coming out is like going through puberty again. It's an emotional roller coaster. It's not good being the test dummy, but I just have to try because if I don't, I'll never know if we could have been something. If I chicken out, I'll never know. Heartbreak might be better than regret. That's what I've decided anyway."

I smile against the speaker. "Thank you."

"Don't tell anyone I'm nice, okay? I'm a Mean Girl!"

I swallow. "Max has a lot of secrets, ya know?"

"We all do, Golden Girl."

"I think his might be worse."

He's quiet again. "Let's be honest. Do you actually care?"

"No. I wish I did though."

We share a long, surprisingly genuine and heartfelt discussion, though not without the occasional drips and drabs of satire and innuendos. However, there are secrets I don't share with him. I don't mention Victoria. I don't mention Butch.

After hanging up and wrapping myself in a towel, I ring

my hair out and twist it down my shoulder so that the water drops fall onto the rim of the towel.

Max stays fast asleep as I wander across his bedroom towards the door. I stop to gaze at him in all his glory. Above the covers. Half-naked.

My Max.

I move toward him and lean over, touching my lips softly to his forehead.

As I turn to leave, I notice his bedside table drawer is ajar. I hold my breath when I see the nose of a black gun poking out from within. My eyes widen and my attention is immediately drawn to Max, who hasn't moved a muscle, and then back to the bedside table. I'm still holding my breath as I pull the drawer out a few more centimetres to reveal the entire black pistol.

It's illegal to own a handgun in Australia.

I don't know what the laws are in Bali.

Looking at it though, I remember what my mum once told me: 'Everyone is made up of little contradictory pieces, and you should never judge another person's decisions because you don't know the pieces they have to choose from.'

A thief is a criminal until he's stealing to feed his kin. A neglectful mother is a bad mother until she is working two jobs to give her children the best opportunities. A gun is terrifying until it's what's keeping you safe, and then you're terrified without it.

Some of us have a lot of contradictory pieces. Some less.

Guns have been banned in Australia since before I was born, so seeing one casually placed beside the bed I sleep in... *This just got real.*

My heart vibrates as I turn to watch Max sleep again. I

don't know much about his pieces, but I know he has a lot of them. And they all have weight.

Slowly, I push the drawer shut.

After getting dressed, I head out to meet the musicians that will be accompanying me tonight at the show.

For most of the day, I rehearse in the luxury Balinese dining club, which is set up not unlike an intimate restaurant with long, banquet-style tables running parallel to a beautiful lily pond. On the other side of the pond is a stage. The orchestra is on a lower level, but I'm going to move from the stage through the musicians as part of a sequence. I've written choreography myself many times; however, I've never had an intimate audience of fifty, inclusive of Max Butcher, Jimmy Storm, and Legend Luca "*The Butcher*" Butcher—whatever that means.

And Victoria...

My pulse races through my neck as I practise my steps. This is all just a bit much for me to take on alone. I wish I was dancing to someone else's choreography because then it wouldn't feel so personal. This mini ballet is about promises. It's about choosing to love unconditionally.

At seven p.m., the club begins to fill with Aurora's and Clay's stunningly dressed families and friends. I can hear shrill feminine laughter and the clinking of glasses from behind the stage. The musicians and I are waiting in a small room. While they warm up out of sequence and independently—violins and flutes whistling different scales—I adjust my white veil and tutu. I'd designed them myself for this occasion. I never—*ever*—wear my hair down when I dance because the line of my neck needs to be seen in union with the lines of my décolletage and arm. However, tonight my ballet bun is a little loose and romantic. It's a little wild, a little flustered.

As I'm wrapping up my toes, a sudden silence descends. I tense, nerves fluttering in my stomach like they do every time I'm about to perform. Breaking the quiet, Jimmy's voice booms through the microphone.

"Sarò breve, caro e breve! Clay Butcher, ha statu sempri patti ra me famiglia. Tomorrow that becomes legal under God. Thank you all for joining us in this union and enjoy tonight's entertainment."

My hands tremble as I finish lacing up my pointe shoes. The musicians begin to move into position and the conductor nods at me. I'm up and jiggling in place, flicking my hands and stretching my body. I clear my mind as the violins start. Mood lighting illuminates the stage. My breathing is slow and controlled. The guests are silent. Beads of sweat run down my brow and over my chest. I hear my musical cue and I'm quickly *en pointe,* moving across the stage like drops of water from a fountain—quick and weightless.

The performance begins with curiosity. Naivety. It's sweet and quirky. The girl matures throughout the sequence, learning fast. It then quickly picks up as she falls in love. It's at this stage, while in a dizzying spell of euphoria, I complete Aurora's twenty-five fouettés, my eyes always finding Max between each spin.

CHAPTER NINETEEN

my max

I'M alone backstage on the floor in my white leotard, unwrapping the silk of my pointe shoes and sliding them off, when I hear Max's deep voice. "That's the first time I've seen what you do."

I peer up at him as he approaches in tan chinos and a navy shirt that's snug around his thick shoulders, chest, and biceps. His sleeves are rolled above his elbows. His collar is open.

My lips part at the sight of him. "You scrub up, don't you?"

"I didn't realise I ever scrubbed down," he says, stopping in front of me.

I quickly pull my shoes off and stand up. "You were definitely scrubbed down when I left you this morning."

"Speaking of which, I didn't like waking up without you there."

I peer up at him through false lashes and shimmering eye shadow. "I had to practise."

He shoves his hands into his pockets, studying my face. "Don’t do that again."

I fiddle with the hem of my leotard skirt. "Max, I have things I need to do."

"Don’t do that again." He grins at me and then circles my body, raking in my outfit. "Next time, wake me." He brushes his fingers along the silk of my skirting. "Look at you."

I follow him with my eyes, but don't turn, letting him move behind me and around again. "Stop it."

He chuckles. "Just when I thought you couldn't get any cuter."

I bite my lip to stop from beaming at him. "Stop it."

"I'd fuck you right here if I thought I could keep you quiet."

I cover my mouth, but part my fingers enough to talk through them. "Am I noisy?"

His face lights up. "Oh, fuck yeah."

Both palms meet my face. "Oh my God."

He peels away my fingers and then bands one arm around my waist. The other grips the nape of my neck. "Oh my *Max.* God has nothing to do with this."

I laugh loudly and he presses his lips to mine. His grip on me tightens as his mouth moves hungrily around my face and neck. He scoops me up so I can straddle his hips with my legs. My arms feed up through his hair.

He walks me into a wall, caging me inside his arms. Instantly, I'm moaning. He stills. Then with a slow smile, he covers my mouth with his big hand, smothering my sounds of pleasure. His fingers rip through my stockings, slide under my leotard and push up inside me. My body tightens with desire, fingers digging into his shoulders and legs tensing around his hips.

My eyes squeeze shut as he presses me harder into the

wall, moving his fingers in deeper. Groans come from my throat, so he tightens his hand around my mouth. He kisses my nose and eyes and forehead as he starts to really penetrate me. His hips move with the rhythm of his fingers as if it's his penis inside me. My thighs begin to shake. I open my eyes and look into his. They are only inches from mine, dark and determined.

He moves his mouth to my ear. "This is the sweetest pussy I've ever touched."

I tremble. He licks my ear and neck as his fingers curl inside me and my internal muscles rub against them.

"Fuck," he bites out. "You make me ache."

My breasts are hot from the friction against his chest and my insides are aching from his touch. He slides his fingers in and out, up to my clit, and back inside me again. His tongue and mouth are all over my neck and ear. My senses are drenched in Max Butcher.

I buck against him, my breaths hard and fast.

"Good girl," he rasps. "You know what you want now. Take it." Pressure builds through my spine. I blink at him. A tear beads in the corner of my eye as the sensation builds through me and with a final jerk of my hips, I explode over his fingers.

He continues to move them inside me until I'm sated and weak.

Releasing my mouth, his lips press to mine, soft and sweet. We kiss slowly as I catch my breath. I never knew anything could feel this good. Being held by him and kissed by him makes me feel complete. If I could get closer, have more of my body connected to his, I would. His fingers slide from inside me as he lowers me to the ground. My legs shake as they take my weight.

We finally break our kiss.

I gaze up at him and reach to stroke his freshly shaven jaw. "That was nice."

He grins wickedly and puts his fingers in his mouth, sucking on them. "I agree."

My cheeks burn. "How do you go from being so sweet to so crude in the space of a few seconds?"

"I was never sweet."

"Okay, Max. You keep telling yourself that."

Walking a few steps away from him, I begin to undress. My eyes stay trained on his as I slowly expose more skin. He clenches his jaw as he studies me. I walk around in front of him, completely bare, and feel his eyes everywhere as I bend over and search for my knickers, bra, and thigh-length red party dress.

As I turn to face him again, my gaze drops to his groin. He's grown, his erection a clearly defined ridge in his tan chinos.

I peer up into his dark, narrowed eyes. "You must struggle to hide that sometimes."

His lips become sharp and menacing. "You're very lucky that there are people out there."

"Are you bigger than most guys?" I ask, ignoring his provocative tone.

"You wanna talk about cocks with me? That'll help hide it."

I giggle and begin to dress. "I've only ever really seen yours up close."

His brow lifts. "Up close?"

"Well, I saw Bronson's, but only for a moment."

"Hmm." His lips twitch. "Let's keep it that way."

My fingers fumble for my zipper as Max moves behind me, closing the space between us. He kisses my shoulder and

I quiver. His fingers touch the slither of skin between the open zip. I inhale, waiting. *Wanting...*

The zip slides up.

"No. You're not sweet at all." I breathe out fast, spinning to face him.

My body melts under his smile. It's boyish and real.

"I wanna hold your hand, but it's not a good idea out there," he says as his smile loses its shine. "Stay close to me. Let's go get a drink."

I follow him out, passing the banquet tables and groups of people standing around talking, until we get to the bar where Bronson, Xander, Clay, and three other men I don't know are sitting on bar stools. One of the nameless men is hard to ignore with his craggy face, scratched and craterous. He isn't drinking or conversing; I get the impression he's not simply a guest.

A guard perhaps.

The Butcher brothers all look dapper in their dress pants and shirts. My God, they have good genes.

I peer around the room. "Where's Flick?"

"She's with Stacey. They left just after the show," Xander answers me as he peers around the room, his eyes missing nothing.

Bronson smirks. "You look flushed."

I smile back. "Thanks for pointing that out."

Aurora suddenly appears in front of me. "You were wonderful. Thank you so much. You did my twenty-five fouettés!" She engulfs me in her long, elegant arms.

Bronson mouths over her shoulder. "You were."

Clay gives me a thumbs up and a wink.

I smile. "Thank you. I'm glad you liked it."

"You're coming tomorrow, right?" She holds my shoulders out in front of her. "You know you're invited. I've placed you next to your sister."

"Thank you. I'd love to."

"Aurora," someone calls.

She glances over to them and nods. "Sorry to rush off, Cassidy. Today is all about me."

Max laughs once. "As opposed to every other day?"

Clay clears his throat to disguise a chuckle and Aurora slices him up with her eyes. Bronson and Xander make whipping sounds as I swallow a giggle.

She smirks at Max. "Just this once, I'm going to find your snide remarks amusing."

Aurora disappears and several middle-aged men approach me to thank me for the performance. They shake my hand and kiss my cheeks, enveloping me in the smell of smoke and alcohol. Max hands me some champagne before positioning himself behind me with a stance rather business-like and stiff.

I'm on my third glass of champagne when the boys begin to argue over who won at paintball yesterday. I swivel on the stool to look around the club. Many people seem to have retired for the evening. I notice Jimmy Storm's and Luca Butcher's table is empty, the two having relocated to a booth with several other men. They are consumed in a private conversation as they drink liquor from short glasses and grit cigars between their teeth. Their wives are still greeting other guests, giving them light hugs so as not to crease their dresses and kissing cheek to cheek so as not to smear their lipstick. They nurse red wine in large glasses as they natter on with polite smiles.

Max's lips touch my ear, making me shiver in the best kind of way. "We'll be back. Stay with Xan."

I want to grab him and feel his mouth on mine. We have

been so close all night and yet so far away it's excruciating. I watch closely as Max, Bronson, and Clay approach Jimmy and Luca's group. They converse and it's all very formal. The whole table suddenly shifts their gazes to me, so I dart my eyes to Xander, but he's leaning across the bar, trying to get the staff's attention. Willing myself not to look back at them, I pull out my phone and pretend to read from the display. I peek up just as Clay sits down beside his dad, and Bronson and Max wander slowly back towards us.

Max grins at me. "Alright, Little One, let's make a move."

Bronson sits back down with Xander and addresses the bartender. "Excuse me, lovely, do you mind getting us another round?"

Standing up, I follow Max outside. He straddles his bike and I swing my leg over. Navigating our way through the sea of bikes and scooters, we ride back towards the villa. The streets are lit up with neon signs and a kind of glowing, ambient fog. This time when I press my cheek to his warm back and squeeze him with my thighs and arms, I'm not pretending. And maybe it's not forever, but for right now, he *is* my someone.

As soon as we get off the bike, he lifts me up and I cup his jaw. We kiss passionately, moaning into each other's mouths. His hands massage up and down my back as he walks us through the villa and to the wicker lounge beside the pool. He sits down with me wrapped around him and I kneel, straddling his thighs.

We pet and fondle each other. His lips and tongue move around my face and neck as if he wants to taste me, so I lift my chin up to let him explore. I moan. He moves to my shoulder and chest, then bites my breast through the fabric of my dress. The sudden opening of the door cuts through my whimpers of pleasure.

With my nipple tightly pinched between his teeth, Max grumbles. "Fuck."

Stacey walks outside, stilling when she sees us. "Oh. My bad."

I giggle and cover Max's scowling face with my palm. "All good. Come sit with us. Where's Flick?"

"She's in bed," she says, sitting on the single chair.

Max pulls my hand from his face, his expression tight. "Stacey. We're in the middle of something!"

Stacey turns. "Okay. I'll leav—"

"No, don't go," I plead. "Are you two *okay*?"

She smiles tightly. "We will be. It's okay. Honeymoon period's over, but we—"

As I slide off Max's lap, he groans and drops his head back onto the rest. "For fuck's sake. Boner's gone anyway."

I try not to giggle at him again. "Would you mind getting me a nightcap then?"

His brows draw together, and he's either going to scold me, throw me onto his mattress, or kill me. He chews back a comment and talks through a tight jaw. "What would you like, Your Highness?"

I curl my lips together to squash a smile. "A port, please. Stacey?"

The whites of Stacey's eyes are glowing. "Nothing," she squeaks.

Max walks off toward the kitchen, muttering, "You're in so much fucking trouble."

"Cassidy!" Stacey leans toward me. "I've seen girls get dragged out by the arm for less than that."

"I asked nicely. I think it's good for him."

She sits back. "Never do that in front of his dad... Oh my God, or Jimmy."

I shuffle back. "I wouldn't."

She shakes her head in disbelief. "I'm not even sure what I just saw."

"What? Can't I ask my boyfriend to get me a drink?"

She coughs. "Your boyfriend?"

I glance around nervously. "I didn't mean *boyfriend.*"

Footsteps approach and Stacey's face becomes ashen.

"What did you mean then?" Max asks, taking long casual steps toward us.

I cover my face. "Oh my God. Stop it, Max."

"There are so many better things you could call me," he says. I peek out from behind my fingers and gaze up into his smirking face. "Your Highness." He hands me the port glass, but retracts it inches from my outstretched fingers. "Don't push it," he warns.

I stare at him with sultry eyes. "What should I call you? Like, a menace? Master?"

He presses his teeth together like he's imagining me between them. "Like, *Oh My Max.*"

Stacey shoots up. "If this is your version of foreplay, I should go." Stacey smiles nervously and walks towards the door.

Max glowers at her, his eyes narrowed into slits. "Stacey!" His tone is authoritarian, and she stops mid-step. "Who the fuck do you think you are? Huh? Let me make myself perfectly clear, when I'm with Cassidy, you pretend you're deaf and blind."

Stacey swallows hard. "Sorry." It's meek, submissive, and so not like her. I wince on her behalf. Eyes downcast, Stacey hurries through the sliding door and disappears into the villa.

My back hits the cushion, and I crane my head as I frown up at Max. "What was that about? She made a joke."

He slides down beside me and lifts my thighs onto his

lap. "She thought she could make a remark about our conversation."

"It was... *a joke*."

"So?" He runs his tongue across his teeth and shrugs once. "I don't appreciate the commentary."

"Friends tease each other; that's what they do."

"She isn't my friend."

I touch his cheek. "*Max*."

He drapes his arm over the headrest. "How did you get into ballet?"

"Master of the—"

"Subtle Transition."

We smile at each other.

"Well, how's my transition?" I hesitate, choking on my own words for a moment before I can build up the strength to say them. "I'm going to go on the pill when I get home." I swallow. "Have you been tested lately?" I'm so nervous asking this question that I'm literally trembling.

He just grins. "I never go bare. I get tested all the time. I'm so proud you had the guts to ask though."

My heart fills with him. "*Cool*."

"Now, how did you get into ballet?"

"I went to the ballet with my dad and Konnor when I was six. We saw *The Nutcracker*. The District Academy has performed that ballet at Christmas every year for decades. From the moment I saw it, I wanted to be *Clara*."

He strokes my thigh. "But you're not this year."

"No. But I have been her for the past four years. This year I wanted to show my diversity. And a really great ballerina named Ana got the part of Clara."

He chuckles. "You hate her."

"I don't. She's lovely."

"You want her killed."

I laugh. "No. I didn't audition for Clara this year. She's best suited to a younger ballerina." I stare at him as he gazes at me. The both of us are entwined on the lounge while the sounds of mountainous Ubud echo in the distance.

It's past midnight. It's just him and me. Sometimes I feel as if there is a Max and Cassidy world... and then there's the complicated dark world we share with everyone else.

He caresses my face with his eyes. "I'm kinda pissed I'd never gone with Jimmy to see a performance now."

I cuddle my knees and gaze at him. "Why?"

"I would've had some great wank material."

"Crude."

"I might have met you sooner."

I lean in to kiss him. "*Sweet.*"

"To taste your pussy sooner."

"Max!"

We drink a lot of port as we talk throughout the night and into the early morning. Well, I talk. He mostly listens. I admit I saw him play rugby against Konnor a few years ago and couldn't keep my eyes off him because he was... *oh my gawd*, so hot. He laughs.

I learn that Clay has a business degree. Xander is going to study law next year and Max is in his final semester of his Master of Architecture, which means he doesn't have to attend lectures anymore or go to campus as much.

I get the feeling rugby is his real passion, but he brushes over sentimentalities and offers me short, curt answers to my questions. As such is Max Butcher's way. That doesn't take away from the information offered because, for once, he is actually answering me.

I wonder how he fits being a normal twenty-four-year-old in with the other side of his life.

When we finally crawl into bed, we share a pillow and Max spoons me.

"*Max*?"

"Hmm?" He nuzzles my hair and tightens his arms around me. We lie above the white sheets. The ceiling fan above us is on high. The air is thick. My skin is flushed and my mind is fuzzy.

I stroke his arm. "When was the first time you knew you wanted to sleep with me?"

"Oh fuck, Cassidy, I'm trying to sleep."

"*Please*." I wriggle around in front of him, knowing quite well my bum is brushing against his groin. My heart is beating so fast, I can't relax, and I think I may have drank way too much.

"No," he mumbles. "Another time... sleeping."

"Please? I can't sleep."

"That's because you drank half a bottle of port."

"*Please*."

"Fuck. Fine." He exhales against my shoulder, the heat of his breath cascading down my back. "I was in the alleyway next to Gyspy's—"

"What? We first spoke at my birthday?"

"*Yeah*. But I noticed you before your birthday. Don't interrupt. You were picking up Flick or something, and you must have come straight from ballet because you were in this pink leotard. You were leaning against your car with your ankles crossed and wearing these clunky red sneakers that were way too big for your feet."

"Momma said my shoes would take me anywhere. Momma said they're my magic shoes." I begin to laugh deep from my belly. His silence makes my cheeks burn though, so I stop. "Seriously? *Forrest Gump*?" I giggle nervously. I imagine him wrestling with a smile now. "Don't stop. You know I'm weird. Tell me the rest. What did you think of me?"

He clears his throat. "I just wanted to stick my tongue in you that night. I thought that if pink had a taste, that's what you'd taste like. Why wear anything? Those leotards are like spray paint."

I grin into the pillow. "You remember what I was wearing?"

"When a hot girl is half-naked on the street, I usually remember that."

I giggle. "*Whatever.* You like me."

He pulls me in tighter and rests his chin on my head. "Yes, Cassidy. Let me sleep now."

CHAPTER TWENTY

lazy love

I'M WRAPPED in Max's warm body with his erection pressing against my lower back. His fingers move between my thighs and push inside me. I'm somewhere between awake and asleep. He fingers me slowly. Leisurely. My breathing gets heavier and his tongue licks my earlobe. My body opens for him.

"I won't see you much today," he says, his breath feathering down my neck.

"I know."

I hum as foil crinkles and he shuffles around behind me. He reaches between my thighs and positions his penis between my lips. His erection slowly slides into me. He groans low and long as he grinds deeper, pushing farther. The pressure between my thighs is consuming, yet tender. His fingers are unhurried as they touch me everywhere.

"Beautiful," he murmurs. "Every fucking inch of you. Petite. Perfectly curved. Perfect tits. Fuck me, I just want to eat every part of you..."

"I think *you're* beautiful," I moan, quivering within his

arms and hands. His hips roll against my backside, his penetration gradual and deep. Moans vibrate in my throat as I fist my pillow. His girth forces me to part my thighs and I hook my leg behind his knee, allowing for full-length thrusts. I'm so full of him.

"It should have been like this for your first time."

I breathe. "I like my first time."

"I was rough."

"You weren't."

Fingers move into my mouth and I suck on them in a slow, lavish motion.

We make love lazily all morning.

Afterwards, we wash each other in the shower. I wrap myself in a robe and help Max into his tailed charcoal suit, black shirt, and black tie. My chest feels so full as I reach around his waist to thread his belt and buckle it up. He watches as I dress him with a smile on my face.

He sits down to pull his shoes on. There's a tight line between his brows as he laces them, an internal weight upon his shoulders.

I sit on the edge of the bed. "What is it?"

He stares at me. Pensive. "If you really want this side of me, I won't be able to hide certain things from you."

"I don't want you to hide anything from me."

"Don't ask questions. I'm not prepared to tell you the answers."

"I already told you I won't."

He stands and walks with measured strides to the cupboard, punches a set of numbers into the safe, and pulls out a gun harness. I hold my breath. He turns to face me deadpan and clenches his jaw when he sees me studying the black straps and leather holster. His eyes are anchored to mine as he slides the harness over his shoulders. He reaches into the safe and pulls out the black handgun I saw earlier. Grabbing the magazine, he loads the gun. I flinch when it clicks into place.

Holding my eyes, he tucks the gun into the left side of his holster and fastens it tightly with a clip.

My body swarms with discomfort and fear and... lust? But more than anything, gazing at Max Butcher in a harness, knowing all that I know about his world and accepting that there is so much more that I don't, I just want him safe. I want him *kept* safe. That gun might just do that, and so I decide to like it. I finally breathe out.

"Come here," he orders. "Give me a kiss goodbye."

My heart flutters. I'm immediately on my feet and closing the space between us. Rising onto my tippy toes, I reach up to hold his neck and press my lips to his. He envelops me with big, strong arms. I grasp at them, running my nails lightly along his muscles. Surely, Max is too strong to die.

CHAPTER TWENTY-ONE

he only has to care a little

MAX LEAVES to join his brothers, and I spend the next few hours preparing for the wedding. After slipping into my dress, a nude, backless piece that stops at mid-thigh, I straighten my hair, then spray it to keep it smooth. Positioning myself in front of the mirror, I apply a tiny amount of makeup, contouring my face, adding little ticks to the corners of my eyes, and smacking on natural gloss.

As I stare at my reflection, I feel a flutter of nerves. This is definitely a sexier look than I usually go for. I'd like to see Toni call me an asexual pigeon now. I giggle. I'd like to see him call me an asexual pigeon at all. I'm a falcon now. I giggle again.

It's four p.m. when I slip on my wedges and join Flick and Stacey on their way to the chapel. It's a classic building with stained glass windows and steep walls and is surrounded by lush, green grass. Indonesia might be predominantly Muslim and Hindu, but it's a wedding destination for all faiths.

I try to catch Stacey's eye, flicking her a smile, but she pretends she doesn't see it.

She merely picks up pace and strides ahead of us. "There's going to be over three hundred people here today. If we want a seat, we better get a move on."

I stumble on the cobblestone road. "Wow."

"That's insanity," Flick says, scooping her long red hair to the side.

"I don't even know three hundred people," I say, chuckling awkwardly.

Stacey stares straight ahead at the church. "Family has flown here all the way from Sicily and most of them haven't even met the bride and groom, but it doesn't matter. If you're Family, you're invited. If you're not invited, well, there's a message in that."

I struggle to keep up with her as she charges ahead. "Three hundred is a big family, " I say.

She glances over her shoulder at me. "Yeah, it is, Cassidy."

I still. "*Stacey*, stop walking." She slows. "I'm so sorry about the way Max spoke to you. Don't be upset with me." She halts altogether. When she turns around, she's even more tight faced than she was before.

Flick eyes us both. "What's going on?"

"Cassidy and Max are officially *together*," Stacey says.

Flick forces a smile and looks at me. "Well, that's what you wanted, right?"

I refrain from beaming like a silly little girl. "Yes."

She nods. "Are you happy?"

"Knee-weak happy," I say.

She laughs a little. "But do you trust him?"

"I have to. I've decided I'd rather risk heartbreak than regret."

Flick seems to like that response because she touches my arm and grins. "Well, if you're happy, then I'm happy."

"Cool, we're all fucking happy!" Stacey says. "Max sticking his dick in another girl is the least of your fucking problems." She spins on her heels and continues down the street.

I cringe and call after her. "Please don't be mad at me, Stacey. I'm seriously sorry. Max was a jerk."

She swirls around to face us again. "Stop apologising for him! I'm used to Max Butcher and his moods and his holier than thou attitude. Bronson and Xander have my back, so don't you dare feel sorry for me. Yesterday was just about Max feeling vulnerable and needing to beat his chest... Anyway, I'm not mad. I'm worried."

I sigh. "About Max."

"Yes!"

"Why, though? I'm not going to hurt him."

She groans at the sky. "Because you're everything Jimmy has ever wanted for Max! With you in the picture... he can control him."

I take a step back and frown. "Jimmy has been wonderful to me."

"I'm sure he has." She closes the gap that I'd just made. "Have you ever wondered why?"

I blink at her. "Because he likes the ballet. He's sponsoring me."

She smirks. "That's very nice of him."

I swallow hard and look around nervously. "Max doesn't care that much about me."

"Even if that were true, he only needs to care a little."

"No one can control Max."

"I saw *you* do it yesterday."

I breathe out fast. "You're making me really nervous."

Flick clears her throat. "I don't understand what you two are talking about."

"The Mafia, Felicity," Stacey whispers the words and yet we still flinch. "I'm so sick of trying to keep their secrets when they are just throwing you guys in anyway and asking me to babysit."

"Woah." Flick steps back and crosses her arms. "Babysit?"

"I was told to bring you, Felicity. I was told by Jimmy because he thought Cassidy would feel more comfortable if you came."

I cover my mouth to smother a gasp.

Flick exhales slowly. "*Okay*."

"And he wanted Cassidy here because he wants to see her with Max."

Flick frowns. "So you don't want me here?"

"That's what you're taking from this?" Stacey says, wide-eyed. "What about the part about the Mafia?"

Flick scoffs. "I already knew they were involved in something illegal. The whole fucking District is corrupt. What I didn't know was that you didn't want me here."

Flick withdraws when Stacey reaches for her. "I want to be with you, baby," Stacey says. "But I'd never *willingly* bring you into this world." She shakes her head slowly and swallows hard. "No way."

Flick turns to me. "Did you know?"

"I didn't know anything," I lie. Looking at Stacey, I ask, "Does Max know? That Jimmy has orchestrated this whole thing?"

Stacey nods. "Max isn't dumb, Cassidy."

I wince. "He's just doing as he's told then? He doesn't actually..." My voice breaks. "Like me?"

"Of course he does. None of this was in play until Max hit that cop, dragged you out of the waterpark, and drove you home. That's so uncharacteristic of him. He's a lot more careful than that. One of Jimmy's men saw and well, Jimmy rubbed his hands together. You were invited to dance at the wedding after that, right?"

"*Yes*," I whisper. "I got the call the day after. But he approached me days before that."

"Yes. He likes ballet. He likes you; this is all true. But he wouldn't have invited you here if it wasn't for Max."

Flick hugs my shoulder. "How do you know all this?"

"Jimmy told me. Very casually. He said he thinks you'd make a beautiful couple and he wants to see Max happy. He asked me to invite Flick so that you'd feel comfortable."

I breathe out steadily. "That all sounds kinda nice, though."

"Yeah. But I know what that really means. You're an asset. Leverage. This is what they do. It's the long game. It doesn't look that bad at first, which is how you miss it. It's a favour. It's a kindness. It's a *sponsorship*. But then they have claws in every part of your life and one day, you sit up and you wonder how you'd gotten in so deep..." Stacey's voice stammers and her eyes drop to the ground. After several long moments of thick, tangible silence, she breathes out and looks up at us again. "Now you know. Keep your mouths shut. Behave. Do not tell anyone what I've just said unless you want *me* to go missing."

I tilt my head and bounce my gaze around nervously. "That's a bit of an exaggeration..."

Stacey's lips tighten. "People go missing in the District all the time, Cassidy. It has the highest missing persons rate in the country."

"Yeah, but—"

"But what? You want to be Max's right-hand girl? Then you should know. My advice is to remember what they are capable of."

I cuddle myself and Flick squeezes my shoulder tighter. "The boys are good guys though," I state.

"I love them more than life," Stacey admits. "They are my family, but Max has never allowed anyone to get close before and he definitely doesn't fetch drinks like a Labrador."

"You think they're good guys though, right?" I repeat.

She sighs. "I love them. But *no*. I wouldn't use the word *good*."

Heat builds in my head. "You know nothing about Max!"

She feeds a tremoring hand through her hair before leaning in until I can feel her breath on my cheek. "I've seen *your* boyfriend stomp on a guy's head. I've seen Bronson smash a glass on the bar and then shove it into someone's neck. Xander's climbed through my window, covered in blood, and has cried in my arms more times than I can count. I've seen Butch kill... I've seen a lot. And that's just surface stuff."

Every fibre in my being wants to defend Max and his brothers, but there is a part of me that's known this for a while. When Max hit Luke and saw no repercussions, I knew then that he... I shake my head.

"Max is a good person."

Stacey doesn't respond, but her eyes say it all. Turning, she continues toward the church, where we find a seat at the back on the groom's side. Butch is already in the front row with Victoria, who is peering around with a tight smile.

Nestled against the flower garlands that run the entire length of our pew, I stare at my pink nails, trying to process everything Stacey had said.

At first, I consider grabbing Flick and leaving, refusing to be used against Max, but then I realise we can't. Max would want to know why I'd left and then Stacey might get into some kind of trouble.

Confusion and uneasiness crash together inside me. I'm not sure how I feel about Jimmy now, and Stacey has seen Max stomp on someone's head... No. I can't even picture that. It's too unfathomable to visualise.

I'm yearning for Max to hold me and tell me it'll be fine. That this doesn't change anything. That he's a *good* guy who happens to have done some bad things. My stomach rolls. The moment I'd accepted that gun, I'd accepted his lifestyle. The Ballerina and The Gangster. What a pair we make.

My breath catches when Max passes our pew with the other groomsmen. His eyes bounce over me with hardly a second of recognition. I'm both glad and disappointed. Glad he can't see the confusion in my eyes. Disappointed he didn't reassure me with his. The groomsmen head straight down the red-carpeted aisle, moving towards the front of the church. Along the way, they stop to kiss numerous people on the cheek and share a few words with them in what I can only presume is Italian.

Oh my God. I didn't even know Max spoke Italian.

The boys don't *look* Italian... Maybe Butch, but only slightly.

They stand at the front and a conveyor belt of guests come up after them, all requesting kisses and sharing words. Max grins through all of it, his single dimple on show for everyone to fall in love with. I roll my eyes at all the girls touching his arm and leaning in far closer than they need to.

But he seems relaxed. He's wearing a suit jacket now and I can't help but wonder if the harness is underneath or if he's taken it off for the ceremony.

Would they bring guns into a church?

Seats are filling up fast. Beside me, Stacey is approached by older Italian men who kiss her and request a dance at the reception. She's popular with the Family.

As the organ begins to play, we all swivel around to watch the first bridesmaid walk down the aisle. The rest enter in a timely procession, like models on the runway, all looking beautiful and classy. When Aurora finally makes her entrance in a full-length 1950's style wedding dress, everyone gasps. We turn to watch her walk down the aisle. Clay's face lights up like it's Christmas and New Year's and his birthday all rolled into one. Warmth builds in my belly, and I turn my gaze to Max...

The ceremony switches back and forth between Italian and English. There is a lot of God speak and a lot of traditional readings, so I suppose Toni was right in saying they're Catholic.

As the ceremony comes to an end and the bridal party leaves, I turn to Flick. "They're the hottest bridal party I've ever seen."

Flick sighs. "They're breeding a supreme race."

I glance down at a chip in my nail polish. "I don't fit in."

"Cassidy, get real. You're more beautiful than any of those girls."

I look up and briefly catch Max's gaze as he passes by.

Then he's gone, having followed Clay and Aurora.

Stacey, Flick, and I are some of the last guests to leave the church. The reception is within walking distance. As we approach the three massive marquees, we are herded towards an opening in the fence line. My mouth drops open when I see the metal detectors at the entrance.

I glance at Flick and mouth, "Oh my God."

Flick's face is tight with concern.

Once we are inside, I feel like Alice in Wonderland. There are fire twirlers, a live band, several grazing stations, a cigar bar, and people playing croquet.

Stacey crosses to the bar. "I need a drink ASAP."

While she strides away, I scan the crowd for the boys, but my eyes shift from one group to another to no avail. I approach Stacey and Flick as they order. Pressing my back to the bar, I look around for Max and his brothers.

Giving up, I sigh and turn to face a young Balinese girl. "Can I please have a mimosa?"

The server smiles. "We are serving Louis Roederer, miss."

"Coolios. Can you please put some OJ in there, *terima kasih,*" I say with little shame.

"That is basically a crime," a masculine voice says from behind me.

"Salvatore!" Stacey hugs a handsome man who looks a lot like the male version of Aurora. "I'm so happy to see you. I need to get drunk."

"Music to my ears," he says, feeding his hands through his slick black hair. "My cousin is on a rampage because they don't have the salmon puffs."

Stacey gasps in mock horror. "Not the salmon puffs!"

He eyes me, his grin lopsided. "Ballerina girl."

"Don't talk to her," Stacey says. "Max will have a heart attack."

"Excuse me?" I falter.

His eyes widen and he beams. "Are you Max's?"

Flick nearly coughs up her drink. "No one owns her."

I hesitate. "Um..."

"I've known Max Butcher my whole life and have never known him to claim territory," he states smugly.

Stacey looks at Salvatore. "Trust me. He has."

I blink at them. "I'm standing right here."

Stacey puts her hand on Salvatore's shoulder. "Salvatore and Max don't really get along."

Salvatore scans my body and grins as if I were a new toy. "Well, I love ruffling Max's feathers. So, ballerina girl—"

I shudder under his gaze. "Um, it's Cassidy."

"Where did my uncle find you? You're amazing." He ogles me. "Nubile. Flexible. I went from six-to-midnight instantly watching you perform. Was it The Doll House? It was at The Doll House, right?"

"Are you fucking kidding me?" Flick snaps.

My mouth drops open. I wish I didn't know that The Doll House is a strip club in the District, but between Toni and Konnor, the place has been mentioned more than once.

"Salvatore!" Stacey yells. "How much have you had to drink already?"

He shrugs. "It's a compliment. No, seriously, I'm sorry. You were wonderful. And to get Max Butcher to claim turf"—he gazes at my thighs and I'm sure that if his eyes could crawl up my dress they would be—"you must have something very special up your dres—"

"Are you finished?" My eyes narrow on him. "I'm not a stripper. I'm a professional ballerina. And what's up my dress would bite you!" Snatching my expensive and *criminal* mimosa, I head off towards the croquet lawn. Before I'm out of earshot, I hear Flick and Stacey crack up. Despite my annoyance with Salvatore, that makes me smile. Maybe that exchange will loosen them up enough that they can enjoy the wedding.

For a few moments, I just watch the game being played. It looks like fun. Like hockey and golf combined.

"Do you want to play?" a young red-headed girl asks me as I watch from the sideline.

I beam. "So many yeses!" She hands me a mallet and explains the instructions. It takes me a while, but eventually I'm annihilating the other contenders. By the time I finish playing, the sun has dropped below the horizon.

After wandering around the marquees for a while, I finally see my name on a table.

Soon after I sit down, Flick comes up beside me. "Have you seen Max?"

"Nope, but I'm having fun. I've just won at croquet."

She sits down next to me. "You're just like Dad. You're good at everything you try. It's really unfair."

The tables slowly fill. Despite the hour, beads of sweat form on my chest and neck, and I mentally thank Aurora for organising overhead fans in the marquees.

As the waiters begin to serve the evening meal, I glance up at the bridal table and finally get my first glimpse of Max since the ceremony. The sight of him steals my breath away.

He's taken off his jacket and opened the first few buttons of his shirt. His hair has been messed with as if he's run a hand through it a couple of times. Smiling, he turns to talk to a man standing beside him. Though Max is trying to appear casual and carefree, it doesn't hide what he is inside. It doesn't hide his burdens. They are in his eyes, in his gestures. I can see them.

I stare at him like a lovesick puppy throughout the entire four-course meal, watching as he's attacked by women eager for conversation and kisses. A knot in my belly twists every time anyone gets his attention while I sit here.

As I'm finishing off Stacey's chocolate fondant, Butch stands up to make a speech.

"Having googled a bit about wedding speeches, I've learnt that Jimmy is copping out." Everyone laughs as Butch turns to look at Jimmy, an exaggerated mien of expectancy on his face. "Father of the bride speech?" he goads as Jimmy laughs deep from his belly. "Alright, I'll do it then. Well, firstly, Aurora, sweetheart, welcome to the family. You're a Butcher now."

Butch relays a few stories about Clay and Aurora sneaking around, but they're all so innocent that if I didn't know any better, I would have presumed they were both from regular upper-class Catholic families.

After Butch finishes his second story, Bronson jumps up and pats his dad on the back. "Okay. Sit down, old man." Smiling, Butch takes a seat as his son turns to face the groom. "So... handsome, enigmatic, infectiously fun." He pauses, his eyes flicking to the crowd. "Yeah, that's enough about me."

After more laughter dies down, Bronson continues, "These things usually start with, 'When I first met Clay... But *oh wait,* that doesn't work too well because I was shitting myself when I first met Clay. So, just like my old man, I googled this and Google says the best man—" He pauses and grins. His silence is enough to make everyone laugh again. "Yep. So as *the best man*, I need a killer opening line... Well, I think I nailed that. Then I need to thank the other speakers... Cheers, Dad. Jimmy, where ya been, mate? Huh?" Bronson says something in Italian. Everyone laughs, and Jimmy chuckles and waves his hand. "I also need to congratulate the couple. Clay. Aurora. Congratulations! I need to compliment the bride. Well, Aurora, you look hot. I need to make a joke about the groom, but do I really need to though? Just look at that head. And finally, I need to propose a toast... To lots of sex." He raises his glass and people cheer. Victoria barely looks up from her wine. "On a more serious note though, Clay, you will leave today with someone to share your life with, a strong, elegant, and insanely beautiful woman. Aurora, you will be leaving with a great dress and some very overpriced flowers."

The speeches have ended and the bridal party has scattered around the reception. While licking the sweet taste of port off my lips, I remember Max's tongue and mouth tasting like this last night. I wish I could go to him. Wish it was *allowed*. But the gender segregation in this world is firmly archaic. Peering across the shadowed lawn and into the cigar tent, I catch a glimpse of him.

Max, Bronson, Butch, Jimmy, Xander, and maybe twenty other men are laughing and conversing. There is no doubting the power of those men. It sits heavily in the air around them, creating a presence that surpasses their physical forms. They move with purpose. They talk measuredly. And although they seem to have affection for one another, there is an aura of tension settled between them.

I watch Max converse with another man. He gestures more exaggeratedly than usual, the stereotypical Sicilian mannerisms appearing once more. He mirrors his companion well. I'm sure that comes in handy in his line of work.

I drain another glass of port and decide to dance my neglect away.

I'm not sure how much time passes, but I dance with Flick and Stacey and a lot of other girls and guys. The band is really good. The orchestra last night was from Sydney, so, of course, Aurora probably had this band fly here from halfway across the world.

As I'm dancing to an upbeat song, sweat beading on my skin, a strong hand catches my elbow. "Do I know you?" the man asks.

I spin to a stop and blink up at an older gentleman with dark-brown eyes and a wide, chiselled jaw. "No... I don't think so."

The air around us is charged.

"You're the ballerina," he says, his voice smooth and

elegant and with a wisp of an Italian accent. "You were simply stunning."

I shuffle my feet uncomfortably. "Thank you. I'm Jimmy's ballerina." I have no idea why I've just said that, but there is something about this man that makes me uneasy. Something that makes me feel as if I need the weight of Jimmy's name over mine.

"Cassidy, isn't it?"

I swallow. "Yes."

He watches my throat roll. "Cassidy what?"

My eyes drop to the hand still gripping my elbow. "Slater," I whisper.

His fingers release my arm. "Nice to meet you. I'm Dustin Nerrock."

I fix my jaw. My hands ball into fists, shaking violently on either side of my hips. I have not even thought of his name since that night with my dad and Konnor and yet, as soon as I hear it, it pierces my ears.

"May I have this dance?" he asks.

My face twitches in an attempt to stay calm. "I'm not feeling well."

Without any further explanation, I turn and run off the dance floor, not stopping until I'm across the grass and in the forest. My heart hammers in my chest as tears well up in my eyes. I get to a tree and fumble around in my bag, trying to find my phone to call Konnor. My fingers won't work.

That man...

Sold my brother.

Paid to have him kidnapped.

Finally managing to find my phone, I band it with my fingers and hold it to my chest. Through the trees I can see the marquee lights and hear the music, laughter, and chatter. It didn't occur to me that I might see *him* here.

It doesn't seem like my dad really knows what happened all those years ago—before I was even born—or was he hiding something from us that night when Konnor had confronted him? There is no doubt he was shaken up by the conversation.

If he's here, then... *no*. Does Max know what happened? He'd have been a child himself when Konnor had been taken. Is he keeping something from me? I know he doesn't like Konnor, but surely, he wouldn't be able to hide such a secret from me. I would have seen it in his eyes. Betrayal lightly veiled.

God, I just need to talk to him.

"Are you okay?" I hear a voice ask. "You're trembling. I'll go get someone. Who are you with?" As a young blond man slowly approaches, I rub my face, wiping the tears away.

"I'm fine. I'm fine."

He steps to my side, but I stare ahead into the darkness. "You're the ballerina. I'll go get Jimmy for you, if you want?"

I reach for him. "No!"

"Okay." He stops mid-step and looks at me, probably thinking I've lost my mind. That I've had too much to drink or am suffering a nervous breakdown. And if I'm being honest, there is probably some truth in such thoughts.

He tilts his head. "Do you want me to leave you alone?"

"*No*," I whisper.

After eyeing me for a few minutes, he leans his shoulder on the tree beside me. "Maybe we start with this. Hi, I'm Erik."

"I'm Cassidy."

I glance at him and catch my first good full look of his face as the light from the lanterns bounce around the spaces between the trees. I try not to stare, instead focusing over his shoulder, but the scars that are etched into his cheek and jaw are hard to ignore. He might have been attractive once, but now he's uncomfortable to look at.

He grins. "Something spook you?"

A twig snaps and I whirl around to see Max striding quickly towards me. I run at him and jump into his arms, relief washing over me. He stills and envelops me, rocking me slightly from side to side. His chest heaves against mine.

"Leave before I finish Konnor's work!" Max barks over my shoulder, and the sound of my brother's name ignites my blood. My arms tighten around him as he holds my weight with one thick, strong arm. The other is tight by his side, hand clenched and pumping.

Erik's voice is snide. "I wasn't gonna touch her."

"Leave!" he barks over my shoulder.

I lean back in his arms, stare into his eyes, and I see it—betrayal lightly veiled. "What do you know?"

Max doesn't shy away from my accusing stare. Instead he just says, "I shouldn't have let them bring you here."

CHAPTER TWENTY-TWO

guarding a bunny

MY FEET LAND on the forest floor and Max squats to stare at me, his face firm and authoritarian. "Did you see that guy's face?"

I squeeze my eyes shut and nod.

"Konnor did that to him."

My eyes fly open. "Konnor did that?"

His brows draw as he seems to wrestle with words. "That's all I'm saying about this. Don't ask me anything else. Ask Konnor next time you see him. Erik and your brother hate each other. Stay away from him... As for Dustin," he growls, "he shouldn't have approached you."

"How do you even know all this? And why is Dustin Nerrock here?" My hands shake violently. "He raised my brother for the first four years of his life and then paid to have him kidnapped!"

He presses his cheek to mine. "You're too small to be feisty and you don't know anything for sure. Don't go around stating that."

My lips begin to quiver as I stare into cloudy grey eyes. "What do *you* know?"

There is a flash of something like disappointment in his eyes and then it's gone. I'm not even sure I saw it. "I don't know anything," he states. "I promise you that. I promise I'm not keeping any secrets from you in regard to Konnor and my family."

"And Konnor and that guy?"

"Not my business to share."

A string of questions claw at my tongue, but when I gaze up into those dark, penetrative eyes of his, the open space of the woods slowly becomes suffocating. He's not going to tell me anything tonight. Tonight he's Luca's son, not simply my beautiful boyfriend. He stands for something else right now. Stands against something... I don't know...

Several beats of silence pass between us.

"And Dustin? Why is he here?"

"He's very close friends with Jimmy, Cassidy."

"He didn't want Konnor. I just can't even fathom that." I want to tell Dustin how amazing Konnor is. How *he's* missed out on knowing the man Konnor has become. How much *we* love him.

Max studies my face. "Talk to me about this. Just don't talk to anyone else."

I sigh. "Konnor is amazing, but I know you don't think so."

"It doesn't matter what I think about Konnor."

"My dad and Konnor said that man had sold him. He was held in a fricking basement, Max."

"They also said they were just speculating." He dips his head. "Remember?"

"But he didn't want Konnor back when they found him. How could a father not want his son?"

"Is he Dustin's son? From what I heard, he might not be."

Shaking my head, I answer, "It doesn't fricking matter. He raised him for—"

"Don't be naive! In my world, to have your wife be unfaithful is—"

"Your *world* sucks." I cuddle my waist. "Why didn't he want him?"

He softens slightly. "It's good he didn't want him, Little One. Then *you* got him."

I try to smile at that comment. "I guess."

"I barely see Dustin," he says. "I can't imagine you will have to either."

"Promise?"

"I promise that if you ever have to speak with him again, I'll be right beside you." He wipes a tear from the corner of my eye. "You still want in this with me?"

I sigh. "I want *you*."

"Then from now on, we do this my way." He entwines our fingers and walks across the lawn towards the main marquee, his strides long and quick.

"Max, slow down," I plea as he drags me behind him.

He instantly slows his pace. "Sorry, Little One. I'm fucking pissed off. They're fucking disrespecting me."

I glance up at him as he stares dead ahead.

If looks could kill.

His jaw works furiously. His whole body is taut with anger. He curses a few times and his eyes dart around as if he's processing something internally.

After we pass Flick and Stacey on the dance floor, he slumps down into his seat at the main table and pulls me onto his lap. We are the only ones seated at this table; the rest of the bridal party is mingling with the guests.

My ears are burning as people covertly watch us and whisper.

I touch his cheek and his stare softens. "Max, what are you doing?"

He looks at me. "Sitting with my beautiful girlfriend."

"Did you just call me your girlfriend?"

"Did you want me to call you something else?"

I smile. "No."

He places his big warm palm on my bare thigh, fingers tracing the hem of my dress. "I like your little dress. It is rather distracting."

I continue to stare at his gorgeous, tightly-wound face. Everyone's staring at me, but I sure as hell don't need to see them doing it, so my eyes stay anchored on Max instead. "How did they disrespect you?"

He glares at me, but the venom in his eyes isn't for me, just merely directed my way. "You're my business. They know that. Dustin shouldn't have spoken to you without my permission."

"Your permission?"

"Cassidy, he knows you're Konnor's sister. He was fucking with you."

Max's world is a matrix of passive aggression. It reminds me of what Victoria said to Bronson: *'It's a game of intimidation.'*

I touch Max's cheek. "And now... Are you trying to make some kind of statement?"

A slight grin tugs his lips out into a dark, dangerous curve. "That's exactly what I'm doing."

"What's the statement?"

A vein in his neck bulges. "Not to *fuck* with my things."

"Your *things*?"

He tilts his head at me. "Not to fuck with my girl."

"I thought you wanted to keep us on the DL."

Another little tug at his lips. "On the *DL*?"

"Yeah."

He lifts his beer to his lips. "That's not working out, is it?"

I shuffle on his lap. "Who were you trying to hide us from?"

"Questions, questions. Wanna know what I'm planning for you tonight?" He sets his beer down and pushes his fingers up my dress a few inches.

My breath catches. "*Yes.*"

He watches my lips part and then drops his gaze to my breasts, my thighs, before slowly raising it back up. "I'm planning on being inside all of your pretty little holes."

I breathe out in a rush and squeeze my legs together, wanting that right now.

"You'd like that, wouldn't you?" he says, and I bite back a smile. "Stick your tongue out," he orders, his voice rough.

When I poke my tongue out, he grabs a handful of my hair and tugs my head back. Crushing his mouth to mine, he sucks on my tongue and groans. His fingers get tighter in my hair as he draws my tongue into his mouth as if he wants to swallow it. Beneath my bum, I feel him growing hard.

Before we can go any further, someone clears his throat behind us. Startled, I lean away from Max, who frowns half-heartedly at his brother. Bronson twists the seat around beside us and straddles it backwards.

I look at him, covering my blushing cheeks and huge smile with my hands.

He grins at me. "I like you for my brother."

My hand goes to my lap. "Me too."

Bronson turns to Max. "So, Maxipad, why do you look like you're guarding a bunny from a pack of wolves?"

Max laughs and it's such a beautiful sound. "I am—"

"I'm not sure I like being referred to as a bunny," I admit.

Bronson reaches into his pocket and pulls out a cigar tin. "Would you prefer to be a deer?"

I raise my eyebrows at him. "No."

He brings a cigar up to his mouth, letting it hang from his lower lip, as he says, "Cigar?"

I hold my hand out and jig a little with excitement. I'll blow this whole gender segregation out of the window. "Yes, please."

He glances at Max. "I was asking Max, but okay."

Max shakes his head at me and then at Bronson. "No."

I pout. "*Please*? I just want to try one."

His eyes never swaying from mine, Max's arm suddenly shoots out and grabs a guy as he walks past. "*Cassidy, mancasti di rispetto*?"

With a quick twist of his hand, Max forces the man to his knees. The guy winces in pain, his fingers getting crushed in Max's vice-like grip. I cover my mouth on a gasp as I stare at Salvatore bowed in front of us, his hand twisted the wrong way.

Bronson lights his cigar as if nothing is happening and looks at Salvatore as though he's waiting for the answer to whatever Max just asked.

Salvatore shoots Max a look of disbelief. "You're at a wedding, Max. You're not on the job." He tries to stand, but it's an attempt to no avail. Max uses little exertion to keep him grounded. "I'll tell my uncle you're starting shit," he warns.

"Jimmy fucking hates you, Salvatore." Unconcernedly, Max applies more pressure to Salvatore's hand. "What did you say?"

At Salvatore's baffled look, Bronson puffs on his cigar and

says, "Max asked if you'd disrespected Cassidy. How about you answer him."

I stroke Max's neck. "It's fine."

He twitches beneath my touch, but ignores my words. "Felicity has already told me what you said, but I want to hear it from your fucking mouth."

Salvatore laughs uneasily. "I just made a joke."

"A joke about what?" Max leans closer to his ear. "Something special up my girl's dress? Enjoying ruffling my feathers? Consider my feathers fucking ruffled!"

"*Ma scusari!* I'm sorry, Max," he whimpers, the whites of his eyes big on his face.

"*Lèviti re peri!*" Max thrusts him away, and Salvatore scampers off.

Bronson draws his cigar in slowly and coughs a, "Don't come back now, ya hear?"

Max grinds his teeth. "Fucking weasel." He closes his eyes for a few seconds before slowly opening them to my stunned expression. "Did that upset you?" He watches me closely as I sigh. Cupping my cheeks, he kisses my thin lips. "I didn't hurt him. He needs to learn some manners."

I don't disagree.

"That'll get their attention," Bronson says casually.

"Good." Max presses his teeth together. "This is what he wanted. This is what he gets."

The discussion with Stacey on the way here suddenly sits heavily in my stomach. I stare at the charismatic, unaffected Bronson Butcher and my possessive, pensive Max Butcher and wonder how it came to be that *I'm* sitting here—the crux of these beautiful men's conversation.

I look at Max, his face tight with defiance. I want to smooth his frown with my fingertips. I want to kiss his tension away.

The dark sky outside the marquee suddenly lights up. I hear a popping sound and then a whirling and a bang. It's fireworks. Everyone floods out onto the grass and I bounce up too, but Max grabs my wrist.

"I wanna see the fireworks," I plead. "Come with me, Menace."

He stifles a grin, but for a split second I see his cheeky dimple. "Okay."

Flick and Stacey appear hand-in-hand and it makes me warm to see them happy again.

"Come with us!" Flick says, beaming widely.

They disappear outside. Max lets go of my wrist and I rush after Flick. We find a space on the grass. The humidity outside the marquee is thick and tangible. Hearing the pop and fizz, I crane my neck and watch as the sky explodes in colour. I feel Max's warm chest pressing behind me. His arms band around my shoulders, resting above my breasts. Relaxing against him, I drop my head back and watch the dome above me being painted with fire.

Bronson stops a few steps ahead of us, looking up at the sky. He rolls his sleeves up, intricate ink work being slowly revealed across every inch of his forearm. I wonder in this moment why he is alone tonight. I wonder why he's always alone. He's beautiful, just as beautiful as my Max, but in a different way—he's a bit wilder.

Appearing beside Stacey, Xander pulls her into his arms and kisses her temple. She smiles as his lips touch her, but she still keeps a firm hold of Felicity's hand. I feel Max's deep sigh against my back. He leans down towards my ear and kisses me quickly on the cheek.

Releasing me, he approaches Stacey. After ducking his head to find her gaze, he grips her shoulder. "You know I'm a jerk. You've known me a long time... But you also know you're my family. You know that's how I feel, right?" Her eyes are instantly glassy. "Don't do that." He coaxes her from Xander and cuddles her against him, kissing her forehead. She returns his hug briefly, then steps back and punches his arm. I beam at them.

Keeping his grip on Stacey, he puts his other hand on Flick's shoulder. He shifts his gaze between them. "Felicity, thank you for telling me about Salvatore. I need you two to do that for me. If you so much as hear Cassidy's name, I want to know about it. Can you do that?" Stacey instantly nods.

I'm surprised when Flick agrees as well. "Sure thing, Max."

"Good girls." He pulls them both in for a quick, firm hug before walking back over to me.

"What a pussy," Xander laughs.

Max chuckles as he slips his arms around me. "Watch the fireworks, dickhead."

CHAPTER TWENTY-THREE
you're not a bad person

WHEN OUR MOTORBIKE stops outside of a different villa, I'm both wary and excited. Max leans forward and twists the front tyre into position as I jump off. He effortlessly swings his leg over the sleek black motorbike and looks at me as if he's ready to eat me.

His tongue lathers his lower lip while his gaze caresses my naked thighs. "What was it you said about that straitjacket?"

I take a step back, feeling my pulse quicken. "Where are we?"

"I want you to be able to scream."

My breathing becomes deep and laborious. "*Okay.*"

Before I can take another step backwards, he's sweeping me into his arms and carrying me inside.

Our last night in Bali is spent having wild, profound, and mind-blowing sex in our very own villa.

We are both athletic and yet, by the end of it, we are flayed out on the mattress, chests heaving, legs entwined, bodies slick with moisture, mouths red and raw. I spread my thighs, humming at the feel of the breeze from the overhead fan licking my swollen parts. God, this feels good.

"Are you sore?" he asks, facing me.

I roll onto my shoulder and peer up at his beautiful face. "A little." Shuffling me about, he places my head on his thick bicep as a pillow, holding me close. He brushes a rogue strand of hair from my face and grins.

"I'll lick you all better tomorrow."

My palm meets his chest and I can feel his heart beating on the other side. Slow and relaxed. "Last time you said that, you disappeared for two weeks."

"I won't be doing that again."

"What's going to happen when we get back to the District?"

He gazes down at me through his lashes. "What do you mean?"

"With us?"

His brows tighten. "Nothing."

The ambiguity in that response causes my breath to catch. "Oh."

He reaches for my face, his thumb running along my jaw. "No, Little One. What I mean is, we'll stay the same. You'll go back to dancing. I'll go back to studying and working. We'll see each other most nights."

I exhale and press my lips together to stop from beaming at him. "Most nights? Really?" My voice gives away my excitement, pitching higher.

I wish I was cooler.

He chuckles softly. "Sure. If you want."

"Of course I want!" I run my nails down the ridges of his muscles, which are taut from exertion. "But... How? How will you fit me in with *Jimmy*? With uni and rugby?"

His pectorals twitched when I'd mentioned Jimmy. He

clears his throat. "I only have uni two days a week. I'm nearly finished. And I've told Coach I can't commit at the moment. He's got me on casual."

"What do you do the rest of the time?"

"I go to the gym. Work."

"And when you graduate... " I stare up at his expression, desperate to know if he'll be moving away from the Family identity and creating his own. "Will you get a job as an architect?"

He glances at me and frowns, the answer in his dubious gaze. "How do *you* spend your days?"

My chest feels a ping of sorrow. "Why get a degree if you don't intend on using it?"

He drags me up onto the pillow beside him. "Don't look so sad, and tell me what you do all day."

"I have ballet like five days a week," I say with a thin smile. "And I teach classes twice a week. I go for runs in the morning. Toni and I have a set date night on Wednesday to watch whatever our series is at the moment. *Game of Thrones* took a big chunk out of our lives. But I also practise in my studio and, when I can, I try to spend time with my family."

He watches my lips move as I speak. "How you gonna fit me in?"

My smile gets wider. "I prioritise."

He grins. "Good to know." We smile at each other in silence for a few seconds before he says, "Jimmy's got us tickets to your show at Christmas."

I begin to trace his perfectly rough jawline with my fingers. His eyes soften when I touch him. "Will everything be alright between you and Jimmy?"

His jaw muscle tics beneath my finger. "Why wouldn't it be?"

"Because of today," I murmur. "I'm not sure what that was or—"

"Just leave it. Jimmy and I are fine. We're family. You don't have to worry."

I sigh. "And I didn't know you speak Italian."

"It's Sicilian actually. And I don't speak it well, or so everyone kept telling me all fucking day."

"Say something in Sicilian for me?"

His stormy grey eyes analyse me. *"Tu, sì a chiù bedda carusa ca ancuntrài nda me vita."*

"What did you say?"

He smirks. "Something filthy."

"I'd love to speak another language."

"I'll teach you Sicilian."

"Really?" I wrinkle my nose and grin a little. "I hear you're not very good at it."

His eyes get dark with warning. "Be careful... I'll fuck you again."

My hand moves from his jaw down to the centre of his chest, where I trace a small tattooed cross with my fingertip. "And you're religious?"

"I don't need God to fuck you again."

I giggle, but it feels strangled by the questions swimming in my head. "No, I mean it. The ceremony was very religious."

"We're Catholic."

"But are *you* religious?" I press.

He lifts a brow at me. "You wanna know if I believe in God?"

"Yes." I tuck my hand under my cheek. "Do you?"

He thinks about the question for a moment. His hand meets my waist, stroking the curve up to my chest and back down to my hip. "The word '*no*' is on my tongue, but... then I've had my tongue inside you, so maybe He does exist."

I giggle again and bat my lashes at him. My smile disappears quickly when I think about my response to the same question. "I don't."

His big hand is hot on my skin. "Why not?"

"I don't want to believe that such a powerful presence exists and yet, such terrible things happen to innocent people."

He exhales slowly through his nose. "Like Konnor."

"Yeah."

There are several seconds of silence in which Max's eyes narrow and fix on me in contemplation. "I have a picture of Butch," he finally says, "holding me and Bronson when we were babies. He's got boxing gloves on. One of us held up by each big fucking bicep. Blood and sweat all over his face, grinning from ear to fucking ear."

I'm surprised my mouth doesn't drop open from him willingly sharing something personal with me. "He was proud of you?"

He scoffs a little. "He'd just won a championship... The guy he'd fought that day died. Brain injury."

My throat rolls. "Oh, Max."

"God doesn't do terrible things to people, Little One. People do terrible things to people."

My face falls. I struggle with the words for a moment before admitting, "I worry about you."

"You don't need to," he assures me.

"Do you mean that?" I study his face. "That I don't need to. You're not gonna get hurt?"

He grins. "It's cute you're worried about me."

"I'm always going to be." My chest tightens and I'm suddenly picturing him stomping on someone's head. "You're a gangster, Max."

"You weren't gonna ask questions," he says, his tone low and smooth.

My pulse begins to race. "That was a statement, not a question."

"What is a gangster?" he bites out. "It's a fucking Hollywood word. We don't use that term."

"Okay." I swallow for courage and mutter, "What term do you use?"

He removes his hand from my waist and the absence of it affects me deeply. Leaning up onto his elbow, he glares down at me. "That's a fucking question."

"Do you hurt people?"

"That's another!"

I feel the backs of my eyes burning and I stifle a little whimper.

He exhales slowly, his jaw working as he reaches for the words. "Only people like me," he states. Stroking my cheek, he adds, "Not people like you."

And my heart sinks and he can see it in my eyes. Unease and disappointment curdle together in my belly and he sees that too. His face gets tighter, his eyes dilate, and I get smaller, crushed beneath his glare.

I sniffle and touch his arm. "But people like you have people like me that love them."

He jumps to his feet. "Cassidy, stop this shit now!" He disappears from our room and slams the door. My heart is in my throat. My breathing is shallow and hard to control.

Hot tears run down my temples and onto the pillow. After a few moments, I hear the front door open and then shut. I curl my knees up and cry, tears falling quick like rain.

"I'D NEVER HURT YOU."

I open my eyes to complete darkness, the sound of the fan clicking as it spins, and those words. The bed dips around me and I soon feel Max's heat on top of me. His hand circles the side of my neck.

His breath hits my cheek. "Don't be afraid of me."

He presses his lips to mine, and he tastes sweet and poisonous. Like rum. Like Max Butcher. His naked body radiates heat against my skin. His erection pulsates hard against my thigh. Opening for him, I wrap my legs around his hips, feed my fingers up through his dark-brown hair, and deepen our kiss.

Neediness takes him over as he thrusts into me on a groan. His palms slam into the pillow on either side of my face. As he rolls his hips against me, my backside curves up.

I grip his shoulders and neck. There is desperation in his movements as he threads his hand under my backside and lifts me up to meet his powerful thrusts. Focusing on his own orgasm—I can feel it by the way he moves—he begins to pick up pace.

When he takes me hard like this, it's as if I can feel his penis inside my abdomen. He's so large and I'm so small. If I placed my palm on my lower belly, I'm sure I'd feel him knocking on the other side.

My pleasure is mixed with pain again, just like the first time, and I cry out his name. He groans deep and long, drops one elbow onto the mattress, and steals my breath as his weight crushes me. His face dips into the curve of my neck. "*Cassidy.*"

There are moments when it becomes too much. Too intense. But he keeps going. Growing more desperate for his own release.

I come twice. My breath is his name*; Max.*

He keeps his rhythm up.

Fierce and determined.

His bicep contracts by my face as he gets rougher. Deeper. His fingers massage my backside, manoeuvring me. Suddenly, his teeth bite down on my shoulder as he comes. His hips keep thrusting through his long orgasm, each pump throwing me up towards the headboard.

He finally stills on top of me, breathing heavily.

He presses his forehead to mine, his body hovering just above me. "You're all I want."

My body trembles, and I *am* a silly little girl because I'd thought love would be warmth in my chest and heart, and peace and contentment in my soul. But it's not contentment. It's not peaceful. It's terrifying. It's so strong that I know it could undo me. It could unravel everything that I am, strip me back until I'm nothing but bare bones and a swollen heart.

As my tears fall, he kisses the corner of each eye. "Don't cry. Did I hurt you?"

I shake my head.

He rolls onto his back, pulling me on top of him. I kiss him desperately. He touches the tears beading by my eyes and then brushes his fingers through my hair, down my back, and up again. "Do you still want this with me?" he says against my lips.

I nod with my heart in my throat. "You're not a bad person, Max," I breathe. "I know you aren't."

He kisses me hard.

CHAPTER TWENTY-FOUR

this is my town too, butcher!

I DON'T TAKE a commercial flight home from Bali. This time, I fly in Jimmy's private jet with the boys and Flick and Stacey. I feel like a celebrity. Not only because of the James Bond style private jet—double O so cool—but also because my phone has been buzzing non-stop with texts from everyone I know. They're asking about the photos of Max and me at the wedding, which are circulating Twitter like a plague.

There is a particularly badly angled photo of me sticking my tongue out and Max sucking on it. I cringe and half cover my face, hoping my parents don't see it. Braving the Twitface platform, I read some of the comments and conclude that people suck.

As always, there are a lot of comments about Max and his never-ending string of conquests, which surprisingly includes me listed as a side piece. At least I'm listed.

There are personal attacks on my character from people I've never met. Apparently, I'm pregnant. A slut. A tart. Too young for him. I have small tits—that one hurts. I'm not very good at ballet, but I've managed to sleep my way to the top, which is funny because all of my ballet mistresses are just that... *mistresses*. I'm apparently really dumb and ditzy and *Jessica* has no idea what Max sees in me. I have also been really busy because there are, like, tons of guys commenting that they'd had me first. And they are *detailed*. I'm also the sister of Konnor, so he was mentioned a few times and that makes my blood boil. Toni has replied to some of the nastier comments and he is so witty and cutting, supporting me and deflecting when he can. He's my rock in every way.

I try so hard not to care. I try to remember these comments are coming from bored people who have nothing better to do than live vicariously through me.

I have several missed calls from Konnor and a few voicemails I'm yet to open. That is a can of worms I'm keeping shut until I'm alone. I doubt Max will take kindly to whatever Konnor has to say about us.

Studying my phone, I sigh. "Max?" When I touch his thigh, he pulls out his right headphone and trains his relaxed eyes on mine.

"Hmm?" He's slumped back in the luxurious plane seat, his thighs spread wide. He's wearing light-grey cotton track pants and a white V-neck. I've never seen him look so normal. Gorgeous and undeniably, uncomfortably hot, but looking like a normal twenty-four-year-old nonetheless.

"Do you use Facebook or Twitter?" I ask.

He smirks. "I don't even have a phone."

My brows shoot up. "Oh my God. What? How do people get hold of you?"

He laughs. "If I can help it, they don't."

"But what about work?"

He shrugs. "I have a pager."

I nod, grinning at him. "*Old school*."

He chuckles. "Want my pager number?"

"Yes. But that's not why I'm asking." I pause for a moment. "People are kinda... talking about you."

He yawns and starts flicking through music on his iPod. "They're always talking about me."

I cringe a little. "About... *us*."

He stiffens and slowly turns to face me. "What about us?"

"About *me*, actually, more than anything." I immediately regret this conversation when his relaxed face is replaced with the irrefutable, tight, and intimidating expression of the Max I know and... well, am obsessed with.

His brows draw in tight. "What about you?"

"Umm... actually, don't worry."

"Cassidy, goddamn it, what are they saying?"

I hesitantly pass him my phone. "Here. Have a read."

He inhales loudly, his eyes darting around the display, getting narrower and narrower until a vein in his neck bulges. "Fuck's sake," he spits out.

My throat constricts. "I haven't been with any of those guys!"

He turns towards me, his scowl still in place. "Are you serious? You think I don't know that?"

I recoil in my seat. "*Sorry*."

"I know everything about your body, what it's done, what it hasn't."

"I know."

"Fuck's sake!" He breathes fast and heavy for a moment and then cracks his neck before turning to seek out my gaze again. His hand lifts to stroke my cheek. "Forget about them." He laughs once. "Your mate Toni has made a come-back in my good books."

I relax on a sigh and smile at him, batting my lashes because flirty and sweet is my default Max Butcher mode.

"He'd be happy to hear he's in your good books. Although, when you told him off at the gym, he kinda liked it."

Max hides his laugh behind a wall of feigned disgust. "Not what I want to hear."

MAX DRIVES me home in his 4WD that I now know is a Range Rover. It's big and sleek and sexy and so him. He rolls onto the lawn next to my studio. Switching off the headlights, he doesn't move for a moment. Instead he stares straight ahead into the darkness. He grips the steering wheel while his face is tight with contemplation.

"I don't like this," he mutters without turning his head.

I know how he feels, but I pretend I don't. "What?"

His jaw clenches. "I don't know... leaving you, I think."

"*Max*."

"It's been me and you. But now... Forget about it. I'll see you on Friday."

Everything he *isn't* saying resonates with me. I've become so accustomed to his warmth at night, the Max and Cassidy world, and... if I'm completely honest, the daily orgasms. "Why Friday? That's like five days away. What happened to 'most nights'?"

"It's just for this week. I've got some things I have to take care of. Toni's at my gym every Friday. Go with him."

"Okay... So I won't see you at all until then? And I can't call you?"

He hands me a piece of paper. "My pager number."

My stomach knots up. "Okay."

Max and I stare at each other, longing in both our eyes and maybe something a little extra. I reach for the drawstring on his track pants, wanting to show him with my mouth how I feel about him, but a thud at the passenger window makes me jump. I swivel to see Konnor waiting impatiently on the other side of the glass.

Frick.

I exhale fast, my hands still trembling a little from what I'd been about to do for Max. And in my own backyard!

Timing...

"Get out of the car, Cassidy!" Konnor grumbles.

Before I can make a move, Max has already leapt from his side and circled around to mine. Unlatching my car door, he stands staunchly between Konnor and me.

Max is only a few inches taller than Konnor, but they are both at least a foot taller than me. I bounce from the car and move towards my brother. Standing on my toes, I sling my arms around him, cuddling his neck so tight because I love him so much, even when he looks like he wants to break something. When he doesn't return my affection, I release him and step back. He's eyeballing Max behind me, his entire body tight with rage.

I swallow and feign ignorance, knowing quite well why his face means business. "Big brother, what—"

"I tried to call you," he says through a tight jaw, his eyes never leaving Max. I wonder what Max's face looks like right now. He's probably smirking. *Menace.*

My pulse quickens. "I know. I was in Ba—"

"I know. I saw the photo."

I squirm a little, imagining Konnor flicking through Facebook and coming across a picture of his little sister with her tongue in Max Butcher's mouth.

My hand meets Konnor's arm. "Are you back for the weekend again?"

Konnor glances at me for a split second. "Go inside. I wanna talk to Max."

I sigh and drop my hand. "No."

He stares at me. "What?"

Max's hand touches my hip. "You don't get to do that," I say while covering Max's hand with mine.

"Get to do what?" Konnor asks, suddenly trained on our hands. Locked onto them.

"Come home and tell me to go inside," I say softly. "You don't get to do that."

Max's hand twitches. "I'm heading off now anyway," he says and twists me to face him. I roll my eyes at Max's cocky smirk, but can't help but smile nonetheless.

"Give me a kiss first, Little One."

Trying not to smile too hard, I rise onto my tippy toes and kiss his cheek. In an instant, I'm lifted to straddle him and he leans back into his car, touching me everywhere he can. His fingers move around my body, exploring and groping. I try to push him away subtly, but he's hell-bent on proving a point.

"Max," I plea between kisses. "Don't."

Konnor growls. "Do you mind not dry humping my sister in front of me?"

Max gradually lowers me to the ground.

Tucking me behind him, he heads straight for Konnor. "You're fucking lucky, Slater. You should stay out of the District. It doesn't agree with you."

Konnor steps toward him and they get within an inch of each other. I hold my breath.

"This is my town too, Butcher!"

Max laughs, but it's not kind. "This is *definitely* not your town."

"You know nothing about me."

"I bet you wish that were true."

"What the hell does that mean?" Konnor shuffles his feet. "You think you know something about me?"

"What's your problem with me, Slater?" Max levels him with a smirk. "Is it because I've made out with your girlfriend or because I know what your sister feels like from the inside?"

Oh my God!

Before I have a chance to react, Konnor throws his fist into Max's face. Grunts of pain spit from them both. Max shoves Konnor in the chest. Konnor hits the grass hard, a winded sound expelling from him. Scowling, Max hovers over him. He presses his shoe to Konnor's chest and pins him to the grass.

"I'm not gonna hit you!" Max barks.

"Oh my God," I yell as I grab my enraged lover's arm, trying to pull him away from Konnor. But he's a solid wall of tense muscles. On the ground, Konnor looks pale and shaky, as though he might throw up. Tugging on Max's arm, I plead with him. "Please, let him stand up."

Max takes his foot off Konnor's chest and turns to face me. The lower part of his lip has a small gash in it. He searches my pained mien and winces, his eyes flashing a silent apology.

"Fuck," he growls, but I think that aggression is aimed at himself.

"Konnor," I hear Blesk call out and Konnor's glare instantly breaks.

Quickly standing, he yells, "I'm fine. We're fine. Max was just leaving."

Blesk appears at Konnor's side, flushed from the run across the grass and yet so naturally beautiful. Her blonde hair bounces around her full breasts as they rise and fall. I notice, of course, because I've always been jealous of big boobs. Her sunflower dress sways over her perfectly curvaceous thighs. She's taller than me, a few sizes bigger, flawlessly proportioned, and simply stunning. '*Is this because I've made out with your girlfrie*nd?' And now I want to analyse Max's words until I go insane.

She smiles nervously at me. "I'm sorry. Konnor isn't himself."

"Blesk," Max says deadpan.

She barely glances up at him. "Max."

I throw my hands up. "You are both cavemen." I stare at Konnor. "Don't you ever hit him again!" Spinning to face Max, I say, "And you're a fricking menace."

Konnor clears his throat. "Just so we're clear, Butcher. I don't have a problem with you because you kissed Blesk once when you two were teenagers. I'm not insecure about our relationship. I have a problem with you because you walk around the District like you own the fucking place and be—"

"I do own the fucking place."

"And because my little sister is way too good for you!"

Max smirks again. "At least we agree on something."

That throws Konnor completely off his train of thought. "Well... good." Suddenly, he cups his forehead. His legs wobble and then he's flat on his back again.

Blesk and I both squat down beside him.

"Konnor. What's going on?" I ask. As the moonlight hits his face, I'm able to take him all in. The hair on his jawline is long and unkempt and his usually bright and endearing emerald-green eyes are dull and bloodshot.

"He's given up drinking. It's been making him dizzy for a few days now," Blesk says, her concern so deep it's etched into every aspect of her expression.

I turn to watch Max approaching us, a tall silhouette that covers the moon, momentarily casting a shadow over

Konnor. Leaning down, he grips Konnor's forearm and hauls him to his feet. Hooking his arm around Konnor's waist, he helps him walk towards the house. I take in a big, slow breath. How do guys go from hostile to helpful in the space of a few seconds?

Once inside, Max guides Konnor over to the couch and Konnor drops down with a grumble. His elbows meet his knees and his hands cover his face. After breathing into them for a few moments, he thrusts his hands through his sandy-brown hair and drags them back down, rubbing his tension away.

"You're my hero, Butcher," Konnor mocks, but I think there is something other than sarcasm in his voice. "Still don't like you."

Max turns from him. "Good."

As soon as he grabs my hand and pulls me towards the door, my heart begins to ache. He's leaving. Stopping by the door, he takes one last look at me.

I stare up at my menace and touch the little cut on his mouth. "Your lip."

He grins wide enough for the dimple on his left cheek to show. "I get hit worse sparring at the gym."

"Either way," I say, glancing at the ground. "I hate what just happened."

He lifts my chin up until my eyes meet his dark, grey ones. "I didn't want to fight with your brother, Little One. But I have zero tolerance towards anyone who gets involved in this thing between us... If he'd been anyone else, he'd be choki—"

"You could tone down the vulgar things you say."

"I could." He cups my neck with both hands and studies my face. "I will."

I lift a blonde brow at him. "And you've kissed Blesk?"

He softens. "*Cassidy.* I was just a kid then."

I stroke my nails through the hair on his tattooed forearm. "I didn't like hearing it though. When you said that, it probably hurt me more than it hurt Konnor."

As his hands caress my face, his eyes follow them. Follow them along my warm cheeks. To the swell of my lower lip. To the tip of my nose. He taps my nose softly and I smile that goofy smile. "And I don't want to hurt any part of you," he says.

I sigh, missing him immensely already. "I have to make sure my brother is okay."

He bites back words. "I know," he manages to say with a deep and sexy voice that makes my thighs quiver. He plants a long kiss on my lips. His arms pull my body in to meet his for a moment, tightening on a deep sigh. Then he releases me, leaving me dizzy, and walks out the front door.

Staring at the open door, I feel the physical absence of him all around me. We have become so close and yet, I don't even know where he lives or how to get hold of him. I literally have to wait for him to find me and that makes me feel sick to my stomach—helpless. Insecure.

"Pipsqueak, I'm sorry," Konnor says from the lounge room.

When I make my way back to where he is slumped over the couch, Blesk is now sitting beside him. They both look exhausted.

After everything he went through, Konnor has always needed a kind of inebriation to function normally. He was on prescription medication for a while, but he'd told us that it had made him feel numb. I close the gap between us and slide onto his lap, cuddling his neck. "Forget about what happened out there. I'm *so* proud of you for giving up drinking." I lean back and measure him up with my eyes. "How long has it been?" I glance at Blesk. "How did you get him to stop?"

Blesk gazes at Konnor, her eyes lapping up the sight of him, full of pride and love. "It's been three weeks. The day after we left here... after that horrible conversation about Dustin Nerrock. He poured all his alcohol down the sink. Just like that. And it has nothing to do with me. He wanted to do it. He's my hero."

"Mine *too*," I say.

Konnor returns my embrace, his body trembling due to the withdrawal. "It's been fucking hard," he says, his voice weak.

I shuffle off his lap and onto the adjoining seat. "Why didn't you tell any of us you were going through this?"

He looks to Blesk and shrugs. "I had Duch."

"Thank you so much for being there for my brother, Blesk. You have been so wonderful. I don't know where he found you, but I wanna keep you." I feel myself getting emotional. "We'd all just accepted he'd always be a drinker. Don't say it has nothing to do with you because it does. Thank you."

"You don't need to thank me," she says. "Konnor is the strongest person in the world. He would have done it eventually. I know it."

A single tear slides down my cheek and now I'm jumping on Blesk and hugging her tight. "I think I love you."

She giggles into my hair. "I'm taken." We both laugh as I return to my seat opposite them. I grab my long strawberry-blonde hair, still straightened from the wedding, and pull it down one shoulder.

I smile at him tightly. "Konnor, I'm with Max now. You two are going to have to get along. Why don't you like him?"

"What's to like?" Konnor asks with a shrug.

Could it be possible that he doesn't remember that day? The day that Max became my secret obsession. "Don't you remember the day we first met him?"

"Cassidy, right now, I barely remember what I had for breakfast."

"You were twelve. That kid across the street, Joshua, I think his name was. He stole my yo-yo. Don't you remember that day?"

"I got the ever-loving shit beat out of me with a cricket bat. Yep. Remember it."

My eyes soften on him. "Do you remember how it ended?"

He rubs his face in contemplation. "Um. I was on the grass. Josh was fucking me up with a cricket bat. Pretty sure, you were screaming. And then some kid we'd never seen before intervened, pulled the bat off Josh and knocked him out—" Realisation crosses his face. "No fucking way... Was that Max?"

I nod slowly. "He's not a bad person, Konnor. Why would he help you if he was? He just stopped the fight and carried on up the street as if nothing had even happened—" When the front door opens and I hear heels making their way through the foyer towards us, I stop talking. I'm relieved to see Flick appear, looking a little dishevelled from the flight and drive. Her face lights up when she sees Konnor.

"Little Bro!" She drops her bags and jumps on him, as such is the Slater way to welcome our family members. She's up straightaway and staring at Blesk. "You must be the famous Blesk."

"I've heard so much about you. I'm so excited I finally get to meet you," Blesk says, shuffling her feet nervously on the carpet.

Flick wanders over to me, hooking her arm around mine. "Everyone in here kinda looks like someone has died."

I cover her hand with mine. "Konnor just got into a fight with Max."

Flick's eyes widen in pretend horror. "And you're still alive to tell your grandchildren the epic tale."

Konnor feigns a chuckle. "Haha. I punched him... once. Fucker barely moved." Looking guilty, he adds, "He was humping Cassidy in front of me."

She pinches my cheek and talks in a baby voice. "No one will ever be good enough for *our little Cassidy*." I make a silly face at her.

Konnor eyes Flick. "So you're okay with this?"

"I wasn't," she admits. "But Cassidy is eighteen, Konnor, not twelve."

"He gets under my skin," he grumbles. "Like, I can't even explain it."

Flick laughs. "I promise that I have firmly expressed my concerns, Little Bro. I'm doing my job. I've mentioned that he's not the boyfriend type... but he's different with her. She makes him a better person. I've seen it."

"So there's nothing I can say, is there?" He exhales loudly before staring at Blesk and then back at us. "Can you please just be very careful? Keep a bit of Cassidy for Cassidy?"

I smile. "Sure."

CHAPTER TWENTY-FIVE
family time

I'D LIKE to say the days are flying by with my Sugar Plum Fairy commitments, but that would be a lie. They're long and mundane. My mum and dad are both working from home this week, and Konnor and Blesk have taken time off from school to help Konnor get through his first few months of sobriety, so we have a full house.

I think about Max constantly and try not to worry. My mum once told me: 'Worrying is like a rocking horse. It gives you something to do, but it doesn't get you anywhere.' I completely agree. Despite that, worrying about him will be something I do often, I feel. It'll be an ever-present state of being for me.

For whatever reason, he can't see me at all until Friday. I don't know why. I should have asked. I guess I'm always hesitant to ask him questions.

The first thing I do on Monday morning is go to my local general practitioner and get a Pap-smear and prescription for the pill.

Tuesday, I dance myself into a coma during the day and

then we share our first family dinner with everyone in over three months. My mum and Blesk talk music while I manage to keep things light and bubbly with Konnor and my dad. I want to pull Konnor aside and discuss Dustin Nerrock. I want to discuss that guy Erik's face. It just never seems like the right time. The other part of me is kicking Dustin's association with the Butchers under the rug to hide from my family. Either way, I'm keeping a secret and that stirs my belly.

After dinner we huddle in the main lounge room and play charades; it's very Brady Bunch and I fricking love it. Konnor and I are both pretty competitive, but we don't keep track of scores tonight.

I'm on the floor in my pyjamas. Konnor, Blesk, and Flick share the couch and Mum and Dad cuddle on the recliner, just like they always do—even when more seats are available. That's what us Slater kids have grown to believe forever love looks like. My parents show and share their affections unconditionally and often.

I find myself studying them in this moment. The heat from the gas fire licks at my cheeks, making me feel that Bali lethargy I now associate with Max. My mum is smiling softly at us, her strawberry-blonde hair cascading over her shoulders, the freckles on her cheeks and nose betraying her age. We share these features. She is petite, like me, and tightly enveloped in a blanket of my dad's big arms.

My dad is a complex man. I model every man I meet against him even though I don't understand him. Even though we're close, a born and raised upper-class girl like me could never understand a self-made man like Ben Slater. Around the District, he's referred to as an honourable man. He is handsome. My friends call him a silver fox. He's loving. He's big and strong, not quite Max big and strong, but not average either. Loyal, yes. But I've always found him protective... mysterious. I realise in this moment how many traits he shares with Max. Not Jimmy or Butch's Max, who is a construct of his upbringing. *My Max*. A fleeting glimpse of a Max without burdens.

After charades, as I read on the couch, I hear Blesk and Konnor giggling on the love seat in the game room. It makes me lonely. Maybe now is a good time to discuss Erik—when Konnor is seemingly relaxed and emotionally stable.

As I walk into the game room, Blesk and Konnor are chatting with big smiles plastered on their faces. Blesk has a tendency to poke her tongue out when she laughs and it's really adorable. When they notice me enter, they unwrap themselves from each other and sit up.

"Hey, Pipsqueak," Konnor shuffles to the edge of the seat. "We were just arguing over the classification of cereal. Soup or not? And why?"

Sitting opposite them, I cross my legs up on the couch. "Well, soup is, like, flavours that have been cooked out into a liquid, right? So soup must be cooked."

They look at each other for a moment.

Blesk laughs. "We have been debating this for thirty minutes and neither of us came up with that answer."

"Glad to be of service," I say, my throat rolling as I carefully consider my next set of words. I shuffle nervously and they both look sideways at each other.

"You alright?" Konnor asks, picking up a glass of water and taking a few sips.

Clearing my throat, I stare straight into Konnor's stunning green eyes. "I met someone at the wedding who knows you. And... I've been feeling a bit weird about it." My brain is sorting through words, fumbling to string them together in an eloquent fashion. "Sorry, cryptic much. His name is Erik. He has all these sca—" I stop talking.

They both stiffen. And there it is. In Konnor's eyes.

Recognition.

Anger.

Bouncing my gaze between Konnor and Blesk, it's clear by their ever paling faces that they *both* know this person.

Konnor talks through a tight jaw. "Stay away from him!"

Blesk's hands are clenched in her lap, but she's trying to keep her face impartial. "He's not well."

"What happened between you two?" I ask. "Max said—"

"What the fuck is he doing hanging out with the Butchers?" Konnor says, draining his glass of water as if it were bourbon—his old drink of choice.

"I don't kno—" I start to answer before realising he'd directed his question at Blesk.

Blinking too fast, she says, "I don't know. I don't know who he hangs out with these days." Her tone has a hint of defensiveness. Of hesitation.

He turns back to me. "Why the fuck was he there?"

"I don't know," I say. "But he spoke to me."

Setting the glass down a little harder than necessary, he leans in closer to me. "Don't speak to him, Cassidy."

My pulse picks up pace. "Well, I won't now, but I didn't know that at the time."

He twists to face Blesk, determined to draw information from her. "Why would he have been invited to that wedding?"

She stiffens. "Konnor, stop looking at me like I'm keeping a secret from you."

His lips twitch. "Have you been speaking to him?"

"No," she says. "I haven't. But Dad said he'd dropped out

of university and moved back home. Apparently, he's a driver or something for some businessman."

Now I'm truly intent on asking a lot of questions, but unfortunately, they both seem racked with nerves. "What businessman?" I ask softly. Is he a driver for Jimmy? Did he drive me to Jimmy Storm's house that evening? I can't remember the driver's face. Does he work for Dustin? If he hates Konnor as much as Max had implied, then maybe he's working for Dustin as a way to get back at Konnor. Am I overthinking this?

Blesk answers without looking at me. "I don't know. I didn't ask." Reaching for Konnor's tight face, she strokes her fingers down his cheek. "When Dad brings him up, I try to change the subject."

Konnor's face makes me wary of asking more questions, but my curiosity eventually wins out. "What happened between you two, Konnor?"

"Cassidy" – he stands, picking up his empty glass – "we got in a big fucking fight, alright? I nearly killed him."

As he walks towards the bar, I follow him with my eyes. "Why?"

He fills his glass up with water from the tap. "It's none of your business."

"Erik's my brother," Blesk blurts out and then holds her tongue for a few seconds. She swallows. "I'm adopted, just like Konnor. Erik was... *attacking* me... forcing himself on me." As those words fall from her lips like acid, I cover my mouth to smother a gasp.

"Oh my God," I whisper, wishing I'd never asked. Wishing I'd thrown a rock at his face. Wishing I'd kicked him in the balls. "I'm so sorry. I didn't mean to bring this up. I didn't know it had anything to do with you, Blesk, or I wouldn't hav—"

"Cassidy, please, it's fine." She leans forward and briefly touches my thigh. "This is actually good for me. I've been working on saying these things aloud." She smiles up at Konnor, who, despite his taut shoulders, returns her smile. "He abused me for years." She looks back at me. "He's sick. There is something really wrong inside him. I know this now. It took me a while though. I've had friends call it a kind of Stockholm syndrome, but I don't think it needs a label. He used to play mind games with me." She gets lost in thought. "Anyway, you should definitely avoid him."

There are tears forming in my eyes now. "Avoid him. Kick him in the balls. Potato patato," I manage to say with a reasonably steady voice, reaching for a soft ending to this conversation.

It works.

She lets out a small chuckle. Even though she is showing signs of resolve that I could never understand, I'm completely devastated for her. There is no possible way a girl like me can comprehend that kind of anguish. And I thought love was the ultimate sensitivity. But abusive love? That breeds unrelatable emotions.

CHAPTER TWENTY-SIX

ice bath

IT'S Wednesday night and my toes and left ankle are in agony from training. I've been overdoing it. The bathtub slowly fills with cold water. The last bag of ice is poured in and it no longer splashes the water, but now settles atop the other cubes. It's been a few weeks since I've had an ice bath, but after today, I feel my body needs it. It's called cold therapy and ever since the first time I'd tried it, after I'd injured my right ankle, I've used it to help with circulation and inflammation.

I stare at the cubes and channel my mind to focus on breathing in through my nose and out through my mouth. Gripping the tub on either side, I slide into the freezing cold water. My breath becomes fitful as the cold consumes my senses and wipes away every other thought. I know that all I have to do is channel my attention through the first sixty seconds and then my body will become accustomed to the freezing temperature and my skin will no longer burn.

My phone buzzes on the floor beside me. Luckily the universe has given me a little distraction from the cold. I reach for it and stare at the screen, suddenly reminded of a week ago when I'd received their first text. I'd completely forgotten about it. I thought it was Max, but now I know he doesn't have a phone.

Unknown number: I wish I could suck on your tongue.

My fingers type frantically across the display: *Not interested, who are you? Seriously get lost.* My heart beats an erratic cadence. Staring at the text, I decide not to press enter. Nothing is the best response for now. Perhaps whoever it is will lose interest.

Focusing on my breathing, I drop my phone to the floor. When I hear a knock at the door, I'm still panting.

"Cassidy? You okay?" My dad's voice comes through the door.

"Yeah. I'm just having an ice bath. I'm not dying." I laugh breathlessly.

"You have a visitor."

It's Toni.

There is no way in hell I'm getting out of this bath and braving the first sixty seconds again. "Okay. I'll be out in about ten minutes. Entertain him for me or just send him up."

There is a pause and then, "Okay, baby."

After ten minutes in the bath, my pulse has gone from frantic to steady. When I step out, I wrap a towel around me, no longer feeling cold at all. As always, after ice therapy, I feel euphoric. The twinge in my left ankle is much better. It can nearly bare my full weight again. I don't let it, though. I'll hobble tonight and let it rest while I'm in bed. Tomorrow I'll use it cautiously. Dressing in a thigh-length pink silk robe and white knickers, I hobble down the stairs. My feet stumble when I see Max and my dad talking in the living room. Unable to stop smiling, I cover my mouth with my palm instead. I do a little happy dance on the step. Will I ever be cool?

Nope.

I backtrack up the stairs and try to eavesdrop, but I can't make out words, only the tones... They are friendly. Chatty. I smooth my hair out, pinch my cheeks, and squat, so I can peer around the wall and observe Max from a distance. He's on the couch, leaning back with his ankle resting on his knee, completely comfortable in my house. He's smiling. My tongue lathers my lower lip while I enjoy the perfection of him like a naughty voyeur. He's beautiful. My dad might have a heart attack when he sees me greet Max in only my robe, but the idea fills me to the brink with excitement.

Act cool.

I take a few steps down and they both focus on me. My eyes anchor on Max as he smirks, dropping his gaze over my body. I bite my lower lip, catching my wide smile in my teeth. I want to run into his arms and kiss him feverishly, but I restrain myself.

My heart pirouettes. "Hi, Max."

"Hey, Little One."

Dad smiles tightly and wanders toward me, planting a little kiss on my cheek. "I'm going to bed. Cassidy, maybe put something more appropriate on for the drive."

The drive?

I blink at Max, who is looking smug. "Okay," I murmur.

Dad disappears up the stairs, surprising me. I'm his youngest child. His baby girl. Why is he allowing me to leave at this time of night and go... where?

Max gradually stands and moves toward me. His throat pulses as he meets me at the stairs and for the first time, we're the same height. He takes me all in for a moment, in no hurry to stop his gaze from stripping me bare. "You're staying at my house tonight."

A smile takes over my face. "Okay."

He chuckles once. "You don't hide anything, do you?"

"I try. I'm just not very good at it."

As I rub my hands down the hard grooves of his chest, his muscles twitch beneath my fingertips. I can feel the breath from his lips, the hot sweetness beckoning mine towards them. My skin is suddenly humming with desperation. Desperate to be touched. Desperate to be taken. We stare at each other, eyes heated. My hands find their way into his hair and then suddenly his lips are on mine. His hands are gripping my arse. My legs are around his waist.

The cotton of my knickers presses against his abdomen as he carries me effortlessly up the stairs and into my room.

This is a different experience altogether. Here I am, in my house, Konnor and Blesk asleep in the room beside mine. But we are still us, Max and me. When we are together, it's like the rest of the world fades away.

Every cell in my body is on fire as his kiss consumes me. The door opens and shuts behind us.

He crawls onto the bed with me, caging me beneath his hot, heavy, needy body. My limbs open to accommodate his breadth. I cry out when he slaps my thigh on a growl. He worships my leg, running his hand down to my calf and up to the soft inner flesh of my thigh.

"You have the sexiest legs," he groans between kisses. "I need to taste you."

Nipping and licking his way down to the little divot between my collar bones, he tongues it suggestively. I squeeze my eyes shut, his mouth overwhelming me. I let out a long, needy moan, thrust my pelvis up into his abdomen, and rub myself on him shamelessly.

He stops suddenly at my chest and raises a hand to my mouth. "*Shh*." He shuffles back up and presses his forehead to mine before looking at me and loosening his grip around my mouth.

My lips part immediately as I breathe hard. "Sorry."

He seems to be gathering his own composure. "Don't ever apologise for those beautiful noises. Just go pack a bag *now*." I slide out from under him slowly, noting the big, defined bulge between his thighs. I smile, loving that I affect him just as strongly as he does me. The urge to climb onto his lap is only held back by my curiosity of seeing his place... Of course, knowing that once we're there, we'll have all night to continue what we started helps me do as I'm told.

While I'm riffling around trying to find my black yoga pants and favourite pink tee-shirt, Max wanders into my ensuite bathroom. I'm debating what panties to grab, knowing quite well they'll be seen and touched and taken off by Max Butcher, when he strides out of the ensuite, the door slamming behind him. Taken aback by the noise, I spin to face him.

He looks at me, but his eyes are unreadable. "Are you injured?" he asks tightly.

My mind shuffles information around in confusion for a few moments before realisation dawns. "Oh, the ice bath. No. Well, a little. I hurt my ankle today."

He mashes his teeth together, blinking unnaturally fast. "Just your ankle?"

I shift my gaze around. "*Yeah*."

"Why the whole bath?"

"I don't know," I say, taking a little step towards him. "I've always done it that way. It's good for you."

"Who told you that?" he bites out.

"*Google?*" It comes out sounding like a question in my confusion. "What's wrong?"

He shakes his head, frowning into space. "Nothing. Get your shit and let's go."

I reach for him, touching his tense cheeks and massaging the lines fixed between his brows. "No, Max. What's this change in mood all about?"

"It's nothing. Forget about it."

"I think it's *something*."

Sighing, his eyes shut for a split second. "I got knocked around a bit when I was a kid." His gaze finds me again. "Ice baths just remind me of a time I'd rather forget."

I wonder who knocked him around. Does he mean fights at school? No, knocked around implies someone bigger and stronger had hurt him. God, he means his mother. A heavy weight settles in my belly, making me want to clutch at it. Claw it out. I hate her. Flashes of him and his brothers as children, beaten and soaking in ice baths, invade my mind, and I can't breathe until they disappear. I shake them away. All of a sudden, I feel as though I'm deceiving him by not telling him I know.

"Who knocked you around?" I find myself asking only to wish I didn't. As I study his tight forehead and pursed lips, my heart aches something awful. "You don't have to tell—"

"My," he chokes on the word. "Mother. Victoria. She liked to take out her frustrations with Butch on us whenever he fucked around. As time went by, I think she started to enjoy hurting us. I think it became a kind of addiction. She has no power and is surrounded by powerful men. It's not an excuse, just a reason."

"*Max*."

"It's okay." He brushes his fingers through my hair, staring at the strands. "She doesn't hurt us anymore. *Can't.*"

"I saw you at my party," I admit, hesitating before adding, "With her."

His eyes are still glued on my hair tangled in his fingers. "I know."

"What did she want?"

His gaze meets mine. "Xander stole her phone, trying to get her attention, but attention from that woman isn't a good thing, so I'd just said it was me."

"Why didn't you tell your dad what was going on?"

"Tell him what?" He laughs with derision. "That our mother was beating us up? Do you have any idea what admitting something like that to Luca Butcher would be like?"

I glance at the floor. "But he loves you."

He lifts my chin. "He does, but he doesn't like weakness."

I feel pin-prickles behind my eyes, beckoning tears to fall. "You were just children."

Looking away from me, his eyes distant, he says, "Butch asked what happened once. So I told him I'd been in a fight at school. He wanted to know what the other kid looked like. I told him *unconscious.*" Max smiles, but it lacks warmth. "He was proud. That's the look I'd wanted from him."

Rising onto my tippy toes, I kiss him softly as a single tear forces its way from the corner of my eye. He has offered me something personal and I never want to take his words for granted as they are rare and hard-earned. "Thank you for sharing that with me."

He points at my half-packed bag, signalling that the conversation is over. I stare at his tempest grey eyes, wanting to tell him all the things in my heart, but in the end, I just lean up and kiss his lips again. He frowns at me, but he's not mad. I smile at him, hoping he can see in my eyes all the things I want to say.

"Finish packing," he orders.

I laugh a little. "Yes, Max."

With my bags ready to go, we wander to his car. I climb inside and he leans across me to buckle me in. Then we head for Connolly. He concentrates on the traffic. I listen to the music and relax. His big warm hand rests on my thigh and my heart is so full of him, I struggle to feel anything else.

Connolly is about half an hour from Brussman, but they're both a part of the District. Max's town was established first and is hard to buy into. The premier families of Western Australia—the Storms, the Butchers, and most of the other old school District families, all live there. Slater is an original District family name, but we never had enough money to buy into Connolly. We do now, though. But we like Brussman.

I turn the music down and twist in my seat to face Max. "How did you get my dad to agree to this?"

He smiles, an arrogant and gorgeous curve to his lips. "Your dad likes me."

"Whatever." I blink at him. "He didn't seem to like you last time."

"That's because you were discussing things you shouldn't and he knew it."

"You think he likes you? The man stealing his baby girl away."

"Can't explain it myself. I'd have shot me." Max's hand shifts on the wheel and I notice a new tattoo on his finger. It's the date of the wedding, I think, in cursive writing. It reminds me of the detailed family tree on both Bronson's and Max's backs. I imagine Aurora Butcher will be added to that soon.

I grin at him. "Does your car have a name?"

He laughs without restraint. It's such a beautiful sound. "No."

"I have a pink Lexus, so my car's name is Lady. Ya know, like Lady Lexus... " I feel my cheeks heat. "You think I'm weird."

"You are."

I smile at him as he tries not to smile. "Can I name your car?"

He chuckles, shaking his head as if he has no choice. "If you have to."

"Hmm." I click my tongue in contemplation as I peer around for inspiration. It's spacious and dark inside. It's masculine and clean. Digital displays glow red and yellow and green. "Range Rover... *Hmm.* Oh, my gawd! It has to be Romeo, Romeo Range Rover."

He cringes. "Fuck, Cassidy, that's the worst fucking name."

"*No.* Romeo is the most famous male ballet character in the world! Yes, it has to be Romeo."

"I'm not referring to my car as Romeo."

"That's fine." I giggle. "I will though."

He glances at me sideways and grins, his dimple showing. "The shit I let you get away with."

Leaning across the centre console, I lightly poke his dimple and then relax into a sigh. "You have no idea how long I've wanted to do that."

It's nearly ten p.m. when we roll onto his driveway and I get my first glimpse of *Casa* Butcher. Most of the houses in Connolly have boom gates at the entrance, but the Butcher's three-story mansion is obnoxiously close to the road, almost daring people to invade their privacy. Streetlamps light the house up on all sides. It's fully rendered in white and has steep, sharp walls and a modernist look with clean lines and simple shapes. It's a new build on an old block.

The garage door rises, and we pull in alongside five other vehicles.

I blink at Max, a proud smile tugging at my lips. "Did you design this house, Max?"

He pulls up the handbrake. "Yes."

"It's beautiful." I gaze at him for a moment as he twists the keys from the ignition. In my mind I say, '*You're* beautiful.'

Max helps me out of the car. I wobble slightly on my bad ankle and his eyes drop to watch me quietly coddling it.

"I'm fine," I say. Ignoring my assurance, he swoops me up and I automatically wrap my arms around his neck. He stares straight ahead, his expression intense.

"I can walk," I press.

"There are three flights of stairs, Little One."

We enter from behind the kitchen. He carries me through the dining room and toward the foyer.

My eyes widen when I see two guards at his front door. Embarrassed I'm being carried like an invalid, I hide my face in Max's shoulder.

"This is Cassidy," Max says, so I turn to acknowledge them with a sheepish smile.

One of them smiles politely at me before looking at Max. "Xander's not home yet."

"Hmm." Max stops at the bottom of the stairs. "Is Carter watching him?"

"Yes," the man says with a quick nod.

"Good." Max carries me up the staircase to the second floor and then the third.

As we continue through the house, I notice that the fixed

décor is always black, white, and beautiful redwood. It's simple and masculine and Max.

I look out through the vast windows and over the top of rooves, spotting the moon glowing large just above the skyline. I count the doors as we pass by them in the hallway. Five. We bump into Bronson, shirtless, wearing only boxers with a toothbrush hanging from his mouth. His eyes light up when they meet mine and he fist pumps the air as if re-enacting the closing scene from *The Breakfast Club*.

I run hot. "Stop it, Bronson."

"I can't help it." He saunters off down the hallway towards one of the other doors.

I look at Max, who sighs, seemingly exasperated by his brother. "Why is he so excited?" I ask.

Max shakes his head. "I've never had a girl here before."

My jaw drops open. Then I curl my lips together to stop from smiling and tense my body to stop from jigging. "Never?"

"No." He shrugs. "Why would I bring a girl back here?"

"Ah, to hang out with her?"

"Yeah. Why would I want to do that? I fuck them at their house so I can leave."

"Max, that's horrible."

"Don't act surprised," he exhales as he walks me into his room. He lowers my feet to the ground and kicks the door shut. "I did the same to you once."

My mind drifts to the first time he came to my house. He'd disappeared out the window. The second time, he'd tried to ditch me after we'd dressed, but I'd shamelessly begged him to stay. Now though, I'm shuffling nervously in his hotel-style room on sacred ground no other girl has touched.

My eyes bounce around his personal space. "So this is where *the* Max Butcher sleeps." I giggle nervously.

Stop being nervous.

It's Max.

My Max.

His room is neat and mature, with sweeping windows that display Connolly from above. There's a rack of dumb-bells in one corner and a boxing bag hanging from the ceiling beside it. A sixty-inch wall-mounted television is hooked up to a PlayStation and an Xbox. The walls are exposed brick, which adds an extra level of masculinity to the space. I like it.

After hobbling over to his large bed, I slowly pivot to face him. I rise onto my toes, scooting backwards along the mattress. As I flex my fingers over the soft black sheets, my breathing labours. Max is staring at me from across the room. My pulse kicks up a notch at the sight of his heated glare. It's serious and menacing. The phrase, 'I do like to chase and eat little animals' comes to mind.

I press my knees together. "So you've never had sex in this bed?"

He smirks. "I'm about to."

CHAPTER TWENTY-SEVEN

I WAS wrong about love not being peaceful and content.

It is.

I am.

Every morning, Max drops me back at my studio and kisses me goodbye with no future plans set. But then every night, usually quite late, he picks me up and drives me to his house. I never say, 'I'll see you tonight' just in case I jinx it or he feels I'm poking fun at the fact that we're acting inseparable. It's been like this for two weeks now. At my house, my bed is always made. At his house, his bed is messy and full of memories and laughter. I'm becoming accustomed to his study and work routine. He's an early riser even if we've been up all night. While I snuggle naked beneath his sheets, he hits the gym. Then we have breakfast and shower together before he drops me home at eight a.m. so I can get to ballet class for nine a.m.

On the third Sunday morning, I pull my favourite skinny jeans up, jumping a little to stretch the denim over my bum. I can feel Max's eyes lingering on my backside as I grab my white long-sleeve crop top off the floor.

After putting it on, I turn to acknowledge his eyeballing. "Yes, Max?"

"I like you in jeans."

I try not to beam like a massive dork because I've been planning this outfit for days.

In an hour, I'll be sitting on the bleachers at Preston Retreat University, watching Max play for The Dingoes. Two wingers on his team have dropped out and his coach has begged him to fill in.

I raise a blonde eyebrow at him. "I thought you liked me in skirts and dresses?"

"I do. But... your arse in those jeans." He bites his fist as he grins, his mouth a slash of mischief that cuts up his beautiful face. "I'm gonna be all over that after the game."

My cheeks pinch with a smile. "Stop it."

Still grinning to himself, Max leans down and starts filling his sports bag with his jersey and shoes. I let my eyes take him all in. A powerful physique wrapped in taut, tattooed skin that's both a young man about to enjoy a recreational sport and a dangerous heir to an underground empire. He's so much more right now than most people are in their entire lives.

I wander across his room to the punching bag and lay a few light hits on it. My knuckles ache immediately.

"Frick. That's *hard*."

He laughs and pulls on a shirt. "What did you expect?"

I giggle a little, cupping my fist. "Some padding."

"No. You'll have bruised knuckles after a session on the bags."

"So, do you guys all box?"

He slings his bag over his shoulder. "Just for fitness."

"But Butch is a professional boxer?"

Max opens the bedroom door, waving me through. "*Was*."

As we take Romeo to the game, I jiggle in the passenger seat, nervous about sitting on The Dingoes' side of the bleachers because they're playing against The Browns—Konnor's team. I'm not even sure if my brother will be on the field or if he'll be sitting the whole game on the bench. After taking time off to focus on his abstinence from alcohol, maybe he's also deferred from rugby... I doubt it though. He has a partial athletic scholarship, so I imagine that only stands if he's playing.

My belly churns and Max glances at my leg, watching it vibrate with nervous tension.

"You nervous?"

I look at him. "You know you're up against Konnor's team."

A huge grin spreads across his cheeks, his dimple mocking the world with its irresistibility. "Can't wait."

"Max. I love my brother. Play nice."

"I will." He is still grinning, and it's cool and confident.

"*Ugh*. You're a menace."

Once we arrive, Bronson takes over as chaperone—apparently, I need one—and Max disappears into the sports block after demanding a good luck kiss. Bronson and I find a spot on the bleachers, and I buy a hotdog and chips.

Game food is the bomb.

The sky is crystal clear, blue and picturesque, but the wind has a nasty nip to it. I'm relieved my skin is completely covered.

As I search for Konnor or Blesk, I take a big bite out of my hotdog.

Bronson laughs and I tilt my head at him, searching his clear blue eyes. "What?"

"Nothing." He chuckles and helps himself to my chips. "Who are you looking for?"

I sigh a little. "My brother. He's playing for the opposite team."

"Ah. I'm sure he'll go easy on him. If Maxipad wins this one, he's gonna be in the best fucking mood tonight. Note that. If you want something, ask tonight."

"I have everything I want," I say, smiling at the freshly clipped grass. In the corner of my eye, I see Bronson staring at me with the same unapologetic gaze Max has, and then he smiles. "You love my brother."

I grin down at my lap, my cheeks hot. "*Stop it*, Bronson."

My attention is drawn to the field as a voice introduces the away team. They run on and I scan the faces and numbers, hoping I don't see...

Frick.

But at least Konnor looks stronger than the last time I saw him. Maybe I won't wince every time Max tackles him...

At the introduction of the other team, I uncross my legs and lean forward in anticipation of Max's entrance. All the players jog onto the field. My Max: number three.

I hold my breath as Konnor stares in Max's direction. When he turns to search the bleachers, I breathe out slowly. His eyes land on me. I wave at him and smile. The one he returns is tight, but still visible even from a distance.

The players move to the sideline. The crowd quiets. Then the whistle blows and the two teams are slamming against each other in the scrum. The ball is fed through the centre.

And it's game on.

I absolutely love rugby, always have. It's the perfect combination of agility, speed, and strength. It's fast-paced and unpredictable. Of course, I'm rooting for Max and Konnor and not a specific team. When Konnor lands a try, I jump up to applaud. When the people around me glare, I let out a nervous laugh and sit back down.

I watch intently when Max is passed the ball. My breath catches in my throat. He runs, clutching the leather to his chest and moving with an agility that leaves me in awe. When he gets to a tight blockage in the line, he passes to someone else, who quickly scores a try. Max is then tossed the ball at the sideline where he kicks it through the goal.

We all go wild.

Bronson stands up and claps. "Fucking yeah!"

The girls in front of us call out Max's name between whistles and cheers. Max's teammates mob him, bounding around and patting his back. The huge easy grin on his face makes my heart flutter.

There really are two Max Butchers.

As the game progresses, I watch with pride. Max is powerful and tackles person after person as they attempt to break through the line. He's an aggressive player. My pulse races. Watching him out there has me in physical discomfort —needy in a way I've never felt before. I shuffle in my seat as I imagine letting him use my body for whatever deviant act he desires.

It's the third quarter. The score is forty to thirty-three in favour of Konnor's team. Konnor has the ball, but he is heading straight for Max and a tight barricade of big bodies. Max lowers his shoulder and darts to the side, preparing to tackle Konnor as he tries to weave through the defence. One of the other players aims for Konnor. It's all happening so fast. I want to close my eyes, but I don’t, despite expecting to see Konnor brutally tackled.

Just as he is about to reach him, Max trips. Falling to the

grass, he takes out his own player. Konnor leaps over them as they tumble to the dirt, then sprints to the try line and grounds the ball.

I blink at the field.

Did that just happen?

Did Max just pretend to fall and take out his own player?

My proud, arrogant Max?

No, my beautiful, family-orientated Max.

"Let me guess, number ten is your brother?" Bronson says, amusement in his voice.

I catch him smirking and shake my head in disbelief. "Did he do that on purpose?"

Bronson's expression says yes. "I've never seen him take a fall like that. I'm gonna give him so much shit."

Max is up and watching the commotion. Konnor glares at Max from the try line as his mates jump around him and celebrate. Max raises his fist in the air and then points in my direction, his eyes still trained on Konnor. I breathe out fast as Max jogs back into position as if nothing even happened. And it reminds me of the first time I saw him...

The Dingoes win fifty to forty-seven.

Konnor finds me as Bronson and I wait for Max to leave the shower block. Konnor eyeballs Bronson, his closeness to me, the licks of ink crawling up his neck and down his hands, his staunch stance. There is a confidence to The Butcher Boys that can't be described. It is in their faces, their posture, and their eyes. Bronson's confidence is accompanied by mischief, while Max's is by warning.

"Did you hire a bodyguard?" Konnor asks, wiping sweat off his brow.

I rush to him and we embrace. He lifts my feet off the ground and spins me. "How's my beautiful sister?"

"How's my beautiful brother? I've missed you."

He places me on the ground. "Well, for once, I'm the one at home. You're the one who is always away."

Feeling Bronson behind me, I get a tingle of shame. "Sorry. This is Bronson. Have you two met?"

With a cool grin on his face, Bronson leans in and offers Konnor his hand. "No. I haven't had the honour. You must be the brother. Slater, am I right?"

Konnor looks at Bronson's hand and then takes it. Their shake is firm. "Yeah."

My breathing becomes a little shallow as I observe their interaction. I glance from one man to the other. Konnor's clearly wary, but Bronson's grin is charismatic and easy going.

Konnor looks back at me, his gaze going down to the slither of skin peeking out between my jeans and shirt. "You look all grown up."

My hands fumble with the hem before pulling it down. "I've been *all grown* up for a while."

He sighs. "You just look... *different*."

"I'm not," I assure him.

Konnor reaches for the corner of my mouth and wipes something off. He shows me his finger, which has a bit of tomato sauce on it. "At least you still eat like you."

My face radiates heat. "Oh my God! Bronson, why didn't you tell me I had sauce on my face?"

Bronson laughs. "I thought you were saving it for Max."

Konnor cringes at Bronson's words, but doesn't comment. Two pretty girls approach Bronson and he gives them his attention while I catch up with my big brother.

"You were so good," I say, gazing up into his lovely emerald-green eyes. "You look so good. So strong."

He grins, his boyish double dimples on display. "Thanks, Pipsqueak. I feel pretty good."

"Cassidy feels good too," Max taunts, walking toward us. He stops just shy of Konnor and looks down his nose.

I frown up at him. "Menace, stop it."

"With that, I'm out of here." Konnor wraps me in his big arms and squeezes. He speaks into my hair. "I love you, sis. Come home soon and spend some time with us."

As Konnor walks away, I turn to face a cocky looking Max. "Why? Why do that?"

"I can't help it. He's so easy to wind up." Max pulls me to him and presses his lips to mine. My mouth opens for him, allowing his tongue entry. I never can stay mad at him. He's playful. I consider for a moment whether he's being playful with Konnor, treating him like he does his own brothers. Taunting harmlessly. I wonder whether he knows any other way to interact... I'm not sure... because now I'm being dragged back to Max's tongue. And my legs buckle. And he lifts me to straddle his waist. "Excuse us," he says against my lips as he walks us towards the toilet block.

We move into the disabled bathroom and he locks the door behind us. He's impatient, rushed—as if lust has been building through him for hours and is now ready to erupt. He unbuttons my jeans while I run my fingernails down the taut muscles of his abdomen.

"Did you like watching me play?" he says against my lips.

I'm already moaning and rubbing myself against him. "Yes."

He spins me to face the mirror. I grip the cold ceramic sink with both hands as he yanks my jeans and knickers down. They bunch around my ankles. He pulls me towards him and kneels behind me, his tongue licking my lips from behind.

"*Beg* me, Cassidy."

"Max, *please*." I push back into his face, inviting him to

take what he wants. I can't believe how shameless I am with him.

He massages my bum cheeks, then spreads them. My face goes bright red when I feel his fingers replace his tongue so he can fervently lick my bumhole.

He works my body well, jaw rough against my skin, tongue greedy, fingers curling to massage the muscles inside me.

Oh my God.

"*Max.*"

My legs tremble and shake. My bum flexes against his tongue. My thighs tighten around his hand as I come hard over his fingers.

His mouth moves away and his fingers slip from inside me. Standing quickly, he tugs down his pants. He fists his penis and not wasting any more time, he thrusts his thick hard ridge into me.

I cry out.

"Good girl. Now watch me fuck you."

He studies me in the mirror, his eyes near black with arousal. He buries himself deep, draws himself out, and drives into me again and again. I gasp and then moan with each slap of his pelvis. I can feel him everywhere. My cheeks are blotchy and pink. My body is thrown forward and then pulled back. I grasp the vanity with all my strength, my hands growing numb. Max's grip on my hips tightens as he pumps into me fiercely. It's near impossible to stay upright. My eyes flutter shut, the sight of him overwhelming my every sense. The pleasure is so intense. A destructive force thrashes through me with every thrust of his hips.

"Open your eyes," he growls.

My eyes flicker open. He wraps my hair around his fist

and pulls until my back bows and my chin rises, revealing my neck and the pulse that runs rampant through it.

"Fuck." He grunts. "Take me, Little One. Take all I have to give you."

I watch his gorgeous face. It's tight and intense. His eyes are a wicked storm of danger and ecstasy—brows drawn in, teeth bared and pressed together. "Good girl. You're doing so good."

I brace myself against the sink, mewling his name. "*Max*."

Grunting, he pumps me with more force. And then he lets out a deep, long, almost excruciating groan as his cock pulses with his orgasm.

His head dips back, mouth open and panting. I try not to collapse into an overwhelmed puddle at his feet.

He finally finds my eyes in the mirror. "Are you okay?"

I swallow and nod. It's all I can manage. As he looks down to where he fills me, he watches his cock slip from between my thighs. I straighten and slowly turn to face him, my ankles tied together by my jeans.

His mouth is still open. His breathing is still laboured. He stares at me with those lovely, wild ocean-blue eyes of his and strokes both hands through my hair before cupping my cheeks. "Was I too rough?"

Moving into his gentle touch, I shake my head. "No."

His eyes narrow. "If I'm ever too rough, you have to tell me to stop."

I nod. "I will."

He grins, and I love that I'm the only woman who gets to see this side of him. "That was *unreal*," he says.

We clean up, Max taking care of me like he always does. As we exit the room, he entwines our fingers. Several people stare at us. My eyes dart to the grass and I don't look up. My cheeks feel hot with embarrassment. I was loud. Max was loud too, but his head is held high, completely unaffected by the attention we have.

"I'm so embarrassed," I murmur as we walk to the car.

Max just laughs. "Don't be. You sound beautiful when I fuck you."

CHAPTER TWENTY-EIGHT

prince not charming

IT'S eleven p.m. on a Wednesday night. Max's fingers are threaded through mine, pinning my palms to the mattress. He's thrusting deep inside me from behind when an erratic knocking shakes the bedroom door.

"Fuck," he groans as he flexes his penis inside me. "Not now!"

I moan laboriously into the pillow. "*Max*," I beg. I do that now, when he teases me, when I'm desperate for him. I beg. He's made me this needy. I wasn't before. Now, I struggle to go a day without an orgasm.

"Max! I got a page." Xander's voice shakes.

He growls, thrusts two more times, and then crawls off me. His erection squeezes out from between my thighs and slides across my leg. I whimper at the feeling of being so empty and unsated. Rolling over, I sit up straight in his bed and watch him move around the room. Grabbing his clothes, he tugs them on. I'm breathing so hard and wild. I'm so wet and needy, but I wait frozen for him to acknowledge me.

I think I whisper his name. "*Max?*"

Finished dressing, he closes the miserable gap between us and kisses me quickly on the lips. "I'll be back soon."

Then he's gone.

I blink at the closed door he has just rushed through. My belly fills with unease. I want to run after him and beg him not to go, not because I'm clingy, but because nothing good can come from whatever they need to do in the middle of the night on a Wednesday. Closing my eyes, I will the anxieties away. It'll just be family drama. He'll be fine.

The "Family" drama...

Shuddering, I pull the covers up over my body even though I'm not cold. After several minutes alone in his room, I decide to see if Toni is still awake. Retrieving my phone from the bedside table, I find his name and hit dial.

The ringing drops and his lovely voice sings through. "So apparently, we don't do Toni and Cassidy Series Night anymore because you're too busy getting humped by Max Butcher. I haven't gotten a boner for Uhtred, son of Uhtred of Bamburgh, for weeks now and that's all on you."

I laugh, but it's a little weak. "I'm sorry. I'm sure he'll get bored of me soon."

"*Right*. You remember when I said you won't marry and have annoying little brats with the first guy you sleep with? Well, you proved me wrong, Golden Girl."

I place my phone on speaker and shimmy off the bed to retrieve my knickers. I usually sleep naked, but I don't feel comfortable completely bare unless Max is beside me.

"*Oh my gawd*, Toni. Stop it. We are just..." I hesitate.

"In love. You can say it."

The truth is undeniable. Concrete. I know how I feel. My heart is in a constant frenzy because I am so fricking crazy in love with Max Butcher. There is no other word that comes close to describing this feeling, so that one will have to do... Love. I step into my underwear and pull them up. "*He's* not."

"Oh, okay," Toni says dubiously.

"He's not. Stop it. It's not fair on me for you to say that when you don't know if it's true."

He scoffs. "I do know it's true. He's *obsessed* with you. You spend every free moment together."

I smile to myself as I slide back beneath the sheets and look through the large, full-length window. "I'm obsessed with him."

"Yeah. I bet you guys look great fucking. You should film it."

My palm meets my face. "Stop it. How's Braidy?"

"He's good. We're good. We're good at it. I like it." I can hear his smile.

"*Aww*, I like hearing you happy. How are you guys handling his journey from the closet into the bright lights of Gay Land?"

"It's been bright and gay." He laughs. "On the surface, it appears like everyone has accepted us. The only problem is that his parents adore me, so ya know, something must be wrong with them."

"Toni D'Annunzio! Liking you is not a defect."

"You have to meet them. They would love you! And every time I go there, they tell me I'm too skinny and try to feed me." He sighs. "It's really good for my soul. *Oh*, we should double date!"

"Oh *yeah*," I mock. "Let's get your cop lover and my less than reputable boyfriend together and see what happens. Let's just see how crazy stuff can get."

"Oh my giddy aunt. I haven't thought of that. How are we going to work this sitcho?"

"I honestly have no idea."

"So where is Prince Not Charming?"

"Well, he kinda rushed off about five minutes ago and left me alone in his house."

"Was it a call? Another virgin?"

"No, nothing like that." I pause and squirm on the mattress. "I don't think..."

"*Oooh,* go snoop around his house." He claps. "Take pictures. Send them to me."

I roll my eyes. "No."

He squeals with excitement. "Go into Xander's room. Steal me a pair of his underwear. I'll wear them when I feel pretty."

"Oh my God, Toni."

"What?" he says. "Would you prefer to analyse why he left until your fanny dries up?"

I tuck the sheets between my thighs. "Not really."

"Do you think it has something to do with his *work?*"

I sigh. "I know it has something to do with his work."

"You need to talk to him about it." I want to tell Toni what happened the last time I tried that, but it doesn't feel right betraying Max's trust. Talking about it isn't going to change anything. It's not just a job. I don't think he can just quit because his girlfriend doesn't like that kind of behaviour.

These deeds are part of his responsibility, his duty as the son of Luca Butcher. He's the son of a gangster. For him, corruption and intimidation are the norm, a privilege and burden of his last name. I wonder if he's ever asked to break free of it. Hating the thought and wishing I'd never had it, I also wonder if he *likes* being a gangster.

I imagine the power can be intoxicating.

"I can't." I snatch my phone and mute the speaker before pressing it to my ear. "We can't really talk about this here."

"Well, why did you call then?"

I yawn, snuggling deeper into the bed. "I just wanted to hear your voice."

"That's gross. I love you too."

I eventually fall asleep with the phone wedged between my cheek and pillow. My body rolls further towards the edge of the mattress as I hear movement around the bed. Caught in slumber, it takes me a while to draw my consciousness back into the waking world.

My breathing must have changed, though, because I hear Max's deep, raspy voice. "Go back to sleep, Little One."

I settle back into the mattress, spooning my Max pillow tightly to my chest. Sleep numbs the feelings and questions I have, and I begin drifting back into my dreams.

With a slight thump, his shoes come off. His keys jingle. His jeans drop to the floorboards and then something metal clinks onto the bedside table.

My eyes snap open and I stare dead ahead.

My heart leaps into my throat.

Oh my God.

I know what that sound is. It's not like I've ever heard a gun being placed on a bedside table before, but I still somehow know.

I know he keeps his gun in a safe. At least, he did in Bali. The last time I saw it placed out in the open was after he'd passed out with another woman pressed to his body. A little unease stirs me further to suspicion. Is he drunk? It must be late.

The bed dips as he moves in behind me and envelops me with his big, warm body. His chest presses against my back. His hot breath feels like warm silk on my neck. The smell of whiskey, smoke, and shoe polish surrounds me. Despite the heat radiating off him, I'm suddenly freezing. I pull the blanket up, trying to get warm again.

I'm left in two states of mind. One wants to slide out from beside him and investigate. The other wants to fall back to sleep in his arms. I'm supposed to be at peace with the gun. I like the gun. It keeps *him* safe, him in control.

My eyes close. Wiggling my toes, I slide my feet along the soft sheets. I try to concentrate on how his beautiful body is pressed to mine, try to remind myself how lucky I am to even be in his bed. Reminding myself I'd promised not to ask questions, I try to follow him into slumber.

It doesn't work.

I wrap my fingers around his hand and lift the whole heavy weight of his arm off me as I shuffle out from under it. I hold my breath when the mattress moves around, but he's only rolling to face the other direction. My bare feet hit the floorboards, but there is no sound. I tiptoe my way over to stare at his gun.

It looks heavy.

Like, I'd struggle to hold it up and point it at someone. I've never given much thought to the weight of a gun. In the movies everyone can hold one up—even the children. But staring at Max's gun, I think I could probably point it and shoot immediately, but if I was hesitant or holding up a bank or threatening someone... *Oh my gawd*, why am I even on this train of thought?

I shake my head and swallow hard. Stepping backwards, my feet suddenly get caught in his clothes on the floor and I nearly trip. I lean down and scoop them all up. After carrying them into the ensuite, I drop them into his clothes basket.

All the warmth and colour drain from my face.

There are blood splatters all over his shirt.

He's hurt.

My chest tightens so hard that I want to gasp for air. Rushing to his side, I switch the bedside lamp on and pull back the covers, terrified that he's... perfect.

Clean.

My hands tremble on the blanket. I stare at his bare torso as it rises and falls, then glance up to catch his eyes open and fixed on mine. When I jump backwards, he lunges for my wrist and pulls me onto the mattress. He rolls me beneath him, pinning me. Inadvertently pressing my palm to my throat, I feel my pulse thrashing beneath my fingers.

A hard, sad, and determined gaze nails me to the mattress. "What are you doing?"

"I thought you were hurt," I barely whisper. Despite my unsteady voice, I'm not scared. I know he'd never hurt me. He's drunk and naked on top of me. His penis is pressed to my thigh and I'm startled, aroused, and concerned, but not afraid.

"What made you—" He stops talking and looks back over his shoulder at the gun. He squints at it as if he's confused by its presence. "*Fuck*," he hisses.

"It's okay." I touch his cheek, drawing his eyes back to me. "I saw it."

His stare penetrates me. "Yeah. And?"

I gaze into the defensive grey eyes of the man I love. "The blood on your shirt. I thought you were hurt. I panicked."

His lips twitch. "You were worried about me?" He lets out a cynical chuckle. "That's the first thing that came to your mind? Even after you saw the gun?"

"Yes," I admit.

He presses his forehead to mine on a sigh. "You know I'm a bad guy, right? I thought you knew that."

I kiss his lips chastely and we close our eyes. I cup either side of his neck and rub my forehead against his. The feelings between us are thick and overwhelming. "You're many things, Max Butcher, but bad isn't one of them."

He laughs and it's sad and dubious, and his tone forces a sob from my throat.

"I watched a man die tonight," he says smoothly.

Tears fall down my temples. More pool in my ears. I'm not sure I truly register his words or maybe I'm so full of him, I no longer have regard for others. Or maybe I'm selfish. Or maybe I've just been waiting for something like this to happen and now that it has, I'm somewhat prepared. I remember our conversation in Bali.

"DO YOU HURT PEOPLE?"

"Not people like you. Only people like me."

"But people like you have people like me who love them."

"OH GOD." I whimper. "Are you okay?"

"There you go again... Yes, Cassidy. *I'm* okay."

Even though I know he's physically okay, I'm not so sure his soul is settled. I can feel a darkness in him tonight. In the way he breathes. In his taut body.

"What did he do, Max?" My voice falters and my palms tremble against his neck. "What does a person have to do?"

He kisses my lips softly. "It was him or us."

I sob into his mouth. "Max, *no*. It's not that black and white. It can't be."

"He was a bad person, Little One."

"But he was *a person*."

He shakes his forehead against mine, groaning. "I thought you knew this!"

"I don't know what I know!"

When he lifts his forehead, my chest tightens, preparing itself for the hole of his absence. I know he's about to leave. I cover my face, not wanting him to see my anguish.

Fingers link through mine, pulling my palms away and exposing my pain. Our eyes meet. He runs his thumb possessively over my quivering lower lip and studies me closely. I weep quietly from confusion and the truth and my self-imposed naivety.

He winces ever so slightly. "Do you still want this with me?"

My heart aches. "I love you, Max Butcher. I'll *always* want to be with you."

He blinks at me slowly and, oh my gawd, I can't believe I've just told him I love him. I can't believe I've done it right after he's admitted to watching a man die.

I'm so messed up.

But then he rolls onto his back, pulling me on top of him, and manhandles me until I spread my thighs to straddle him. He caresses my spine before gripping the nape of my neck and pulling me for a kiss.

His tongue skates inside my mouth, causing me to moan.

"I want you," I say, desperation in my voice. I need to be close to him right now. I need to get lost in our Cassidy and Max world.

He kisses me as if he's in physical pain. Then he helps me slide my knickers off before repositioning me above his erection. I've never been on top before. He likes to be in control.

My nipples skim his chest, the sensitive buds tightening. I start to whimper as he slides me down his length. It's a new level of penetration. No angle obstructs the depth.

Breaking our kiss, he pushes me upright. And then his hands are back on my hips, controlling the level at which I take him. I stare at him. He stares at me and then his eyes flutter as he forces me down all the way. My body strains to consume the final inches of him. As I recoil slightly, he curses and holds my hips in place, stirring his penis inside me.

"*Max*," I think I cry out.

My eyes squeeze shut.

"It's okay, Little One. It'll only hurt for a moment." He barely gets the words out through a long deep groan.

He doesn't thrust up into me.

But he also doesn't let me inch away. I can feel him pulsing inside me. We stay very still for several seconds, panting, as I become accustomed to the feeling of being wrapped around the root of his erection.

"Look down," he breathes. "Look at your pretty little pussy swallowing my cock."

Oh God, the way he talks.

I force my eyes open and stare down at where he's opening me, spreading me wide. His penis flexes. My clit is pressed into his neat dark-brown pubic hair and the sight of us has me dripping with pleasure. Encouraging me, Max moves my hips again, rolling me along him in slow, deep, long waves. I'm full, so crammed with him. My orgasm beckons me, so close...

I curl my hips, brushing my clit against him.

He groans, his fingers flexing around my hip bones as he wrestles with his need to *take* me. Longing, feverish and intense, brews inside me.

"Do that again," he begs.

Max Butcher is begging *me*.

I roll my hips again and his hands move to my breasts, palms stimulating my tight nipples. "*Max*," I moan.

"*Good* girl. I like it when you moan my name."

I move faster on top of him. The feeling of his erection inside me, pressing against my cervix, is consuming.

His eyes—heavy and carnal—lap up the sight of me working his erection from on top. He's giving me the control and he's lost all composure in the process. I feel a sense of power. I have given myself to him willingly and often, and he takes and I love it... But right now, I have the reins. I control the speed. The movement. I curl my hips on him until more moisture slides from inside me, until a tingle twists my clit. Until hot pressure forces its way up my thigh and invades my abdomen before crashing together between my legs.

I come hard. "*Max!*"

He bares his teeth, but doesn't move.

I think I'm torturing him.

Once I regain my senses, I slowly move my hips in circles. Panting and buzzing from my orgasm, I try to keep my stamina up. I watch his face, his beautiful, tight, pleasured, and curbed expression. He glares at me through his lashes and his hands glide around my body.

They stroke my trim stomach, cup my breasts, and then fist my hair.

He tugs ever so lightly, sexual rage flaring in his irises. "Fuck me like you love me."

Oh God.

Anchoring myself in his eyes, I lean back and grip his toned thighs. I start to really work my pelvis, lifting and then sliding my backside down to take all of him in again. Over and over. So deep. So overwhelming. My breasts bounce. My hips roll down to draw him in and curl up to squeeze him out.

"Fuck!" He grips me harder, fingers biting at my skin. Then they are on my thighs with a slap, clasping so tight, stirring me along his hips. And now as his hands hold me to him, he's thrusting up into me as he comes. His groaning is long and intense. His penis pulses, forcing cum up into me, but there is no room, so it explodes down the shaft of his penis and spills out from where we connect.

Feeling his orgasm as intensely as I do my own, I spiral into another, coming again. My hands cup his face as I lean forward to kiss him, riding the wave until my body drops to his.

I kiss him hard and desperately.

I kiss him with every piece of unconditional love I hold for him.

Unconditional.

CHAPTER TWENTY-NINE

keep that breathless charm

I'M LEANING over the vanity, applying clear lip gloss and giving myself a thorough examination, when several girls enter the toilet block. They freeze when they see me. It's as if I have a 'kick me' sign on my forehead. I glance at them sideways while continuing to check my hair and makeup. They whisper to each other before separating into different cubicles.

After adjusting my little baby-blue dress, I comb my fingers through my hair, puffing it up to add volume. I feel like a big fake. I don't know why I care so much right now about being perfect. It's just—I haven't been out on a real date with Max in the District before tonight and everyone already thinks he's too good for me.

The girl in the mirror looks happy though.

I *am* happy.

Sometimes I feel guilty that I'm so happy given the moral compass of the man who inspires it. But most of the time, I don't. As nervous as it makes me, I accept my boyfriend is a gangster.

I accept the gun.

I accept what he does with it.

I trust in his character enough to believe he'll make the right decisions for his family. Because in the end they are all that matter. His family and mine. Him and me. Max is beautiful, just a little broken at the moment, but I believe one day he'll go straight.

As the girls leave their stalls one by one, scrutinising me so obviously, I sigh aloud. Collecting my gloss and purse, I leave them to gossip about me in peace.

I can feel Max's eyes following me as I move across the room, so I catch his gaze. Feigning a flirtatious walk, I exaggerate my strut, my hips swaying pendulously and over-the-top. He laughs, and that's why I'll never be cool. He likes me as I am.

I slide in beside him on the booth seat.

So relaxed.

He's dressed in a dark-blue shirt and black vest tonight, looking like a powerful young man. Resting his thick tattooed arm on top of the seat, he plays with my hair and neck as we watch the live jazz band on stage. I sip my port while Max nurses a whiskey. I've never been here before, but Max knew that I'd love it due to the music and, of course, the elaborate menu.

It reminds me of a 1950s club where live music and fine dining collide. It's loud, active, vibrant, and classy. The Minister for Agriculture is sitting a booth over from us. It's a scene.

It's *elite,* I suppose.

And fun.

My favourite Frank Sinatra song comes on—*The Way You Look Tonight.* Max keeps his fingers moving on my shoulder and neck and hair. I glance at him, and he grins at me and mouths the words in time to the song. I'm in heaven. If I could feel any more love right now, I'd die of a heart attack.

Max's nose touches my ear. His breath cascades over my neck, making my skin hot. While I'm trying to concentrate on the music, his tongue feathers the shell of my ear. My knees press together at the exact time he turns towards me. His left hand slides between my thighs and hikes my knee up onto the cushion. Fingers move inside my knickers. Up into me.

"Max. No," I whisper, smiling and breathless.

I turn my back to the other tables, hiding his hand and my face from everyone's view. He fingers me slowly, curling in the right spot. I try to pretend it's not happening, but I want to drop my head onto his shoulder and moan.

His fingers move around, touching every sensitive spot as if he has a road map for each nerve ending. Oh God, I can't restrain myself. Shamelessly, I roll my hips into his fingers, taking more of what I need from them.

I'm halfway through a soft moan when he jerks his hand from between my legs. His knuckles hit the underside of the table, rattling glasses. Startled, I look up at him, but he's glaring over my shoulder. Cheeks burning, I glance over to see a man standing behind me, shuffling nervously beside our table. I hurriedly turn my eyes back to Max.

"Sorry, Max," the man begins. "But there's someone I think you'll want to see in the cigar lounge."

Max holds the arch of my neck. "Are you fucking crazy? Can't you see I'm here with my girl?"

"You'll want to see him," he presses.

"I don't!" Max puts the two fingers that were just inside me into his mouth and sucks on them, all the while glowering at this other man. I am not sure if the man knows what Max was doing but I cover my face with my palms, smothering a mortified smile. I peak through my fingers at Max. He grins at me and I shake my head with a giggle.

Menace.

Max then dips those two fingers into his whiskey, swirls them around, and drains the glass. "I've got better things to do. Go get me another drink."

Shuffling nervously, the guy presses, "You told me to look out for him... Remember? When you got back—"

"Yeah alright. Alright. Fine. Send Nina over here to sit with Cassidy."

My heart jumps into my throat. "Max, no. Where are you going?"

He tries to scoot me from the booth so he can leave. "I won't be long. Five minutes."

I refuse to move. "Don't. I don't want you to." I prepare myself for a scolding, but instead he once again glowers at the man behind me. With quick steps, the man walks away, leaving us alone. Max's expression is soft and playful now, and I have all of his attention.

His hand massages my neck and shoulder. "Five minutes, Little One."

"No." I shake my head. "What could you possibly need to do right now?"

He grins at me and tilts his head. "*Little One*, I'll be five minutes. How much trouble can I cause in that time? Clock me."

I roll my eyes. "Fine, *Menace*. But then you have to dance with me."

"Do you think I wasn't already going to?"

"Really? You were going to dance with me? In front of everyone?"

"Why are you surprised? I'm a fucking majestic dancer."

I laugh and he slides out from the table. As he follows the

other man into a room behind the bar, I sigh. He knows exactly how to work me.

A tall barmaid with burnt umber hair wanders over to me and sits on the opposite side of the booth. "I was told to sit with you. I'm Nina." She rubs her hands down her apron as she smiles sweetly in my direction. With a cute pleated upper lip and violet-blue eyes that are circled by dark lashes, she is very attractive.

I cross my legs. "Okay, well, you don't have to if you don't want to."

She nods. "Yes, I do."

"Okay." I bite my lip idly. "What's back there?"

She tilts her head towards the door, questioningly. "There? The cigar lounges."

"Cool. Can anyone go back there?"

She leans on the table and taps her nails. "No. It's just for VIPs."

I feel a wave of excitement. "Can *I* go back there?"

Her lovely eyes shift around. "I guess. You're with Max."

A wicked grin takes over my face. "So I could get up right now and walk in there and you'd let me?"

She sighs. "Yes. I don't know why you'd want to though."

"Why?"

"Because it's just full of businessmen talking shop. And skimpies. Not the right place for a girl like you."

I blink at her. "Excuse me? A girl like me?"

"Calm down." She shuffles slightly and her breasts move beneath her shirt, voluptuous and heavy. She's striking. I imagine outside of her work attire, she'd be a showstopper. "I didn't mean to offend you. You're Max's date. He's not back there to see them. He's out here with you. You're better than them and he's very protective of you."

I try to listen to the intent and appreciate the words, but I can't help but feel uneasy when a total stranger gives me insight into my boyfriend's intentions and feelings. "I'm sorry, what?"

She smiles despite my tight face. "He will want to keep the world beautiful for you."

"What?" I sip my port. "How do you even know this?"

"Because I can tell. I've known Max for a very long time."

My brows draw together. "How long?"

She's had sex with my boyfriend.

I feel sick.

She deflects my question. "When you see men drunk and surrounded by women who will do anything to get their favour, you see things that make you realise how perverted the world is. How sick men can be. He doesn't want to taint you with that scene. But clubs that bring in an aristocratic demographic also need a private retreat for them to handle their business. That's the cigar lounge."

I roll my eyes and wrap my arm around my stomach protectively. "I'm not a delicate little flower. I know men."

Her head tilts. "Do you?"

I swallow. "Yes."

She smiles at me again. "You don't know *these* men."

My arm tightens around my stomach as it rolls with nausea. "How *well* do you know Max?"

"Very well. I used to live next door to them," she states emphatically. "For many years."

"And?" I stare at her questioningly. "You've slept with my boyfriend."

She laughs. "No."

"Why don't I believe you?"

She laughs louder. "I used to sleep with Bronson. Not Max."

Suddenly, I can breathe again and the wave in my belly calms. *Bronson*. "Oh. Wow. What happened?"

She shrugs and tries to smile, but her forehead is tight as if she's forcing it. "Nothing. He just never really liked me."

"Oh." I sigh and feel a tingle of compassion for her. The Butcher Boys are addictive. If my love for Max was unrequited—and maybe it is—I'd never be a whole person again after we split. I find her sad but resolute gaze. "But you *liked* him."

She laughs as she flicks her hair around. "Liked? I'm still in love with that crazy son of a bitch."

"In this case, you actually can call her a bitch too!" The words just tumble out.

We both laugh and share a knowing grin that only girls in love with a Butcher boy could understand. That love is consuming. I'm sure Bronson is just as intense to be in love with as Max. Just as overwhelming. "Go find him. He's single!"

She releases a little sigh, but a smile still plays on her lips. "He'll probably always be single."

I nod. "I've noticed. He's alone a lot."

"He's a romantic and has never been able to see past Shoshanna."

I lean across the table. "Who is Shoshanna?"

Her mouth drops open. "You don't know about Shosh?"

Max clears his throat and his shadow is suddenly blanketing us. "Shosh is my brother's business. And you, Little One, owe me a dance."

I look up and scrutinise him, searching for something that would tell me what he'd been doing... Like blood. But the dark colours he's wearing camouflage any trace of an altercation.

Smiling, he offers me his hand. When I take it, he pulls

me to my feet, bands an arm around my middle, and lifts me onto my tippy toes. I kiss him deeply.

Then we walk onto the dance floor. As the music turns slow and romantic, I envelop his waist with my arms, cuddling him as we sway.

"What did you just do?" I ask as I listen to his heart beating on the other side of my ear.

He holds me to him, both arms around my shoulders, a hand stroking the back of my head, his fingers running through my hair. "Remember that picture of us on Twitter?"

"How could I forget?" I say, breathing slow and heavy in rhythm with his heartbeat. "My brother had a nervous breakdown."

"Remember some of the comments? Specifically, the ones about you and other guys?"

I exhale in a rush. "*Yes*."

"I've been making sure that they don't do that again."

"Max." I blink into his shirt. "You said to forget about it."

"No. I said for *you* to forget about it. I took care of it. Did you honestly think I'd let some random guys say the things they said and not have words with them?"

I have no answer to that question, but I'm suddenly reminded of the random text messages I'd received. It's probably not a good idea to ever tell Max...

Sighing against him, I listen as the jazz band plays a smooth tune and the blonde girl on stage sings about Chicago in the fall. Her voice is sweet and melodic. A perfect match to this fairy-tale setting. Even after we'd made our relationship official, I'd never imagined moments like this. In the open. For all eyes to see. I'd accepted a kind of hidden, secret love affair with Max Butcher. This is so, so much better.

"Have you had other girls tell you they love you?" I ask, even though I already know the answer. How could they not?

I feel his sigh through his chest. "Yes"

"And did you ever tell them you loved them back?"

His fingers tighten in my hair slightly. "What are you doing, Little One? Don't you think if I had, *you* would have heard it as well?"

"No." I squeeze his waist. "I don't know.

"Look at my actions, Little One. I'm telling you every fucking day how I feel with my actions."

Shaking my head against his chest, I grow disappointed in myself for bringing this up now. After what Nina said about Bronson, I suppose I just want to hear Max say he returns my feelings. I want him to say he loves me. "Does it mean anything to you that *I* love you?

"Of course it does." He holds me away from him, cradling my head with his hands. Lifting my chin, he looks into my eyes. "It means *everything* to me. Why are you asking me this shit?"

"But you've heard it before," I say.

He smiles as if that is the stupidest thing I've ever said. Shaking his head, he pulls me back into his chest and sways with me. "From girls who don't know me. They love it when I'm inside them. They love my cock, not me."

"You express a lot when you're making love, Max. I feel sick when I think about you with other girls," I say as I cuddle him tighter.

"They never meant anything. And I definitely didn't make love to them."

"You still gave a piece of yourself to them," I say. Those words alone make me feel ill, but he doesn't seem to understand. "Don't you see that? Don't you see me? Don't you see me when we make love?"

I feel the rumble of his growl. "Yes, I see you. But I'm looking."

"They do too. They see *you*. What if you weren't my first? This other person would have seen me like that. Wouldn't that bother you?"

His back gets very tight beneath my fingers. "Come here," he whispers and entwines our fingers. He pulls me toward the door he'd entered earlier. The door shuts behind us and it must be soundproof because I can't hear the girl singing anymore.

Curious, I look down the hall. A rich-red carpet leads to an ominous door. Mirrors hang on the walls. Max directs my gaze back to him as he presses me into the wall.

He lifts my chin, his eyes dilating as they fix on me. "What do you want from me? I can't not have sex with all those girls. It's done."

"I know."

"So, what do you want?"

"I just want..."

"Let's get really serious, Little One. That's really what you want, isn't it? This is how I feel." He points at the door. "Out there you're Cassidy Slater. Ballerina. You're a fucking angel." Both of his palms press onto the wall on either side of my head. "But with me, you're *my* Cassidy Slater. You do all the things you won't speak aloud. You let me use your sweet little body for my dirty pleasure. And the other night, *you* fucked *me,* Cassidy." His hands flex on the wall as his lips meet my ear and I nearly stop breathing. "It does things to me, thinking about you being that Cassidy with someone else. I'm the only guy to taste you. To make you come. I filled you the other night and it felt like a goddamn religious experience. I may not tell you I love you, but I'm a scary kind of possessive over you, Cassidy. So do us both a favour and don't ask me how I'd feel if you were with another guy unless you want me to lose my fucking mind."

And my breath leaves me in a rush.

Cupping his cheeks, I pull him close for a quick, soft kiss. "I'm sorry. I was unfair." We breathe slowly together. "I just wanted to hear you say the words. That's all."

He moves into my caress, tight-faced, teeth grinding. "It's not that—"

"You've said everything I need to hear. Keep telling me through your actions, Max."

Suddenly frowning, Max turns his head towards the door at the end of the hallway. I look over to see Jimmy standing with his arms wide and welcoming.

"*Cassidy,*" he coos. "What a lovely sight you are. Max, you've been keeping her from us."

Max stands up straight. "I'm not taking her back there."

"No, of course not," Jimmy states, appearing confused by Max's tone. "It's not suitable for your *bedda* girlfriend. But you have to bring her tomorrow night. You have told her about the auction, *se*?"

Max shakes his head. "She's busy."

"Oh, Max. No." He walks towards us, his black coat swaying, the harness underneath peeking out slightly—purposefully. "I have the perfect piece for her to showcase. You know the one with the half-carat *Diamante rosa*? *Se.* Bring her? *Piffavuriii?* Who could resist it after seeing it around her neck?"

I study Max's stern expression as he says, "She's busy, Jimmy."

My feigned smile widens and I bat my lashes at Jimmy sweetly. "I have a family dinner," I lie.

He claps his hands together in front of him. "*Nun m'anteressa.* I really must insist."

CHAPTER THIRTY

glass is fragile. it also cuts

WHILE WE WAIT on the porch, I straighten Max's black bow tie and try to ignore the desire building between my legs. He looks like sex and danger in his tailored charcoal vest and black shirt. Even knowing his gun is tucked into the back of his pants, hidden by his shirt, doesn't dampen my arousal. An arousal that's stoked by Max's hot stare as he gazes down my body.

I'm wearing an ankle-length, body-hugging ivory gown. A wide slit runs the full length of my leg. The fabric crosses at my bust, sleeves hanging off my shoulders. I wear my hair mostly pulled up, but with a few tendrils falling around my crown and for the first time outside of the ballet, I'm wearing red lipstick. I part my lips to breathe and Max's gaze is instantly there. I know what the menace is thinking. He's not subtle.

Innocently, Max presses his lips to my forehead. His arms find their way around my middle and squeeze me lightly. Rubbing his nose through my hair, he finds my ear. "Your lips look so fuckable."

With my heels on, I barely need to crane my neck to look at him. Fixing him with my most flirtatious gaze, I slowly trace my lips with my tongue. When his eyes drop to watch the show, I giggle. He laughs.

Yep. Nailed sexy.

Bronson appears by Max's side in a black bowtie, white shirt, black fedora, and black suspenders. A glimpse into the intricate artwork that paints the canvas of his body is offered at his hands and neck. I giggle. His choice of attire seems satirical and reminds me of the Chopper moustache he'd been displaying the day I'd met him. He's since replaced that look with a manicured beard.

Max rolls his eyes at his brother. Bronson snaps one of his suspenders and winks at me. "Sister Cassidy, you look stunning."

"You look stunning yourself," I say and when he tips his hat, I giggle again.

We watch as the limousine pulls up, but none of us take a step towards it. Instead, we wait patiently for the rest of our party.

Bronson clears his throat. "Did you know we were supposed to become boxers like Dad?"

I shake my head, smiling.

"But we're just too pretty, hey Maxipad?"

Max stifles a grin and kisses my hair. Xander and Stacey are the last to join us. Xander is in a navy three-piece suit and Stacey is wearing a wine-coloured strapless gown. They're both effortlessly elegant.

Stacey halts when she sees me. "*Ugh*. You're so petite, Cassidy. It's not fair. I used to be the hot one!"

"It's five hours a day worth of training," I say. "And I'd prefer your big boobs and curves any day."

"Oh, get fucked," she says. "You have curves. Your whole *little* shape is perfect."

"I'd still like bigger boobs," I admit.

"Bite your tongue. Your tits are fucking perfection," Max growls in my ear and I giggle.

We climb into the car and it takes off, leaving the prestigious streets of Connolly as it heads towards Stormy River, where the auction is hosted. I want to ask questions. Instead, I stare at the flickering lights of the city on the thirty-minute drive to the outskirts of the District.

I know a little bit about what to expect when we arrive. The diamond auction is an annual tender of Argyle Diamonds, known for its coloured and rare-to-acquire diamonds. I was gifted a white Argyle by my dad on my sweet sixteenth, but its value is pennies compared to the pink diamond I'll be wearing for Jimmy.

As we pull up alongside a sleek black limousine, I watch several people step out wearing masquerade masks. They are dressed to the nines and buzzing with excitement.

Xander and Stacey slide on masks and step out of the car. I turn to Max questioningly and he lifts his hands, sliding a mask onto my face. I shuffle to see my reflection in the mirror. The new addition to my outfit is ivory and lacy and covers me from my upper lip to the middle of my forehead. My lips appear even more red and my usually hazel eyes glow almost gold in contrast to the fair colour of my mask.

I beam at Max. "*Pretty*. I like it."

A mischievous grin tugs at his lips as his eyes scan my face. "No straitjacket. No muzzle. This mask. That lipstick. Your mouth. My cock."

I grin at him. "Crude."

His face softens. "You look fucking *beautiful*."

I grin hard. "*Sweet.*"

"And we all know I look beautiful," Bronson says as he opens the door and slides out of the limousine.

Words dance on my tongue. My cheeks burn at the thought of them, but watching Max's gaze drop to my lips again gives me the courage to speak. "Stick your tongue out. I'll give you a preview."

The grey in his eyes darkens as he sticks his tongue out. I take his tongue into my mouth and suck on it. He fists my hair hard, his grip biting at my scalp. Groaning into me, he reaches for my hand and presses my palm to his erection. His hips buck. My heart pummels inside my chest.

He pulls his tongue out abruptly and nips my lip. "Naughty girl! I have to go out there and as you once pointed out, I'm not easy to hide."

I breathe hard and lick the taste of him from my lips. "Sorry."

He reaches down to adjust himself, his eyes never leaving mine. My hand finds his thigh before he can exit the car.

"Max. Why the masks?"

"These people like anonymity."

I laugh nervously. "But they don't hide anything. You'd still recognise me."

"It's something Jimmy started doing. It offers a sense of privacy and it's infinitely harder to identify a person in a photo with a mask on."

My mouth and throat get really dry. I decide to just nod in lieu of asking any more questions. Gazing through the tinted windows at the gallery, I watch as gowned ladies and tuxedoed men stroll leisurely up the steps and through the arch. Privilege drips from them in the form of clothes, jewellery, and attitude.

"You trust me, right?" Max asks.

I tear my eyes away from them to look back at him. "Only with my heart."

His eyes soften as he squeezes my hand. "And I'm gonna take care of it. Just be the good girl I know you are. The one that read me yesterday when I told Jimmy you were busy. I don't give you enough credit sometimes, Little One, and I should. You read my play. Just do the same in there. And remember, I'm working tonight. I might have to leave you every now and then, but in that dress, I can assure you, I'll have my eyes on you. Nothing should go wrong. We aren't expecting any surprises."

He lifts my mask and kisses me softly. His tongue skates over my lips, tasting me. I moan and he breaks our kiss, sliding the mask down again and ushering me from the car.

"Wait, aren't you wearing a mask?"

"No," he says, entwining our fingers. "I'm six foot four and everyone knows me. It's pretty hard for me to go incognito."

He tries to tug me from the car again, but I pull my hand from his.

"Wait," I plea.

He stills.

"Little One, I can see you're stalling. It's going to be okay. You might even have fun tonight."

I sigh and draw courage from his attentive grey eyes. "*Okay.*"

We step onto the red carpet, where Bronson waits for us. The whole frontage is lit up, lights shimmering in the dresses and heels that pass me by. I understand the appeal of the mask now that I'm wearing one. Just like a pair of sunglasses seem to hide emotions—eyes shifting, pupils dilating—a person's *tells*, the mask hides expressions—weaved brows, blushing cheeks. The mask allows me to observe the other guests inconspicuously.

Bronson and Max flank me, both boys tall and powerful and standing so close that I can smell them. Even though the mood between the three of us is light, their positions warn me to exercise caution.

We are pat-down at the door. The guard touches Max's gun, but ignores it. The female guard frisks me gently, barely touching me. With the slightest hesitation, I enter the bright gallery.

The space is wondrous. It's white on white. Glass. Shiny. Men in suits with earpieces stand staunchly in every corner. Stunning girls walk elegantly around, almost untouchable in their perfection and yet, they display product on their being, beckoning guests to approach. Necklaces. Earrings. Rings. Bracelets.

The overhead lights are absorbed by the facets in the diamonds, making them flicker with additional colours. Colours not found in the diamond without the addition of light.

A lady in a suit approaches us with a silver tray. I expect to be handed some liquid courage, but instead I'm staring down at a thin, softly-looped, white gold chain holding a delicate deep-pink solitaire diamond.

"This is yours for the night, Cassidy," the lady says. I hold my breath as she picks the necklace up and moves behind me. Max's fingers slip from mine, the absence of him seeping deep into my bones. She touches my shoulder with her wrist as she places the piece around my neck. I stand very still even though about twenty sets of eyes have fallen to my décolletage. I desperately try to steady my pulse, but it's an attempt to no avail. My breathing becomes laborious and my mouth parts. I dare not touch

another suited lady who holds an empty silver tray. Before she can reach around and remove the diamond from my neck, I unclip it myself and place the piece on her tray. I don't look at Max as I excuse myself, slowly walking towards the bathrooms.

Once inside, I grip the basin and stare at my reflection. "What are you doing?" I whisper to myself. "Why are you even here? This isn't your scene."

My scene is lounging around in my pyjamas, eating pizza and listening to jazz or playing PlayStation or reading. It definitely isn't elaborate galas filled with passive-aggressive chitchat.

I hate Dustin.

I hate Victoria.

I don't know how I feel about Jimmy, although I like him less and less the more I see the strings he holds. Max's strings. Bronson's strings.

Mine?

Everything Stacey warned me about swims in my mind. My stomach rolls, a thick mixture of unease and champagne curdled together. Bile moves into my throat and I throw myself over a toilet to vomit.

After cleaning myself up, I gather my purse. I'll tell Max I'm not well and hopefully we can retire early.

When I re-enter the main gallery room, Xander's eyes are glued to me. Before I can wander over to him, Dustin blocks my path. "Cassidy, let's see that diamond back around your neck."

Shuddering at the way he articulates the word neck, I shake my head. "I need to get some air. Where's Max?"

"Not feeling well again." He takes one long step towards me before cupping his hands in front of him. "You should really get that checked out."

He gazes at the column of my neck. His eyes are dark-brown voids that scratch at my skin and leave goosebumps in their wake. The champagne is currently doing nothing to aid in calming my nerves.

Max promised me that I would never have to talk to this man alone. "Where's Max?" I say again.

He nods in the direction of a door. "Still with Jimmy. They might be a while."

Xander appears at my side, smiling tightly at Dustin. "Everything okay?"

"Yeah," I say, my voice definitely shaking now. "I just feel a bit strange. I think I'm coming down with something."

"All right." Dustin's hand touches my waist and it takes everything inside me not to slap it away. He walks me a few steps towards a corridor and points down a long run of doors. I stare back at Xander, his eyes still trained on me. "Go to the end. There's a little courtyard out there."

Xander joins us by the corridor. "I'll go with her."

Dustin tsks. "And leave Stacey unattended?"

"Stacey has three guards in this room, Dustin." Xander almost barks the words, and his tone makes Dustin straighten.

Then Dustin relaxes.

It's chilling. His stance. Like the quiet of the sea at night. You know that there are monsters beneath its dark depths, but all you can see is still glassy blackness. "Are you still talking, little Butcher?" he finally says, his voice smooth.

Around the room, several guards watch our exchange closely. Xander clenches his fists on either side of his body as he acknowledges them with a nod. It's not clear where their loyalties lie. With Jimmy, I suppose.

"It's fine," I say to Xander, honestly just eager to get away at this point. I reach for Xander's arm, stroking the tense muscles beneath. "I'll just be outside." Walking away from both of them, I head straight down the corridor, passing five doors as I do. It's well lit. My stomach rolls again, so I clutch at it, wincing slightly. At the end of the corridor, I push the door open and the fresh air greets me. A crisp wisp of air fills my lungs... and then something else. Something smoky. The atmosphere is not quite right.

The door behind me closes on its own. A shadow in the corner moves.

"*Ah*, thank you, God! This is a sign," I hear someone say.

Squinting as the shadow moves towards me, a face is gradually revealed. Erik. He's smoking something that is definitely not tobacco. The herbal remedy wraps him in thick, pungent smoke.

"Stay away from me," I say as I turn for the door handle, only to find it has locked behind me. Erik is quickly beside me, pressing his fist to the door. Tugging on the doorknob, a shaky breath expels my mouth. I spin to scowl at him, my lips curled up in disgust. My eyes well, but I wrestle with them so they don't expel tears like rain. But they want to.

His gaze shifts around my face before fixing on a single tear as it slides down my cheek. "We got interrupted last time I found you. This is a little gift from God. He owes me."

I narrow my eyes with defiance.

He grins. "Did you get my messages?"

Oh God.

My throat tightens, but I manage to say, "Are you crazy? Max is going to kill you."

He laughs and the hysteria in it chills me to my core. "Max is going to kill me?" he mocks. "Do you think I care if I die? *This* is all I want. This is all I asked for. Revenge. It's the only item on my bucket list. Dustin wants my revenge as well, ya know?" He leans in, his eyes wild. Crazed. "He doesn't like your brother either."

A whimper escapes me without my permission. His hand slides up the slit of my dress and I tense, willing myself not to break down as I begin to vibrate with fear against the door. My eyes drop to his hand as I feel two fingers push against the thin fabric between my legs.

Where are *my* hands? What are they doing?

Push him away!

My head screams Max's name.

Max!

But my lips do nothing but draw in air.

"I have no life. I have no interest in living like this... with this face," he hisses.

My teeth tighten as I stare at his disfigured face. I will myself to hold my own. Don't break down. His cruel brown eyes crinkle in the corners at my attempt to stay strong. He chuckles a little, which causes another tear to fall from my eye.

As he talks, he leans in until his lips are pressed to my wet cheek. "I want to take something from him. He took Blesk from me. She was mine first. The only girl I've ever loved. I didn't even know that he had a sister until I saw you in The District News. So pretty as well. Such was my luck that day. And now this day. Of course, I didn't realise that Max Butcher had already put his cock inside you. That was a bit of a disappointment."

It's hard to breathe as he presses his forearm into my neck, pinning me, near airless, against the door. His other hand—oh God. It begins to rub me through my knickers. I squeeze my eyes shut, pleading with my body not to respond, not to betray me. Although I'm frozen, my heart is riotous in my ears. I imagine fighting back. I imagine slapping him. Frozen by fear, my body isn't responding to my demands. To move. To fight. To scream.

"Don't worry, I'm not going to kill you. I just want to fuck his sister like he's fucking mine." His hot, smoky breath slithers down my neck as he slides his fingers under my knickers and inside me. "Women were created to be so weak. Small. Fragile. And with this little part of your body, men can control you. Max controls you with it too. Doesn't he? We literally enter you. Like the devil himself. We enter you."

As Erik moves his fingers inside me, my teeth fix tight, but my throat groans my discomfort.

He chuckles at me. "Does that feel good?"

My mind shifts to a different place. And now I see Blesk. I hear her words about mind games. This is her brother. A driver. He's not nearly as powerful as my boyfriend. Or his family. My eyes narrow on him. "You could never make me feel good!"

As laughter erupts from him, my hands flex at my sides, reminding me that they are there. In an instant my fingers meet the crevassed plane of his face and my nails dig in hard, splitting skin and drawing blood.

Growling, Erik grabs my wrists and throws me forward onto my knees. "You cunt!"

"Max!" I scream, stumbling to my feet just as Erik lunges for me. He fists my hair, my scalp burning as he drags me across the alfresco. My elbows go up to protect my face as he throws me headfirst through a glass table. Shards scatter in the air and drive into my skin. Blood drips down the length of my forearms and onto the floor. With fingers knotted in my hair, he drags me across the ground and drops down on top of me.

"Feisty little bitch. I was just going to fuck you, but now I think I'll cut that pretty little face up."

Oh God!

I gyrate beneath him, flailing my limbs and body, trying to buck him off. His weight compresses my chest, but my knee meets his groin and he keels over onto his back, grasping at his balls. Before I can get to my feet, fingers enclose my ankle, yanking me backwards. A big shard of glass in my forearm digs in deeper as I'm dragged under him.

I claw at the pavement. "Max!"

He grunts with exertion as he slams me onto my back. He rears up and drops his fist into my face, the blunt force of his knuckles blackening the world around me. I let out long, deep groans as I roll around, disorientated.

Squinting up at him, I try to focus on the blood splatter on his jagged face. Try to pull myself out of the haze that has settled around me. Try to ignore his hands. He starts to touch me. The breath on my cheeks is hot, musky and makes my head spin. He's suddenly squeezing my breasts so hard that pain shoots under my arms and around the back of my shoulders.

When I regain my sight, nasty bloodshot brown eyes scowl at me. I feel the shard in my forearm shuffle between gashed skin.

Glass is fragile. It also cuts.

I reach for it, pull it out with a long throaty cry and thrust it into the side of Erik's neck, pushing it through the soft, mushy flesh.

Those cruel eyes widen.

Instantly, blood begins to pour from the incision. I kick him off, straining for breath, and scamper on my knees to the door. When I reach the door and he still hasn't come after me, I turn to watch as he rolls onto his back. Blood splutters as guttural sounds escape him.

Pressing my back to the wall, I watch him choke on his

own blood. The piece of glass in his throat moves as he swallows and groans. Fearful glossy brown eyes stare at me.

I'm not shaking anymore. My body is perfectly still. A little cold, perhaps. My breathing is deep, steady, and precise.

The door beside me opens and Max strides out, his back to me for a moment.

Then he turns.

Narrowed grey eyes wrap themselves around me. Bronson and the scarred guard I'd seen at the wedding are beside Max in an instant. Their eyes fall to me on the floor, taking in the blood and glass. Xander bursts through the door next.

Completely ignoring Erik gargling on his own blood a few metres from my outstretched feet, the Butcher brothers drop to my side. One of them immediately wraps the wound on my forearm with something soft; a piece of fabric—a tie, I think. Big warm palms cup my cold, wet cheeks. Max searches my expression. Dropping his eyes, he studies each cut, scratch, and gash on my body as if creating a record in his mind. The stormy grey rings around his pupils thin to near nothing.

"She's in shock," Bronson murmurs, his voice soft, chilling. The voice of Mr. Hyde to his Jekyll. So, unlike the man I know. He gently strokes my hair.

Xander's eyes are frozen open. "I'm so sorry, Cassidy! Max, I'm so sorry."

I watch Max's face contort. Snap.

Break.

He jumps to his feet, swiftly and deadly. Pulling his gun out from the back of his pants, he points the muzzle between Erik's eyes.

"Stop," I say as I try to climb to my feet.

And to my absolute disbelief... Max does.

Bronson helps me stand. My legs are weak and sore, having been twisted and hauled around. Xander stands like a statue—stone cold. The other man merely steps back inside the corridor and closes the door behind him.

Max lowers the black pistol to his side as I approach him. While I stare at his profile, he doesn't seem able to break his pointed watch of Erik—or maybe he just can't look at me...

His eyes glisten in the low light of the courtyard. Something is very wrong in his dark mien... irredeemable pain. Unimaginable rage.

My gaze bounces from the lethal look in my lover's eyes to the look of fear in Erik's. Briefly, Erik looks relieved to see me standing over him. Doesn't he know he's going to die? I told him as much a few minutes ago and now his blood is pooling around his neck so deep it appears near black.

Max grabs the barrel of the gun and offers me the black handle to take.

"Max, no," Xander begs. "She shouldn't—"

"Hush, Xander," Bronson orders.

I blink at the gun for a moment... And then my fingers enclose the cool, hard piece with little more thought.

"Both hands," Max states, his voice toneless—almost disembodied.

Clenching my jaw, I grip it in both hands. It's not nearly as heavy as I'd originally envisioned. Should I feel remorse right now? Or is this just another contradictory piece of myself being discovered? A piece that's sick of people underestimating me. Sick of people calling me weak and fragile. A piece so very sick of people *fucking* with my family! I lift the gun, stare at the whites of Erik's eyes and pull the trigger.

I feel the power in the piece as it unloads. Like a pulse within my palms. The bang should be loud, but I'm not sure I can hear it properly. A kind of fog has settled in my mind and it's as if my feelings have been cauterised to the point they no longer exist. It's like confusion, but without the loss of information. I understand everything happening, but my response isn't natural—isn't Cassidy.

I pull the trigger again. Before I can pull it a third time, Max wraps his hand around the barrel and takes the gun off me.

Erik isn't choking on his own blood anymore.

CHAPTER THIRTY-ONE

there are secrets here

IT'S ONLY BEEN a few minutes, but as I try to recall what just happened, it feels like I'm reaching for a vague memory from childhood. I envision myself holding the gun and shooting Erik in the face, but in my memory I'm a spectator. Not the one holding it. Not the one shooting. There is a disconnection between my body and my mind—a severance of soul from form.

Sadness. Desperation. Feelings are slowly re-emerging inside me, but they have nothing to do with Erik's death. Or the fact that I've killed someone. A person. A person who has people like me who care about them. None of my feelings are for him or them. They centre around Max. My Max. The man unable to tear his eyes away from the corpse on the floor.

I squeeze my eyes shut and pray this is nothing but a nightmare. That I'll wake up and be back in bed with him. We won't go to the auction. Instead, we will stay cuddled up together in the peace our love offers us. I'd stare at his relaxed mien and he'd touch me, fingers declaring his love for me more strongly than any word could.

But now, as I open my eyes to the dark courtyard and that corpse... our peace and his relaxed face are a distant memory.

And so I don't care that Erik's dead.

"Dustin wants my revenge as well, ya know?"

"Dustin..." I murmur the name as Erik's words tumble back to me. "He sent me out here." *Oh God*, is that what my voice sounds like?

"Fuck!" Max barks and strides towards the door, but his brothers form a barricade with their bodies. I take a step backwards, my hand now gripping the fabric around my gashed forearm. It stings. Like a burn.

"Don't open the door, Carter!" Bronson yells through to the man on the other side.

"Open the fucking door, Carter!" Max states.

"Don't be stupid, Max. What are you going to do!" Xander yells.

"I'm going to shoot Dustin in the fucking head," Max replies, his voice lacking any warmth. Or rationality. Or hope. His face is racked with grief.

I'm frozen in place, wanting to reach for Max's arm. Wanting to comfort him, but I'm in slow motion compared to him because he's pulling his gun out now and pointing the muzzle at his brothers. His arms shake violently with restraint. His heart may be broken, but his body is a live wire ready to burn anything or anyone that gets in his way.

"Get out. Of the. Fucking. Way," he hisses.

Something inside me screams for him to stop, but the words won't reach my tongue. His brothers stare down the barrel with understanding; both sets of eyes are pained and sympathetic. The whole scene makes my soul shudder.

"Max, don't be stupid," Xander pleads, his brows slumped.

"Put the gun away, you crazy son of a bitch," Bronson orders, pulling Xander behind him, clearly unsure at what length Max might go to avenge me.

Slowly shaking his head in warning, Max's narrowed eyes dart from one brother to the other. "Signùri pensaci tu! Move. Now."

He looks at me briefly and his expression *kills* me. Where his heart used to pump is a black pit. I want more than anything to press my body to his so we can share mine. Because mine is still there, beating fast. For him. For us. Tonight changes nothing for me. But for him... I don't see us in his eyes. I don't see hope for the future. Our future.

My breath catches when the door swings open and out storms Butch and the crater-faced man.

"What the hell is going on out here?" Butch orders, his complexion instantly reddening at the sight of Max with his pistol raised. The cords in Butch's neck pulse as he charges at Max. A powerhouse of muscles and training, he throws his fist into his son's stomach. They both grunt on impact.

Max drops the gun on the pavement and keels over, gripping his abdomen. He releases a long deep groan and that sound is enough for me to lose what little content is left in my stomach.

I choke out his name. "*Max.*"

Bronson is beside me before the second convulsion racks my body. He holds my hair away from my face and rubs my spasming back.

"Who did this?" Butch orders.

All three Butcher boys reply in unison. "I did!"

"Bronson, get back inside before Jimmy notices we are all gone," Butch barks. "Xander, you too. No one is to disturb Jimmy tonight! I will take care of this. Now go!"

The hand on my back disappears and my stomach twists again, wringing the dregs of water and bile out. "*Max...*"

Suddenly, a hand grips my waist, the other my shoulder, and even though I'm bent over, facing the floor, unable to see who is touching me, I know that it's him. Nothing feels quite the same as when he's near. As when he's holding me.

"I'm sorry," he whispers, his voice raspy. Fractured. It almost doesn't sound like him.

When I finally straighten, I'm alone with Max, Butch, and the man I now presume is Carter.

"What happened here?" Butch growls, looking from Max to me and back again. Carter stands behind him, a solid and unwavering presence that means business.

Max wipes my mouth and rubs bile and saliva onto his pants. I find his black eyes and they wince at the sight of mine. In this moment, for the first time since Erik punched me, I feel pain in my cheekbone and below my eye.

I find my voice, but am unable to divert my gaze from my Max. "I wasn't going to let him rape me."

Max winces. His eyes squeeze shut for a brief moment. I hear Butch take a step towards us and I turn to look at him. The light from the courtyard flickers around his face as he takes another step, stopping an arm's length away from Max and me.

He studies me, his eyes calculated in their path around my body. From scratch to cut to scratch to gash and back to my bruised eye.

"Good," he finally says. I didn't expect that response. I'm not sure I'd ever painted him as an enemy in my mind, but I'd never placed him as someone I could trust.

Butch speaks frankly. "Was this about the diamond?"

"She took it off." Max wraps his arms around me. There's a tightness to them that might have once scared me, but now it's something I love and need. "This was about her brother," Max says, and my breathing turns shallow.

"Carter, drive my son and Cassidy to the hospital," Butch says, his eyes glued on me.

"Dustin did this!" Max growls, his body vibrating around mine.

Butch's expression doesn't falter. His blue eyes and firm face are unreadable and yet, contemplative. It's as if he's not surprised by the accusation but merely considering his response. Deliberating. I think he knows that Max won't let what has happened tonight rest. It'll fester.

I almost expect an exchange in Sicilian, but then Butch speaks in English. He includes me, offering me an explanation of sorts. Perhaps I'd earned that from him when I'd fought back. All that I know about the head of the Butcher household is that he respects strength.

"Dustin is threatened by us, Max. You know this. Keep that cool head of yours. You're smarter than them. He's a fucking uneducated Australian mutt. Not a slice of Sicilian in him. And we are Jimmy's family now! My son will take over his empire and Dustin threw away the only son he had. I have four sons! We're the most powerful name in this District, son. They just don't know it yet."

"Why Cassidy?"

Butch looks at me. "Two reasons I can see. I doubt he wanted it to go this far, but... To scare her would work to his advantage, yes. Push her away, *se*? He doesn't want the sister of the Slater boy associated with our business and,"—he looks straight at Max—"Jimmy has daughters. Dustin has daughters. I have sons. He's been trying to arrange a pairing between our families for years. There are secrets here. One day, I will tell them to you. Not today. This conversation is over."

Max sweeps me up into his arms, cradling me against him. The warmth from his body is like a radiator pressed to my skin. He's running hot. Maybe he won't let this change us. Maybe he won't withdraw. Disappear into his guilt. No, I won't let him. I'll dig him out with my bare hands if I have to.

My head dips into the curve of his neck and I close my eyes, thinking about the blood all over my dress. Erik's and mine. I feel disgusting. Dirty. The need to shower becomes more important than that of drawing in air.

A hand lightly grips my shoulder, strong and slightly curled—the hand of a boxer. "You have my word, Cassidy Slater. Someone will pay for what happened tonight. *No one* is above my family."

CHAPTER THIRTY-TWO

wish upon a star

AS I SIT in the gallery's kitchen, Max wraps my forearm up with a bandage from the first-aid box. The gash is deep; it'll need stitches. But I don't care about the wound in my arm. It's the distance Max is putting between us that hurts more than a thousand pieces of glass.

He's right beside me and yet so far away. His eyes are a tunnel of darkness with no light at the end. I'm not sure he has actually looked at me yet. Like, has really looked into my eyes since before I'd shot Erik.

After I'm patched up, he leads me to the rear loading bay, where Carter sits behind the wheel of a black limousine.

We drive away from the gallery. Away from that whole nightmare. The car is dark and silent. Too silent.

Staring down at my bloody dress, I begin to whimper. "Get it off me." Desperation controls my movements as I scratch at the dress. At the seams. At the zipper. "Get it off!"

Max is immediately kneeling in front of me, helping me shed that revolting layer. Once I'm sitting in my underwear, he slides back onto the black leather seats, pulls me to straddle his lap, and buries his face in my knotted hair.

With shaky arms I embrace him. I finally feel a wave of sorrow submerge me.

Drag me down.

Sink me.

Max must feel me trembling because his thick, strong arms tighten around my waist. His breathing turns jagged and heavy, weighed down by emotion. I rub my face against his shoulder. My eyes well, the sting of tears biting at the heels of my anger towards Erik. They fall. Down my lips. Down my chin. And now I'm sobbing violently into the curve of his neck.

Max holds me close. One hand moves up to cup the back of my head, fingers brushing my hair. The other bands my waist, pressing me to his warm hard torso. Our heaving chests beat together in a collective erratic tempo.

He leans into my ear and whispers, "If you were me, what would you do to make *you* feel better?"

"My mum sings to me."

"What song? Sing it for me."

My breaths wobble as I begin to sing. "Someday I'll wish upon a star." Suddenly frozen, Max seems to have almost stopped breathing. I know he doesn't understand the love of a mother. A mother singing to her child—the whole concept must be completely foreign.

As I continue to sing, my voice breaks and everything in this car is swallowed up by my grief.

CHAPTER THIRTY-THREE

his words

MAX HAD a change of clothes in the trunk of the limo, so I wore his oversized shirt into the hospital.

They almost didn't let him stay with me. When they saw the black eye and bruises, they immediately thought he'd done it. That I was a victim of domestic violence. The way he held my elbow and scowled at everyone like a dog being backed into a corner didn't help. But he wasn't going to take no for an answer.

We told them I'd been in a car crash, but the finger marks on my thighs and breasts exposed that lie. Eventually I told them that I was attacked. Almost raped, but that I'd fought him off. They sutured my arm, took a blood test, and put a cannula into my hand to administer fluids. Apparently, I was severely dehydrated.

Now all the tests are done, and Max and I are finally alone in my hospital room. I've barely been able to look at him; it's an effort at the best of times, he's so tall. But tonight, he's hard. Stone.

We move into the bathroom and I keep my eyes downcast. Max turns the shower on hot. Steam fills the white clinical room. There is a rail for safety in the large shower bay. It's big enough to get a wheelchair in; I suppose that's the point. Max kneels in front of me to slide my knickers down and I grip his shoulders, stepping out of them. I feel smaller than normal. Like I've somehow shrunk.

After rising to his feet, he begins to underdress himself. Clothes drop to the ground, reminding me of our first intimate time. Floors always look better when Max Butcher's clothes are all over them. I look up at him. The sight of his powerful, muscular body brings me a new kind of comfort. I know how strong he is. How fiercely he'll protect me as long as I'm by his side. A place I don't plan on leaving.

His penis is erect, thick, straight, and solid, and knocking at his navel. I want him. Want him to take away the feeling of another man's fingers on me. Touch inside me. I'm his. All my parts. The ones that are tangible and all the invisible, contradictory pieces that make up me.

They are all his.

We step into the shower together and I rest my cheek on his chest as he begins to wash my back and arms. Our naked bodies touch. That beautiful long ridge is squashed between my stomach and his hips. His fingers move around my body with gentle possessiveness, lathering me with soap and water. The hot water has brought a pink glow to my skin, especially around the mound of my breasts. Max probably can't see them; they are squished against him, but I'm sure he can feel my nipples. Hard. Aching. In any other situation. On any other day. He'd have taken me by now. But tonight his touch is like a feature. His hesitation makes me feel like a broken bird. A broken pigeon.

Not a falcon.

The sorrow I'd felt in the car is replaced with a frantic

need to feel normal again. As quickly as possible. I want to run a marathon to normality. To have every emotional state settle into their rightful places and not change the perfect world Max and I have created for ourselves.

I want him to look at me. In the eyes. I lift my head, resting my chin on hot, smooth tattooed skin. "Look at me, Max."

He peers down at me, his gaze vacant—like something is missing. "I am."

"Properly," I say as I drag my fingers up his back and down again. "Like you used to."

His brows draw together. "I am, Little One."

"You're not. You're looking right through me," I say, my voice faltering. "It's like you can't stand the sight of me."

Shaking his head, he narrows his eyes. "That isn't what this look is."

"I want you to touch me." I reach for his hand and bring his fingers down to the delta between my thighs. As desire builds through me, I become desperate for him. He clenches his jaw, trying to stifle his groan as I use his fingers to stroke my lips. "I'm wet for you already, Max."

"No, Cassidy. Not tonight."

Sinking like a boulder into the pit of my belly is fear. Fear he's going to leave me. Fear he doesn't want me anymore. Need me anymore. "Please, Max. I'm not ruined."

"What?" He pulls his hand away from mine and grabs the side of my neck, finally staring into my eyes like he used to. Penetrative. Intense. "Don't ever say shit like that to me!" he growls, low and deep, and I love the angry undertone.

Wanting him to channel that energy and release it between my thighs, I whisper, "He didn't touch me that much. Just a litt—"

"Stop trying to downplay what just happened to you,

goddamn it! You don't need to do that." Stroking the bruise below my eyes with his thumb, he winces as if it causes him physical discomfort.

I put my hand over his. "I want to."

"Well, if you want to, then fine. But don't you fucking dare do it for me. This can play out however you want it to. No one is going to tell you how to feel."

"Please touch me then. That's what I want," I beg. "Please. I want to feel your fingers. Your tongue. Your penis. Anything. Everything. Please."

He leans into my ear. "Do you want me to fuck you with my tongue, Little One?"

Relief fills my chest when he kneels in front of me. His hands adore my legs and thighs, tracing the curves, squeezing the soft flesh. I shouldn't want this after what happened. This is shameful. But it's normal. For us. This is normal and that's what I crave. Our world. Our thing.

He pushes me back until I'm wedged between him and the shower screen before lifting my leg onto his shoulder. His tongue dives between my lips. I buck immediately at the feeling of his penetrative, greedy kiss.

"*Max.* More," I moan and his tongue assaults me from every angle. "*More.*"

His mouth closes around my clit like a vice, sucking hard. Arching on the wave of pleasure he's summoning, my thigh twitches on his shoulder. His hand slides up between my legs, and a thumb pushes between my lips, rubbing the muscles inside me as they knead back in want. In desire. The intensity of his strokes and the heat of the shower is consuming.

"Fuck, Little One," he groans against my skin. "I'll always want you. I go insane for you."

God, he's so good at this. Squeezing my eyes shut, my

head drops back onto the shower wall. I purr into his face, rubbing myself against the rough stubble on his jawline. His lips and tongue are hot on my clit. Fingers stimulating every nerve ending inside me. Steam blankets us. That sweaty, wet lethargy of our world settles into my soul. He's greedy tonight, insatiable, unrestrained. It's dizzying.

Weakening...

"WOMEN WERE CREATED SO WEAK. *Small. Fragile. And with this little part of your body, we can control you. Max controls you with it, too. Doesn't he? We literally enter you. Like the devil himself. We enter you."*

I FREEZE.

No breath.

Max gets wilder between my legs, but now it makes me cower.

I want it to stop.

I start to sob, loud and unsoundly. Pushing him away, I fall onto my bum.

Max is staring at me now. "Cassidy?"

I pant, taking shallow breaths. I'm not sure how much time goes by while I try to swallow air, but it's long enough for Max to scoop me up and into his arms. Pressing his back to the shower wall, he holds me between his outstretched legs. My face presses against his warm chest. His arms wrap around me, rocking me.

Pulling wet hair from my face, he whispers in my ear, "I got you. We'll go as slow as you want. For as long as you want."

"Tell me something good," I sniffle, staring at the spray of water hitting the tiles around our bodies. Tears sting my eyes, but nothing falls. I've run out of tears. I didn't know that was possible. When I recall the feeling of Erik's breath on me, his fingers between my legs, my pulse quickens further, and I clutch my stomach as it rolls with nausea. But I've already emptied it. Now it's just pulsing to no avail.

I really have been *A-less* for such a long time. But now, Action, Angst, and Anguish are a part of my being. If I was to dance Nikiya tonight, the audience would weep...

Wrapping my hand around his bicep, I say, "Tell me something so I can stop thinking about his words." Words that have changed acts exclusive to an intimate and trusting world with Max alone into something that makes me feel weak—used.

"Okay, think about mine," Max says. "Do you want to know how I feel about you?"

I nod against his chest.

"I never knew how good it would feel to have someone in this simple way. Someone to hold, like this." He squeezes me closer. "If I knew, I would have come looking for you the second I could think for myself... But I never knew how much I'd want it. I had no idea how good it would feel to make *you* smile. *Fuck me,* I'd do just about anything to make you smile. When you smile at me and I'm the reason... it feels better than being inside you. I'd give up sex to make you smile."

I think I giggle, but it's strange. Choked. Half a sound.

"The weirdest things start to happen when I'm with you. I wanna talk to you. Fuck, yeah, we do that a lot. I didn't know I had anything to say... but when I'm with you, I wanna tell you about my day... and I wanna hear about yours." He gently pushes me from him and cups my cheeks as if they were made of glass. He tilts my head up to see the intensity in his eyes. "I will *never* let anything like this happen to you again. *Never.* Do you hear me? Never." His hands shake on my face. "Say it. Say, 'Max will never let anyone hurt me again.'"

As saliva builds up in my throat, I swallow hard.

"I let you down," he continues. "I won't do it again. I'll never forgive myself for what happened tonight. I thought I was impenetrable, and *I* am, but then you came along—*fuck.* Just say it for me."

"Max will never let anyone hurt me again," I whisper because I know he needs to hear it... Not because I believe anyone—not even Max Butcher—can promise such a thing in the face of the world we now share. Either way, I know he'll try. And at this point, there is no going back. If he leaves me, I'll hurt. If I stay with him, I may get hurt.

Enveloping me in his body, his arms around me tighten. "I failed you, Cassidy."

I shake my head against his chest. "No."

"I should have known better... What happened tonight —*Fuck."* He pauses and the silence isn't nice. It's rich in guilt and anger. "I'm going to kill him, Cassidy. I'm going to kill him for you."

CHAPTER THIRTY-FOUR

loving me

"*GOLDEN GIRL*."

My eyes slowly bat open. The first thing I see is Max asleep on the hospital chair in front of my bed. Then I roll towards the door and find Toni quietly approaching me.

It takes only two seconds for all the images and conversations from last night to spit into my mind like a dramatic woodchipper, throwing the blended chips of events at me. As I remember those cruel brown eyes, my breath catches. I see myself pushing Max away in the shower, falling to my bum, and trembling in his arms like a stupid, traumatised little girl. I can't let last night control me. I won't.

My eyes land on Max again. His arms are folded across his chest—thick chiselled biceps bulging under his tucked hands. I've been a part of his world for three months and in that small amount of time, I've already seen my fair share of violence and intimidation. How does he have any gentleness left inside after twenty-four years surrounded by murderers, kidnappers, and cruel bastards?

I remember a few months ago when he'd told me that I

soften his life. I really understand that today. His world is hard. Hard physically. Hard mentally. Hard to navigate. Hard in every aspect of the word. His face twitches for a moment, so I wonder if he's dreaming about last night. About me.

God, I love him.

He deserves a little softness in his life. There is no way I'll be taking that from him.

Rolling my shoulders, I'm pleased to discover that I'm not as sore this morning and that my nausea has settled. I peer down at the cannula in my hand; it moves beneath my skin when I flex my fingers, and I hate that feeling. When I find Toni again, he's in an emotional state—eyes welling up, swallowing hard.

Stopping beside me, he says, "I don't have words."

I lick my dry lower lip as I whisper, "That's a first."

The emotions spill through him almost uncontrollably. Turning to hide his face from me, he takes a few moments to collect himself.

Sitting up straight, I feign a sense of composure. "*Jebus,* do I look that bad?"

He turns back toward the bed, and through a teary giggle, he quietly replies, "Yes."

To my absolute surprise, I grin at him. "What are you doing here?"

"Max called me." His gaze bounces to Max. "Are we going to wake him up?"

My eyes land on Max again. Usually his face transforms when he's deep in slumber, reminding me he's just a young man; it's easy to forget such a thing when he's taking on the world, standing staunchly, power radiating from him. Right now though, he's tight faced and his breaths in and out are rough—angry.

"I think he's out for now," I say through a sad sigh.

"Let's go get a coffee from the hospital canteen."

I glance around, attempting to decipher the hour, but the curtains are drawn shut and the lights are dim. "What time is it?"

"Nine in the morning."

"There is no way I can leave this room without waking him up first. If he wakes up and I'm not here, he won't handle that well."

Toni nods. "Usually, I'd insert a caveman joke here, but given the circumstances, it doesn't feel right. I'm sure I'd also come up with a good innuendo to do with inserting things into cavemen, but I'm not on my game this morning."

I smile at his attempt to lighten the mood. When I shuffle over to make room on the bed for him, Toni kicks his shoes off and slides in beside me. As he wriggles in to share my pillow, I'm enveloped by his scent. Mint and cologne and Toni.

"Max told me you got attacked by some guy," he whispers and I hold my breath, wary of how much Max might have disclosed about last night. "But you managed to fight him off? Oh my giddy aunt. He better hope we never find him."

Of course, Max didn't tell Toni everything that had happened. Not only is it incredibly unfair to share such a burden, but I won't put Toni in a position where he has to lie to the man he loves. Although, I know he would lie to Braidy. For me, he'd lie on his death bed and then again at the heavenly gates.

I raise a brow at him. "We?"

He smiles gently. "Yeah. Max and me. We're in a gang now."

I try for a laugh, but it's sad.

"I brought you clothes. Panties. Bra. Jeans. And your Bert and Ernie yellow tee."

"Oh my gawd, thank you." My arms find their way around my best friend, clutching at him. Sighing hard, he pulls me in even closer and we hold each other in silence. Tremoring with restraint, he fights to hold back tears, but my shoulder can feel the drips flowing.

"I'm okay," I say, but as soon as I do, my voice shakes and then breaks on a small whimper. "I'll be okay."

"I'm so angry. I'm so... fucking... *fuck*," he says through a low growl.

I shake my head against his, trying not to cry. "Stop it."

"I want to take you away," he whispers, arms tightening around me. "Away from everyone."

Aware of how secretive my beautiful boyfriend is, I lower my voice further. I'm sure if he wakes up, he'll hear us whispering, but I'm hoping he won't be able to decipher our words. "It's not Max's fault."

"I'm sure it's not, but you're getting hurt. I feel like you have cried more in the past three months than the whole time I've known you. And you have disappeared from your home. You pretty much live with him now."

"I'm in love with him... and he needs me."

His nose touches my cheek. "But what do *you* need, Golden Girl?"

"I need him too," I admit, and nothing has been truer in my whole life.

Toni nods in the crook of my neck. "Oh fuck." A bit of tension has left his voice. "I've already hired a dragon to guard the tower I was going to lock you in. I wonder if they'll give me my deposit back."

"I hope you're not bisexual, Toni." Max's deep, gravelly

voice interrupts us. "'Cause you're touching my girl right now."

Toni relaxes his grip. Kissing my nose, he grins at me and says loud enough for Max to hear, "I find all your female parts completely revolting."

"Excellent," Max says as he appears at my side. He's a beautiful, big presence made up of taut, tattooed skin, lean muscles, and lots of contradictory pieces—pieces that fit perfectly into mine. "More for me."

As I stare at him, my heart wants to dive inside his chest and find its other half. He bares me down with those stunning, intense irises to my bones—to my swollen heart. "Hi, Menace."

His gaze diverts to the door just as I hear footsteps approaching. I sit up and Toni slides off the mattress as a nurse stops by my bedside.

"I'm going to get you a real coffee, okay?" Toni kisses my forehead.

When his lips touch my skin, I smile. "Love you."

"Gross," he says, walking from my hospital room.

Giving the nurse my attention, I twist to face her. She lifts my chart up as if to read from it. "Morning, Cassidy. You slept so well. We administered fluids twice during the night and you slept right through." She lowers the chart. "You must have really needed it."

"I feel a lot better."

She smiles and flicks Max a look. "That's great. Convince your boyfriend to sleep tonight. He refused to go home and get some rest. He's a stubborn one, hey?"

I look at Max, who shrugs indifferently.

"He is," I say adamantly with a light smile.

"We can discharge you today. You've had plenty of fluids over the past ten hours. We would recommend keeping your fluids up though. Drink lots of water. Your sutures are dissolvable, so they won't need removing. However, you should get the incision checked in seven days."

"Okay," Max says from beside me.

When she turns to leave through the door, I notice Carter standing just outside. His back is to Max and me, legs a hip's length apart—a business-like stance.

I peer back at my beautiful, tall lover, who is watching me intently, eyes filled with that gentleness I can't believe he can still manage—for me.

He nods towards the door. "There is someone I want you to meet."

Out of the corner of my eye, I see Carter casually stroll in. A grin meets his lips and it must be the first time he has smiled in my presence because he's not so scary to look at right now. Actually, he has a boyish, mischievous type of grin that hints at an attractive face beneath the scars.

"Miss Slater, I've been wanting to introduce myself since the wedding," he says, his black suit buttoned tight around his broad shoulders and thick waist.

As I turn back to Max, he brushes a few rogue strawberry-blonde tendrils over my shoulder. His eyes are still glued to me, searching my thoughts and feelings and diving beneath my layers. The way his stare can penetrate doesn't feel uncomfortable anymore. In fact, it's very reassuring knowing he's trying to figure me out—wanting the truth. "Carter has worked for my family for over two decades. He used to be Xander's." Max pauses, and his eyes follow his knuckles as they stroke the bruise along my cheekbone. "But he's yours now."

My eyes widen, darting between Carter's cool, calm face and Max's serious, authoritarian one. "I'm sorry, what?"

A little grin tugs at Max's lips. "You don't need to feed him or anything."

Carter just laughs. "I'm pretty low maintenance."

"And he doesn't need a place to sleep, right Carter?" It wasn't a question despite being phrased like one.

Carter nods. "I don't plan on sleeping ever again, boss."

Although I appreciate the attempt at humour, it's not settling the discomfort rolling through me. For a few moments, they let me absorb what they are saying without further information. "I'm sorry. I'm confused," I finally say.

"You don't have to acknowledge him if you don't want to." Max squats down beside the bed until his eyes are set lower than mine, and it makes me wonder whether that move is strategic. Max is excellent at observing body language. He's no fool.

Is he trying to appear less domineering? Is he lessening the blow of giving me a fricking guard dog—who is human?

He smiles at me, his blue eyes intense in a way I've never seen before. Assured. Ready. For what?

Me?

Us?

"He can drive you anywhere you want to go. But you don't have to drive with him. I know you might want to drive..." He stifles a tight smile. "*Lady*... but he'll be driving behind you."

I clear my throat. "This is weird. You're acting weird."

"No. Well, to the first part anyway." He shakes his head a little. "Our biggest overhead is security. It's very common. Aurora has four guards. Stacey has three."

"And I only get one?" I say it as a joke because the whole concept is laughable.

A slow, sly grin meets his lips. "Only one you'll see."

I breathe out fast. "This is insanity."

When he reaches for my hand, I look down to watch his tattooed fingers stroke mine. Running the full length of his ring finger is a new tattoo that I'd never noticed before. It reads: *Ardente One*.

"If I'm busy, at work, or you want to go out somewhere, he'll take you. To the movies. To dinner. Whatever you want."

My mind is swimming. "Aren't you going to take me to the movies and dinner and—"

"Of course, Little One. This is just for when I can't be around. You can get him to take you on dates or watch you rehearse. And I don't need to worry about you falling in love with him because he's fucking ugly."

Carter laughs again. "But I'm not as scary as I look."

Somehow, I doubt that...

Between this conversation and Max's hand stroking my fingers with such gentle, chaste love, my breaths become shallow and uncontrollable. "I don't—"

"I'm taking this thing between us very fucking seriously now." His eyes leave mine for a moment. His jaw tics. "*Fuck*. It's how it should have always been done. You kinda snuck up on me, Little One. Our relationship wasn't something I was planning on."

"I'm not sure—"

His other hand reaches up, sandwiching mine between his big warm palms. "Do you still want in this with me?"

My breathing stops altogether for a second. "*Yes*."

"This is part of the package."

Still holding my hand tightly between his, he stands and then sits beside me on the bed. I crane my neck to look up into his grey, emotion-ridden eyes. Dark. Intense. *Ready*. Leaning in until his nose touches my cheek, his hand slides along my thigh and up to grasp the nape of my neck. With worshipful fingers, he strokes the skin at my neck, summoning flutters throughout my body and deep within my heart.

When he turns his face until our lips lightly touch, my mouth opens and breathes into his. His into mine. Then his mouth presses against mine. Deep. Humming. Loving. Loving me with his kiss. With his actions.

Loving me...

And when he pulls his lips from mine, I feel my heart hammering against my ribcage in the best, most dizzying way.

His mouth moves to my ear as his grip on my nape tightens. "Max is never going to let anyone hurt you again."

And this time, I believe him.

cosa nostra - book two

Get book now!

"I love you, Max Butcher."

Those words are dangerous. Just about as dangerous as the world I was born into. As dangerous as the people I call my family.

They hurt her.
My. Little. Ballerina... My piece of purity.
They hurt her...

I wanted to keep the world beautiful for her.
I failed.
So I should let her go. For her own safety and my sanity.
But she crawled into my bed. Settled in my head.
Cassidy Slater.

Her sweet-talking mouth says those dangerous words.
Words I didn't know that I craved. She waits for me at night.
Accepts the darkness around me.
Now that's not something a man just lets go of.

I'm a selfish bastard too.

And she's mine.
I'll protect her; it's an eye for an eye and I'm willing to blind the whole damn lot of them.

For her, I'll start a damn war.

Get book now!

a butcher boy short story

14 years earlier.

"Come in here, boys."

Max and Bronson shut the lounge room door and press their backs to it. They hold their breaths, trying to pretend that they aren't here.

"Come on, Max. I saw you."

Glancing at each other nervously, they shuffle their feet before pushing the door open and entering the foggy room. Tobacco hangs in the air in a thick cloud. They strain to see through the dense atmosphere as they move to sit opposite Jimmy, Butch, and the Family associates.

The men sit on the lounge, cigars in their mouths, smoke filling the air, liquor on the table. They sit expressionless. Their suits look freshly pressed and impeccable.

Jimmy shows his teeth as he bites down on the thick cigar between his lips. "What did you hear?"

They glance at Butch. The weight of their silence grows dangerous and dense. Their father folds his arms across his chest and nods at Jimmy. "Go on, boys. Tell Uncle Jimmy what you heard."

Max clears his throat. "Nothing."

"That's a very good response, Maxwell, a very good response... For anyone besides me." Jimmy sucks the contents of his cigar in, puff by puff.

His eyes narrow on the boys.

Bronson leans against Max. "You got problems with Mr. Mallick."

Jimmy bursts into a fit of laughter so loud the boys flinch. They straighten, frowning at Jimmy's derision and feigning fearlessness.

But they are definitely scared of Jimmy.

They'd be damn fools if they weren't.

Jimmy curls his lips around the cigar and leans towards them. "You want to help Uncle Jimmy?"

The boys look at each other, unsure but wanting to please, fearful but eager—all those conditions at once.

Eventually, they nod.

"Tomorrow at midday, I want you to go into Mr. Mallick's shop and take your cricket bats. Demolish it, *se*? I own the space and I've been meaning to... How do you say it?" He turns to a colleague.

"*Renovate*," this man says.

"Yes, renovate for a while. The more you bring down, the more I will pay you. It is mine, so don't listen to them. Just bring it down and then come straight back here for payment." Jimmy leans towards Max and Bronson, holding open a tin. "Cigar?"

Bronson picks one up and places it between his teeth. Max watches the other men as they eyeball him and his brother. He feels his stomach contract as they interrogate him—intimidate him. Max knows those words: interrogate, intimidate. Even at the age of ten, he knows them well. He's a Butcher.

One of the Family's associates leans in to light Bronson's cigar for him. Bronson stares at the ember burning inches from his face. A string of smoke snakes through the air, but he's unsure of what to do now.

"Just draw it into your mouth, Bron," Butch says with a smile. "Swirl it around. No need to inhale."

"What if Mr. Mallick tries to stop us? What if he grabs us or something?" Max asks.

The tin is offered back to Max. "Then take your bats to his knees."

Max stares wide-eyed at Bronson, who is now sucking away on his cigar. He looks back at Jimmy and whispers, "But he's old."

"Exactly," Jimmy says, glancing down at the open tin and then back at Max. "He has bad knees. Remind him of that."

After taking one final look at Bronson and Butch, Max accepts the cigar.

her way - bronson butcher's story

I'm a medical resident, engaged, and settled. Just when I thought I was happy, *he* turns up on my operating table with a bullet wound in his chest.

And all the love and devastation we shared darkens my perceived happiness.

Bronson Butcher.

My high school obsession.

We were desperately in love until I made a mistake that severed our shared heart.

So when he wakes up in the hospital and hears my voice, he stalks me down the corridor.

He pins me to the wall and inhales me as though starving...

But he's not that wild boy anymore. *No.* He's a ruthless man who takes what he wants, and what he wants is to punish me for running from him, remind me how my body hums beneath his—

What he wants is to take me back to his city with or without my consent.

Get book

facing us - the prequel

Have you read Konnor & Blesk's story?

He is desperate to remember.
She will destroy everything to forget.

Konnor: Up until now, my life has been a mirage of sorts. Of dark, lonely places. Of bourbon and women. I don't care. I think I'm pretty happy really.
But then she happens. . .

Blesk: He wants me. He'll do anything, drop everything, to have me. But when he uncovers who I am and what I've done, he'll rue ever facing me.
I've already buried everything he loves. . .

We both have secrets. Mine are harrowing. His, heart-breaking. Just merely being together threatens to expose everything we have tried to escape.

Will finally facing our past bring us peace or. . . spark chaos?

the district-origin story

Jimmy Storm—1979
Controllare le strade; control della citta
(Control the streets; control the city.)

My father was a ladder-man in the late 1940s. In the old country—Sicily. He was the boy the Family trusted with their money, for he was the one with the clearest vantage point. The expression ladder-man had come about back in the early gambling days when young men would stand on ladders on the casino gaming floors, watching and waiting for misconduct.

My father was the most trusted and feared man in Sicily—a complete oxymoron, I know. But it all depended on who was doing the trusting and who was doing the fearing.

The Family paid him ninety lira an hour, which was good money back then, and so, of course, the crooks of the club—the ones on the gaming floor pocketing chips, counting cards, and winning too much of the Family's money—found death quickly. There was very little chance for rebuttal once my father had them in his sights. He was an adolescent then and rather engrossed in the power bestowed upon him, as would any young man be with the strength of many at his beck and call.

Things were irrevocably simpler back then. If there was a misdemeanour, it was handled quickly, quietly, and strictly; very few people lived to talk about it. Which is how it should be.

According to gossip, my grandfather was a 'likeable type' and had no knowledge of his son's activities. Luckily for us, my grandfather had died when my father was sixteen, leaving him without any relations. Luckily? Yes, because there is little I can learn from a 'likeable type' of man.

After three years of being the boy up the ladder on the most notorious gaming floors in Sicily, my father became an orphan. And an orphan he was for exactly two days before the Family picked him up and officially made him their own. They bought my father. They owned him then. It wasn't until then that he really understood what he'd signed up for.

He had married the mob.

When you marry the mob, as when you marry a woman, you are contractually, spiritually, legally, and emotionally bound to them. The key difference being, there is no such thing as divorcees—only widowers. That is where it all had started—humble beginnings and a life of servitude to the Family.

When I was a young man, my ego was larger than Achilles', rivalling my father's in every way. It would be fair to say I flexed my muscles every chance I could—at the boys at school, at the people on the sidewalk offering me less than obedient glances... at everyone. I was a sfacciato little shit, and partly because of that cheekiness, I learned to thrive on the sensation people's submission gave me. I'd usually be hard as a rock beneath my trousers in the midst of a power play.

I am Jimmy Storm, son of Paul Storm, and my name is legendary. Storm is not our real name, of course. My father named himself when he became a made-man.

Half of Sicily owed the Family money, which meant we owned half of Sicily and her people. We managed people with ease, for their lives were worthless to us and priceless to them. I grew up around the cruellest, slyest, dirtiest bastards in the country and they set the benchmark for my behaviour as an adolescent; they were my idols.

When I turned twenty-seven, my *zu* Norris and I left Sicily, taking with us blessings and funds from the Family, with our sights set on a new place of profit. We flew to an area of Australia renowned for its wealthy residents—a secluded section on the coast consisting of four towns: Brussman, Connolly, Stormy River, and Moorup. I recently learnt of an Australian idiom for this kind of unmonitored and isolated area—'Bandit Country.'

I was out to prove myself at any cost.

Which brings me to today, and the reason I have my shoes pressed to a man's trachea.

"I am Jimmy Storm!" I state. The rubber of my heel presses very slowly on his windpipe, and when he tries to buck away, I know I have found the *puntu debole*. He tries desperately to claw at my foot, attempting to relieve some pressure. He can't, but that doesn't save my shoe from getting covered in fingerprints, and that is just so inconvenient.

My *zu* and I have been in this miserable part of the world for three godforsaken weeks and have found nothing short of disorganised, disrespectful, and inferior versions of la Cosa Nostra. The young man whose trachea I'm currently crushing is Dustin Nerrock, and he is 'the name' about these parts. A slightly hostile *parràmune* has taken place and I am simply establishing my dominance.

We'd met under casual terms, but this disrespectful man forgot his manners along the way. I've been told, 'What the Australian male lacks in brains, he makes up for in brawn,' and I truly hope so. Since being here, we have found a lack of connections, a lack of muscle due to scope—all of Sicily is smaller than this area of Western Australia—and far too many new legalities to... manipulate without consultants to advise us. Despite my indelicate means of conversing, the end game is to get Dustin Nerrock and a few other big-name families in this area to work with us.

For us...

Dustin's father died last year, leaving him with businesses scattered throughout the area, but with no idea of how to utilise them. Money and dominance are the game. The man under my shoe has more money than sense, an ego that rivals my own, and a name people know. And soon, here, people will know mine.

"Do you have any idea who—" Dustin chokes, struggling to force words out while my boot is pressed to his throat.

Pity...

"Oh, *scusari*," I say, feigning concern. "Did you say something?" His face looks so feeble; I want to crush it 'til it goes away. Men who bow are ants, small and helpless, but infinitely useful when put to work. I've been told my temper is an issue. Apparently, it is obvious when I'm irate; I speak a mongrel version of Italian, Sicilian, and English, and my accent seems to thicken... Personally, I don't hear it...

"Madonna Mia, are you going to cry like a *paparédda,* Dustin. You're the man about these parts. Stand up!" I yell and then press my heel further into his jugular... so he can't.

"*Alzarsi!* Stand up!" He can't. I won't let him, and the whole idea of that makes my dick twitch.

I find myself tiring of his weak attempts to fight me off. I remove my shoe from his neck, allowing him to gasp and drag some much-needed air into his lungs. And he does, sucking like a man possessed. His palms meet the pavement under the dimly lit street lights and I take a few steps back to allow him room to stand. He pushes off his hands and climbs to his feet, a scowl firmly set on his face. Dustin all but growls at me and then spits blood to the side, his body shuddering slightly while he regains air and stability.

I mock, "Are you okay, *paparédda?*"

"You're in deep shit," he hisses, coughing at the pavement.

The bitterness in the air is tangible, an entity apart. It is time to switch the play and lead the conversation in a more mutually beneficial direction. I've humiliated him, and now I shall woo him.

"Let's talk like gentlemen, Dustin," I begin, removing a handkerchief from my pocket and offering it to him as he coughs and clears his throat. "Please oblige me?" I wave the folded white material in front of him, a feigned gesture of a truce.

He takes it and uses it to wipe away the little pieces of gravel pressed to his cheek. "Talk..."

"Perhaps we can start again. *Se*?" This is my favourite part of conversing—switching the play, manipulating the conversation. "You know who I am now, and I know who you are. You also know what I do, se?"

He stares at me, his brows drawn together, his eyes narrowed. "Yes."

"Well," I say, clapping my hands and grinning widely at him. "That's an excellent start. May I recommend we take this little *parràmune* to a more appropriate place? I know an establishment not too far from here... Will you join me for a drink? Put this little and unfortunate indiscretion behind us..."

It didn't take long for me to gain Dustin Nerrock's favour. In fact, it took less time than I'd imagined. The man is hungry, power-hungry. I recognise it in him. It is indeed a trait we share. After three hours with Dustin, I'm even more convinced that this area holds infinite possibilities. To start with, there is a high crime rate, which, of course, is a huge benefit to my cause as protection comes at a cost. There are strictly governed gun laws, which, of course, means demand, and I am happy to supply. There is a vast class division, which means two things: an opportunity to clean up the riffraff at a cost, and addicts—I love addicts.

My father once told me to never choose a side, but to rather find out their motivation(s) and make them beholden to you. 'Control the streets; control the city.' I share this philosophy with Dustin. The final and most tantalising piece of information is that this country is bursting at the seams with minerals and is far too big to secure thoroughly. There are gold, diamonds, and unsealed access roads.

"I have never met a rich man I didn't like," I declare, clinking Dustin's glass with mine.

A grin stretches across his face. The grin of a man whose eyes are suffused in dollar signs. "Well, that said, there are others we need in on this..."

"Yes." I raise the glass to my lips and the smoky whiskey fumes float deliciously up my nostrils. "A man who my Capo told me about. Big pull in the old country." I use my hands to talk. My Sicilian mannerisms are hardwired. "Big pull. But he seems quite the enigma. I could not track him down. He has recently married some beauty queen from England and is probably just... How do you Australians say it? Fucking and fucking. No time for business when there is pussy. Se?" We both laugh and I play the game of equals; that is what I want him to believe. "So this man," I continue, "he is a half-Sicilian, half-Australian, mongrel. But the Family... They seem to love him. The name I was given was Paul Lucchese."

Dustin's gaze narrows, his amused expression slipping. "I know who you're talking about... We can't trust that bastard." And I'm immediately intrigued...

"He is very important to the Family." I feign a sigh, but I'm eager to meet the man who has inspired such a reaction. I have never liked 'likeable people'; it is the unlikable ones I prefer. They have attitude and spirit. They make excellent soldiers.

Dustin seems to study my expression. "He will never agree."

"He will. I assure you—" My attention is redirected to a clearly inebriated character as he swipes a collection of glasses off the bar; the sound of them smashing rudely invades my senses. I tilt my head and watch from our booth as he begins to yell and threaten the bartender.

Well, this is a pity.

I was having such a peaceful drink, and I have my favourite shirt on. The inebriated man's grasp of the English language shocks me, and it makes me wonder whether it was his mother or father who has failed him so profoundly, perhaps both.

"Listen, 'ere," he starts, pointing a shaky finger at the bartender. "I ain't sellin' nufin. I'm just 'ere for a drink."

Interesting...

I shuffle from my seat and excuse myself politely. After walking slowly over to the man at the bar, I lean beside him and smile.

"Wah you want?" He lowers his voice. "I ain't sell nufin." His mouth opens and expels words only vaguely fathomable. It is a damn pity about this shirt.

"*Scusa.*" I motion across to my table. "I was drinking over there with a very important colleague of mine and you're making it rather hard to concentrate. May I suggest finding a different establishment, se?"

It has been a long time since a man dared strike me, and it is apparent why over the course of the next few seconds. He stumbles backwards and then jolts forward, throwing his fist into my face. The smell of his breath knocks me harder than his knuckles do. My cheek burns for a short moment.

I shrug apologetically to the wide-eyed bartender and jab the bastard beside me twice in the throat. Jab. Jab. His knees meet the floor with a thud. My knee rises to connect with his chin. Crack. A guttural groan curdles up his throat. My knee rises again. Another groan. The back of my hand collides with his cheek. How *irrispettoso*. I can't stand disrespect in any form. As I stare down at his swaying body, I notice a small stain on my shirt.

"*Madonna Mia. Fare le corna a qualcuno,*" I hiss at him. "Look what you did."

Dustin's brawn most definitely comes in handy as we relocate my new friend to a more private locale—an old building Dustin inherited. He doesn't look quite as lively laying bound on the cold concrete floor. Although, my dick does like the bindings...

I can already tell that after this exchange, I'll be in dire need of a lady's company.

"Will you drag Mr...?" I stare questioningly at our bound captive.

"Get fucked..." He chokes on his own words.

"Very well, will you drag Mr. Get Fucked so he is sitting against that wall just there, se?" I smile calmly in my new partner's direction, pointing at the rear brick wall. "Thank you, Dustin."

This disused warehouse would make an excellent abattoir; perhaps I will recommend a new business endeavour to Dustin. I ponder this as I remove a few items from my bag and set them down on the wooden workbench behind me: a blade, a bottle of aqua, and a Luna Stick. Pouring a small amount of water onto my shirt, I gently wipe at the stain. The chill from the liquid sends shivers down my spine.

"Such a pity," I mutter to myself. When I tilt my head to watch Dustin manoeuvre our intoxicated captive to a more suitable position, I feel serenity wash over me. These are the moments where I truly shine. In the grit. When others usually waver, I am at my most contained. Perhaps, it also has to do with my new partner's eager and obedient behaviour; after all, I did nearly squash his throat into the pavement a mere few hours ago. A sly grin draws my lips out. Who said money can't buy happiness? Money can purchase the most loyal of comrades, and fear has no limit. Empires have been built on the foundations of both.

"I am Jimmy Storm. You know me?" I query, though I know the answer.

"No," our barely coherent friend snaps, pulling away from Dustin's grip.

"Well, this is Dustin Nerrock. You know him?" I ask, once again knowing the response. Our inebriated friend glances up at Dustin and nods, appearing to exhibit a suitable level of unease. “Well, now you know me too. Jimmy. Storm. I would like to know who you work for.”

“I’m not fucki—”

“A-ta-ta-ta." I wave my finger at his rude interruption. “Before you say no, we found ten grams of heroin on you. Now, don’t lie to Jimmy. Tell me who in this town supplies you... And then I will give you an offer you can’t refuse.”

“I’m neva snitchin’. He’d fuckin’ kill me.”

“I see.” I sigh and turn to my assortment of items. “I respect that.” As I pick up the switch knife and feel the cold metal in my palm, I run my finger over the blade, the rigid edge grating my pad. The excitement of what's to follow forces blood directly to my groin and I find myself in a state of impatience, eager to show Dustin how I assure success.

I spin on my heels and walk directly to my captive. I lean down. The blade slices through his flesh like a zipper parting fabric. The knife ruptures the nerves within. The deed is done. His eyes widen and his hand grips his left wrist. Blood trickles through his fingers and drips onto the concrete.

“Shit,” he cries. “Wha tha fuck? You said you respected tha.”

“I do, very much,” I state adamantly. “I hope you live. Loyalty is my favourite virtue.”

“Christ,” Dustin mutters from behind me. Yes, this is how we interrogate in my Family.

“You will die from exsanguination within ten minutes.” I squat at the man's side and grin, watching his face pale and his head bobble on his neck as nausea floods him. I have seen this look many times. "I am a spiritual man. You would not know, but I am a Catholic. And I could swear to Mother Maria..." I stare at him as he struggles to hold his head up, narrowing my eyes to better study his. “I could swear you can see death take a man. The seconds just before... in his eyes... you see death enter him."

Something akin to a whimper splutters from his throat and panicked tears burst from the corners of his shallow eyes. This poor, underprivileged street rat will not be missed and without any evidence, his disappearance will be stamped as drug-related. Which, in a way, it is. "Now, tell me where I can find your boss and I will help you live."

"What? How?" Dustin asks me.

I laugh from deep within my abdomen; I just can't help it. "I told you, I'm a spiritual man."

My weeping captive tries to speak, "He is... he owns..."

"Can you feel that chill?" I ask him, moving so close my lips brush the shell of his ear. "He is near, my friend."

"He owns Le Feir. The bakery." He passes out, seven minutes before closing time. The smell of his blood, metallic and tangy, hits my nose. It pools around his outstretched legs, creating small glistening puddles. Yes, I think to myself, this warehouse would make an excellent abattoir.

Deciding to keep my word, I stand and walk briskly over to the workbench, retrieve the Luna Caustic nitrate stick—one of my favourite tools. While I roll up my sleeves and wet the stick's tip, I think about what a real shame it is that my captive won't be conscious to feel the burn. I hear it is quite a unique sensation. My dick is throbbing like a stubbed toe below my zipper as I approach my captive and squat by his side. I begin to cauterise his slit wrist. The blood makes it rather difficult, however, not impossible, and I've had plenty of practise. "So, young Dustin," I call over my shoulder, my eyes unwavering as I work. "We will pay Mr. Le Feir a visit tomorrow. Make a deal. We don't want any product besides ours hitting these streets. This is now our *quartier*, our District. Why is this?"

"Control the streets, control the city," he replies, his nerves stammering through his voice. A chuckle escapes me. I think I may have scared my new partner; how quaint. It appears Dustin Nerrock doesn't get his hands dirty; he must be a proficient delegator. But as my father once told me, 'It is the dirt that makes the man appreciate the sparkle.'

"More importantly than Mr. Fier," I say, "is organising a meeting with the man my Capo spoke about... You know him. Where will we find him?"

I hear Dustin release an exaggerated breath. "He doesn't go by Paul Lucchese anymore. His name is Luca Butcher and he lives in Connolly."

nicci who?

I'm an Australian chick writing real love stories for dark souls.

Stalk me.

Meet other Butcher Boy lovers on Facebook. Join Harris's Harem of Dark Romance Lovers

Stalk us.

Don't like Facebook?

Join my newsletter

It's taken three years into my author career to write a biography because, let's face it, you probably don't care that I live in Australia, hate owls, am sober, or that my husband's name is Ed—not Edward or Eddie—Ed... like who names their son 'just' Ed? (love my in-laws, btw). Anyway, you probably don't really care that my son's name is Jarrah—not Jarrod or Jason—to compensate for his dad's name *Ed*...

I ramble...

Here's what you really want to know. I'm a contradiction. Contradictory people are my jam. I am an independent woman who has lived her entire life doing things the wrong way, the impulsive way, the risky way... my way. I'm not from a rich family but I've taken wealthy people chances... I'm my own boss. I'm a full-time author, an Amazon best-seller, all despite the amount of people who said I couldn't, shouldn't, wouldn't... I'm that person.

So while I live a feminist kind of life... I write about men who kill, who control, who take their women like it's their last breath, pinning them down and whispering *"good girl"* and *"mine"* and *"you belong to me"* and all the red flag utterances that would have most independent women rolling their eyes so hard they see their brains.

I write about men who protect their women. Men who control them because they are so obsessed, so in love, they are terrified not to... Do I have daddy issues? *Probably.* Did I need to be controlled and protected more as a child and this is my outlet? *Possibly.*

So... if you don't like that... if you don't see the internal strength in my heroines, how they are the emotional rocks for these controlling *alphahole* men... then don't read my books. You won't like them. We can still be friends.

But I want both. I want my cake and to have a six-foot-five, tattooed, alphamale eat it too.

facebook.com/authornicciharris
amazon.com/author/nicciharris
bookbub.com/authors/nicci-harris
goodreads.com/nicciharris
instagram.com/author.nicciharris

Printed in Great Britain
by Amazon